# BY THE SAME AUTHOR:

*The Dark Frontier*

# FLOWERS FROM THE BLACK SEA

## A.B. DECKER

The Book Guild Ltd

First published in Great Britain in 2024 by
The Book Guild Ltd
Unit E2 Airfield Business Park,
Harrison Road, Market Harborough,
Leicestershire. LE16 7UL
Tel: 0116 2792299
www.bookguild.co.uk
Email: info@bookguild.co.uk
Twitter: @bookguild

Typeset in 11pt Adobe Garamond Pro

Printed on FSC accredited paper
Printed and bound in Great Britain by 4edge Limited


ISBN 978 1916668 430


British Library Cataloguing in Publication Data.
A catalogue record for this book is available from the British Library.

Forever indebted to Penelope for her patience and support

# CHAPTER 1

The cool wind that blew across the tarmac caught Matt Quillan off-guard as he negotiated the steps down from the plane. The shock of that early-morning breeze on his face was punctuated by a solitary drop of rain that hit him in the eye. He had not expected Istanbul to be so cold and damp in the dying days of September.

Picking up his bags `from the carousel some thirty minutes later, he headed outside for the buses. It was not a fear of flying with the local airline that prompted him to shun the transfer desk for domestic flights. He needed time to get his head around what he was doing on this southeasternmost fringe of Europe. For Matt, it had the hallmarks of a country moving into the fast lane to tyranny.

He really had no wish to be here. But a long-distance bus ride to the south coast of Turkey would at least delay his arrival by the best part of a day and give him time to think.

Walking out into the chill of the morning air to get the bus, he could not escape the presence of heavily armed guards. They lurked on every corner. At every exit. And did nothing to ease Matt's apprehension. Or to allay his doubts about ever agreeing to come here in the first place.

His sense of foreboding was not diminished by what was about to follow.

He had agreed to locate a person of interest for his old friend Ben Braithwaite. Matt was no sleuth and had no idea what awaited him or what his first move should be. Ben had suggested only that he start the search in a resort on the Mediterranean coast. As to why he was even looking for the person, he had remained stubbornly evasive.

Matt felt forever indebted to his old friend for funding his start-up in the security business. Without this help, he would likely still be battling his demons of alcohol, cocaine and poker tables. Or at best floundering on a zero-hours contract somewhere.

So, when Ben called in the debt one day, Matt knew he had no other option. It was a good six weeks ago when, out of the blue, Ben called to say he was in town and why didn't they meet for a drink. They had not seen each other for a good seven or eight years. It proved to be a drinking date he would never forget.

"This has nothing to do with company business, Matt. So, I'll be paying you out of my own pocket, but you'll be rewarded handsomely," he said, before lifting the empty glass again.

"Another one?"

Matt nodded and mulled the prospect of financial compensation. With a divorce to deal with in the months ahead, the extra money was not to be sniffed at.

"So, just supposing I go along with this," he said, when Ben returned from the bar with two more glasses of beer, "who am I looking for?"

"The man's called Ahmet. Ahmet Karadeniz. He was last known to be in or around a tourist resort on the south coast of Turkey called Karakent. Runs a property business, so he should be quite easy to find."

"If he's so easy to find, why don't you go and look for him yourself?" Matt asked.

"I'll be sailing down that way in October. I'm hoping you'll have found him by then," Ben said.

This was no explanation. And it was his friend's evasiveness that nagged at Matt's thoughts now as the bus headed over the Bosphorus and into Anatolia.

While he pondered every angle of Ben's motives and of what might lie ahead for him, both here in Turkey and back home in London with the pending divorce, the flicker of passing trees cast his thoughts adrift. His eyes closed, and he fell into a deep sleep.

It was the harsh sound of a jangling ringtone that rocked him from his slumber. On the opposite side of the aisle, the only other passenger still remaining – a young man in his late twenties perhaps – gazed out of the window. He spoke a few muffled words into his phone. Then slid the device furtively back into his pocket, peering over the seats in front as he did so, and glanced across the aisle towards Matt. Only a fleeting glance. But it was enough to give Matt a sense of being measured up.

The young man turned his gaze back to the road ahead. He appeared nervous. The bus was beginning to slow down. He picked up a laptop bag that lay at his feet, unzipped it and, slipping his hand quickly in and out of the bag, crossed the aisle and parked himself in the seat beside Matt.

"My name Rekan," he said, extending a hand.

Matt was taken aback by this unwanted advance, but did his best to remain unfazed by the intrusion.

"Matt," he said in return and took Rekan's hand.

"You go to Karakent," the young man said, making an imperative of what Matt took to be a question. Matt assumed it was his reddish-blonde hair that prompted the young man's use of English, since he could not by any stretch of the imagination be taken for a Turk.

"Yes," Matt replied, unable to conceal the suspicion in his voice.

"Please, go to Trabzon Ekmek Fırını and ask for Murat," Rekan said, pressing something into Matt's hand. "Give him this."

Matt looked at the object. It was a USB stick. His suspicion hardened.

"Where?"

"Trabzon Ekmek Fırını," he repeated, hastily pulling pen and paper from his pocket, writing out the words in bold capitals and thrusting the paper into Matt's hand.

"Why don't you give it to him yourself?"

"I must go," he said. Then, as the bus eventually ground to a halt and the engine stopped, he implored Matt again with a "please" as he slipped back across the aisle to his seat, adding in a whisper, "Give it to Murat. Only Murat."

At that moment, the door of the bus slid open and two uniformed men in berets climbed on board. One of them exchanged some words with the driver, while the other surveyed the rows of seats ahead of him before slowly making his way up the aisle to the back of the bus. He inspected each row of seats as he went, then turned and made his way back towards the only two passengers on the bus.

The gendarme stopped just behind the row where Matt and the mysterious Rekan were sitting. He muttered a few words in Turkish that Matt was unable to understand. The young man fished a document out of his pocket and handed it to the gendarme, who inspected it briefly as he gestured towards the door. Rekan rose from his seat, picking up his laptop bag, and made his way down the aisle towards the door.

"Pasaport," said the gendarme, turning to Matt with a complete lack of expression in either his voice or his face. Matt presented his passport. The gendarme took it – with a long, piercing gaze at Matt as he did so – and slowly leafed through every page. He meticulously studied every visa and every stamp that Matt had accumulated in the last five or six years since he last renewed his passport. Still leafing through the document, he strolled back down the length of the bus, turning as he reached the door, and beckoned Matt to follow.

Matt had enough experience of the Jandarma from his very first trip to Turkey as a student to know that they are not to be messed with. He had almost been landed with a long jail term over a vestigial gram of cannabis found in his pocket. Fortunately, they had proved more inclined to bribery than they were to upholding the law. But this was a character trait he could not count on now with the country's new taste for cracking down on freedoms of any kind and incarcerating anyone it takes a dislike to. So, he tamely followed.

When he emerged from the bus, he saw the gendarme disappear into a van. Its red and blue flashing lights cast an eerily pulsating hue over the early evening sky around the bus. Rekan was already seated in the back of the van. Matt was left to wait and contemplate what lay ahead of him in the chill of the mountain air that bristled through the cedar trees. He walked a few metres off the road to escape the reach of the van's pulsating lights, lit a cigarette and watched the white mountain in the distance gradually absorb the growing redness of the sky.

There was a portentous quality about this mountain. The way it would not let go: it had tracked his journey south for the best part of half an hour. As if it carried a message and would not give way until it was delivered.

The sound of the van door sliding open butted rudely into his stream of thought. He flinched and turned to see the gendarme approaching.

"Where you go?" he asked Matt.

"Karakent."

"Otel?"

"Kelebek," Matt replied. Ben had recommended he stay there.

"Good," was all the gendarme said in reply. He returned Matt's passport and walked back to the van. Rekan remained inside. Matt climbed back onto the bus, where he was now completely alone, apart from the driver, who had sat impassively in his seat throughout. As Matt relaxed back into his seat, the only sign that the driver was there at all was the sound of the engine starting up and the motion of the bus as it continued on its journey.

Matt had a sense of being cast adrift in a huge puzzle, none of whose pieces fitted. He had set out on this journey as a favour, although Ben had never made clear to him exactly what it was all about and left him no idea where it would lead. And now, acutely aware of the lump in his pocket that was Rekan's flash drive, he had the distinct feeling he had just been thrown another huge piece in a completely different puzzle that had nothing to do with him.

When the bus emerged from the mountain landscape and lumbered now along a winding coast road, his mind wandered out across the vast expanse of sea to his left. The turquoise of the water had already turned a dark blue, as the peninsula jutting into the sea ahead swallowed up the crimson sun. Only another twenty kilometres to go if the road sign they had just passed was to be believed. But Karakent itself would prove not to be quite the tourist resort he had imagined it to be.

# CHAPTER 2

As Matt stepped off the bus, he caught the cadence of the call to prayers. It drifted off through the eucalyptus trees beside the road, carried by the wind that blew in from the sea. He mopped his brow. It seemed to him, some five hundred or so miles south of Istanbul, to be unseasonably warm and humid for the time of day in late September.

There was little activity in the centre of town when he stepped onto the pavement. The only signs of life came from a solitary figure in an otherwise deserted restaurant and the call to prayer from a minaret that peered over the rooftops as if designed to vet the new arrivals in town.

Alone on the pavement in this off-season resort, Matt surveyed the scene before him by the light of the street lamp beside the bus. His eyes wandered over a row of small single-storey outlets. A car rental firm. The ticket office of the bus company. A carpet shop with kilims stacked either side of the door. And the restaurant. It sprawled out towards the street beneath a magenta canopy of bougainvillea. From the canopy hung a board bearing the name Osman's Kitchen.

Matt's gaze settled on the tables that spread out onto the pavement, where the solitary figure, a stout fifty-something, sat sipping tea. He watched the man take a handful of almonds from a small bag beside the glass of tea, place them on a block of wood alongside his chair and, with the single blow of a brass mortar, crack open a nut and slip it into his mouth. As he chewed on the nut, he hummed to the music that played faintly in the background. It came from a radio: the plaintive yearning sound of a clarinet which competed with the call to prayer.

Most of the tourists had long since left. Of the few remaining stragglers, a passing middle-aged couple stopped on the roadside opposite. They glanced up at a flag that fluttered in the wind, the white crescent bobbing on a sea of red, and exchanged a knowing look – as if they saw in this a signal. Then continued on their way past a string of yellow taxis that stood idly at the rank, waiting for the promise of a fare.

Matt gripped his rucksack tightly over his right shoulder and ambled over to the tea drinker.

"Good evening," he muttered, exhausted from the long journey, and let the rucksack slip from his shoulder onto a chair at the table opposite the tea drinker.

"Iyi akşamlar," came the response.

The man's reply was almost inaudible through the almond nut that he was chewing on. But Matt recognised the words. It was one of the few Turkish expressions he had managed to memorise before setting off on his journey: 'Good evening' according to his phrase book. But he had little trust in the evening that lay ahead. It had all the makings of a very awkward one.

Glancing up at the flag that had caught the middle-aged couple's attention earlier, the tea drinker rose to his feet and sauntered back into the darkness of the restaurant. Matt's gaze now drifted from the flag, through the bristling eucalyptus trees, up to the building behind. Although it tried to hide the state of disrepair behind the trees – its broken or missing windows, the cream and red paint now faded and flaking off – the building was an imposing presence in the heart of this small town. A statement on the skyline that was destined to capture the attention as it looked out over the bay below Karakent. It left Matt with a deep sense of unease that he was unable to explain.

He was still running this edginess around in his mind when he became aware of an arm beside him. It reached down and planted a tulip-shaped glass of tea in front of him, nestled in a saucer with two sugar cubes and a spoon. Matt looked up to see the tea drinker.

"Welcome. My name Osman," he said, putting his left hand to his chest and gesturing with the open palm of his right hand.

"Present. For you."

"Oh, I think you mean it's on the house?"

"On the house," Osman repeated slowly. There was the trace of a smile on his lips as he practised the words.

"That's very kind. I'm Matt."

He was more in the mood for a beer than a glass of tea. But after the long trip from Istanbul, he was in no mood to press the point. As his host returned to his seat, Matt dropped the sugar cubes into the tea, gave it a vigorous stir and raised his glass to Osman.

Edging closer to the purpose of his visit, he took a pack of cigarettes and a box of matches from his pocket, reached over to Osman's table and offered him a cigarette. His host declined with a wave of the hand, which he then placed on his chest and said simply "heart."

"Do you mind if *I* do?" Matt asked, putting a cigarette between his lips and lighting up without waiting for a reply. "Can I ask you something?"

Osman's dark eyes cast a doleful look that lay somewhere between suffering and suspicion. He said nothing. Had he understood? It was hard to tell.

"Ask something?" Osman repeated as Matt puffed on the cigarette. Then: "You want room?" he asked.

"I've been recommended to try the Kelebek," Matt said. He was irritated by the deflection.

With a disdainful snort, Osman waved his hands in a gesture of dismissal.

"Şimşek Pansiyon better," he said. "My brother. Ergün."

When Matt asked how to find the place, Osman lifted his hand from his chest, ran it over his face, and wiped a smile onto his lips as he did so. His teeth still bore the trace of almonds as the lips parted, and he raised his arm, gesticulating up the hill in the direction of the dilapidated building.

"Thanks, I'll try it," said Matt, before finally getting to the question: "Do you know a man called Ahmet?"

"I know many Ahmets," Osman said.

The smile was instantly replaced by an expression of downright suspicion.

"Ahmet Kara-something-or-other," Matt added hopefully. Then hesitated. Fishing out of his wallet the card with the full name that Ben had given him, he dragged with it the piece of paper entrusted to him earlier by the young man on the bus. It fell onto the table and landed right under Osman's nose.

Osman pounced on the paper, flattened it out and instantly lit up with the excitement that comes with recognition, as he read the words Trabzon Ekmek Fırını.

"Ah!" said Osman with a note of triumph in his voice and seemingly happy to change the subject.

He stood up, gesticulating and waving his left hand in the direction of the dilapidated building, past the eucalyptus trees and up the hill, as he curved his right arm around the other arm, pointing to the left. Then he turned back to Matt, waved a finger at him and added in a solemn tone, "Ahmet no."

Matt had been hoping the additional mission thrust upon him on the bus would fade away through lack of oxygen. At least for a time. But, in view of Osman's obvious reluctance to speak about anyone called Ahmet, it struck him that he might stand a better chance with Murat and maybe kill two birds with one stone. He put a coin on the table for his tea, but Osman immediately pushed it back into Matt's hand with a hurt expression in his eyes.

"Please. On the house."

Matt thanked him and made his way up the hill, past the crumbling building and the bristling eucalyptus trees. At the first junction, signposts pointed to a cluster of hotels, including Hotel Kelebek, further up the hill. Matt turned left in what he assumed to be the direction Osman had intended.

There was little to recommend the street he now found himself in. The few restaurants appeared to have closed. While he passed one or two shops whose English hoardings told him they were there for the tourists, the unlit interiors told him their season was over.

After a five-minute walk, he came to the neon-lit Şimşek of Osman's brother. It was offering rooms at prices lower than those he had been quoted for the Kelebek. So, at least in that respect, it seemed a better option.

But there was nothing on the street that bore the sign he was looking for until he had almost reached the end of the surfaced road. In the gloom stood a plain single-storey building. Painted above the door were the same three words that Rekan had written out for him.

A solitary light shone within. As Matt approached, he could see from the shelves inside that it was a bakery. But apart from the single naked light bulb shining over the counter, there was no sign of life. He pushed open the door and called out.

"Hello."

His cry was greeted with silence. The bakery was plainly not closed, since a few loaves still lay on the shelves behind the counter. Matt called out again, and this time he caught the sound of movement in a back room, before eventually an old woman emerged through the shadows dressed in headscarf, black cardigan and floral-patterned pantaloons.

"İyi akşamlar." Matt was first with the greeting this time in an effort to make a good impression.

The old woman reciprocated.

"Murat?" Matt asked.

He lacked any of the verbs and other trappings of language needed to get across his message. But the name was enough to elicit a response. It sent the woman into a howling outburst of emotion. She raised her hands to cover her face, cried and wailed in obvious distress, before fleeing into the back room from which she had just emerged. Her place was instantly taken by a man – young, slim, unshaven, his eyes glistening. He stood defiantly in the doorway.

"I'm really sorry," said Matt, in shock at the impact of his question. "I didn't mean to startle your mother."

"What you want?" growled the man in the doorway.

"I'm looking for Murat."

Matt was relieved that at least this man spoke a rudimentary kind of English.

"Murat not here."

"Where will I find him?" Matt persisted.

The man gestured to the heavens, mumbling in an incantation that included the unmistakable word Allah, then added in his perfunctory English, "Murat dead."

"Dead?"

"Heart," the man explained, nodding, as he put his hand to his chest. "Why you want Murat?"

Matt was about to take the flash drive from his pocket, then recalled those last two words Rekan had spoken on the bus: "Only Murat." Matt was perplexed. This was not why he had come to Karakent. He had been entrusted with a mission by a complete stranger. He had not accepted it, because he had not been given any time to accept. But equally, he had not refused it. And he had had every opportunity to do so: he could have handed the flash drive to the gendarme and have done with it. But he didn't. So, implicitly, he had accepted the mission. All these thoughts were racing through Matt's mind as he stood there, hand poised in his pocket.

"I was told he bakes the best bread in town," he said.

Suspicion was etched into the man's expression. Not even the most plausible of explanations would alter that. He moved around behind the counter, took a loaf from the shelf and placed it on the counter in front of Matt.

"Ten lira," he said, not taking his eyes off Matt for a second.

Matt placed a ten lira note on the counter and picked up the loaf.

"Thank you." Matt gave a courteous nod of the head. "I'm sorry for your loss."

He had plenty on his mind as he snuck back into the darkness and made his way down the road to the Şimşek. They were offering rooms a hundred lira cheaper than the Kelebek that Ben had recommended. That would do just fine. But it did not deter him from trying to negotiate his way down further. It was off season, after all.

Ergün was a slim, almost emaciated forty-something with aquiline features that made him so unlike Osman that it was impossible to imagine they were of the same parentage. But as soon as Matt mentioned the name Osman, a beaming grin lit up his face, and there was plainly no need for haggling. A fifty-lira discount would be just fine for any friend of his brother, he assured Matt in a fluent English that was streets ahead of his older brother's.

And for this discounted price, Ergün even gave Matt a room with a view, albeit in darkness by now.

"But in the morning, you will enjoy the beauty of the ocean," Ergün assured him, as he flung open the door.

So, if his trip to Turkey was looking more complicated by the minute, at least the trimmings were beginning to make Matt feel a little more comfortable. But he was not ready to let his host off the hook just yet.

"I have a question before you go," Matt said, as Ergün was about to close the door and leave his guest to settle in. Matt fumbled in the inside pocket of his jacket for his wallet and took out the card with the name Ben had given him.

"Do you know this man?" he asked, handing it to Ergün.

"Ahmet Karadeniz," Ergün said slowly as he examined the card. A wary smile crossed his lips.

"Why you look for this man?" he asked.

"Do you know him?"

"I'm sorry. I can't help you," Ergün said bluntly, the smile now faded to a look of what Matt took to be concern. He handed the piece of paper back to Matt and left the room.

Plainly the search for Ahmet would have to wait until tomorrow. In the meantime, a different curiosity was exercising Matt's patience. The object of his other mission. He slipped the rucksack off his shoulder, took out his laptop and started it up.

Normally, this would be the moment in the day when he would check his mail. But the day had long since ceased to be normal. And the flash drive was burning a hole in his pocket. He slid it into one of the USB ports on his laptop and opened it up. It contained a PDF file, bozkurt.pdf, two videos and a clutch of audio files. There was no password to the PDF, and it opened instantly. But it proved as enlightening as it would have been if it had been password-protected. As far as he could tell, it was a collection of lists, accounts, bills and so on. What text there was on these pages was entirely in Turkish. It told Matt nothing at all.

He opened one of the audio files, but that too was way beyond his grasp. And even the video clips, peopled with shady-looking characters speaking Turkish, remained obscure.

These files had clearly been important to the man called Rekan, who wanted to be sure they found their way into the hands of Murat. And only Murat. This made it all the more of a mystery to Matt why they had not been given the security of a password. Unsure exactly what he was going to do with this flash drive, but intrigued by the circumstances surrounding it,

Matt zipped the files, assigned a password – his date of birth backwards – and copied the zip file onto his laptop as an added precaution.

Removing the flash drive, he placed it on the table beside the laptop, lay on the bed and pondered his next steps. As if one obscure mission were not enough to handle, he had now been encumbered with another that saddled him with incriminating evidence of some kind.

Reason told him he should ditch the flash drive and get on with locating Ahmet Karadeniz. But for once in his life, Matt felt driven by a counterintuitive feeling deep in his bones. A feeling that went against every principle of safety that he now lived by as the director of a security firm. An inexplicable instinct to hold on to the flash drive.

# CHAPTER 3

Matt's night was riven by a troubled sleep that left him exhausted. By the time he rose from his bed, the morning was already half over. The journey and the two obscure missions entrusted to him by Ben and the stranger on the bus had taken more out of him than he cared to admit. But it was the heat that really did it. And the cicadas.

The room had no air-conditioning. When he opened the window, he was assailed by an endless chorus of the creatures practising their mating calls. Closing the window brought him only the relief of a dysfunctional ceiling fan that simply churned up the hot suffocating air above the bed. It was not until the cicadas settled down around midnight that he was emboldened to open the window again. And found the heat from outside no less suffocating than the heat within.

The view may be great, he told himself as he drew back the curtains onto the azure bay below and the rustling of resplendent grey-green olive trees in the foreground, "but if a fifty-lira discount won't buy you a decent air-con system, perhaps I should have checked into the Kelebek in the first place."

As if it were not enough that Ben had posted him to this unlikely location on the other side of Anatolia in search of the mysterious Ahmet. He now found himself also burdened with cryptic data, which had all the hallmarks of an assignment that was not entirely legal. But he put this part of his plight to the back of his mind for now, packed his rucksack and ventured out in search of the Hotel Kelebek.

Ergün was nowhere to be seen when Matt left. He placed the agreed fee on the reception desk and stepped out into the late-September day. Unlike the heat of the night he had been through, the gentle breeze blowing up from the bay told him that, even here on the Mediterranean, autumn could not be far off.

Matt retraced his steps from the previous night, back to the signpost he had seen for the Kelebek, and headed on up the hill. After a hundred yards or so, another sign pointed him down a lane off to the right. A few yards along this side road, he glimpsed the name Hotel Kelebek plastered across a building. And over the door, a large sign with a butterfly painted in red.

The young woman at reception beamed a bright smile every bit as cheerful as that butterfly when Matt approached the desk. Her long black hair fell over her shoulders free of the headscarf that Matt had seen so many of the older women wearing since his arrival in this country.

"Can I help you?" she asked in immaculate English.

"I hope so." Matt was pleasantly surprised by her command of his language. "Do you have a room free for a week or two?"

"Yes, of course," she said, taking a book from under the desk and leafing through its pages. "I just need your passport."

Matt reached into his pocket and handed her his documents along with the plaintive words, "With air-conditioning?"

"Of course, Mr Quillan," she repeated, briefly examining the passport as she placed it on the photocopier and glanced up at Matt with her disarming smile, which left him feeling ludicrously at home.

"Mr Matthew Quillan?" she repeated slowly when she took the passport off the copier and studied it more closely. The smile had now turned to a look of nervous suspicion.

"Yes, that's right."

"The Jandarma were here earlier this morning," she explained. "They wanted to know if you are staying here."

An awkward silence filled every inch of the small lobby.

"Of course, I had to say no," she added.

"So now if they return you can say yes," Matt replied with a grin, as she handed the passport back.

This outward show of cool indifference concealed an unease made all the more acute by the ominous files tucked away in his rucksack.

"Is the room ready?" he asked.

"Of course. No problem."

She handed him the key, mistrust still written into her expression where the welcoming smile had been just a few minutes earlier.

Matt nurtured his own suspicion that she would contact the gendarmerie as soon as he was out of sight. And he was keen to sort his baggage before they reappeared, as he was certain they would. In the sanctuary of his room, where he was pleased to find a functioning air-con system, he took the laptop from his backpack, started it up and deleted the mysterious files from the USB stick. He then changed the name of the zip file on the laptop to an innocuous vacationplans.pdf, saved it in a folder full of photos from his foreign trips and saved a copy onto one of his mini-flash drives as an added precaution. He then slid this into the ticket pocket of his denims, where it could lie safely without drawing attention to itself.

After emptying the backpack of the few clothes he had brought with him, he returned the laptop to the rucksack. Slipping this over his shoulder, he then closed the door behind him and walked out into the sun.

There was little shade on the walk down into town. But it was a thankfully short stroll. Osman still sat outside his kitchen cracking almonds and sipping çay to the accompaniment of a clarinet from deep inside the restaurant. He showed no sign of recognition as Matt passed.

Matt saw no reason to distract him and explain the sudden departure from his brother's hotel. He walked on past and down into the narrow streets of the old town. Steep streets that ran parallel with each other in the direction of the marina and were criss-crossed by equally narrow streets that ran horizontally along the hillside.

Many of the buildings were immaculate two or three-storey houses built in the classical Turkish style with wooden bay windows and lattice-work screens. Matt could imagine the wives and daughters of the houses peering out from behind them at the men on the streets below back in the days of the Ottoman Empire.

Other buildings were more modern and slightly run down. Every street was decorated with the whole array of offers for the discerning tourist. From tours around the local sights, through fashion, ceramics and jewellery, to upmarket property. He was struck by the number of real estate agents in such a small resort. On almost every street.

This discovery kindled a moment of quiet excitement. Ben had explained that Ahmet ran a property business. So, he must surely be on one of these streets, Matt told himself. He took a notebook from his backpack and drew a rudimentary map of each street – there were only four down and five across – then combed each one, marking every estate agent he passed on the map. There were twelve in total – most of them not yet open.

Comforted in the knowledge that he could have this wrapped up by lunchtime, Matt decided to take a break and enjoy a beer down by the marina before knocking on doors. Watching the gulls as they circled in the sky above and listening to the melodic lapping of the water on the boats below, he took a deep breath of the sea air and wondered what business Ben could possibly have in an idyllic Mediterranean resort like this. Unless he was invested in the property market. Was that his beef with Ahmet?

He sensed a hint of darkness about the mission he had been tasked with. It did not fit with the sunlit peace and quiet of this marina, interrupted only by the gentle sound of music wafting from the restaurant above: a tired old hit from years back. Carly Simon and 'You're So Vain'.

But the peace was short-lived when all at once, the loudspeaker on the white mosque above the marina started blasting out its call to prayers. The mismatch with the western music playing at the restaurant some hundred metres down from the mosque struck even a philistine like Matt as an insult to the locals.

There was little sign that it was an eatery, apart from the music signalling that it was designed for western tourists. Indeed, it was barely visible at all behind the bright magenta of the bougainvillea that crept over the white-painted struts of the pergola and down over the high wall on which it perched. But it looked the perfect place to eat, and he liked their taste in music. So he set his mind on getting a table there as soon as he had checked out all the real estate agents.

The first on his list called itself Akdeniz Properties. He was hopeful that the similarity in the name might be a sign of ownership by a Mr Karadeniz. The office lay just a few metres up the road from the mosque. The door was open, but Matt had the impression as he walked in from the bright sunlight that the place was empty. It was not until his eyes had accustomed themselves to the dimness that he saw someone sitting at a desk in the far corner. The dark-haired young woman who greeted him could have been the sister of the receptionist at his hotel. Her captivating smile, as with all things of beauty, engendered a sense of optimism in Matt – an impression as ill-founded as it was irrational.

There was no one called Ahmet Karadeniz working there. And she insisted that she had never heard of him.

From here, Matt worked his way back up the hill, checking out one agent after another on his list. But the response was always the same. No one knew an Ahmet Karadeniz. And everyone he asked politely repeated the mantra that they had never heard of the man. Until he reached the last agent on the list.

This one bore the name Bay View Properties over the door. And the lady who rose from her desk to greet him as he entered was plainly no more Turkish than the name of the business. With her shoulder-length red hair and her green eyes, she could have been Irish, but she spoke a very middle-class English.

"Good morning," she said brightly, extending her right hand and fanning her face with a brochure in her left. "I'm sorry. The air-con's packed up again this morning. Can I help you?"

"I hope so," he replied, pointing at the motionless arms of an overhead fan with a questioning look as he shook her hand.

"I know," she said with an apologetic shrug. "That's been dead for days as well. So, what can I do for you?"

"My name's Matt Quillan. I'm looking for someone who I believe works in the property business here. And I'm wondering whether you might know where I could find him."

"We all know each other in the business here. What's his name? Oh, I'm Pearl by the way."

"He's called Ahmet Karadeniz."

Matt pronounced the first syllable with an accentuated guttural sound, dragging the aitch over the back of his tongue, as if to burnish his credentials as a man of the world who knew a thing or two about foreign names.

The brightness of her welcome instantly dimmed at the mention of this name.

"Ahh-met," she repeated, emphasising the softness of the first syllable in the manner of a teacher. "The aitch is always silent in Turkish. They don't appreciate being likened to Arabs."

Matt sensed that the dimming of her mood had more to do with the name itself than with his pronunciation of it.

"So, do you know him?" he persisted.

"He moved his office to the next town east of here along the coast," Pearl said. "Why are you looking for him?"

"Business," he replied, mopping his brow. He was uncertain himself what the answer to this question was. But Pearl had at least put a little more flesh on Matt's curiosity about the mysterious Ahmet.

"You said just now that you all know each other in the business here."

Pearl nodded, almost imperceptibly, but said nothing. He caught a sense of nervous anticipation in her manner.

"Which makes me wonder why everyone else I've asked until now says they've never heard of him."

The edgy silence that followed seemed unremittingly endless to Matt. He had the feeling there was something she wanted desperately to say but could not find the words. Finally, she gestured to Matt to take a seat in one of the comfortable chairs reserved for prospective buyers. Then took a chair facing him from the other side of a large coffee table.

"Ahmet was not well liked," she explained. "And people prefer not to be reminded."

"Reminded of what?"

The flicker in Pearl's eyes betrayed a tension that told Matt his question was not about to be answered. A further uneasy silence followed.

"Is that why he moved his office away from here?"

"He was married to a dear friend of mine," she said. The words were neither an answer nor an explanation of anything that might make any sense to Matt. Her mind was elsewhere.

"It was after she died that he decided to move his business," she added. Then paused again.

The halting poverty of detail in her words suggested that she had more to say than she was letting on.

"Look, I haven't eaten since yesterday. And I'm dying to try that restaurant down the road overlooking the marina. Why don't you join me?" Matt asked, in the hope that the more agreeable setting might encourage her to open up.

"I'm sorry. I can't close the office over lunch. And I have a lot of paperwork to do."

There was an abrupt finality about the way she delivered these words. And Matt had suffered enough brush-offs in his life to know it was pointless pursuing their chat any further. But he could not escape the feeling that she wanted to say a lot more.

"Can you at least tell me where to find Ahmet's office? And how I get there?" Matt asked, as he got up from his chair.

"Just follow the coast road to the east," she said, waving her left arm in a random direction that could just as well have been north or west. "It's about fifteen miles from here. He calls it ASK. Can't miss it. You'll see the oversized letters splashed in bold capitals across the building as you enter the village. You can get the dolmuş there. Or a taxi if you're feeling flush."

"Seems a strange name for a real estate business."

"That was his idea," she explained. "**A**hmet and **S**usie **K**aradeniz. And 'AŞK' also means love or passion in Turkish. Susie fell for it straightaway."

The sense of distaste in her words was not lost on Matt. This piqued his curiosity all the more. But he knew it was pointless trying to dig deeper just yet.

"I'll let you know how I get on," he said as he left Pearl's office to stroll back down the road past the white mosque to the restaurant.

The name Zeytin was crudely etched into a wooden plank over the entrance. Apart from an elderly couple in the far corner, the place was empty. He opted for a small table under a tree that was helping to prop up the horizontal struts of the pergola along with the abundance of creeping bougainvillea. Looking out over the yachts that bobbed on the water in the foreground and the expansive blue of the bay beyond, it seemed the ideal place to eat.

Carly Simon had been replaced by another tired old hit from back in the day: 'Albatross' by Fleetwood Mac. It may not go down well with the imam at the mosque, Matt told himself, but the gentle sound of the timpani mallets on the cymbals was a perfect match for the lapping water below.

He ordered a selection of mezes with a glass of rakı. The kitchen lay across the road from the seating area, and his order arrived within minutes. The waiter filled his table with aubergine and pepper salads, stuffed vine leaves, courgette fritters and various dishes he could not identify. He topped up the glass of rakı with water and watched the liquid instantly turn a cloudy white. Memories of a misspent youth in countless Mediterranean haunts were instantly evoked with his first sip of the milky, aniseed-flavoured spirit. Memories that carried him all the way to the last sip of the glass.

"A bit early in the day for lion's milk," came a disembodied voice as he placed the empty glass down in front of him.

Matt looked up to find Pearl standing at his table. He did not immediately recognise her, as she was wearing dark glasses and a wide-brimmed hat that cast a shadow over her face. And her words left him baffled.

"Lion's milk. That's what they call their national drink," she said, pointing to the empty glass. "It makes the men here feel better about themselves when they drink it."

"Well, everyone deserves one guilty pleasure in life. And better this than the white powder that plagued my life for far too long."

Matt paused and regretted for a moment that he had let his guard down with these words.

"Look, if you've changed your mind about lunch, I'm afraid I've just finished," he said, and made a sweeping gesture with his right arm over the empty plates to drive home the message.

"No, I had a sandwich in the office. I just wanted to warn you about Ahmet. He may not have many friends around here. But he has some very unpleasant acquaintances."

From the edginess of her shifty posture, Matt knew she was here for more than a word of warning.

"I appreciate your concern," he said and gestured towards the chair on the opposite side of the table. "Can I offer you a coffee at least for your trouble?"

Pearl hesitated for a moment, then pulled out the chair and sat down. When she removed her sunglasses and placed them on the table, Matt saw the same edgy flicker in her eyes that he had seen in the office earlier. An awkward silence followed as they waited for the coffee and a second glass of rakı to arrive.

"She was so full of beans when I first met her," said Pearl at last, after taking a first cautious sip of her piping hot Turkish coffee.

"Who's she?" Matt asked.

"My friend Susie. She was here with a friend. Only just arrived for a couple of weeks' holiday and, as she was walking past the office, she slipped and fell. It looked a really nasty fall, so I dashed out to help. But she brushed herself off and insisted she was fine. No damage done. And that was how we met.

"That same evening we had dinner together. Me, Susie and her friend Jo, who was a bit of a pain, to be honest. Hardly let anyone get a word in edgeways, telling me Susie's whole life story, how Susie had arrived home from work one afternoon to find her husband Mark dead on the lawn from a heart attack and how she needed to get away from it all. I assumed the death was just too painful for Susie to talk about herself. But why couldn't her friend just show a little discretion?"

By now the edgy flicker in Pearl's eyes had turned to a look of anger and frustration.

"So anyway, the dinner continued like that until Ahmet appeared. Selling roses. He was quite dashing for a flower seller. And he had charm, as so many Turkish men do. He certainly charmed Susie.

"For all Jo's faults, at least she was perceptive enough to see the effect he had on Susie, so she bought a lovely red rose for her friend – and with it the persistent attention of a flower seller that would be Susie's downfall."

"What do you mean?" Matt asked.

"Every time Susie and her friend went out for dinner after that first evening, she told me later, Ahmet would appear selling his roses. Except that when he reached her table, his roses were suddenly not for sale. He simply presented her with a rose and refused to accept any payment 'from such a beautiful woman'. And as the evenings went on, it became two roses, then three and so on."

"So, how did that become her downfall?"

"A relationship that's fed with a staple diet of roses and little else is never going to get very far, is it?" she said, then added with a sense of bewilderment in her voice, "I mean a flower seller for goodness' sake!"

Matt stared across the table into her visible anger. He needed more than elliptical turns of phrase. And she saw the impatience in his glare.

"He was far too young for her," she said. "Almost twenty years, which I suppose added to the excitement after almost thirty years with Mark, who was about twenty years older than her."

She paused briefly, as if gathering her thoughts.

"All I can say is that the liaison with Ahmet was not a happy one for long, despite appearances. But I can't tell you the exact details of how it ended. You should speak to the doctor."

"The doctor?"

"Hauke Schmitt," she said. "He's from Frankfurt originally. But retired here some years ago. He has his own theory about what happened."

"And?" Matt said, probing further when she fell silent.

"I'm sorry. I really find it too hard to talk about," Pearl replied, rising from her chair. Matt caught the trace of a tear as she put her sunglasses on. "Like I say, you should speak to Hauke Schmitt. Now I really have to be getting back."

"No worries," said Matt. "It's really nothing to do with me, anyway. My business is with Ahmet."

"Well, you be very careful," she warned him. "Karakent might seem a pretty little resort. But it's not without its dark sides."

# CHAPTER 4

Pearl's cautionary words nagged at Matt as he finished his second glass of rakı. He settled the bill and strolled up the hill, past the various estate agents he had canvassed earlier. Pearl was now back in the office engrossed in her paperwork as he passed. At the restaurant where the bus had offloaded him the day before, Osman still sat blinking into the sun through the eucalyptus trees that bristled in the early-autumn breeze. It was another slow day for Osman.

Matt continued up the hill until he came to a car rental place that he had noticed on his way down before lunch. It was clear to him that he would need a vehicle over the coming days. He booked a car for two weeks. A white Citroen Elysee.

Fully aware that he was probably over the limit after two glasses of rakı, he still fancied he could handle the traffic here quite easily since he had often driven on the right before and there were not many vehicles around to contend with. He had not reckoned on the tight bends, the slippery surface of the coast road and the fondness of the few drivers he did meet for overtaking blind.

When Matt eventually stepped out of the car in the next town, he convinced himself it was all thanks to the rakı that he had kept his nerve and arrived there in one piece. He smiled at his powers of self-persuasion and closed the door with a gentle thud.

The building stood on the opposite side of the road. Pearl was right about one thing: it was impossible to miss. The huge blood-red letters ASK across the front of the building were so stark they were enough to make any traveller stop and think before venturing further. It had the air of an exhortation by some obscure religious cult: just ask, and the truth shall be yours.

With a sense of caution that tipped into trepidation when he set eyes on a menacing Rottweiler chained up outside the building, he crossed the road. Happily for Matt, the beast was asleep, and continued to doze quietly in the shade as he passed and pushed open the door.

The cool of the air-conditioned office brought a sense of relief. And the fresh yet harsh smell of polish on the wooden floor, a sense of renewal. The combination swept away the last remnants of rakı swimming around his head. At the solitary desk on the far side, behind a coffee table and two leather-bound chairs, sat a young woman. Matt judged her to be in her mid-twenties at most. She had a round, almost oriental face, and wore her black hair tied back in a way that accentuated her Asian appearance. He had noticed on previous trips to this country how many Turks there were with oriental features. He took them to be descendants of Genghis Khan's marauding hordes.

This young woman sat at a computer screen and only registered Matt's presence in her office when he planted himself down and occupied one of the leather-bound chairs in front of her desk.

"Merhaba," she said. "Can I help you?"

She peered around the screen as she spoke and gave Matt an unconvincing smile that made him feel he was not entirely welcome – that he had intruded on something private.

"I'm looking to buy some property," Matt lied.

"My husband is not here at the moment," she said, handing him a card. "He will come in at about five or six this evening. You can talk to him then."

Matt examined the card: a kitschy Ottoman-style border in gold; the blood-red letters ASK splayed across the inside of this frame in bold; and beneath them the name Ahmet Karadeniz complete with phone number and email address.

"Perfect," he said, and smiled back.

He could not believe his luck. This card more than fulfilled the mission for his old friend: he had not only located Ahmet; he now had all the contact details Ben might need.

"See you later," she said, as Matt disappeared back onto the street and crept cautiously past the dozing Rottweiler to his car. Before starting up the engine to set off back to the hotel, he texted Ben: 'Located target. See you soon?'

The sun was getting low in the sky as he motored back along the twists and turns of the coast road – more carefully now that the effects of the rakı had worn off and the sun threatened to dazzle him each time he turned a bend.

Driving up to the Hotel Kelebek, he felt his heart miss a beat at the sight of a familiar van parked outside. It bore the telltale colour blue with a red strip around its midriff and red and blue lights on the roof. It should have come as no surprise. He had been expecting a call from the Jandarma. They were in the lobby talking to the receptionist when he entered. Two of them. Both in dark glasses.

With the memory of Rekan still fresh in his mind and the flash drive in his ticket pocket, Matt did his best to stay cool, ignored the two men in uniform and strolled past the desk towards the staircase up to his room.

"Mr Quillan?" the taller of the two men asked as Matt passed.

Matt stopped and looked around with all the nonchalance he could muster. First at the receptionist. Then at the two men.

"Yes?"

The tall one walked over to Matt with the kind of slow, demonstrative purpose so unique to officialdom and power. He stared at Matt through his dark glasses and said nothing for an unnervingly endless lapse of time. Simply stood there like a living statue, frozen, until Matt relented.

"Can I help you?" he asked, doing his best to give an impression of innocence.

"You come, please," was all the gendarme was prepared to offer in response. He placed a guiding hand on Matt's left upper arm and gestured towards the exit. By the time they reached the door, the shorter gendarme was on the other side of him with a guiding hand on his right arm. And they led him off to the waiting van.

The gendarmerie lay on the outskirts of town. A sprawling, single-storey building, half enclosed by a garden of pink and white oleander bushes. The prettiness of the scene against the sun, which hung low in the sky by now, was at odds with the sense of menace Matt felt as he was escorted through the garden to the entrance.

He was taken to a bare room furnished with only a couple of wooden chairs and a desk that had seen better days. The only window in the room was barred. Clinging to one of the iron struts was the motionless figure of a praying mantis. It had the look of permanence about it, as if posted there to petition Allah for mercy on behalf of anyone locked in the stuffy room. The window was at least open, allowing an occasional swirl of air to blow in from the olive grove around the building. It was a tepid swirl. And did nothing to take the heat out of the dusty room.

Matt stood by the window, almost eyeball to eyeball with the praying mantis, watching for signs of movement. Only its head rotated slightly when he edged closer, as if to acknowledge his presence. Otherwise, the creature remained stock still. For Matt, it seemed to accentuate the stifling inertia in the room – until the door behind him swept open.

He spun around to find in the doorway a tall, distinguished-looking man with a head of thick, salt-and-pepper hair. The three stars on his epaulettes told Matt that this gendarme was several ranks higher than the two who had brought him here. He was also somewhat older. Fifty-something, Matt reckoned. All of which lent the man an air of authority that was underscored by the official-looking folder he carried under his arm.

"Good evening, Mr Quillan," he said in perfect English with an overly welcoming geniality that told Matt he should be on his guard. The man sat down behind the desk, placed the folder in front of him and flicked it open. "Could I see your passport, please?"

Matt pulled his passport out of the backpack he still had with him and placed it on the desk.

"You travelled here from Istanbul by bus," the officer said in a questioning tone as he leafed through the passport. "May I ask why?"

"What do you mean 'why'?"

"Why did you not fly?" the gendarme persisted, still thumbing the passport. "It's much quicker."

"Quicker's not always better. And I like buses. I wanted to see the countryside."

"And did you like our countryside?"

"Very much," Matt said. And instantly regretted his words of such fawning approval.

The gendarme closed the passport, placed it on the folder in front of him and fixed a long, piercing gaze on Matt. But said nothing. Pushing the passport to one side, he then spent some minutes sifting through the papers in the folder. Matt grew increasingly uncomfortable.

"How do you know Rekan Yavuz?" the gendarme said at long last without looking up from the folder.

"Who?"

"The man who was with you on the bus from Istanbul," Matt's inquisitor said.

"No one was with me on the bus. I'm travelling alone."

A smile crossed the gendarme's lips. Matt sensed it was an expression of disbelief.

"Why?" the man asked, raising his head and looking Matt straight in the eye.

"Why not? I like travelling alone. I like my own company."

"But why here?" the man asked. "Why come here?"

"I'm here for a friend back in the UK," Matt said. "He's looking for someone."

This piqued the gendarme's curiosity all the more. He fixed Matt with a piercing stare across the desk.

"Who is he looking for? What is the name of this person?"

"I think it was probably a holiday romance," Matt lied. "He didn't go into details."

For all its apparent geniality, the smirk that greeted this information went beyond disbelief. It carried a hint of menace.

"Could I see your phone?" he asked. And, as Matt handed him his mobile phone, added: "Are you sure the name of the person is not Rekan?"

"No, it's Samantha," Matt lied again. "I wasn't given a surname. So, it's not going to be easy finding her."

"Şifre?" the gendarme asked as he fiddled intently with Matt's phone.

"What?"

"Şifre, şifre," he repeated impatiently.

"Oh right," Matt said.

He took the phone, entered his PIN code and handed it back to the gendarme, who then spent the next five minutes scrolling through all Matt's messages. Visibly irritated that he could find nothing to hint of any contact with a Rekan, he finally pounced on his last text message to Ben.

"What does this mean?" he asked, showing the message to Matt and reading the words: "Located target."

"Oh that," Matt said with contrived nonchalance. "I was asked to look out for some real estate while I'm here. My friend's in the market for a nice villa to buy."

The gendarme pursed his lips in concentration. His suspicions were not quelled by Matt's discovery of such impromptu storytelling skills.

"This Samantha," he said. "Does she have a villa here? We can check the records with the Belediye."

"No, she was on vacation. Staying with someone."

"Perhaps the name of this someone is Rekan?" The gendarme probed and prodded further, increasingly sceptical of Matt's explanations.

"Look, I really don't know what this is all about. I'm here for an old friend of mine. And I don't know anyone called Rekan, never met anyone called Rekan," Matt added, lying this time with an impatience that was born more of creeping nervousness than frustration.

He had no idea who this Rekan was. But he had been entrusted with the young man's information. And while he had no wish to play the martyr for a complete stranger, his distrust of authority made Matt wary of giving up the mysterious flash drive to a gendarme whose trustworthiness was as tenuous as the smile on his lips.

These thoughts were running through Matt's mind when the corridor outside the room exploded with the sound of crashing doors and raised voices. A fierce argument appeared to be under way. Matt's interrogator did not bat an eyelid. He calmly picked up the folder with the passport and rose from his chair.

"Wait here, please," he said, and disappeared out through the door, leaving Matt to contemplate the bareness of his surroundings once again.

Nothing had changed during the surrealistic rambling of their conversation. Dust still covered the floor. The air in the room was no less sultry. And the praying mantis continued to cling motionless to the bars over the open window. Only the sound of angry voices intruded on the stifling air and ruffled the inertia in the room. He waited, pacing up and down for a good fifteen minutes while the disturbance ran its course.

"What's going on?" Matt asked once the noise had died down and his inquisitor swept back into the room.

The gendarme stood at the door, that now familiar gaze fixed on Matt, who had the impression that the man had dire news. But he said nothing – until he threw the door wide open, stood to one side and declared:

"You can go."

There was a sense of disappointment in the man's expression that was not lost on Matt as he picked up his backpack and made to leave.

"Your passport," said the gendarme, and handed Matt the document. Then added with an ominous caution: "Be careful of the friends you make here."

As Matt passed through the station lobby, he could not fail to notice a stranger in the middle of the room, pacing up and down, as if waiting for the bizarre interview to end. He cut an imposing figure. Tall, wearing an immaculate white suit, white tie and white shoes, with a red pocket square in the breast pocket, he was plainly not a gendarme. But he carried an air of authority even greater than that of Matt's interrogator.

By the time Matt walked out onto the streets, the place was shrouded in the dusk of early evening. His inquisitor's words of warning stuck with Matt, and haunted his every step all the way back to the hotel. He had the distinct feeling the Jandarma would be watching his every move from now on.

When he arrived at his lodging, the reception desk was in the charge of a portly man he had not seen before. His hair slicked back and clearly dyed a pitch black to disguise his fifty-something years, he sat frantically fanning himself with a magazine. Matt's heart sank the moment he entered the building, laid eyes on the fluttering motion, and was immediately hit by the stifling heat and the realisation that the air-conditioning had packed up.

The man on the desk looked up.

"No electricity," he grumbled. The smile that came with these words was more an expression of resignation than apology.

Matt attempted a smile in return and went upstairs to his room. As he was sliding the key into the lock, he felt the vibration of the phone in his back pocket. Closing the door behind him, he put his backpack in the chair, threw himself onto the bed and checked the phone.

It was a message from Ben:

'Great news! Currently in Rhodes. Be with you soon.'

# CHAPTER 5

When Matt drew back the curtains of his room in the morning, he had to admit that Osman's brother had the edge over the Hotel Kelebek in one respect. There was no view over the sparkling blues of the sea here. Only a concrete mass of dusty building works that crawled relentlessly up the mountainside behind. One half-finished villa after the other, all waiting to be snapped up by sun-seekers who could think of nothing better to do with their money. And now he did not even have the air-con to crow about. With the electricity still off, he had been treated to a suffocating and sleepless night that had left him exhausted and drenched with sweat.

He took a long, cold shower, slipped yesterday's clothes back on, and ventured out into the morning air in search of breakfast.

Most of the cafés and restaurants were only just opening up. Or were still closed. But the air at least was refreshingly cool. And the streets were slowly coming alive with the darting sound of mopeds and scooters.

There was no sign of life in Osman's restaurant when Matt passed by. The bars and cafés beyond were also closed. He decided to try the marina, where he imagined the cafés might open earlier for the yacht owners. But the seafarers plainly catered for their own breakfasts on board. The only sign of life here was the occasional stray dog sniffing around the hibiscus bushes that lined the street separating the cafés and restaurants from the marina.

It was just as he reached the restaurant where he had enjoyed a beer the day before that he caught a familiar sound. The gently muted tone of timpani mallets on cymbals and the dreamy, floating effect of a guitar. It wafted out over the bougainvillea above. 'Albatross'. It told Matt that at least the Zeytin must be open for business.

Matt wandered back up the winding street to find a lean, sixty-something man with a thick mop of white hair laying the tables. He was deep in concentration.

"Are you open for breakfast?" Matt asked. The man span around.

"Welcome! Hoşgeldin!" he said with a sweeping gesture of his arm and a gleaming grin. "Please."

Matt was spoiled for choice, but went for the table he had occupied the previous day. Before he had a chance to place an order, the white-haired man had disappeared across the street into the darkness of the kitchen. Within a minute or two, he returned with a platter of olives, cucumber and tomatoes together with bread and a large tulip-shaped glass of tea.

"Not quite what I'm used to for breakfast," he said with an air of disappointment, as he dropped two sugar cubes into the tea, "but thank you."

"You are in Turkey," the man remarked.

The needless observation irritated Matt for the way the man lingered by the table, as if he had a whole lot more to get off his chest. Matt simply wanted to be left alone to enjoy his tea.

"You were here yesterday," the man added. "Talking with Pearl."

"Mmm," Matt nodded, increasingly vexed by the stream of superfluous remarks and the thought that his every move in this town appeared to be under surveillance. He looked around for any sign of a gendarme watching from a shady spot. But saw none.

"Your name?" the man asked.

"Matthew."

"My name Yusuf," the man said, placing a hand on his chest as he did so.

Despite the welcoming grin, Matt was innately suspicious of anyone who was given to watching him. So, he was more than a little dubious about exchanging first names. And to find himself nevertheless doing so disquieted him even more – until the man's next intriguing words:

"You speak about Susie."

"Pearl was speaking about Susie," Matt corrected him. "I was more interested in Ahmet."

Matt was struck by the sense of darkness that swept across Yusuf's face at the mention of Ahmet's name. Like a shadow cast by the movement of a dense cloud. And he saw what looked like the moisture of tears as Yusuf quickly turned and disappeared into the kitchen. Only moments later, Yusuf returned with a glass of tea and the same beaming grin that had greeted Matt a little earlier, yet this time with a hint of earnestness in his eyes. He sat down at the table with his tea.

"Why your interest in Ahmet?"

Matt had not reckoned on sharing breakfast time. He wanted it to himself, and the unwanted company bothered him – until he caught sight of a man further up the street from the restaurant. A slim, well-dressed young man with greased-back hair and thin moustache. He sat in the shade of a tree, playing with a set of red worry beads.

When Matt glanced casually in the direction of the figure with the worry beads; he had the impression the man was watching the restaurant. Or was it Matt he was watching?

He recalled his visit to the Jandarma the day before. The interrogation. Their fixation on Rekan from the bus. And the words of warning when Matt left. These memories fuelled his curiosity about the files that still lay snugly in the ticket pocket of his jeans.

"Does the name Bozkurt mean anything to you?" he asked, ignoring Yusuf's question. "Or Ergenekon maybe?"

Matt's words injected a darkness into Yusuf's mood. All trace of a smile evaporated. Dropping three sugar cubes into the tea and stirring them with painfully slow deliberation, he contemplated every granule of sugar until all three cubes were completely dissolved. And said nothing all the while. Matt sensed that he was mulling over some private disquiet.

"My brother is writer," said Yusuf when eventually he found the words to speak. "Journalist. He write many reports, articles. The Kurdish problem. The AK party. The corruption. Many things. Now he is a guest of the government in Izmir."

Yusuf took a sip of his tea, before adding with a sigh of resignation:

"Some things it is best not to talk about."

Hidden in the back of the kitchen across the street, someone had changed the music from nostalgic western rock to the plaintive sounds of Anatolia. A gently wailing reed flute combined with the strings of the bağlama lent an almost mystical quality to the atmosphere. It conflicted with the sudden darkening of Yusuf's mood.

Matt glanced up the street at the man with the worry beads. He still sat there in the shade of the tree. Watching the restaurant.

It brought to mind the gendarme's last words the evening before: "Be careful of the friends you make here."

Listening now to the tale of Yusuf's brother, Matt wondered whether maybe it was Yusuf who was the object of their interest. This train of thought was brought to a jarring halt by a new voice calling from across the street.

"Baba! Baba!"

It was the cry of a young woman who Matt reckoned to be in her early twenties. She came running over to them from the kitchen. Yusuf instantly broke into his irresistible grin and put an arm around her as she stood beside him.

"This is my daughter, Belgin," he announced with beaming pride as he turned to Matt.

"Matt," he said in return, and Belgin smiled sweetly in reply.

"What is it, my love?" Yusuf asked his daughter.

"Oh, nothing important," she said, still smiling at Matt, yet obviously dying to know what her father had been confiding in this stranger.

"You look so sad. What were you speaking about?"

"We were talking about your Uncle Adnan," Yusuf replied, then turned to Matt. "My daughter loves her uncle very much. She misses him. Don't you, my love?"

Belgin nodded.

"But we also talk of other things," Yusuf continued, visibly uncomfortable with the talk of his brother and keen to change the subject. "Matthew wants to know about Ahmet."

"Ahmet?" Belgin repeated.

"Karadeniz," her father said.

Belgin stared down at her father with a look that spoke of complete incomprehension and carried more than a hint of disapproval. Ahmet was plainly a no-go topic of discussion for Yusuf's daughter.

"How can you go from one sad story to another like that?" she said in disbelief. "How does it help when you change the conversation about Uncle Adnan to a conversation about Susie?"

"Why is it," Matt chipped in, "that, whenever I say the name Ahmet Karadeniz, everyone starts talking about this Susie woman?"

"She was a lovely woman, very special. Always try helping people," Belgin said, as if this explained everything.

"So I gather from Pearl."

"Susie and Pearl were very close," she added, "and my father, also."

"She was a good cook. And she give some interesting ideas for our menus," said Yusuf. He chuckled at his private memories. "I remember the first evening she come to our lokanta – our restaurant – and she ask why we have no horseradish on the table. 'English people love horseradish,' she say."

Belgin smiled.

"I think she was only speaking for herself."

"That's true," her father admitted. "But she had such heart."

"He was in love with her." Belgin laughed, nudging him with her elbow. Yusuf ignored his daughter's teasing.

"She promised me that evening she would bring me some horseradish from England and show me how to cook it. But she was wrong. The English tourists who come here are not so happy with it."

"Perhaps it doesn't go with the sun," Matt suggested.

"You may be right, my friend," Yusuf replied, and took another sip of tea from his glass. "Susie say to me that Ahmet have same in the mountains of the Black Sea region. It's much colder there and they have more rain. So, you may be right. But what he bring from the Black Sea not good."

"What do you mean?" Matt asked.

Yusuf's last words had cast his mind into a deep pool of reflection. The tense mood was heightened by the mystic wailing of the reed flute from across the street. He looked hopelessly lost in his thoughts. His daughter took over for him.

"My father was the last person to see Susie alive," Belgin said. Her words came with the air of an explanation. Yet they told Matt nothing.

He slipped a black olive into his mouth and pondered the way his short stay in this country had so far been shaped entirely by innuendo and half-meanings that brought him no further to the truth behind his mission. He may have tracked this enigmatic Ahmet down, built a vague picture of the man and gotten his contact details, but the connection with his old friend Ben

Braithwaite was as elusive as ever.

From what he had gleaned so far, there seemed to be only two possible explanations. Either Ben's interest in the former flower seller had something to do with a dodgy property deal. Or it involved this Susie woman in some way. Whatever the explanation, it left Matt with another set of questions: What were Ben's plans now that Ahmet had been located? Where did Matt fit in, since his part in the mission had been completed? And what else might his old friend expect from him?

Matt had begun to feel way outside his comfort zone as soon as he became a person of interest to the gendarmerie. And now, to top it all, the conversation with Yusuf and his daughter gave him a sense of being drawn ever deeper into someone else's story around a mysterious death.

Ben's arrival could not come soon enough for Matt. Now that he had fulfilled the mission for his old friend and located Ahmet, there was nothing to keep him here any longer than necessary.

It was Belgin's voice that broke his train of thought.

"Why are you interested in Ahmet?" she asked.

"I'm not," Matt said. "A friend of mine is looking for him. Just don't ask me why, because I have no idea."

He finished his çay and slipped a last olive into his mouth.

"Could you bring the bill please?"

"Please come back tonight," Yusuf beseeched, as Matt reached for his wallet. "This is your table. I will reserve it for you and we will speak again."

Matt assured him that he would. With little else to do while he waited for Ben to arrive, he was intrigued to learn more about Yusuf's imprisoned brother. But he was equally curious to know who the stranger under the tree might be.

"Do you know that man?" he asked, nodding discreetly in the direction of the stranger with the worry beads, as Yusuf opened a bottle of yellow liquid and sprinkled a lemon-scented cologne on Matt's hands before he left.

Yusuf screwed the top back on the bottle and glanced up the street.

"No. He is not from here," he said.

But Matt detected a cagey concern in Yusuf's voice.

# CHAPTER 6

The moment Matt made a move to stroll back up the street, the man with the worry beads got to his feet and sauntered casually into an alleyway that led behind the mosque. By the time Matt had reached the junction with this alleyway, the man had disappeared.

The shops and estate agents had begun to open up by now, and when Matt reached Bay View Properties further up the road, he found this office was no exception. Pearl was seated at her desk talking to another woman, who lounged in one of the comfortable chairs. Pearl caught sight of him as he passed, waved and sprang to her feet.

"How did you get on?" she called from the doorway. "Did you find him?"

"I found the office. But he wasn't there."

"Come on in for a çay and a chat," she said with an inviting swish of her right arm.

Matt followed her into the office and was immediately comforted by the cool freshness of the air that told him the air-conditioning was up and running again. He hoped this was a sign that he also had power now in the hotel.

"Matt, this is my gorgeous baby sister, Amber. She just arrived last night for her annual fortnight."

The sister wore a lime-green top and white culottes that combined perfectly with her strawberry-blonde hair and matched the freshness of the air in the office. From the comfort of her easy chair, she offered Matt her hand with an engaging smile, accompanied by the jangling sound of two thick white bangles on her wrist.

"She makes me sound like a chore," Amber said.

"You are," Pearl insisted with a grin. "Have been since the day you came into the world."

"So, Matt," Amber said, ignoring her sister's remark, "who is it you're trying to find? Or is it none of my business?"

"It's a long story," Matt replied, unwilling to admit that yes, it was none of her business.

"He's looking for Ahmet," Pearl chipped in. "And the way you told it to me, Matt, it sounded like a pretty short story."

Matt refused to be drawn any further on the vagueness of his mission and changed the subject.

"I was talking to Yusuf and his daughter earlier," Matt said. "He seemed pretty cut up. His daughter said he was the last to see Susie alive."

"This sounds juicy," Amber promptly chimed in, as her large blue eyes grew bigger still with expectation.

"You know the story already," Pearl said, dashing her sister's hopes of any new gossip and gesturing her to sit back in her chair. Matt eased himself into the chair beside her.

"So, what is the story?" Matt asked, turning to Pearl as he sat down. "And what's Ahmet's part in all of it?"

Pearl said nothing, but disappeared into the back room to make the tea, leaving him to admire her sister's deep blue eyes and the delicate symmetry of every feature from the faintly dimpled chin through the Goldilocks lips to her slender eyebrows. There was something about her manner, as well as her looks, that was trying to remind Matt of someone. But he could not put his finger on the memory.

"Why are you looking for him?" Amber asked in turn, equally keen to know where Matt came into the story.

"Here you go," Pearl said, interrupting with a tray of Turkish tea glasses, which she set down on the table.

"Yes, he was very cut up," she added, absolving Matt of the need to answer Amber's question.

"When Yusuf heard the next morning that she'd died, he was heartbroken, especially as he'd noticed how unwell she looked and had said nothing. He felt it was partly his fault. That if he had said something, she might have seen the doctor and still be alive today. But that wasn't the only reason he was so cut up."

She hesitated, her lips moving almost imperceptibly, as if on the brink of forming words. Matt sensed that she was carefully pondering what to say next.

"I probably shouldn't mention this, but the thing that really upset Yusuf was what Ahmet said to him on the evening of her death."

She paused again.

"Go on," Amber said.

Pearl took a deep breath.

"Ahmet told Yusuf they'd just changed her will that day."

After a sharp intake of breath by Amber and a "No! You never told me that before!" the three of them fell into an embarrassed silence that lasted for some minutes. They sipped on their tea, each waiting for someone else to speak. It was eventually Pearl who broke the stillness in the room.

"I shouldn't have told you."

"Are you saying Ahmet killed her for her money?" Amber asked, still in shock.

"No, I'm not saying that," Pearl insisted. "There has been talk of course. As you can imagine. It was Hauke Schmitt who first raised the suspicion, but I'm not sure how much truth there is in it. It's only conjecture and gossip, really."

"Hauke? The German doctor?" Amber asked.

Pearl nodded.

"So, what's the gossip?" Amber persisted. She was not about to let go now, while Matt looked on, gripped by the exchange between these sisters.

"It could have been accidental," Pearl said.

"What are you saying, exactly?"

Amber frowned.

"What was accidental?"

"As I said to Matt yesterday, Hauke Schmitt's the one to talk to. He's the one who came up with the idea that she might have been poisoned."

"Poisoned?" Amber shrieked. "That's horrible!"

"What's horrible?" came a deep, gravelly voice from the doorway.

Matt turned to see a tall man of slim build strolling into the office, his long face framed by curls of dark hair tied back in a ponytail. Just behind him, in the doorway, stood another figure silhouetted against the sunlit street. Matt had the impression from the way he stood there that he was connected with this newcomer in some way.

"Hamza! I didn't expect you back already," said Pearl, getting out of her chair and leaning up on tiptoe to land a kiss on the man's lips.

"You know my sister, Amber," she added. "And this is Matt."

Hamza beamed a big grin at them both and shook hands with Matt.

"Hamza's my husband," Pearl explained. "He helps me run the business alongside his own shop."

"So, what's horrible?" he asked again.

"We were just talking about Susie," Pearl confessed, "and Hauke Schmitt."

"Ahh," was all her husband had to say in reply. This one long, drawn-out syllable and the look of displeasure that came with it piqued Matt's curiosity.

"But don't forget we have to take a look at the books this morning," Hamza reminded her.

"I hadn't forgotten."

"Well, perhaps we should let you get on with your work," Matt said in a show of discretion that disguised a more selfish ambition. "Do you fancy a drink, Amber, while we leave them to their work?"

Amber gave him that same bewitching smile that she had seduced him with the moment Pearl had introduced them to each other. If only he could access that compartment in his memory that was jogged every time she smiled like that.

"I'd love to," she replied. "But I have one or two things to do first. Could we say half an hour?"

Matt gave a casual nod of approval. It was meant as a dispassionate, almost non-committal gesture. But he was feeling a buzz of anticipation and only hoped it didn't show.

"There's a bar up the road called the Utopia. You'll have passed it on your way down," Amber added, as she rose from her chair and gathered up her shoulder bag. "I'll see you there."

"Bye sis, bye Hamza," she added with a wave and swept out, smiling at the silhouetted stranger in the doorway as he moved back into the street to let her pass. Matt found the man's presence unnerving, until Hamza said something over his shoulder in Turkish, and the man instantly turned and headed off down the street towards the marina.

It was only then that Matt noticed Hamza's silent sidekick was accompanied by a woman. Wearing a headscarf and traditional pardosu that was so long it almost touched the ground; she gave an impression of complete obscurity. And when the man turned to go, she followed in his footsteps without a sound. Like a shadow.

"That's Amber for you," Pearl said, interrupting Matt's contemplation of the shadow woman in a tone that came across almost as a health warning. "Here one minute, gone the next."

"Who are *they?*" Matt asked, ignoring Pearl's words and gesturing in the direction of the couple.

"That's my assistant Hasan," Hamza said. "And his wife, Fidan."

Matt was struck by the apparent servility of this shrouded woman, the way she dutifully followed her husband without a word. For Matt, there was something almost medieval about the scene. But he gave no further thought to the pair. He was keen to keep his appointment with Amber. So, taking his leave of Pearl and Hamza, he headed for the bar.

Amber had been correct about one thing: he had passed it on the way down; he had simply failed to notice the place, perhaps because the bar itself sat on a platform above the patio of empty tables and lounge seats extending out onto the pavement. As he approached it now, he saw signs of activity inside. But the lounge seats on the patio, with their enticing view through a row of eucalyptus trees and over the bay, still showed little sign of custom. All the tables were empty except for one. This was occupied by an elderly bespectacled man in a light linen suit and Panama hat. He was nursing the standard glass of Turkish tea.

Matt took one of the lounge seats at the far end. Barely had he sat down, than he was greeted by the sound of an ungracious crusty voice. It was a good match for the dowdy owner of the voice: a grey-haired man in his mid-sixties coming down the steps from the bar. The man wore a brown T-shirt and shorts that looked as if they had not seen a washing machine all season. But his appearance was at odds with the sparkle in his eyes and the faintly Irish lilt in that otherwise sullen tone.

"What can I get you?" he asked.

It was too early for beer. Matt knew this. But he had already had more than enough Turkish tea for the day. And he had no stomach for coffee. He called for a beer. The man turned and vanished back into the bar.

"It's never too early for a cool Efes," said the man, as if he had been reading Matt's mind all the while, when he placed the glass of Turkish Pilsner on the table.

"Haven't seen your face around here before," he added. "Your first time in Karakent?"

Matt nodded.

"Thought so. I've a good memory for faces, and I've been here over ten years now. I'd have recognised you if you'd been here before."

"Ten years is a long time. What brought you here?"

"Ah, that's a long story," the man said, pulling up a chair and sitting down at Matt's table. "Most of us who've put down roots here are running away from something."

He left this remark to linger in the air, before adding, "How long are you here for? Um... I didn't catch your name."

"I didn't give it."

"No, quite. Of course you didn't. Thomas Moore," he continued unabashed, offering his right hand to Matt and extending his left arm with a sweeping gesture towards the name UTOPIA in large letters over the doorway to the bar.

"Which explains the name. I have one O too many, of course, but what the hell? And when you look at that view over the bay, you have to agree. It's paradise, isn't it?" he added with a look of self-satisfied pride in his eyes. "You can call me Tom, by the way."

"If you've been here so long," Matt said, "you probably know Ahmet Karadeniz."

"The locals don't drink here," Tom replied curtly.

Matt was struck by the contradiction between Tom's apparent geniality on the one hand and his evasions on the other. It was a conflict that dovetailed neatly with the mismatch between the sullen crustiness of his voice and the twinkle in his eye.

"You found it then," came a softer and more welcome voice to interrupt his thoughts.

"Amber! You're looking as lovely as ever," Tom said, getting up from his seat. "When did you get here?"

"I flew in last night," she replied with her inimitable smile.

"With your latest conquest?" he asked, nodding in Matt's direction.

"Good heavens, Tom," Amber said, the smile now in full retreat and a look of mock horror on her face. "We've only just met."

"Ah well, there's plenty of time yet. And if you do find you're in the mood for conquest, Utopia's the place to be."

"Tom, you're embarrassing us both. Could you just bring me something to drink?"

"I'm sorry," Tom said, hands raised in a gesture of apology. "Your usual?"

Amber nodded, and Tom disappeared up the steps into the bar while she took the seat he had just vacated.

"He's a bit over the top, isn't he?" Matt said. "But he's right. You do look lovely."

The smile she had shown earlier reappeared now with a vaguely apprehensive look about it that told Matt his flattery was not as welcome as he had hoped. He instantly regretted his forwardness. And begrudged Thomas Moore the familiarity that he enjoyed with Amber.

"Here you go," Tom said, placing Amber's drink in front of her, then withdrew to attend to a table of new guests that had just arrived.

"That looks delicious. What is it?" Matt asked, still racked with a certain envy at the thought that sullen-but-affable Tom was privy to any of Amber's favourite things.

"It is. Utterly refreshing. Fresh lemon juice with mint."

"So, tell me about yourself," said Matt.

"What do you want to know?"

"Anything. Everything. What do you do, for example?"

"Everything is really quite uninteresting," Amber replied. "I live with my cat, run a little bookshop in Brighton and take a holiday in Turkey once a year. I can't afford to take the time off. And can't really afford holidays either. Which is why I stay with my sister when I need to get away. It's the cheap option. That's about it."

"I've always found the idea of running a bookshop quite romantic," he said.

"Really?" She cast a look of tired incredulity at Matt. "We're not talking City Lights and San Francisco here, you know. Those days are long past. This is Brighton in the age of Amazon. Browsing bookshelves is one of those pleasures enjoyed by an ever-dwindling population."

At that moment, a stray dog limped around their table. It stroked Amber's leg with its tail as it passed, then wandered off down the street. She sat watching the lame mongrel in what seemed to Matt to be an anxious silence until it disappeared.

"But I'm sure you have a much more interesting story to tell," she continued, peering at him as she sipped on her lemon juice.

"I really don't," Matt said. "Father died when I was in my early teens. That was pretty tough. So, I settled for a quiet, settled future and studied economics. Worked at a bank for a year or two until I couldn't stand the life of those pin-striped louts any longer. Then drifted through life as barman, bouncer and whatever else I was completely unsuited for.

"Insane really. I mean, if you're looking for a quiet life, you don't go working in dubious clubs and wild bars. Sums me up, I suppose: one big walking contradiction."

He paused, looked up to see a smile of amusement in Amber's eyes as she sipped on her drink and persuaded himself it was a look of affection.

"Always on the lookout for the main chance, I guess," he added. "Then opportunity knocked and I started my own security business."

"Security?" Amber said in a questioning tone that left Matt uncertain whether it spoke of disbelief or a kind of satisfied approval. He opted for the latter.

"Sounds exciting, doesn't it?" he said. "Truth be told, I feel a bit of an imposter. I'm no action man, just a pen pusher. But it pays the rent – and divorce fees for my soon-to-be ex-wife who got fed up with me being so focused on my business."

"Oh."

There was a look of awkwardness in Amber's eyes that he was unable to read. Had he overshared, Matt wondered – until she added:

"Kids?"

He shook his head and took a deep swig of his beer, as if to wash down this part of his life and let it be forgotten.

"That's good," was all she said, and sipped on her lemon drink in synchrony with Matt. "So, is it business that brings you here in search of Ahmet?"

"Ahmet?" came a disembodied voice from over Matt's shoulder. "Are you still talking about that awful man?"

He looked around to find an elegantly dressed man in a Panama hat, probably in his late sixties, early seventies. Matt recognised him as the solitary man he had seen nursing a glass of tea.

"Dr Schmitt," said Amber with a tone of pleasant surprise in her voice. "It's so nice to see you again."

"The pleasure is all mine," the man said, taking Amber's hand in his and bowing gently to plant a kiss on the back of her hand.

Matt now detected the hint of a German accent in his voice. 'So, this is the Hauke Schmitt they keep talking about,' he told himself. He stood up and gave the man his hand.

"Matt Quillan."

"Schmitt," the doctor said with a formal bow of the head as he shook Matt by the hand.

"Do join us Dr Schmitt," said Amber.

A part of Matt was fervently willing the doctor to refuse her invitation. He still knew far too little of Amber and wanted her company to himself. But there was another part of him that was curious to learn what this mysterious Dr Schmitt had to say about the man his old friend Ben was looking for.

# CHAPTER 7

"So, you know Ahmet?" Matt said, when the German doctor accepted Amber's invitation and settled into his seat.

"Of course," the doctor replied with the kind of firm certainty of tone that seems peculiar to German speakers.

"Amber's sister told me of his humble start here a few years ago selling flowers," Matt said. "But when I visited yesterday…"

"You visited?" Hauke Schmitt interrupted, peering over his gold-rim glasses with a look of astonishment.

"He wasn't there so I didn't see him," Matt explained.

"I'm happy to hear that. And it makes me very happy indeed to say that no one has seen him for months."

"Why is that?" Matt asked. "I mean, why does it make you happy? And why does no one have a good word to say about him?"

The doctor looked across the table at Amber as Tom brought another glass of tea and placed it on the table in front of him. He adjusted his Panama hat to shield his eyes further from the sun and took a deep breath.

"Ahmet Karadeniz seduced… I believe that is the expression," he said, lingering uncertainly on his choice of word, "seduced a lovely Englishwoman to marry him, to convert to Islam even. Then he destroyed her."

Hauke Schmitt drew the glass of tea closer to him. His hand shook as he dropped two sugar cubes into the tea, then began frenetically to stir them around the glass.

"Are you talking about Susie?" Tom chipped in. "Aye, she was lovely all right."

"Indeed," Dr Schmitt said as he put the teaspoon back in the saucer and said no more.

The stiff posture of the German doctor made it clear to Matt that this intervention was unwanted. It had the effect of closing down any further conversation until Tom eventually slunk back up the steps to the bar without another word.

"Pearl says you think she might have been poisoned," Amber said, finally breaking the silence.

"Did she?" was all he offered in reply.

Hauke Schmitt was reluctant to be drawn any further.

"Are you a medical doctor?" Matt asked.

"A cardiologist. But I'm retired now. When I bought my holiday home here many years ago, there were no roads to speak of and it took two days by donkey to reach the closest town of any size. After a lifetime in Frankfurt, it seemed the perfect refugium, so to speak, for peace and quiet. I only hope we are not soon overrun by Russians, like so many other places in this country."

Matt had the impression Dr Schmitt was thankful for this chance to change the subject. But Amber was not about to hide her obvious impatience for more detail.

"So, *do* you think Susie was poisoned?" she persisted.

"Let me put it this way," he said. "I have always had a special interest in pharmacology. And I observed signs in that lady during the time I knew her, which on reflection – post-mortem, so to speak – made me sit up and think."

"What signs?" asked Amber.

"There is a condition known as mad honey disease, which is sometimes reported here, especially in the Black Sea region," Dr Schmitt explained.

"Grayanotoxin poisoning," Amber said. There was a flutter of excitement in her voice, as if she had just rediscovered a treasure thought to have been lost forever. "I've read about that."

Her eyes were alight now. She appeared instantly engrossed.

Matt flashed a look of shock across the table at Amber. He was taken aback by her grasp of such arcane detail. And he could see that Hauke Schmitt was no less startled, fixing a gaze on her that fell somewhere closer to suspicion than surprise.

The doctor took his last sip of tea, placed the glass carefully back in the saucer and sat forward into the sun that shone through a gap in the umbrella above them. Enlivened by Amber's apparent knowledge of the subject, he looked her in the eye and said with a pretentious engagement in his German accent that came across to Matt as pompous bluster,

"*Nomen est omen*, as they say." He adjusted his hat again to keep out the sunlight. "The disease is caused by the consumption of honey in excessive quantities. But this is not the honey you buy in the shops. It's made from the blossom of a plant they call alpine rose. Or pontic rhododendron to give it its true name. It has a deceptively pretty flower.

"Have you read Xenophon's account where he describes the March of the Ten Thousand over the mountains to the Black Sea?"

Dr Schmitt tapped the saucer with his teaspoon two or three times with the air of an impatient professor. Matt and Amber exchanged the quizzical glances of two students embarrassed by their ignorance. And the doctor smiled, as if pleased to have put Amber back in her place.

"It was probably the very first report of mad honey disease," he continued. "Almost two and a half thousand years ago. Xenophon's army was flattened by it. If you consume too much of this honey, you see, it will make you very sick."

"Sick?" Matt repeated. "You mean sick as in vomiting?"

"Vomiting, yes," he agreed. "That can be one of the signs. But it has many effects. On the central nervous system. And the heart. Sinus bradycardia and… um," he hesitated. "Mobitz, atrioventricular block, for example."

"I'm sorry," Matt interrupted. "Your English is excellent, but you've completely lost me now."

Hauke Schmitt smiled across the table at Matt with a wave of the hand as if to dismiss the flattery.

"Oh, I spent many years in Britain's African colonies. So, my English may seem slightly odd at times."

"It was the medical jargon I had in mind," Matt said.

"Well, I won't bore you with the technical details," Hauke Schmitt replied with an air of loftiness that rankled with Matt, who fell into an aggrieved sulk. But Amber still hung on the doctor's every word.

"The early symptoms often go unnoticed," he said. "It may start with slight dizziness, tingling or blurred vision. But in time, with large doses, it will lead to a loss of coordination and weakness of the muscles."

"And you saw all this in Susie?" asked Amber.

"No," he said. "I did not see all these things. But what I saw in that lady disturbed me immensely. She looked increasingly unwell. She lost her sunny manner. Her hair lost its shine. She no longer dressed so well. And yes, perhaps there were coordination problems and such. But if they existed, I only noticed them post hoc, so to speak."

Dr Schmitt looked visibly troubled as he fell into quiet contemplation. The uneasy mood that followed was interrupted only by the return of the stray dog. It limped along, weaving from table to table and back again, stroking its tail on Amber's legs every time it passed, until it finally settled at her feet.

"It was only after her death that I made the connection," Hauke said, breaking the silence at last.

"What connection?" asked Matt.

"I remembered that she told me one day about the jars of honey, which Ahmet brought back for her every time he returned from his home near the Black Sea. She said that he insisted she should use it in her tea instead of sugar, that it was much better for her than sugar and tasted sweeter. I had noticed that she used more and more of the honey whenever I visited. She also mixed it in her yoghurt, spread it on her bread, she almost seemed addicted. Then suddenly it occurred to me when I was talking to Yusuf after the funeral. Do you know Yusuf?"

"The Zeytin restaurant?" Matt said.

"Exactly. He was very upset by her death. And when he told me about the way she looked in the days and weeks before her death, I thought of her stories about the honey and remembered an article I had recently read about mad honey disease."

"So, you think that's what killed her?" asked Matt.

"Oh no. I think that's quite unlikely," Dr Schmitt said, and added darkly, "He is much more cunning than that."

"What's that supposed to mean?"

Matt fired his question at the doctor as, much out of irritation as interest. He was growing ever more frustrated with the doctor's mix of innuendo, medical jargon and obscure classical references. But before Dr Schmitt had any chance to enlighten Matt, the peace of the bar overlooking the tranquil blue of the bay was shattered by a crashing salvo of noise more deafening than a dozen thunderbolts shot from the sky. The air was rent with such fury by a pack of yapping, growling dogs around their table that Amber was almost thrown out of her seat at the shock. Matt leapt up to beat back the onslaught. Dr Schmitt retained his Teutonic composure and simply retorted to the fracas with a snarl of resentment on his lips at being so rudely interrupted.

By the time Tom emerged from the bar to see what the commotion was all about, Matt had chased off the aggressive beasts. Only the lame dog remained, sprawling at Amber's feet and whining pitifully. With a visible gash in its muzzle and a part of its left ear torn off in the attack, the animal lay slumped on the ground in such a wretched state that Amber was moved to tears.

"Oh, the poor creature," she cried and knelt down to comfort the injured animal.

"I shouldn't worry," said Tom when he eventually reached their table. "It'll pull through. Happens all the time around here with these strays."

"But you can't just leave the poor thing," Amber protested as she stroked the animal's quivering belly. "It needs treatment. There must be a vet here somewhere."

"If you're really so concerned, Amber, my love," Tom said with a humouring tone that was attempting to show sympathy. "The best people to talk to are the Bennetts up the road."

"Who are the Bennetts?" Amber asked.

Dr Schmitt eyed Tom with suspicion. But said nothing.

"Luc and Betty. They're good with animals. They have a dog sanctuary up in the hills in Palamut," Tom explained. "About half an hour by car."

"I have a car at the hotel. We could drive up there now," Matt said.

From the flicker of hesitation on her lips, the tinge of reluctance in her eyes, he sensed that his offer did not play well with Amber. Had he been a little too eager, he wondered? But her concern for the injured dog won through, and she accepted with a smile. So, while Tom drew a map for her with detailed instructions explaining how to find the Bennetts, Matt returned to the Kelebek to pick up the car and drove it back down to the bar.

"It's right out in the sticks," Tom shouted after Matt and Amber, as they carried the dog to the vehicle, "but if you follow the map, you should be okay."

"I wouldn't be so sure of that," Dr Schmitt chipped in ominously, looking on while they carefully settled the animal down on the back seat.

"Betty is the animal person and I'm sure the dog will be in good hands with her," he conceded, before adding in an odd turn of phrase that Matt took to be an idiom peculiar to his native

German: "But Luc Bennett is another pair of shoes altogether. I advise you to be careful."

Matt could not fail to notice the reproachful look that Tom gave the doctor.

"Don't mind Hauke," he said through the open window of the car, as Matt got behind the wheel, closed the door behind him and started up the engine. "He's got a bit of a grudge to bear. But don't ask me what it's all about. I have no idea."

While Matt and Amber drove off up the hill, the doctor raised his Panama hat, mopped his brow and sat down for another glass of çay.

# CHAPTER 8

The white Citroen Elysee accelerated out of town and swept up the hillside above the ocean. Amber tapped the switch on the armrest to roll down her window. A gleaming smile lit up her face as she let her strawberry-blonde hair blow freely in the breeze.

"Isn't that beautiful?" she said, dangling her hand out to feel the cool air between her fingers. "The way the coastline and islands just keep getting smaller and smaller. It feels like we're taking off."

Matt glanced across the cockpit and grinned. He saw little more than her blonde hair against flickering glimpses of the blue Mediterranean behind her. But he got the picture and put his foot down to lift them up the hillside faster still. Amber grinned back with delight at this added sense of speed.

It was a good fifteen minutes before the road flattened out to become a winding country lane that guided them between gentle slopes of pine trees and oleander bushes.

"It should be the next road on the right," Amber said, looking up from the map that Tom had drawn. "About a mile, according to this."

The sound of cicadas in the trees almost drowned out the sound of the engine.

"Could you close your window please, Amber?" Matt asked.

"That noise really gets to me. I'll turn up the air-con if it's too hot for you."

"That's okay. The air's a fair bit cooler up here, anyway. This is it, by the way," she said, pointing at the road ahead. "This is Palamut."

Matt turned right onto a gravel road. It took them through a village that seemed almost deserted in the midday sun. Only at the next junction in the heart of the village did they find any sign of life. At a café on the corner, in the shade of a large oak tree, a group of men sat sipping çay and playing backgammon. They looked up and peered at the car.

"Straight on here," said Amber, still reading from Tom's instructions. "For about 500 yards. Then there should be a dirt track off to the right."

The dirt track wound endlessly through one olive grove after another around the hills overlooking the sea. They had already been driving for well over Tom's estimated half an hour. And when an unmarked fork loomed in the road ahead, Matt was certain they had got it wrong.

"Hey, are you questioning my navigation skills?" Amber said. "I've been following exactly what he wrote."

Matt smiled.

"Maybe he missed out something."

"Don't forget," she assured him, "Tom said they live way out in the sticks."

When they reached the fork, Matt stopped the car.

"So, left or right?" he asked with more than a trace of impatience in his voice, and reached out his right hand. "Can I take a look?"

Amber fixed him with a look of fury in her eyes, and thrust the paper with Tom's map into his hand. It was the sound of barking dogs that rescued them from their budding squabble. Barking dogs and a tap-tap on Amber's side of the car.

She rolled down her window.

"Can I help you?" came the tapper's voice. It belonged to a woman in her late fifties to early sixties with mousy unkempt hair that trailed down over the straps of her blue dungarees.

"Are you Betty, by any chance?" asked Amber.

"I am," the woman said in a tone that lay somewhere between curiosity and suspicion.

"We're told you're good with dogs," Amber said, pointing to the back seat. "We wondered if you could help."

"Oh my goodness," said Betty when she caught sight of the pitiful creature with its bloodied muzzle and severed ear. "Let's get the poor thing inside."

Matt lifted the dog out of the car and followed Betty down through a grove of olive trees to a house that he had not seen from the road. At the back of the house was a large fenced-off area, and it was from here that the sound of barking came. He saw a good half dozen dogs roaming around this area and others in kennels along the far side of the fencing.

Betty led Matt and Amber inside the building – a rambling single-storey construction. It looked as if it had been erected in a single day and was at risk of collapsing any moment. She took them into a back room that reeked heavily of animals and instructed Matt to lie the injured dog on what looked a workbench.

"What's going on, Betty?" asked a man's voice from behind Amber.

It came across as the growl of a heavy smoker. Matt and Amber turned around to see a grey-bearded man leaning in the doorway behind them. He wore a timeworn black T-shirt emblazoned with the gothic letters of AC/DC in red and gold, jaded check shorts and a red baseball cap faded by the sun, which he lifted slightly to scratch his head revealing a noticeable absence of hair beneath.

The man stood patiently clutching the lintel of the door with his left hand while Betty was absorbed in her examination of the injured dog.

"Betty?" he repeated.

"Your wife is kindly looking after our dog," Amber said.

Matt was irritated to find himself included in ownership of the beast. Yet he was also quietly enthralled by the thought of sharing something with this woman.

"Matt Quillan," he said, offering the man his hand.

"Luc," the man replied, keeping his left hand on the lintel and the right hand firmly in his pocket.

"With a C," he added.

Matt had the feeling they were not entirely welcome.

"And I'm Amber. Actually, it's not our dog strictly speaking," she elaborated. "We found it hobbling around town, and suddenly it was set on by a pack of other hounds. Tom down at the Utopia, told us about your dog sanctuary."

"Well, that's Betty's field. I'm just the assistant," Luc said with the pleasing lilt of a Welsh accent that had failed to make itself heard earlier with his offhand introduction. "But the creature's in good hands. She'll look after it all right. Why don't you come outside and have a drink while Betty gets on with it?"

"It'll need stitches," Betty said, looking up at Luc.

"I think I'll stay," said Amber. "You go on, Matt. I'll join you later."

The Welshman fetched two cans of Efes from the kitchen, gave one to Matt and led him back out to the olive grove, where a table stood with half a dozen chairs parked randomly around in the grass. Clutching two of the chairs in the crook of his right arm as they went, he placed his can on the table and let the chairs drop out of his arm.

The leaves of the olive trees around them rustled affably in the breeze. And despite the occasional barking of dogs in the background, Matt felt curiously at peace as he took his beer can in both hands.

"Where are you staying?" Luc Bennett asked, pulling the tab on his can with his left hand and letting out a whoosh of carbonated gas as he spoke.

It was only then that Matt noticed the disfigurement of Luc's right hand as he used it to cradle the can against his chest when he opened it. The fingers, of which there were probably only three left, were so mangled and disjointed that they looked incapable of grasping anything at all. Matt assumed it was the aftermath of a catastrophic injury. He now realised why this otherwise welcoming Welshman had refused the handshake.

"The Kelebek," he replied.

Luc Bennett gave a wry smile.

"Why?" Matt asked. "What's wrong with that?"

"Nothing at all. I believe it's quite comfortable. But it doesn't seem the most romantic of choices for a vacation."

"Oh, don't get the wrong idea. We're not an item," Matt said. "We only just met today. Amber's staying with her sister, Pearl. Of Bay View Properties."

"Pearl's her sister? Okay, that figures. I can see the resemblance now you mention it."

"You know Pearl then?"

"Of course. All the expats know each other," Luc said. "In fact, it was her husband, Hamza, who gave us the idea of this dog sanctuary. Somewhere for the villa class to leave their animals when they fly back home for the winter. Come December, we'll have a lot more dogs to look after."

Matt sipped the cool Efes beer and mulled over this information. He was thinking of the doctor, his apparent grudge against Luc Bennett, and what Tom had said about how many expats here are running away from something.

"But why all the way up here?" he asked. "Out in the sticks?"

"Privacy. It's so underrated these days. And we have it in spades up here. No trouble. No intrusions. Except for the dogs, of course."

His words served only to stimulate Matt's curiosity all the more. With an enigmatic German doctor down the road bearing a grudge and Luc Bennett's exaggerated need for privacy, Matt could not help thinking this Welshman was one of those expats that Tom Moore had been talking about.

"You say that you and your young lady have only just met. So, what brings a good-looking young man such as yourself to holiday here all on your own?"

Matt stared into his beer.

"It's no holiday," he said. "I'm here for a friend. Looking for someone."

Luc Bennett showed no outward sign of curiosity. But Matt had met too many cagey people in his line of business not to recognise a shrewd old fox when he met one. It was plain to him, as Luc toyed with the beer can in his hand, that the Welshman was burning to know more. But he said nothing. Simply fiddled with the beer can in silence, waiting for Matt to accommodate him. It took little more than a minute.

"A man called Ahmet Karadeniz," Matt said. "Do you know him?"

Matt saw a flicker of recognition in Luc's eyes.

"The guy who married Pearl's friend, Susie?" he said. "Only met him once. Can't say I took to him."

He paused and continued to finger his beer can, as if measuring whether now was finally the time to take a swig.

"Nasty business all around," he added, lifting the can to pour a slow stream of beer into his open mouth. Then, placing it back with careful deliberation in the exact same position on the table, he looked up and shot a piercing gaze at Matt.

"Why are you looking for him?"

"There's a German doctor down in Karakent," Matt said, ignoring the question. "Seems to think he's a cunning bastard who was involved in her death."

"You mean Schmitt?"

The Welshman smiled, picked up his can and poured another stream of beer into his open mouth.

"Tom Moore at the Utopia Bar says he bears a grudge against you," Matt said.

Luc took a cigarette from the breast pocket of his shirt, slipped it between his lips, and offered the pack to Matt.

"Why was Hauke Schmitt even a topic of conversation?" he asked.

"He was with us when the dog was attacked," Matt said, as he accepted Luc's offer, took a cigarette from the pack and put it to his lips.

"He was with you?" Luc repeated, a puzzled expression in his eyes. "And yet you were talking about him?"

"It wasn't quite like that. We were talking about other things with Schmitt. Then the dog was attacked by a pack of strays, Tom came out and…"

"What other things?"

"Oh, all kinds of stuff," Matt said. He sensed an indefinable need to play his cards closer to his chest. "Roses, honey, the Black Sea. And some guy called Xenophon."

"Schmitt likes his classical literature," the Welshman said with amusement on his lips. Or was it a look of relief at getting away from any talk of grudges?

"Just out of interest, how did you get to know him?" Luc asked. "He's never been one to talk easily to strangers."

"It's a long story."

"They always are." Luc took a last swig of his beer, got up from the table, and waved the empty can in the air. "Another one?"

Matt gave a nod and watched his host's broad yet slightly stooped shoulders in their black T-shirt vanish into the darkness of the house as Luc Bennett dropped his empty can into a box by the door. At that moment, he felt a chill in the breeze that blew through the olive trees around him. And the light in the olive grove dimmed. He glanced up to see a dark cloud gathering over the mountains behind. It was moving south, menacing the sun.

"If that comes to rain," Luc Bennett said, looking up at the sky as he emerged from the house with two more cans of beer, "you need to take care driving back. The roads can be treacherous when they're wet."

Matt took one of the cans and opened his second beer.

"Especially if you have too much of this stuff," Luc added.

"You have a point," Matt agreed. "I don't even know if Amber drives."

"So, what's the story, Matt?" Luc asked once he had settled into his chair. "What's your business?"

"I run a small security outfit."

"Security." Luc repeated, mulling over the word as if to make a mental note for future reference. "That's interesting."

"Like I say, it's a small business. We provide protection for SMEs that can't afford the fees charged by the big guns. These days it's mostly about online safety."

"So, what's the Schmitt connection?" Luc asked.

"There is none. Not with my business," Matt said, before correcting himself. "Well, only indirectly."

"Indirect connections are often the most interesting part in a long story."

The olive trees sighed in the breeze. It was only the prelude to a hefty gust of wind, which caught Matt's empty beer can and swept it off the table. Matt felt the goose pimples rise on his arms and looked up at the looming darkness of the clouds.

"You did say it was a long story," Luc prompted him further as Matt rubbed his forearms in silence.

"It is," he said eventually. "Probably too long for now. Those clouds tell me we should be getting back soon before the storm comes. I don't fancy driving back down those wet bends if the road gets as treacherous as you say it does."

"As long as you take care, it's not a problem," Luc reassured him. He took a swig of beer, lit up another cigarette, and leaned back in his chair. Matt made it plain he was reluctant to expand any further. And it was equally clear that this intrigued Luc Bennett.

"Look, discretion's in my DNA," he said after a prolonged pause, waiting for Matt to say something. "It's been my USP ever since the day I went for my first job interview. Now, I can see you're loath to open up on your connection with Hauke Schmitt. I respect that."

Matt watched him take a deep drag on his cigarette. He could almost see the thoughts forming beneath that baseball cap as an attempt to blow smoke rings was stymied by the breeze.

"I've known Schmitt for longer than I care to remember," he continued. "Off and on. Called himself Josef Wasenmeister when I first met him. And whatever your involvement with him, there are one or two things it might be worth your while knowing as well."

"There is no involvement," Matt insisted. "We were simply chatting."

But Luc Bennett was not listening.

"I first came across him in Cairo," he continued. "Said he was working for the embassy. But as far as I could tell, he spent most of his time at the SSIS."

Matt looked across the table with blank frustration.

"State security," Luc explained. "That was just before Sadat disbanded it. Schmitt had only recently qualified, and I couldn't understand at the time why a young German physician might be involved with the SSIS. He was well-read, very cultured and proved a good drinking companion."

He took another long drag on his cigarette, then sank into a pensive moment as he contemplated the smoke.

"Soon after the SSIS was broken up, Schmitt moved on, and I heard nothing more of him until the firm posted me to DSM."

"DSM?" Matt repeated.

"Dar es Salaam," Luc said.

"What were you doing there?" Matt asked. "Or in Cairo for that matter?"

Luc stubbed out his cigarette, plucked Matt's empty beer can out of the grass, slowly crushed it in his left hand, and placed it back on the table. Matt had the impression he was playing for time, searching for a plausible explanation without disclosing too much of the truth.

"I was an agronomist, working in agrochemicals," he said as he rose from his chair, scooped up the crushed beer can with the fingers of his left hand and threw it into the box by the door. "So, one evening in DSM," he continued as he walked back to his chair, "I was sitting in a bar that was popular with FO types and other expats, when in walked Josef Wasenmeister. Hauke Schmitt as you know him. We'd both gone a little native over the intervening years in Africa, but we recognised each other instantly. We got chatting and then met up for drinks over the next few evenings, exchanging tales and getting nostalgic about Cairo. Apparently, he had just arrived from Zanzibar and was set to leave for Mozambique at the end of the week.

"That was when it twigged. They only sent loyal party members to African outposts like Zanzibar. And moving on from there to Mozambique was a sure sign he was with the MfS."

Matt was increasingly irritated by the way this man spoke in arcane abbreviations and acronyms.

"State security," Luc explained in the tone of a teacher grown impatient over Matt's interruptions. "You probably know it better as the Stasi."

But Matt's irritation was not placated by the footnotes Luc Bennett threw into the conversation. He had the impression these obscure ciphers were intended to confuse him.

"You surprise me," Matt said, thinking he had caught the Welshman out. "He told me he's lived in Frankfurt all his life."

"An der Oder," Luc snapped back. "Didn't they teach you geography in school? There are two Frankfurts. One in the west of Germany and one in the east."

Luc was audibly irritated by the suspicion implicit in Matt's words. But this geography lesson and the years that Hauke Schmitt said he had spent on tour around East Africa brought home to Matt the inconsistency in Schmitt's telling of his history. If he had spent so much time in Africa, Matt told himself, he could not possibly have lived all his life in Frankfurt. So, either his advanced years had robbed him of his deception skills – if he really had worked for the Stasi – or Luc was embellishing with a vivid imagination.

"You need to listen to this," Luc added, interrupting Matt's thoughts in a tone that had suddenly turned earnest. "That is, if you plan on seeing any more of Schmitt."

The Welshman paused and glared across the table.

"So, to get back to the story: after our brief encounter in DMS, he disappeared off the radar. And didn't show up again until a few years later. I was in Harare keeping an eye on events around the summit of non-aligned countries being held there at the time. And lo and behold, Schmitt pops up.

"That summit was the last time I saw him until we moved to Turkey four years ago. And ultimately it was that last meeting in Harare which is at the heart of the grudge you mentioned earlier."

Matt leaned forward, his arms resting on the table. His suspicion had finally surrendered to a burning curiosity.

"Why? In what way?" he asked.

"Well, that was back in the early days of Mugabe's rule, so you can imagine there was a lot of hush-hush business going on there. But something quietly spectacular happened at that summit. The presentation of what came to be called the Harare brochure. It was the start of a disinformation campaign to plant the idea in people's heads that HIV was all part of an American biological weapons project gone wrong. And of course, the Stasi were in the Kremlin's pocket. So, when I saw Wasenmeister at the meeting, I realised at once that, with his medical background, he likely played a part in compiling that document.

"In fact, he more or less admitted it one evening when we met for drinks. Made no secret of his admiration for the brochure. Kept going on about all the hard work that had been invested in exposing the truth about HIV. Finally, the Americans had been revealed as the villains they were, he said.

"Then the Berlin wall came down, the Stasi files were opened up and the time of reckoning came for a lot of people. It took years to wade through all the files in search of any evidence that pointed to the operation behind that brochure. And I have no idea if they ever found any proof of Wasenmeister's involvement. But whether or not they did, he eventually had his licence revoked and was no longer allowed to practise medicine in Germany."

"He told me he'd retired," said Matt.

"Of course he did. After all, he must be well over seventy by now. But the fact remains he was banned from practising medicine any longer. And he blames it on me. He's convinced that I grassed on him and that's why his licence was revoked."

"And did you?" Matt asked.

Luc Bennett paused. And as if to accommodate him, the wind through the olive grove briefly eased, prompting him to reach for another cigarette and light up. He ignored the question.

"You know, I've often wondered if it was his Stasi past that brought him to Turkey when he was kicked out of the medical profession. They had people all over the place at the time, especially in Ankara and Istanbul, because they were getting increasingly worried about the Bozkurt and had a network of local agents here."

Matt's ears pricked up. He felt the first drop of rain on his face. And the cloud above was growing ever darker. But Luc had grabbed his attention with that one word. He was reminded of the flash drive that still lay buried in the ticket pocket of his jeans. And he was hooked.

"Worried about what?"

"The Bozkurt," Luc repeated. There was a hint of relief in his voice that Matt's earlier question had now been left behind. "Ever heard of the Grey Wolves?"

Another fat drop of rain hit Matt in the eye. He blinked and wiped it away.

"The Bozkurt is a wolf. A grey wolf to be precise. For some people here it's an important mythical figure in their country's identity. And the Grey Wolves have taken it especially to heart. Some fanatics dream of a Greater Turkey stretching from Western China to the Mediterranean. Quite bonkers, really. They've gone pretty quiet in recent years, perhaps because of the government's tough line against the Kurds. In fact, many of them have even allied themselves with the ruling AK party. But they're still a bunch of far-right fanatics and gangsters with a gruesome taste for violence. And to make things worse, a whole pack of mobsters were even released from prison not long ago under a Covid amnesty. It's becoming a dangerous place to be.

"It was their fanaticism that made them such an easy target for another of the Stasi's fake news campaigns when they were implicated in that attempt on the Pope's life back in the eighties."

"What's all this got to do with Hauke Schmitt?"

"What I'm trying to say, Matt, is that he's not all he might appear to be. His history of working for an organisation where disinformation was a way of life, and truth was routinely treated with contempt, is something you must always keep in mind."

"For an agric, you seem to know an awful lot about these things," Matt said. "About covert operations, the Stasi, and so on."

"You just bear it in mind. That's all I'm saying," the Welshman muttered, stubbing out his cigarette as the rain began to make itself felt. "I think it's time we moved inside."

He picked up his beer can and hurried over to the door. Matt followed on behind. He had the distinct feeling that Luc Bennett was more than happy to let rain stop play. But he was not about to let his curiosity hang unsated.

# CHAPTER 9

"We were beginning to wonder where you two had got to," Betty said, as Matt entered the dimly lit front room and closed the door behind him. At the very moment when the door clicked shut, a flash of lightning lit up the place. It briefly revealed a sparsely furnished room dominated by two armchairs and a sofa in the heavy, ornate style typical of many older Turkish homes. Matt could not imagine it was either Luc or Betty's taste. He assumed the furniture had come with the house.

"Your dog is all sewn up now and resting in one of the kennels," Betty added. "Once I'd washed off the blood and calmed him down, I finally recognised him. He belongs to a couple who own a villa here. They have a habit of leaving their dog to roam free when they fly home to the UK. So, we'll keep him here safely until they get back."

"But that's awful," Amber protested. "How can people be so thoughtless?"

Her words were almost drowned out by a sudden clap of thunder, and the room turned an even darker shade of gloom. Betty flicked a light switch by the door.

"I shouldn't worry," she said. "You can be sure they'll get a bill when they get back. Would you like a cup of coffee before you set off down the hill?"

Amber cast a questioning glance at Matt, who was quietly probing his ticket pocket for the flash drive. Luc Bennett's story of the Grey Wolves still preyed on his mind.

"If Matt's going to be driving down that road in the rain," Luc chuckled, "I think he could do with it after the beer."

"But preferably not Turkish," Matt said. "That stuff is too strong for me."

"We don't do that here anyway," Betty assured him. "Too complicated. I can only offer instant."

"That's perfect."

"For me too," Amber chipped in.

"Luc," Matt said, "do you have a computer?"

"Of course, come on through," Luc said and led Matt off to a back room.

"I'll be with you in a moment, Amber," Matt called over his shoulder as he followed Luc into the next room. Betty cast a knowing men-will-be-men glance at Amber.

"We can chat while I make the coffee," she said, and Amber followed her into the kitchen.

The back room was even dingier than the front. The only aspect of it that gave any clue to its purpose did not suggest to Matt that it was a normal office space. Against the facing wall stood an array of electronic equipment that would not look out of place in GCHQ and left Matt wondering precisely what function this room served in Luc Bennett's private life.

Matt stood in the doorway, hesitating. For all the technology in that room, Matt could not see any sign of a computer, until Luc strolled over to a trestle table nestled against the opposite wall. He flashed a look of quiet anticipation at Matt as he sat down at this makeshift desk and opened a laptop that lay before him.

"So, what have you got for me?" Luc Bennett said, the expectation in his eyes now replaced by a broad grin that filled his entire face. As the laptop was starting up, Matt fished the USB stick from the depths of his pocket. He handed it to Luc.

"What's this then?" Luc asked, his Welsh lilt now further whetted by his growing curiosity when he inserted the flash drive in the USB port, clicked on it, and found a single folder named Pics. "Holiday snaps, is it?"

"If you open it and scroll down, you'll find a zip file."

"Vacation plans?"

Luc cast a mystified look up at Matt.

"Not exactly," Matt said. "I was given a flash drive on my way here. It contains a PDF, along with a bunch of video and audio files. The PDF was originally called Bozkurt. After a run-in with the Jandarma, I changed the name and buried all the files in this folder of holiday snaps on a flash drive of my own. I had no idea what it was all about, but I began to suspect it might land me in trouble if it was found in my possession. Then you mentioned Bozkurt earlier and it got me…"

"Who in hell's name gave you something like this?" Luc asked, glaring up at Matt. There was a startled, almost panic-stricken look in his eyes.

"Open the zip file. The password is 0791rebmevon51," Matt said, and slowly pronounced every character as Luc Bennett typed each one in. "The letters all lower case."

Luc clicked on the zip file.

"Oh, my goodness! Who did you say gave you this?"

"I didn't."

"Well, you're right about one thing. You'll be in deep shit if you're found with this stuff in your pocket."

"So, what's it all about?" Matt asked. His voice trembled slightly with a mix of excitement and apprehension.

"Well, the title of the first page in the PDF tells you all you need to know. Ergenekon. A clandestine group of nationalists who hate the ruling party and are reckoned to be part of a deep state organisation bent on overthrowing the government."

Luc paused as he scrolled slowly through the PDF.

"They seem to be bills, accounts and the like," he said, intrigued, and continued scrolling through the pages. Then stopped.

"Shit," he muttered to himself.

"What's up?"

"Those mobsters I was telling you about, released under the Covid amnesty," Luc said, and paused, rubbing his injured hand.

"Yes, and?" Matt said, when the pause became a prolonged silence, as if Luc was steeped in some unpleasant memory.

"One of them is here," he said at last. "A nasty piece of work who goes by the name Erkan Suleyman. Has a massive villa down in Karakent and likes to swan around all in white. White suit, white tie, white shoes. Looks like Peter at the pearly gates. You need to steer well clear of him.

"And so does your lovely young companion next door," he added. "Suleyman has left a long trail of damaged women behind him."

Matt recalled the tall, imposing figure he had seen at the gendarmerie. To judge from Luc Bennett's description, they were plainly one and the same person. He made a mental note of the image and attached the name Erkan Suleyman to it.

Luc looked up at Matt, his dark eyes wild with the drama of this discovery.

"So where does your target fit into all this?" he said.

"My target?"

"Karadeniz. Ahmet," Luc Bennett said.

"Ahmet? He doesn't. There's no connection."

"Maybe," Luc said with an audible scepticism in that Welsh lilt. "But with Suleyman in the frame you can never be sure. We had the misfortune of crossing his path when Hamza recommended that he bring his injured dog to us. It had obviously been in a vicious fight and was beyond saving. But Suleyman blamed us for its death."

Luc paused, as if reliving his memory of that day, and looked at Matt with a disconcerting darkness in his eyes.

"Believe me, he's not a man you want to cross. He'll always want his pound of flesh."

He paused again.

"Look, I don't know what this is all about, Matt. But you need to ditch this now. It's dynamite."

"And the other files?" Matt said, ignoring his words.

Luc opened the first video file to find a clip showing a group of men around a table. Neither Luc nor Matt could understand what they were saying, but still it kindled a moment of excitement in Luc.

"I recognise a couple of them. He's high up in the army," he said, his eyes alight now as he pointed a finger at the screen. "And that one works in intelligence."

Luc closed the file and eyed Matt with a look of deep concern.

"Like I said, if you want a quiet life, you need to ditch this. And do it today."

Matt's life in the security business may have drummed a keen sense of caution into him over the years, but he was still a romantic at heart. A shy adventurer. And these words sent an instant thrill of adrenaline coursing through his veins. For reasons he was unable to explain even to himself, he felt that a charge of dynamite in his pocket could be not so much a risk as an asset.

"We'll see," he said, almost in a whisper, as if to underline how cool he was with Luc Bennett's warning. "I have a soft spot for explosive stuff."

Yet Matt was sufficiently self-aware to sense that the smile on his face was not so much that of the cool operator, but more the overcautious security officer. He knew it spoke of apprehension just beneath his would-be cool exterior. And he could see that the Welshman was bemused by the conflicting message between his words and his affected smile.

In his distraction, Luc Bennett's attempt to remove the flash drive from the computer resulted in a clumsy and ineffectual tug. The awkward movement attracted Matt's attention again to the disfigured hand.

"That looks like a really nasty injury," Matt said, looking at the gnarled and twisted fingers when the Welshman eventually freed the flash drive and handed it to him.

"Oh, that." Luc Bennett glanced down at his hand. "That was a stupid farming accident years ago. I hardly notice it these days."

Matt knew little about agriculture, but he was pretty sure agronomists were scientists, not hands-on farmers. He could not escape the feeling that Luc Bennett was not being entirely straight with him.

He recalled how Luc kept rubbing his injured hand when Erkan Suleyman's name cropped up. Was he the source of the injury? Matt wondered, and was turning this thought over in his mind as they made their way back to the lounge.

By the time the two of them emerged from the Bennetts' office, the coffee was waiting for him. And getting cold. Amber had already finished hers.

"What's going on?" she asked as Matt sat down and took the cup in his hands. "You're looking very pensive."

"It's all good," he replied. But the strain of his attempt to maintain a cool exterior was too obvious. She fixed a suspicious glare on him as he drank his coffee.

"I just wanted to check something on the computer," he added. "But we really need to get going soon before the storm gets any worse."

The thunderclap that greeted their exit when Betty opened the door for them to leave almost shook it off its hinges. The shock sent Amber recoiling back into Matt, who instinctively reached his arms out to keep his balance and clutched Amber around the waist.

"I'm so sorry," he said. "I really didn't..."

"My pleasure," Amber replied with a teasing grin, and tossed a flirtatious glance over the shoulder with her strawberry-blonde hair.

It was a glance that tantalised and enchanted Matt in equal measure.

"When you two lovebirds have finished," Luc taunted as he followed them out to the car, holding an umbrella over Amber's head, "you have a slippery road ahead of you. You need to give it your full attention Matt."

"No worries," Matt shouted cheerily over the noise of the rain beating on the roof of the car as he slammed the door shut.

Luc delivered Amber to the passenger side of the car, walked back around to the driver's side, and tapped on the window as Matt started up the engine. Matt lowered the window.

"If you find that Ahmet guy, you take care. He has some unsavoury friends. In the meantime, get rid of that other stuff today," Luc said. "And if you need any more help, just let me know."

With the noise of the rain beating down on the car, Amber only caught the tail end of Luc's warning.

"What was all that about?" she asked, as they drove back up the track and onto the road through the village, where the group of backgammon players had long since beaten a retreat from the storm.

"What?"

"If you need any more help," Amber said, repeating Luc Bennett's words. "What did he mean by that?"

Matt feigned a need to concentrate on his driving, aided and abetted in this by the cloudburst that hit them at that very moment. He kept his eyes studiously on the twists and turns of the road ahead and said nothing. His hands remained firmly on the wheel as the car was buffeted by the wind that blew down from the mountains, and he negotiated the branches and other detritus strewn around the road by the gusting storm. The oleander bushes, so peaceful and resplendent on the drive up earlier, struggled now against the squalls of driving rain that brutally stripped them of their pink and white blossom.

"Help with what?" Amber persisted, raising her voice above the noise of the windscreen wipers and the beating rain.

"I was just asking him for some information," Matt replied at last.

"About Ahmet?"

"No," Matt said, and hesitated. "Not directly."

He said no more. Amber admitted defeat, finally caving in to his avoidance behaviour and the lashing rain on the windscreen, as the road brought them back onto the hillside looking out over the sea.

Gone now was the deep azure blue that had waved them off up the hill to Palamut earlier in the day. The sea now stretched into the distance like a dull grey carpet; unsold and unwanted in an abandoned bazaar.

The rain had eased by the time they emerged onto the hillside road. The storm had blown itself out in the mountains behind them. And far below, nestling in the bay, the whitewashed houses and hotels of Karakent were lit up by a bright beam of sunshine through the clouds. It lent them an atmosphere that was in stark contrast to the leaden carpet of water.

By the time they reached the outskirts of Karakent, the rain had stopped altogether. The sunshine had now spread to the entire bay. And the dusty streets they found when Matt steered the car off the highway and onto the main boulevard into town flaunted the bay's happy escape from the ravages of the storm. Amber asked Matt to drop her at the roundabout in the centre of town.

"That's a shame. I was hoping we might continue our drink at Tom's place," Matt said as he brought the car to a halt.

"My sister's expecting me, I'm afraid," Amber replied, stepping out of the car.

"How about dinner this evening, then?"

Amber closed the car door behind her, leaned in through the open window and simply smiled.

"Shall we say seven?" Matt said.

"Pick me up at Pearl's office," Amber replied, still smiling, and left Matt to gaze after her as she sauntered off in the direction of the marina. He could tell from the mannered sway of her hips and the swing of her hair in the afternoon sunlight that she knew full well he was watching.

It was three hours later, at six thirty, when Matt strolled out of the Kelebek into the dimly lit street. He was still not used to the early onset of the night in these parts. It took him by surprise every evening. But despite the darkness, he could not fail to miss a familiar figure seated on the other side of the road. It was the luminescent motion of the red worry beads shining in the street light above that caught his eye. The same well-dressed man in a smart suit that had been watching him at breakfast in the Zeytin restaurant early that morning.

It occurred to Matt that any half-decent snoop assigned to keep an eye on him would be in the shadows. Not sitting brazenly under the street light fiddling with his worry beads. This one wanted to be seen.

Matt stood on the pavement opposite and watched. Aside from the repetitive movement of the fingers on the beads, the man remained motionless, watching back, until Matt stepped off the pavement to cross the road. The moment his foot touched the tarmac, the beads vanished into a pocket of those smart trousers as the man quickly rose, scurried off down a side street, and faded into the shadows.

# CHAPTER 10

When Matt arrived at Bay View Properties, Amber was waiting in the doorway. She appeared edgy and flustered.

"Sorry if I'm late," he said, looking at his watch. He was ten minutes early.

"No, it's okay. I just feel a little *de trop*," Amber reassured him, glancing back into the office, where her sister was deep in discussion with a sixty-something couple. "Pearl has some prospective buyers."

"Okay, let's go then," Matt said. "What are you in the mood for this evening?"

"What about the Zeytin?"

"Is there anything else?" Matt asked. "I've already had breakfast there today."

In truth, he was concerned by the thought that those worry beads may still be lurking. And, while he had promised Yusuf that he would return that evening, a second visit to the Zeytin in one day could make life a trifle too monotonous for his stalker. Might even create the impression he was conspiring with the brother of a dissident journalist.

"I know the perfect place," Amber said, taking Matt by the arm and leading him out of the doorway onto the cobbled street. "A rooftop restaurant. Quiet and cosy."

Matt happily let Amber lead him through the narrow streets to her perfect corner of cosy intimacy. It took no more than ten minutes. The eatery lay on the other side of town, overlooking the far end of the marina. Turning to climb the steps up to the rooftop, Matt glanced behind him. He could not escape the movement of red worry beads glistening beneath the street light. About fifty metres up the road.

From the top of the steps came a disembodied voice with the customary "iyi akşamlar", as Amber strode ahead of Matt, who remained caught in a web of concern over the mysterious stalker. On reaching the top of the stairs to the dining area, they were greeted by the owner of the voice, who introduced himself with an effusive handshake and the offer of his first name: Ahmet.

Matt was reminded of Osman's words on his first evening in the town: "I know many Ahmets." And he wondered just how many there were. This waiter was of the unctuous variety. His long black hair, greased back, left the field of his face free as if deliberately to accentuate his bulbous eyes and prominent nose.

There were no other guests in the restaurant and no tables reserved, so Ahmet invited them to choose whichever table took their fancy. It struck Matt as an ominous sign of what to expect from the kitchen. He concluded that the emptiness of the place probably explained the waiter's obsequious welcome. The expression on Matt's face was not lost on Amber.

"It's end of season," she explained, and led him to a corner table that looked out over the water. "We're lucky they haven't closed down already."

Matt was not convinced that 'lucky' would prove the best word to describe the dinner ahead. His mind was still troubled by the worry beads on the street below. And the prospect of the food on offer was doing little to distract him from these thoughts when Ahmet handed them the menus.

"The local wine is quite good here," she said. "I recommend the Angora. White."

Matt's troubled mind was open to any suggestion she chose to make.

"Okay. A bottle then," he replied with a beseeching look at Ahmet the waiter. "And a bottle of water."

"They do a really good hummus for starters," Amber continued as the waiter disappeared. "On the other hand, they'll also bring us a freebie starter anyway. So, you'll need a hearty appetite if you want to follow that with hummus. And for the main they also do a fabulous Urfa kebab if you like your food hot and spicy."

"Sounds great. I'll have it all." Matt was in no mood for trawling through the menu. Amber was in control, and he was happy to trust her taste.

After Ahmet had disappeared with their order, they sat in silence and watched the gently rolling sea below. Only the chug of a boat leaving the harbour invaded the quietness of the air until the gently plucked strings of a bağlama weaved their way into the evening. The waiter had switched on a piece of his native music to underscore the Anatolian backdrop to their dinner. He plainly wanted to please. Bathed by the background melody, Matt watched the fishing boat as it rounded the squat lighthouse at the end of the harbour mole and made its way out to sea.

"So idyllic, isn't it?" Matt said, turning back to Amber and gazing into her deep blue eyes. He saw something between irritation and resentment in her expression, a vulnerability, as if she found his gaze intrusive. This bothered him.

"Karakent may seem pretty and romantic," she said with a tired smile on her lips. "But it has its dark sides, too."

"Your sister said the exact same thing when I first arrived."

"Oh, she was probably just alluding to the name," Amber said, switching all at once to a more flippant tone, as if regretting her remark. "Apparently it means 'black town' – quite fitting really."

If this casual afterthought was an attempt to quell Matt's curiosity, it failed. And, as an awkward silence descended on the table, he wondered what darkness it was that prompted Amber to parrot her sister's words.

"One thing intrigues me," he added at last, when the waiter emerged to place the promised freebie on the table: a bean puree with olives and a flat bread.

Amber plastered the bean puree on her bread with a faintly quizzical smile in the corner of her lips. But said nothing, simply waited for Matt to continue.

"When Schmitt was talking all that stuff about mad honey disease, you were really on the ball. You seemed to know an awful lot about it with your talk of grey toxins – whatever they are."

"Grayanotoxins," she corrected him and smiled again, this time with amusement in her eyes. "I learned about it during my studies. But most of what I learned I've already forgotten."

"What did you study, then?" Matt asked.

"Pharmacology."

"So how come a pharmacology graduate winds up running a bookshop in Brighton?"

Amber pushed the remainder of her bean puree to one side with a sigh that Matt read as a hint of fullness even before the hummus had arrived. But with hindsight, he realised it was more a sigh of existential relief.

"It's a long story."

"They always are," Matt said in imitation of Luc Bennett's words earlier that day. And he waited. In the meantime, the waiter had removed the remains of the bean puree and brought out the hummus.

Returning to the kitchen, he left behind a prolonged pause in the conversation. It was as if she needed time to rehearse her words.

"My pharmacology degree took me into the drug industry," she said at last. "Working for an American company. I spent a few years at the research labs in the States. And that's probably what did it for me, because it was there that I started getting strange allergies. It was odd, because nothing like it ever happened in the university research labs. It was only when I arrived in America. And it became quite debilitating. The doctors even thought it might be lupus at one stage. The upshot was that I had to give up working in the labs. So, I returned to the UK and let the company train me up for a position in marketing. What a huge mistake that was," she said, and paused to take a sip of wine.

"But on reflection, it was actually my salvation. I'd always felt good about joining the drug industry. It seemed such a worthy business, developing treatments for all the ailments of the world. It felt as if I was doing something for the health of humanity."

"So, what changed your mind?" Matt asked, tucking into the hummus.

"The marketing. The push to sell your product at all costs, even when it's not a wonder drug and is little better than a placebo. The drive to extend the patent life of a drug by any means possible on the flimsiest of grounds. There was so much dishonesty. Even bribery and corruption at times." She took another sip of wine. "It's good, isn't it?"

"As good as anything you'll get at Tesco," Matt agreed. "And it goes perfectly with the hummus."

He paused, expecting Amber to continue. But she simply nodded, busily spreading hummus on a piece of bread.

"So, you quit?"

"Yes, I quit," she said, as she placed the slice of bread on her plate. "And fulfilled an ambition I'd harboured ever since my teenage years."

Matt detected a curious crack in her voice as she spoke these words. And an expression in her eyes he was unable to fathom.

"I opened a little independent bookshop in my home town by the sea," she proclaimed, as if to conceal the crack. "The best move I ever made."

"And the allergies?"

"Gone," she said, raising her hands in a gesture of triumph.

"Even my cat's been unable to bring out the slightest allergic reaction in the eight years she's been living with me. I put it all down to my books and the sea air."

"That's good. And I have to say, in the few hours we've known each other, you give me the impression of someone much better suited to a bookshop than a research lab."

"What makes you say that?" Amber shot an aggrieved glance across the table. "Are you saying a research lab is no place for a woman?"

"God no! That might be the kind of view shared by a man like Schmitt, but do you really imagine I might think like that?"

"I've no idea. As you said, we only met a few hours ago." Her words were unintentionally brusque. She smiled as if to compensate, then added: "Do you really believe that's what Dr Schmitt thinks?"

"Well, I couldn't miss the startled look on his face when you went all scientific on him," Matt said. "Don't forget, he's German and very old school. Women belong in the kitchen for men like that."

"I find him quite sweet."

"Do you really?"

Matt was genuinely surprised – and certain she would think differently about the man if she knew what Luc Bennett had told him about the Stasi doctor.

"So, what do you think about that mad honey disease he was on about?" he asked.

"Well, from what I recall of my pharmacology days, it sounds pretty plausible. But it was what he said after that."

"What do you mean?"

"That he thought it unlikely the honey would have killed her and that Ahmet was much more cunning than that. What did he mean? I so wanted to hear more."

"Really?"

"Absolutely. I was totally hooked. And then those bloody dogs. They killed the whole thing."

Amber's fascination for the story and her interest in Ahmet's cunning gave Matt an idea. He had been pondering a return to the real estate office all day.

"Would you be interested in going to see Ahmet?"

"Going to see him?" Amber gawped at him with a look of alarm in her eyes. "Why would I want to see him? By all accounts he's not a very pleasant man."

"You've never actually met him then?"

"He's never around when I'm here. But I've heard enough to know he's not someone I'd care to meet."

"That's a shame," Matt said, popping the last portion of hummus into his mouth and pushing his plate to one side.

"Why?"

Before Matt could even consider his reply, Ahmet, the waiter, appeared from the shadows of the kitchen to clear away the bread basket and empty plates. In almost perfect synchrony, Matt and Amber each raised their glasses and sipped on their wine in silence while they waited for Ahmet to return with the Urfa kebab.

"You know I was asked to locate him for a friend?" Matt said, his fork raised and ready to sink into the kebab. Amber nodded. "So I found his office a little way along the coast. He wasn't there at the time. Now, I've no idea what Ben's business is with him, but after everything I've heard, I'm curious to get to know him before Ben arrives. The idea of playing a prospective buyer with an interest in one of his properties, kind of appeals to me. I thought maybe you'd like to come along."

He paused, before adding with a mischievous grin: "Play the wife. Or my partner."

"I really don't think so."

Matt had gone too far. Her words were enough to tell him there was no point trying to change her mind. So, he stayed clear of the subject for the rest of the meal and focused his attention instead on the Urfa kebab with a side of culinary small talk. It was only after the meal, as they sat waiting for the bill, that he found her dismissive words had merely been a front.

Along with the bill came two cups with lids on and a small tray containing little cubes of Turkish delight.

"What's this?" Matt asked.

"Turkish coffee. On the house, sir," Ahmet said in his softly obsequious way.

"No, not for me." Matt pushed his cup away. "That's too strong for me."

"Good God, Matt. As a security expert, you need to man up." Amber tossed a look of rebuke across the table. It stung.

"After all, it's rude to refuse a gift, so at least try it," she added. "Suck on a little cube of that Turkish delight, then sip the coffee through it. It's divine."

She slipped a cardigan over her shoulders against the advancing chill in the air, as she watched Matt cave in, pop a piece of Turkish delight in his mouth, remove the lid and put the cup to his lips.

"Damn. It's hot."

"Of course it's hot, Matt. I didn't say do it right away."

Ahmet withdrew with amusement in his eyes and left the two of them alone. As the cup cooled in the night air, Matt negotiated a peace settlement with his coffee to the point where eventually he was compelled to agree with Amber.

"You're right. It is delicious."

Amber gave a smile of quiet triumph. The gentle strings of the bağlama continued to weave their enchanting melody around the night. And Matt gazed out to sea, watching another boat chug its course towards the lighthouse on the harbour mole as it made its way back to port.

"When were you thinking of going?" she asked.

Matt looked across the table at Amber. The sparkle in her eyes betrayed a quiet eagerness.

"Late afternoon early evening's probably best," he said.

Matt settled the bill and they agreed to meet at Tom Moore's place at four-thirty the next day.

Coming out onto the street again and turning to walk up the hill, his mind was now too preoccupied with the date in Utopia and the prospect of finally meeting Ahmet to give any further thought to the stranger with the worry beads. So, he failed to notice the man slip out of the shadows behind them and slither away up the hill.

# CHAPTER 11

It was four-fifteen. Matt was early. So, he was surprised to find Amber already on the patio outside the bar. She had changed into a marine-blue sleeveless blouse with the same clunky white bangles on her wrist and was carrying a blue shoulder bag. He smiled at the way she was always so perfectly coordinated. She sat at a corner table deep in conversation with the unmistakable figure of the German doctor.

"Dr Schmitt," he said, pulling out a chair to sit down. "So nice to see you again."

Hauke Schmitt immediately rose from his chair to shake hands. But Matt was already in place before he could reciprocate, leaving the doctor to sink awkwardly back into his seat. Matt was not sorry to have caused him this slight embarrassment. The German doctor's arrogance and Luc's tales of his Stasi past had given Matt a visceral dislike of the man.

"We did agree four-thirty, didn't we?" Matt asked, turning to Amber, fearful that he might have got the time wrong.

"Don't worry. You haven't kept me waiting," she said, as if reading his thoughts. "I was on my way to the boutique down the road and saw Dr Schmitt here as I was passing. So, I stopped for a chat. Then it became a drink."

"And what can I get for you Matt," came the unmistakable Irish lilt of Tom Moore from behind him. Matt wondered how the barman came to know his name, since he could not recall having given it. The implication of friendship irritated him. But he ignored it.

"I'll have the same as Amber," he said, not wanting to repeat his first trip to Ahmet's place under the influence of lion's milk.

"I hear you're planning to visit Karadeniz," Schmitt said, peering over his gold-rim glasses.

Matt shot a look of both censure and disappointment across the table at Amber. After what Luc Bennett had told him, he did not trust Schmitt one inch and would not be surprised if the man was best buddies with the Jandarma. The last thing he wanted was to have the Stasi doctor knowing his every move.

"How was Harare when you were last there?" Matt asked. It was not a smart question. But he was keen to let the German doctor know he was no less privy to Schmitt's history than Schmitt was to his movements.

The German doctor removed his gold-rim glasses and placed them carefully on the table. Amber cast a nervous look at the two men that darted back and forth from one to the other. She had plainly caught the abrupt sense of tension in the air.

"So, you've been talking to Mr Bennett," Schmitt said with slow deliberation and a curious smirk on his lips. "You should not believe everything a man from MI6 tells you."

"He said he was an agronomist."

"Indeed."

With this one word, the smirk on Schmitt's face morphed into a look of supercilious contempt. Matt wondered whether this disdain was for the Welshman or for his own artless words. And yet, he thought, if Schmitt knew Luc Bennett was a spy, then this would lend credence also to the story that the German doctor had worked for the Stasi.

Matt looked across the table at Amber as his drink arrived at the table. The fragrance of fresh lemon and mint wafted from the glass. It seemed tailor-made to clear the atmosphere.

"I phoned the agency before I came out," Matt lied as he picked up the glass. "We agreed to meet there at five. So, we should drink up and get going soon."

Hauke Schmitt picked up his gold-rim glasses, returned them to their perch on the bridge of his narrow, beaky nose and said no more. The expression on his face beamed a sense of satisfaction that he had put Matt in his place.

As soon as Amber had finished her drink, Matt leapt to his feet, gave her his hand to steady her as she rose from her chair and put a fifty lira note on the table.

"That should cover it," he said, sliding the note over the table towards Hauke Schmitt. "We must be off."

As they made their way up the road past Osman's place, Amber could not contain her curiosity any longer.

"What on earth was that all about?"

Her question came in a whispering tone of disbelief, as if conscious of a secret that should not be shared.

"What?"

"You and Dr Schmitt. All that talk of Zimbabwe and MI6."

Matt pressed the remote on the key fob to unlock his vehicle at the far side of the car park. And kept her in suspense. He said nothing until they reached the car, when he walked around to the passenger side and opened the door for her.

"If Luc's to be believed," he said, as Amber eased herself into the seat, "your sweet old Dr Schmitt has a very colourful history."

Nothing more was said as they drove out of town. Yet he could see that her curiosity was aroused. Her mind almost visibly raking over his words. But Amber remained patient. She waited. Enjoyed the view of the surf below them, the breeze of the sea air through her window. And sat tight, ready for Matt to reveal more as they drove along the coast road. Until her patience grew so thin that it finally cracked.

"Go on then," she said.

"What?"

"Tell me about the colourful history."

"Let's deal with Ahmet first," Matt said, pointing to the building ahead with huge blood-red letters ASK across the front. "That's his office."

They drew up on the other side of the road opposite the building. The Rottweiler lay still chained up outside the entrance.

"Oh, my goodness, look at that poor creature," said Amber, as she opened the car door the moment they stopped. They crossed the road. "Why do people keep their dogs chained up? It's so cruel."

The dog sat up on its haunches as they crossed the road. And growled. Its eyes wild with a tortured kind of menace.

"It's a Rottweiler, for God's sake," Matt said, taking her by the arm and guiding her away from the snarling beast. The animal was on all fours by now. It edged towards them, tugging on the chain.

"Listen to that growl, Amber. I'm afraid your love for it's not reciprocated."

"You'd be growling if you were chained up like a dog."

"Well, thank God I'm not then."

Matt held her arm more tightly as he spoke and led her through the door into the dimly lit office of the estate agent. He recognised the young Asian-looking woman he had met earlier sitting at the same desk behind her computer screen. She seemed flustered by their sudden appearance in the doorway and hastily donned a pair of sunglasses, as if wanting to cover her face.

Standing behind her was a man, short and chunky, wearing a pair of mirrored aviator sunglasses. They were as out of place in the dim light of the office as they were on the man's chubby face.

The two of them, in their shades, presented a bizarrely comical picture. Yet oddly disquieting at the same time. The woman at the desk, still visibly flustered, looked up at her partner and exchanged a few words with him. The tension between them was palpable. He placed a hand on her shoulder, as if to offer comfort, then walked around the desk to greet his visitors.

The sinister quality of the shades was not even faintly eroded by the jovial chubbiness of his face. Nor by the gesture of welcome when he held out his arms to Matt and Amber as if they were old friends.

"Hoşgeldin," he said with a beaming grin that spread the entire width of his face. "Welcome."

Matt was not prepared for the warmth of the handshake when Ahmet took Matt's hand in his. After all he had heard about Ahmet, he fully expected the sinister air, but not the geniality. He was forgetting that the man was a real estate agent.

"I'm Ahmet," he said, still beaming. "My wife tells me you're looking for property here. Please, take a seat."

Ahmet made a sweeping gesture with his right arm that guided them to the two leather chairs in front of the desk.

"May I offer you and your charming wife some tea? Or maybe something stronger?"

Amber smiled awkwardly with what seemed to Matt like a mix of amusement and embarrassment at Ahmet's assumption. But he was not about to put the man right. She had a role to play.

"I don't suppose you have any fresh lemon juice with mint?" she asked.

"Not in the office, I'm afraid. But Yamur can arrange it," he replied, flicking his fingers and switching to Turkish as he turned to the woman behind the desk.

"No really, it's not necessary," Amber said. "I'll just take some water."

"It's not a problem, madam," he insisted. "My wife will be happy to do it for you."

Without a word, the woman called Yamur was already on her feet before Amber could protest any further.

"Make that two then," Matt said, tired of the tea he was

offered everywhere they went and in need of something more thirst-quenching.

"Where did you learn to speak such good English?" he added, turning to Ahmet, who had taken Yamur's seat behind the desk as she vanished through the door on her errand.

"We must speak good English here for our tourist friends," Ahmet replied.

Irritated by this evasion, Matt exchanged a brief glance with Amber, then pressed the point further. "You have very good teachers here, then."

"Yes, very good."

Matt watched for signs of discomfort. An awkward shifting in the chair. A slight tremor of the lips. But there was nothing.

"What kind of a property are you looking for Mr…"

"Luke. Call me Luke," Matt said. Amber looked across the coffee table at Matt with an uneasy smile at this subterfuge.

"What can you offer us?"

"That depends on your budget, of course."

Ahmet looked questioningly at Matt. He was waiting for a response, but Matt said nothing, simply waved his hands dismissively, as if to say money was no object.

"We have a whole range of properties," Ahmet said, now happily into his element. "Apartments, duplex, triplex, villas with sea views, mountain views. You name it, Luke, we have it."

Matt looked across at Amber. Her smile was wearing thin.

"We were thinking of a villa with a view over the bay, weren't we, my love?"

The smile now vanished altogether as Amber looked daggers at Matt. But Ahmet failed to notice. He was too busy fussing over his wife Yamur when she came through the door with the drinks. She dutifully placed the glasses on the coffee table and retreated to a back office without a word. While Matt and Amber took a sip of their juice, Ahmet threw himself into his sales pitch.

"We have some amazing villas overlooking the bay in Karakent, pure luxury," he gushed. "Do you know Karakent?"

Matt nodded.

"I could take you there tomorrow and show you some of our finest properties."

"Tomorrow." Matt repeated the word slowly, as if weighing every syllable. He recalled Ben's message from Rhodes. That was two days ago.

"He could be here any time now," he muttered under his breath.

Ahmet leaned forward, straining to hear Matt's words.

"Pardon me?"

"Could we make it the day after tomorrow?" Matt said. "We have something already arranged for tomorrow."

Amber cast a deeply quizzical look across the table at Matt.

"That's perfect," Ahmet said, interrupting their unspoken exchanges. "Shall I pick you up from your hotel?"

"That's okay, we'll come to the office. What time should we be here?"

They agreed on two in the afternoon.

Matt and Amber rose from their chairs and made to leave. As they did so, Matt noticed Yamur emerge from the back office. It was as if she had been listening all the while, although he had the impression that she had no English whatsoever and would probably not have understood a word.

"You have my card," Ahmet said, as he opened the door, "just in case you need to contact me."

"Yes, I have it." Matt checked his wallet for the card and fished it out. "You have a very interesting name for your business. ASK. Does it have any special meaning?"

Matt would have liked to look into his eyes for some sign of unease. But those mirrored aviators remained loyal to Ahmet's inner thoughts. And his smile was too deeply ingrained for any hint of betrayal.

"AŞK is Turkish for passion," Ahmet said, pronouncing it 'ashk', as he held open the door.

"Oh, I didn't see the cedilla, the curly bit, under the S," Matt said, taking a closer look at the business card, then back at Ahmet when he still failed to see any hint of a cedilla. And finally caught the faintest hint of a crack in that smile.

"The printer we used for the cards was not good," Ahmet shot back in reply. He was ruffled, and it was beginning to show. But Matt had no reason to press the point. Since Ben could be in Karakent any time now, he needed to get back.

"So, we'll see you here at two o'clock the day after tomorrow," Matt said, giving Ahmet his hand and guiding Amber out past the Rottweiler.

When they reached the car, Matt looked back at the office before opening the door. Ahmet still stood there, watching, beneath the three blood-red letters over the door. In block capitals. ASK.

"No sign of a cedilla there either," Matt remarked and climbed into the car.

"So, what arrangements do we have tomorrow?" Amber wanted to know, as Matt started up the engine. She was plainly irritated by the way she had been roped into something without any discussion.

"Don't worry. My arrangements. You don't have to be involved."

Matt's words annoyed her all the more.

"Doesn't it occur to you I might want to be involved?"

"You can stop the role play now, Amber," he teased her. "You're not my wife any longer."

"God, you're impossible!" she cried. "I can't imagine any woman ever wanting to put themselves in that position."

Matt laughed.

"Please Matt. I'm serious. Don't you wonder why that man lies about the name? Just denies any acknowledgement of Susie? As if she never existed."

"What has me wondering is why he didn't just wipe out the

S altogether and include the cedilla when he set up business here? That would have been a denial. But he didn't. Is that the act of a guilty man trying to expunge someone from his memory?" Matt asked.

"Are you saying he's innocent?"

"I'm just trying to keep an open mind," Matt said, bringing a frown to Amber's expression, and she sank back into a brooding silence.

They drove back along the coast without exchanging another word until the phone in Amber's handbag pinged. Matt glanced over and saw a look of unease on her face when she took out her phone and read the message.

"Problem?" Matt asked.

"No, it's all good," she said and sank back into the silent divide between them. It was not until they were approaching Karakent that Amber spoke again.

"You never explained what arrangements you have for tomorrow."

"I'm meeting an old friend."

"When?"

There was a breathless, anxious quality about Amber's question, as if apprehensive of where it might lead.

"I don't know. He'll message me when he gets here. It might even be this evening."

"We could have dinner this evening then, if you like," she suggested in a more confident tone. "And maybe he'll text you over dinner."

"Okay, good idea. Let's make it early dinner and go to Yusuf's now, he said as they drove into the car park."

"Yusuf's?" she repeated.

"The Zeytin. Do you know it?"

"Yes, of course."

"Of course you do," Matt said. "You've been here so often, you'll know it far better than I do."

"How do you know how often I've been here?" Amber asked.

He said nothing, and they strolled down to the Zeytin in silence until Matt spotted Yusuf on the street outside his restaurant. He had also spotted them.

"Well, I assume it's pretty often," Matt said in reply at last, and giving Yusuf a wave as he spoke, "judging from Pearl's comment about your annual visits."

Matt was already a step or two ahead of Amber as they came close to Yusuf.

"You should never make assumptions, Matt."

Matt looked back at Amber and caught the glimpse of an ominously familiar motion some way up the street behind her.

"You're damned right I shouldn't!" Matt replied.

It was the steady roll of red worry beads. They glistened in the light of the next street lamp up the road.

Matt put his arm around Amber's waist and sensed her flinch.

"What are you doing, Matt?"

She shot an icy glance at Matt with a tone of voice that was clearly intended to express shock. But the protest was not matched with any resistance. It was followed instead by a loose but reciprocating arm around Matt's waist.

He smiled as they came close to Yusuf, who spread his arms with an expectant welcome and gestured for them to take a table.

"Good evening, Yusuf," Matt said. "We have other plans tonight, I'm afraid. Book a table for tomorrow. I'll be here. That's a promise."

With these words, Matt steered Amber past the Zeytin restaurant and on down the road to the marina.

"What on earth's going on, Matt?" Amber asked in bafflement once she had disentangled herself from the arm around her waist. "I thought we were going to Yusuf's to eat."

"Change of plan, that's all. Let's take a table down on the marina by the boats, and I'll explain when we get there."

Matt guided Amber down onto the promenade along the

marina, which was lined with a string of al fresco dining areas, all with identical menus to choose from. He settled for a place at the furthest end of the string.

Matt sensed Amber's impatience, could see it with every flicker in her eyes and every movement of her lips. He was acutely aware that he owed her a whole bunch of explanations. He had still not enlightened her about his chat with Luc Bennett. And now there were those worry beads to add to this muddled equation. But he wanted to get the food ordered and the wine on the table before he could even consider how much it was wise for her to know.

They sat sipping their white Angora, watching the yachts tied up in the marina. The silence between them was broken only by the water lapping around the boats. Neither had any appetite for the freebie which the waiter had placed in front of them.

"Well?" Amber said at last. "Are you going to tell me what that was all about?"

"The diversion you mean?" Matt said, knowing full well what she meant.

"If that's what you want to call it. Just now it was simply a change of plan."

"We were being followed."

"Followed?" Amber repeated in disbelief. "What do you mean followed?"

Matt reached for the wine bottle to top up her glass. But he was beaten to it by the waiter, who rushed to the table, took the bottle from his hand and poured it for him. The eager attentiveness, which Matt had grown used to in this country, irritated him at that moment. The interruption put him off his stroke.

"That man with the worry beads up the road behind us. Did you notice him?" he said.

Amber looked across the table at Matt in a bewildered haze, a mood that came fully orchestrated with the sudden blast of a clarinet. The music wafted out from behind the bar across the road. A snaking eastern melody that sang of shisha and dingy cafés.

Matt recounted the story of the flash drive he had been given on the bus by the man called Rekan, his interrogation at the gendarmerie and Luc Bennett's fears about the implications of the data on the flash drive.

"He told me it was explosive stuff and I should get rid of it."

"And did you?"

The bafflement on Amber's face had turned to a look of deep concern by now. But the way her nose wrinkled as she spoke these words lent an expression to her eyes that Matt found deeply seductive. A feeling that was only heightened all the more when she put her lips to the glass and sipped on the wine.

"There were other files on the flash drive as well," he said, ignoring Amber's question. "But it's all in Turkish. I can't understand a word."

Matt paused and took another sip of his wine.

"It was after I was questioned by the Jandarma that the man with the worry beads started to appear. He never lets me out of his sight," Matt said.

He went on to explain how Yusuf's brother had been jailed as a dissident journalist and how he wanted to avoid dragging Yusuf into the suspicions of the stranger following him by being seen there too often.

"That's why I thought it best not to dine there tonight and to come down here instead. I'm sorry, but there was no time to explain."

Amber placed her wine glass carefully down on the table and gave Matt a probing, almost challenging look.

"So where does Dr Schmitt come in?"

"Schmitt?"

Matt was confused by this change of direction.

"You muttered something about Dr Schmitt's colourful history according to the gospel of Luc."

"That's another story altogether." Matt smiled wryly. "But you make it sound as if you don't give much credence to what Luc Bennett says."

"What am I supposed to believe with all this fanciful talk of grey wolves and MI6?"

"It was your Dr Schmitt who brought MI6 into the equation," Matt reminded her. "And when it comes down to it, who would you prefer to believe? The man from MI6 or the Stasi doctor, who's probably not called Hauke Schmitt at all?"

"What do you mean?"

"That's what Luc tells me. Apparently, he used to call himself Josef Wasenmeister."

Matt went on to explain how Luc Bennett and Hauke Schmitt became acquainted in Africa, of the Harare report with the fake HIV story, and of how the doctor lost his licence to practice. Amber hung on his every word, finding it hard to comprehend that the earnest, but kindly, doctor she knew had worked for East Germany's notorious state security service.

"This is the problem with disinformation," Matt added. "It makes you so suspicious of everything that you end up not knowing who or what to believe. But if I had to choose between Bennett and Schmitt, I know where I'd put my money."

He called the waiter for the bill. While the gentle music in the background continued to weave its atmosphere of shisha and dingy cafés, inviting them to stay, Matt could see that she was unsettled. That she was in no mood to linger any longer.

"Do you think Mr Worry Beads will still be following us?" Amber said, looking up at Matt as they stepped back onto the street.

"I wouldn't be surprised. Perhaps you'd like to see me back to my hotel," he said with a grin. "Make sure I get home safely."

Amber returned the smile with a look somewhere between unease and amusement that Matt was unable to decipher. And he was in no mood to attempt cracking cryptic codes. He had enough of that in the ticket pocket of his jeans. So, he took the bull by the horns.

"What do you think Pearl would say if she were to get up in the morning and find you hadn't slept at her place?"

The smile this time came with a twinkle in her eyes that sparkled like two bright stars. No more was said, as they slipped their arms around each other's waists and strolled back up the streets, letting the eastern melodies of the clarinet fade away behind them in the dark.

They took a circuitous route back to the Kelebek to avoid the Zeytin restaurant and any worry beads that may be lurking. It was not until they reached the hotel that Matt saw him again. Sitting on a wall on the opposite side of the road. Waiting. The red worry beads glistened in the light beaming out from the hotel.

"There he is," Matt said, nodding in the man's direction. "Mr Worry Beads."

They stood and stared at the man for some time. And all the while he remained seated on the wall. Staring back. Watching them. Until Matt let go of Amber and made a move across the road. The beads instantly vanished into the stranger's pocket; he stood up and slipped quickly into the shadows before Matt had even taken more than a couple of steps.

When Matt turned back onto the pavement, he could not escape the troubled look on Amber's face. He put an arm around her shoulder and guided her to the hotel entrance.

"Come on. There's nothing to worry about. I'm more anxious to know how we're going to get you past reception."

"I've been followed by too many strangers in my life to relax and tell myself there's nothing to worry about," she said.

Her words unnerved him, left him uncertain what to say. But at least his concerns about reception proved unfounded. There was no one on the desk, and he was able to get Amber up to his room and soothe away the disquiet in her smile with little effort as he closed the door behind them.

"Funny," she said as she looked about the room. "I had expected an untidy mess. But it looks almost unlived in."

"I always travel light. So, there's not much to make a mess with. You should see my flat back home."

"And where's home?"

"North London," Matt replied. "Haringey, to be precise. In amidst the Turkish community, so I feel quite at home here in a way."

"You make it sound as if you're planning to stay."

"Oh, there's no denying they can be lovely people. Like Yusuf here. So welcoming. They'd do anything for you. But there can also be quite a dark side to the ultraconservative types, and they seem to be on the rise here judging by all the new mosques they're building," he said, and paused for reflection.

"So, no chance," he added, putting his arms around her waist and planting the gentlest of kisses on her lips. "I'd much sooner move down to Brighton."

He was unsure whether her quiet chuckle was appreciation for the idea or embarrassment.

"I was only joking," he added to put her mind at ease, then changed the subject.

"Do you know the wife of Hamza's sidekick, Hasan?"

"I wouldn't describe him as Hamza's sidekick. But no, I've never spoken to her. Why?"

"I can't get the picture of her out of my mind. The way she followed Hasan in silence down the street, looking isolated from everyone around her. It was like she was in total servitude.

"You know, when my father died, my mum was utterly devastated. In her devotion to him, she had shut herself off from the rest of the world so completely that she was lost when he was no longer there. Hasan and his wife remind me a little of them. Only the relationship between these two looks far worse. Not so much devotion, more like bondage.

"That's what I mean about the dark side to the conservative Turk."

Amber was not listening. She had already slipped out from under his arms during his meandering talk and undone the belt around his jeans.

"You know, I often wonder," she whispered, slowly pulling down the zip on his jeans, "if the worry beads that the men here play with are a substitute for their balls?"

She was thinking of the stranger in the shadows. And the image drew an appreciative chuckle from Matt as he looked down and caressed her strawberry-blonde hair in his hands. But he was abruptly put off by a tutting sound from Amber.

"So, what's this?" she said, looking up at Matt.

Running her fingers over the rigid object and tugging on his jeans, she gently slid her thumb and index finger into the ticket pocket. Matt looked down to see an expression of concern tinged with triumph in her eyes as she knelt before him with the flash drive in her hand.

"Is this the explosive file you were telling me about?" she asked. "I thought you said you'd dumped it."

"I never said that."

Matt stepped out of his jeans, took the flash drive from Amber, and placed it on the bedside table, pulling her onto the bed with him as he did so. She sighed in a demonstration of surrender and did not say another word.

They eased their way into the remainder of the night, teasing the clothes off each other, one by one, to drink in the perfumes of the body before eventually falling into a deep sleep in each other's arms. So deep that neither of them heard the ping on Matt's phone beside the bed just after three in the morning.

It was not until they woke around seven and disentangled their sweat-drenched bodies from each other that Matt reached over to the bedside and grabbed his phone. He could just make out through the early-morning bleariness that he had a message. He opened it.

"Arrived. See you at the Zeytin in the morning at 10."

It was from Ben Braithwaite.

# CHAPTER 12

"Don't get the wrong idea, Matt," Amber said as she stepped out of the shower and wrapped a towel around her. "I don't jump into bed with every man. In fact, I haven't slept with anyone for longer than I care to remember."

"Believe me Amber, I never thought anything of the kind. I like you. I like being with you."

"Okay, you don't need to go over the top. I'm not looking for commitments or anything. I just don't want you thinking I'm some kind of slut."

Matt was taken aback by this sudden outpouring of nervous, defensive vulnerability. The audible tension in her voice caused her words to quake with an edginess he had not heard in her before.

"Sorry, Matt, I've been hurt once too often," she said. "Last night was so good. And I just don't want you thinking I'm an easy lay…"

"For God's sake, Amber." Matt went to take her in his arms, until she pulled the towel tighter around her chest, and he thought better of it.

"But I also don't want you to get the idea I'm looking for a serious relationship," she added. "And your talk of moving to Brighton…"

"Hey, I was joking," he interrupted, planting a kiss on her forehead as he spoke.

"Yes, I know, I'm sorry. I went through a nasty break-up last year. Then yesterday, out of the blue, I had a message from my ex wanting to meet up again. It's been messing with my mind ever since."

Matt recalled the ping he had heard in the car last evening when they were driving back to Karakent.

"Do you want to meet up again?"

"God no," she cried in horror. "He's the last person I want to see. It just bothers me to think what he might be up to and whether he might turn up on the doorstep when I get home."

She paused, and Matt could see from her furrowed brow that she was raking over all the possible implications of that ping on her phone.

"Or maybe even here," she added with a look of panic on her face. "I know he has connections in Turkey from his timber trading business."

"Just tell him your new boyfriend's in security and will track him down if he bothers you," he said, planting another kiss on her forehead. "But seriously, I also had a message last night. From my old friend Ben. He's arrived and we've arranged to meet in the Zeytin at ten. Do you want to come along?"

Amber reciprocated with a slow, tender kiss in the triangle of Matt's neck.

"I'd love to."

Matt savoured every syllable of this acceptance whispered into his ear. When he took on Ben's mission, he had sworn to himself that he would head back home as soon as it was accomplished. Amber was giving him reason to have second thoughts.

But he had other things on his mind when they stepped out into the morning sun. He looked about for the man in the shadows from the previous night. There was no sign of the silent stranger. Yet, looking up, he saw a different kind of looming threat. Dark clouds gathered over the mountains behind them.

He sensed a change in the weather. In the days since his arrival, he had enjoyed a freshness in the air that hinted at autumn. On this morning, the place was cloaked in a humidity that was not only palpable, but was manifestly creeping up from the sea. It carried the feel of an impending storm. Matt hoped it would stay in the mountains, as it had done when they visited the Bennetts. He took Amber's hand and stepped out onto the pavement.

They were ten minutes early getting to the Zeytin. The restaurant was empty. Yusuf was nowhere to be seen. Only his daughter Belgin invested the place with any sign of activity as she wiped the tables. She looked up when Matt and Amber approached.

"Welcome," she said, running up to them with a smile that perfectly matched the morning sunlight dancing through the bougainvillea in defiance of the clouds which gathered over the mountains.

"My father will be here soon," she added, and showed them to a table overlooking the marina. "You want breakfast?"

"We're waiting for someone, so just some water for now, please," Matt said.

"Is that okay?" he added, turning to Amber for confirmation. She nodded.

The two of them sat in silence for some time, watching the boats as they chugged in and out of the marina and examining the yachts moored at the water's edge. Matt wondered which of these was Ben's and kept his eyes glued to the promenade in the hope he might catch sight of his old friend.

"Which one is your friend's?" Amber asked. The coincidence of the question with Matt's own thoughts teased his growing captivation by this pharmacologist turned bookseller from Brighton.

"I've no idea. Never seen it."

"Matt! Good to see you, mate!"

The fierce slap on the shoulder that came out of the blue caused him to send his glass of water across the table, narrowly missing Amber.

The words were quickly followed by, "Oh Christ, I'm so sorry."

"That's okay," Amber said. "Fortunately, Matt's a lousy shot."

"Good grief, Ben," Matt cried. "You don't have to creep up behind me like that."

"Sorry mate." Ben grinned.

"But it's good to see you," Matt added, getting up to embrace his old friend.

"You don't waste any time, do you?" Ben said, casting a glance at Matt's table companion.

"This is Amber," Matt said,

"Amber," Ben repeated with a look of surprise. "I've heard so much about you."

"You have?" Matt said with a mystified look, as Ben took the seat beside him and placed a thin leather briefcase against the leg of the table.

"I know her sister, Pearl," his friend explained.

"So, you must be Ben Braithwaite," Amber declared, looking across at Matt with a stunned expression. "You didn't tell me this was your friend."

"How was I to know you knew each other?"

"Well, we don't directly," said Amber, and was about to amplify when Yusuf appeared from across the street with his trademark grin and came up to the table.

"Ben, welcome. I'm so happy to see you," he said, resting his right hand on his chest, then added in a serious tone that hinted at an unspoken sadness. "How are you?"

"I'm fine," Ben replied, then turned to Amber and Matt. "Have you guys had breakfast yet?"

"We were waiting for you," Matt said.

"Could you bring us some of your nice Turkish breakfast, Yusuf?"

"You seem to know everyone here," Matt observed, as Ben took the seat beside him.

"So, what have you got for me?" Ben said, ignoring the remark. "Where did you find him?"

Matt pulled Ahmet's business card from his wallet and placed it on the table in front of his old friend.

"His business is just down the road from here."

Ben Braithwaite said nothing. Simply stared at the card.

"We have an appointment with him to view some property," Matt added. But Ben's attention was still fixed on the card.

Matt and Amber watched in silence, exchanging only a brief questioning glance, and waited for him to say something. Until Matt could stand the suspense no longer.

"Are you all right, Ben?"

"Even now he still fucking abuses her," he muttered to himself. "Still uses her name. Still puts her on his card."

"What are you on about?" Matt was bemused by his friend's rambling words.

Before he could get any sense out of Ben, they were interrupted by another familiar voice raised in a tone of pleasant surprise.

"Ben!"

It was the gravelly voice of Hamza. Behind him stood Hasan, the stranger Matt had seen in the doorway when he first met Pearl's husband, and behind him the woman, his wife Fidan. Only today she wore dark glasses and held her headscarf over the lower half of her face.

No longer silhouetted against the light, Hamza's features were more visible to Matt now. His lean face, high cheekbones and fidgety eyes, with the hint of a scar beneath his right eye lent him a slightly menacing air. Hasan remained on the street watching, as Hamza stepped into the restaurant, put his arms around Ben and planted a kiss on his cheek.

"Hamza, great to see you," Ben said. Then, glancing over

Hamza's shoulder when he was released from the embrace, he added a perfunctory, "Hasan. Fidan."

Hasan nodded, shifted nervously from one foot to another and muttered something inaudible. Fidan said nothing.

"How are you, my friend? When did you get here?"

"In the night."

"By boat?" Hamza asked.

Ben nodded, pointing out beyond the confines of the marina. Matt and Amber peered through the bougainvillea hanging over the pergola. Some two hundred metres the other side of the mole around the harbour sat a gleaming white yacht anchored out on the sparkling water. The bright blue strip that ran along the side of the boat was visible even from the shore. It ran like a snake from stern to bow, its head splayed out at the bow to form two extravagantly styled letters: BF.

Matt recalled that Ben said he would be sailing down here, but there was no sign of any sailcloth. This was a fully motorised, ocean-going beast.

"BF?" he chipped in.

"Braithwaite Finance. Others call it Bloody Folly," Ben said, and laughed.

"You don't bring it into the marina?" Hamza asked with a note of concern in his voice. "If there is a storm at night, you would be much safer there."

He fixed a dark stare on Ben, as if summoning the very storm that he warned of. Ben said nothing.

"Okay. See you later then," Hamza added, and disappeared out of the restaurant to walk back up the hill with his sidekick, Hasan, and Hasan's wife in tow.

Matt watched them make their way up past the row of souvenir shops on the right of the street. Some of the shopkeepers were putting their wares on the pavement outside. A group of dogs slept peacefully in the shade of the trees on the other side of the street, outside the mosque. Halfway up, Hasan stopped beneath the trees to speak to a figure seated on a wall behind the sleeping dogs. His wife Fidan stood dutifully behind him.

Matt's heart almost missed a beat when he saw who Hasan was speaking to. It was the man with the worry beads. Matt glanced across the table at Amber and nodded in the direction of the scene unfolding up the street. When she looked back at Matt, unease was etched on her face.

At that moment, Yusuf and Belgin appeared from the kitchen to deliver their breakfast to the table. Tea for all and a variety of plates filled with tomatoes, cucumber, olives and slices of white cheese.

"Ooh, my favourite," Amber gushed with a smile that immediately banished any hint of disquiet and gleamed with a sense of relish at what she was about to receive. "Beyaz peynir. I love this stuff. Like feta, only much tastier."

Matt looked sceptically at the fare on offer, but his mind was on the man up the road with the worry beads and his connection with Hamza's sidekick.

"You seem to know Hasan?" he said to Ben. "What does he actually do, apart from following Hamza everywhere he goes?"

Matt's words were lost on Ben, whose attention was fixed again on Ahmet's business card that lay on the table in front of him. He was rubbing his left eye with his forefinger. Matt had the feeling he was trying to conceal a tear.

"He works in Hamza's shop," said Yusuf, answering for Ben.

"He's a bit of a layabout by all accounts," Amber chipped in.

"You know him?"

"No, I've just seen him about," she said. "Never spoken to him. Pearl says Hamza gives him a job to keep him out of trouble."

"And Fidan?"

"Never spoken to her, either. But it's common knowledge that theirs is not a happy marriage."

The picture she painted of the man, together with his link to the red worry beads, flagged danger. Matt made a mental note to remain cautious of Hasan. He looked back at his old friend, who remained locked in contemplation of the business card.

"Ben, what did you mean when you said Ahmet still puts her on his card?"

At last Matt's words triggered a reaction.

"My sister Peggy."

Matt's jaw dropped. Since his arrival in Karakent, all he had heard was one story after another about a woman called Susie. Was she really the same sparklingly gorgeous person as the Peggy he had met all those years ago?

That was at an anniversary bash Ben held to celebrate ten years since founding his consultancy firm. It was just after he had helped Matt set up his own business, so he invited him along, said it would be a good networking opportunity. But the event was packed with people more interested in crowing about the millions they had made shorting the pound.

The only bright spot of the occasion was Ben's sunny sister Peggy. It was the first time they had met and, although she looked a few years older than him, he was instantly attracted to this woman who had been hidden from him over all the years. Sadly, she was already spoken for and in the company of her husband Mark, who looked a good twenty years her senior and was also heavily into finance. But in crass contrast with Ben's own crowd, Peggy's husband conveyed the kind of cool gravitas that comes with a certain coalescence of age and experience.

It was only now that Matt realised who it was Amber reminded him of whenever she smiled. It was Peggy.

"I thought your sister was called Susie," Amber said.

"My mum and dad were great Buddy Holly fans," Ben said with a pained expression. "So, when my sister was born, it was inevitable they would call her Peggy Sue. She hated the Peggy bit. And I always teased her about it, which made her hate it all the more. So, she insisted on using Sue instead. And it stuck. For me, she's always been Peggy. Always will be."

Matt could not escape the tear in Ben's eye any longer, as his old friend reached down into the leather briefcase leaning against the table. He took out a black cahier notebook and placed it on the table in front of him.

"I was reading through this for the nth time again last night," he said.

"What is it?" Matt asked.

"Peggy's diary. Yusuf sent it to me recently after he found it in the apartment they used above the office. He was the landlord. It's pretty clear from the content that Ahmet wouldn't have known she kept one."

"Can anyone join this breakfast party?"

"Pearl!"

Ben leapt from his seat to embrace Amber's sister as she swept into the al fresco restaurant from the street.

"So," she said, turning to Matt, "I see you've met Ahmet's brother-in-law."

Pearl's words brought a scowl to Ben's face.

"Former brother-in-law," he growled.

"I'm sorry," she said. "That was insensitive of me."

"Oh, we're old friends, actually," Matt said. "It was Ben who asked me to find Ahmet."

"And this is why," Ben said, picking up the notebook and throwing it back onto the table with a smack. "This tells you all you need to know about my sister's marriage to that bastard."

"Why in hell's name didn't you tell me that's why you were looking for him?" Matt asked.

He recalled their meeting in the pub two months earlier, when Ben said he wanted to locate a man in Turkey called Ahmet. And his evasiveness when Matt wanted to know why he was looking for him.

"It seemed better if you didn't know. And I didn't have this diary then, either."

"But you didn't even need my help," Matt said. "He was here all the time."

Ben fidgeted with the black notebook, running through the pages at the top corner with his thumb. "And you say you've arranged a viewing with him?" he added, changing tack.

"Tomorrow afternoon."

"Brilliant." Ben smiled, and appeared to be pondering the implications, before he added, "I couldn't have planned it better myself. We need to talk about that."

"I'll be going along too," Amber chipped in with a gutsy grin. "I'm his wife."

"You what?" Pearl glared at her sister. "I'm sorry, but I'm not going to let you get involved in this. Ahmet is a thoroughly nasty man."

"You sound like Generation Mum. Maybe you hadn't noticed, Pearl, but I'm not your baby sister any longer. I'm thirty-eight years old and I make my own decisions, run my own business, my own life," Amber said, indignation written right across her face, then turned back to Ben.

"Have you heard Dr Schmitt's theory about your sister's death?" she asked.

Ben cocked an eye across the table at Amber. It carried a look that went from suspiciously quizzical to eagerly expectant in a flash.

"The German doctor?" he said. "I remember he didn't have a good word to say about the local doctor who issued the death certificate. But I haven't heard about any theories."

"It was in the months after the funeral that he started talking about it," Pearl explained.

"And you didn't tell me?"

"It's pure speculation, Ben. I didn't see any point upsetting you with wild theories."

"He's a doctor and pharmacologist for goodness' sake," Amber chipped in. "He does have experience."

"And also a reputation for spreading disinformation," Matt added.

Amber glared at him, and Ben looked askance at his friend, as if surprised that Matt already seemed so familiar with events in Karakent.

"What do *you* know about this, Matt?"

"I've been keeping my ear to the ground," Matt replied, glancing up the road at the sound of barking. The dogs had been roused. And the man with the worry beads still sat beneath the tree outside the mosque. Watching.

"Well, whatever Matt says," Amber added, "you should talk to Dr Schmitt. You might find that what he has to say tallies with something in that black book you have there."

Ben looked down at his sister's diary and ran a hand across it in contemplation.

"You're right, Amber. I need to speak to him."

"I'm afraid you'll have to wait a day or so," Pearl told him. "He left for Ankara this morning. Said he had some business there."

"I thought he was retired," Amber said.

"Spies are like dog walkers," Matt quipped. "Even after retirement, they never completely hang up their harness."

Amber sighed. But it was her sister who took up the baton.

"I see you've been talking to our own local dog minder," she said. "But whatever Luc Bennett's views on Hauke, the doctor's theories are very plausible. Amber's right. Take a look at Susie's diary. There might be something in there that substantiates it."

Pearl's endorsement brought a smile of satisfaction to her sister's lips as Amber slipped the last olive into her mouth. Only a few scraps of crumbly white cheese remained on the table. And every glass of tea had been drunk.

Ben leaned back in his seat, ran the palms of both hands over his face as if to wipe it clean, and turned to Matt.

"Look Matt, I have some business to attend to now, but why don't you join me on board later this afternoon? We can relax over a beer, go through the diary together and talk about the strategy for tomorrow."

"The strategy?"

"Okay, your appointment with Ahmet."

"Can I come?" Amber asked and could not escape the instant look of disapproval on her sister's face.

"It would make sense," Ben said, "since you're going to be the prospective buyer's wife."

The disapproval in Pearl's expression had turned to a look of deep concern by now.

"What are you up to, Ben? Whatever it is, I don't like the sound of it, and I don't want you dragging my sister into it."

"You heard what she said earlier."

Amber beamed with quiet satisfaction at Ben's words.

"We're only going to be talking," Matt insisted. "And I'd really value Amber's support."

Pearl watched her sister reach both hands across the table and rest them on Matt's. A gesture that not only spoke of gratitude, but also implied an affection. She was visibly irritated.

"It's what happens when the talking's over," Pearl said. "That's what bothers me."

# CHAPTER 13

Matt watched as Ben embraced Yusuf and then strolled down the street towards the marina with a swagger that spoke of cheerful confidence. But he knew that this was simply window-dressing, that there was a darkness at the heart of Ben's self-assurance.

"You know," Matt said, turning to Amber, "on the journey down here, I told myself as soon as I'd got the job of finding Ahmet done, I would leave him to Ben and be on the next plane home. But look at him. I can't just quit now. He's going to do something really stupid if he's not careful."

"What do you think he meant when he said he has business to attend to?" Amber asked.

"No idea," Matt said. "Pearl?"

"Search me."

"Perhaps he just wants to be alone to visit Susie's grave," Amber suggested.

"He'll be gone for some time, then," Pearl said. "They were all so distressed by the funeral she got here that her daughter, Kyra, first had the body exhumed and autopsied and then returned to England to be buried alongside Mark.

"But in a sense, you might be right. For Ben, the whole of Karakent is her grave. I expect he just wants to wander and be on his own. Talking of which, it's time I wandered too and got back to work."

Matt and Amber sat in silence, absorbing the sounds of the marina below and the warm, tender melody of an oud wafting out from the kitchen. The magic conjured by these strings followed so immediately on from Pearl's goodbye that Matt had the feeling Yusuf was playing it just for them. A feeling that was borne out when drinks appeared before them on the table. An iced lemonade with mint and a beer.

"On the house," Yusuf said, and retreated back to the kitchen.

"Thanks, Yusuf," Matt shouted after him.

He appreciated the generosity of their host and sank back into the melody of the oud strings, smiling across the table at Amber. Yet the warmth of the music did not match the mood reflected in her eyes. She gazed out to sea, her mind adrift in the motion of the water.

Matt hesitated to interrupt her. There was no need. The tectonic plates in her mind were on the brink of forcing a way through the crust that shielded her inner thoughts. She was on edge.

"I think you found me a bit off earlier this morning," she said at last.

"What do you mean?"

"You talked of coming down to Brighton…"

"Hey, I said I was joking," he insisted.

"No, hear me out, Matt." She paused, as if gathering the courage for what she was about to say next.

"The thing is, when I moved back to Brighton, it was all about facing up to my past. I'd been through a bit of a career hell for many years with my allergy."

She paused again, sipped on her lemonade, and let the straw linger on her lips.

"You see, the bookshop was only a small part of my attempt to get my life back on track. Brighton was always something of a double-edged sword. The place where I grew up. In every way."

Amber stopped, but Matt saw that she was still in the throes of a difficult discourse with herself. It was as if she was trying to find the right words until they yielded to the pressure and spewed forth like magma that had nowhere else to go.

"I was raped."

"Oh my God. That's horrific."

Matt was out of his depth. The way his words came out, he was aware of how trivial they sounded, but had no idea what else to say.

"I was eighteen, about to start my studies. I knew the guy. He always seemed so nice, always smartly dressed. Had a penchant for white suits with a red handkerchief in the breast pocket."

Her words put Matt in mind of the man he had seen at the gendarmerie when he was taken in for questioning – and Luc's description of Erkan Suleyman.

"He was quite pretentious," Amber added, "but I liked him, though we never dated or anything. Then one evening I bumped into him down on the seafront. He said how much he'd always fancied me and just dragged me into one of the boats nearby. I lay there in that boat for hours after he'd finished with me. Sobbing.

"But I was lucky. A couple of years later, I read about him in the papers. He killed the next woman he raped."

Amber paused for breath. Matt was still speechless with dismay.

"I never told anyone."

"Not even after you read about the killing?"

"I saw no point. When it happened, I only wanted to get as far away from Brighton as possible. And when I read about the killing, I was just glad to know I'd survived."

She went silent for a moment, visibly trapped in her memories.

"But it stays with you forever," she said at last. "Burning inside you. I sometimes wonder if the whole thing contributed to my allergies and they had nothing to do with the research labs, I don't know. But when I quit my job, I finally realised I had to face up to my ghosts, so I went back to Brighton."

Matt could not fail to see the tears in Amber's eyes when she paused for a moment. He moved around the table to sit beside her, put an arm around her shoulders and said nothing.

"And I'm glad I did," she added, barely acknowledging his gesture as she brushed the tears away with her hands. "But it makes me wonder why I always seem to get it wrong."

"What do you mean?" Matt asked.

"I told you I'd been through a nasty break-up last year. He seemed such a lovely guy at first. I didn't realise what a control freak he was. I mean what's wrong with me that I always get involved with people like that? Why don't I see the signs? Or maybe all men are like it."

"I assure you they're not," Matt comforted her with a squeeze of her shoulder.

She looked Matt in the eye with an expression he was unable to fathom, but it seemed to hover around a vague borderline between anxiety and mistrust.

"I like you, Matt. I really do. And the sex last night was really good. But I hope you can see why I'm not looking for a relationship. I'm just too mixed up."

"I can imagine."

"No, you can't, Matt. You really can't."

Matt withdrew his arm. A wedge of silence was driven into the gap that his last remark had opened up between them. They sat side by side, letting Yusuf's music wash over them and gazed out to sea. The tenderness of the oud had been replaced by the harsher strings of a bağlama. And a cool breeze briefly whipped through the pergola.

Amber pulled her cardigan around her shoulders, pushed her seat back, and rose from the table.

"I have some shopping to do before we see Ben this afternoon," she said, resting a hand on his shoulder.

She spoke in a dull tone that Matt had not witnessed in her before. He could see that she needed space, and time alone.

They agreed to meet down at the marina at three, and she left Matt to ponder her words as he watched her disappear down the street in the same direction that Ben had taken. In the other direction, beneath the tree outside the mosque, the ubiquitous stranger still sat fumbling with his worry beads. The image had become such a constant feature of Matt's time in Karakent that he almost failed to notice him. Almost.

# CHAPTER 14

Viewed from Ben's yacht, the white struts of the pergola peeping through the bougainvillea at Yusuf's restaurant were mere pinpricks in the landscape. Only the gleaming white minaret of the mosque that overlooked it gave any clue to its location on the hillside. Above this, Matt could see the main road cut into the hillside and the occasional truck or dolmuş heading east along the coast in the direction of Ahmet. The clouds that gathered over the mountain backdrop had grown denser over the course of the day. And in the stiffening breeze that blew across the bay, Matt sensed the brewing storm that Hamza had warned of.

Yet there was a joyfulness about the lapping water that sparkled in the breeze. It gave a sense of release from the omnipresence of those red worry beads, tales of the Stasi, and the darkly disquieting flash drive that he continued to carry with him.

From the table on the main deck, Matt watched Amber at the prow of the boat. She leaned on the rails, basking in the sea air. Was she still buried in the memories that she had disclosed to him earlier, he wondered.

Her strawberry-blonde hair glistened in the sunlight. Now and then, the marine-blue, sleeveless blouse beneath her cardigan would billow in the wind to reveal her slim, suntanned waist. He knew that he was growing fonder of her with every day that passed.

"Here you go, Matt. Get this down you."

Catching him off-guard in his thoughts, Ben appeared from behind and thrust a cool bottle of Amstel beer into Matt's hand as he sat down beside him.

"Come and join us, Amber," he shouted, reaching out his arm to her with another bottle. She turned and smiled, before cautiously navigating her way back along the side of the boat. Wrapping an arm around the cardigan to keep it in place, she sat down with them.

Ben fetched another beer from the cabin. He carried with him the black cahier notebook that was his sister's diary when he re-emerged from the cabin. Handing Amber the beer, he laid the diary on the table and placed his mobile phone on top.

"So tell me, Matt. What's this about Schmitt and his theory?"

At these words, a gust of wind whipped around the cabin, almost sweeping both the notebook and the phone off the table. It was only the quick-witted action of Amber, who pounced on them with both hands, that prevented them from getting swept into the sea.

"Thank God for you, Amber," Ben cried above the gust of wind and swiftly planted a heavy ashtray on the notebook along with his phone.

"In more ways than one," Matt agreed. "She's a qualified pharmacologist, so she's much better placed to explain Schmitt's theory."

"Really?" Ben looked surprised.

Amber smiled with a look of shyness on her lips that Matt never would have expected to see in her. It intrigued him. But he could see Ben's impatience to hear the story.

"Go on Amber," he said. "You can tell it far better than I can."

She hesitated for a moment, uncertain where to start, until he added, "As a pharmacologist."

At Matt's prompting, she put on her scientist's hat and began with what she had learned as a student about grayanotoxins. For all Ben's keen interest in what she had to say, Amber had already lost him.

"They're neurotoxins that are found in certain plants," Amber explained when she saw the blank expression on his face. She went on to describe carefully in lay terms the alpine rose and the symptoms of mad honey disease as told by the doctor.

"And Schmitt thinks this is what killed her?"

"Apparently not," Matt chipped in. "He says Ahmet's too cunning for that. Whatever that means. He didn't elaborate, and we haven't had a chance to speak to him again since."

"Maybe there's a clue in Susie's diary," Amber said, nodding at the notebook.

"May I?" Matt added, easing it out from under the phone and the ashtray. He opened it at the first page. It was headed 'Friday, 10 April'.

"When did she marry?" he asked.

"It was all so hurried," Ben said, "and the family weren't invited, so I can't recall the exact date. But it was sometime in September. So, she wrote this seven or eight months later."

"Makes you wonder why she didn't start writing until then," Matt said.

"I wonder why she started writing it at all. I know teenage girls often like to write diaries. But Peggy never did, as far as I know. Why start at the age of fifty?"

"So, what was so important about April the tenth?" Amber said, taking the diary from Matt and reading it aloud:

"*Terrible row yesterday. A. gone home to Ereğli for circumcision ceremony.*" Amber chuckled to herself. "*Says his position in the family demands that he perform the procedure. Horrendous! Back Monday evening.*"

"Oh God," Ben said. "I remember that. Must have been the same weekend. She called me and said he was away for a family circumcision. Told me the last time he'd done it, the boy had cried in pain for days. And I recall her saying she wondered if that was what made the men in this country appear perpetually angry and violent. Like Hasan, for example."

Amber and Matt glanced up from the diary at this last remark.

"Her words. Not mine. God, why didn't she tell me then just how miserable her life had become?" he said. "I could've helped."

"It's not always easy to admit when you're drowning in a pit of despair," Amber said in an effort to comfort him.

Matt darted a look of concern at her, recalling the confession of her nightmare in Brighton. He sensed that she was talking from experience, from her own personal trial. But she did not dwell on the point, and returned Ben's attention instead to the diary.

"That's followed by a couple of other weekend entries," she said. "One about a buyer for a property, and one about dinner with Hamza and my sister. Then on Tuesday: *Not desperately looking forward to him coming home on Monday, but he brought some jars of honey back. Says it's very special. Must admit it's delicious. Especially with Turkish yoghurt. His way of making up I suppose.*

"Making up for what, I wonder," Amber said, glancing at Ben. "Then nothing more for a couple of weeks. It's as if she can only write when he's not around. Sounds very much like he was a total controlling bastard."

With every new entry that Amber read out, the furrows in Ben's brow ran ever deeper. His jaw clenched, the fury burned in his eyes, and the veins of his neck bulged as his anger became ever more visible.

"Ties in with what Dr Schmitt says, doesn't it?" Amber continued, too immersed in his sister's diary to notice his rage. "Then it goes quiet until May the fifth, when she writes: *Relief! Gone back to home for a couple of weeks.* A few days later: *Back with more honey. It seems to be the only decent thing he can offer me.* Then a few days later this: *Such shame! I do try. But it's so difficult living up to his Muslim strictures!*"

These words appeared to take Amber's breath away, as another gust caught the page and blew it from her hand in her momentary distraction.

"Does that mean your sister converted?" she asked with a note of surprise in her voice that was almost lost in the breeze.

"Right after they married."

The bitterness in Ben's voice cut right through the breeze as he rose from the table and went to the cabin.

"All part of the plan," he said, returning with another three bottles. "As she died a Muslim, he could quickly organise her burial with no questions asked. It was fortunate that I just had time to book a flight for the funeral."

"You mean there was no post-mortem?" Amber was shocked.

"No need. The local doctor issued a death certificate. The heart, he said. And when I raised my suspicions with the British Embassy, they said there was nothing they could do."

Ben cracked open another beer.

"So, you reckon he killed her?"

Matt's words were met with a glare of disbelief at the question as Ben raised the bottle to his lips.

"Of course he did! Planned it from the start. Stole her real estate business. Her money. Her property. Everything. Even her sparkle. My niece was left with nothing from her mother."

Amber was reminded of what her sister had said.

"Did Pearl tell you they changed her will the day before she died?"

"That's exactly it." Ben hissed. He continued to seethe with an anger that gave the expression in his eyes a terrifying wildness that Matt had never seen in him before. "And everything I've heard since then just confirms it."

"All of which makes me wonder what Dr Schmitt meant when he said Ahmet's too cunning for that," Amber chipped in, trying to ignore the anger in his voice as she continued leafing through the diary. "He did say overuse of the honey would've have had side effects that could make her feel quite ill. And looking through other entries here, I find she often writes of feeling under the weather. Like here on May the tenth:

"*Can't eat today, feeling too nauseous.* Then a day later: *Dizzy when I got up this morning, almost fell over,* and later the same day: *My left leg keeps giving way, really weak. Still nauseous. Must see the doctor. And remember to buy more foundation first, I'm running out.*"

"God, what a bastard. Even worse than my ex, and that's saying something," Amber said with a venom in her voice that Matt would never have imagined her capable of.

"All this ties in with what Dr Schmitt said," she added. "But he said the honey almost certainly didn't cause her death. So, I'm wondering if there's something here that might give us a clue. Ben, do you think I could take this with me and study it in detail tonight? I'll let you have it back tomorrow."

Ben was deep in contemplation. His anger had now started to ebb away into a dark pool of reflection. It appeared to take a vast lapse of time before her words registered and prompted him to look up.

"Tomorrow," he repeated, slowly mulling over the word. Amber took this as a yes.

"Which brings us to your property viewing with Karadeniz," Ben added.

Matt saw a look in his friend's eyes that took him back to college days. To when they would go out on a bender most weekends, and a moment would invariably come when a gleam of mischief would light up in Ben's eyes. It was always a moment of danger. A signal portending a sudden impulse to go base jumping, to parkour from one high rise to another, or to dive into icy water in mid-winter. Matt could not imagine what trouble he was about to throw himself into now. But that old gleam of mischief was unmistakable. He knew instinctively that his old friend had something up his sleeve. He could only pray that it was not a dead man's hand.

These thoughts were broken by the jingle tone of a phone. It was Ben's. The phone still lay on the table beside the ashtray. Ben picked it up, put it to his ear, and wandered back into the cabin.

"Tony. What's going on?"

These were the only words Matt caught before the conversation became a blur. But Ben's whole demeanour as he disappeared into the cabin gave Matt the impression he was flustered – a feeling that was underscored by Ben's manner when he re-emerged a few minutes later.

"Who's this Tony guy?" Matt asked.

"What?"

His old friend glared at him, a look of anger in his eyes. And anxiety. Something had thrown him off balance.

"Tony?" Ben repeated. "Nobody. Just a colleague."

Matt was not convinced.

"So, what about it then?" said Matt.

"What?"

Ben seemed to be still cast adrift in a different place altogether, brought to him by his phone. He looked nonplussed.

"My property viewing. You said this brings us to my property viewing with Ahmet."

As if in answer, the breeze suddenly grew cooler and stronger. It whipped up the waves around them, causing the boat to rock back and forth. The bottles of Amstel beer began to slide. The light dimmed as the sun vanished behind a gathering cloud.

Matt and Amber exchanged questioning glances across the table and waited for a reply. It was not until the cloud had continued on its path towards the mountains overlooking the bay and left the sun to shine again on the table that Ben's answer finally came. It was delivered with a curious smile.

"I want you to take ownership of my boat tomorrow," he said.

"What?"

The distraction of the phone call had evidently receded. Ben's smile extended right across his face when he saw the bafflement in Matt's expression. He spread his arms wide as if to embrace the yacht, along with Matt, Amber and the entire bay.

"You have a beautiful wife, an ocean-going yacht and a pot of money that you want to splash out on his most expensive villa out there on the point."

With his right arm he gestured towards the promontory at the far side of the bay, where a vast white villa stood like a ghostly sentinel standing watch over this natural harbour. Matt and Amber followed the direction of his arm, saw the villa glistening in the sunshine, and sat in nonplussed silence. Amber's bewilderment was tinged with embarrassment that had her shifting in her seat.

"Supposing for a moment that I do own this beautiful yacht and have pots of money," Matt said, ignoring the wife, "do you know if it's even for sale?"

"That's just an example."

Ben waved a dismissive hand at the villa.

"What you need to do is lay the bait by holding out the prospect of a buy for one of his most exclusive properties and inviting him onto your yacht to close the deal."

"And then?"

"You can leave the rest to me," Ben said.

The wild expression in his eyes returned with a vengeance when he spoke these words. He had lost interest in his sister's diary. Matt was fully aware that Ben's attention was now concentrated on an idea spawned in his mind by the decision to arrange a fake viewing with Ahmet.

Matt could see that this had sparked one of those moments of danger from their student days. And he had an uneasy feeling that whatever it was Ben was hiding so conspicuously up his sleeve might finally prove to be the dead man's hand that he had always feared back in the day. He was beginning to regret the folly of his decision.

Ben placed his hands on the black notebook and pushed it over the table to Amber.

"You take this back with you and see what else you can find of interest, see if there's any clue to what Schmitt was on about. I'll take you both back in the dinghy now, and you can let me know when we meet for lunch at Yusuf's tomorrow."

For all the talk of finding clues in that diary, one thing was clear to Matt: Ben had forged a scheme in his mind, and any clue to the nature of his sister's death was now of secondary interest. Not even the contents of her diary leading up to her death would deflect him from his goal.

This singlemindedness was something Matt had always admired in his old friend during their student years. Even envied. And it had plainly served him well in the finance world. The gleaming white yacht was sure evidence of his old friend's eye for an opportunity to make a killing. And it was precisely this that troubled Matt as they made their way back to harbour in Ben's dinghy.

He knew there was no way now that Ben could be talked out of whatever plan he had in mind. He would have to play his part and make sure his old friend did nothing really stupid.

When they came ashore, Matt's attention was immediately drawn to the fumbling motion of fingers on a set of red worry beads. The man sat on the wall at the entrance to the marina. He appeared to be casually watching everyone who came and went. Matt knew it was him the stranger was waiting and watching for.

The sight of the ominous figure had escaped Amber. Her attention had been caught by the drama of a mewing kitten caught in the lower branches of a tree outside the al fresco restaurant where they had dined the evening before. A small crowd had gathered to watch and gesticulate at the hapless man from the restaurant attempting to rescue the kitten. The animal was within easy reach of his long arms, but rather than take the tiny animal in his hand, he was vainly attempting to coax the kitten down instead.

"Matt, look at that poor little kitten."

Amber nudged Matt's arm and pointed to the scene, which was steadily morphing from drama to tragicomedy. "That man's never going to get the poor creature down like that. Unbelievable. I think he's actually afraid of it."

Jolted from his reflection on the worry beads, Matt was glad of the distraction. He strode over to the tree, lifted the kitten down and placed the creature carefully on the ground. The man smiled awkwardly and retreated to the back of the restaurant with a look of discomfort on his face, and the onlookers dispersed.

"Thank you," Amber said.

She caressed Matt with her eyes, put her arm in his, and they strolled along the promenade together. The unexpected intimacy of that moment put any further thought of worry beads to the back of his mind, and he said nothing of the sinister watchman to Amber. When they turned the corner to walk up the hill past Yusuf's place, they were greeted by the sound of another blast from the past wafting from the Zeytin restaurant. Simon and Garfunkel's 'Bridge over Troubled Water'.

"Yusuf likes his golden oldies, doesn't he?" Matt said.

"It's just a business choice. What Yusuf really loves is his Turkish music," Amber said. "He plays this boomer music to attract custom. Hadn't you noticed that there aren't many young people to speak of here?"

"You're right. I hadn't noticed. Too focused on other things."

Amber squeezed his arm, as if to reassure him after their awkward conversation earlier in the day. Glancing casually back over his shoulder and seeing no sign of the man with the red worry beads, he put his arm around Amber and quickened his pace, as if to urge her up the hill more quickly.

Pearl was in her office when they passed. She looked up just as they stepped into view and called her sister in.

Seeing the look of disapproval in Pearl's eyes, Amber expected further objections over getting involved in any schemes dreamed up by Susie's brother. She hesitated for a moment, then released her arm from Matt's and walked in. To her surprise, there were no words of censure from her sister.

"We're having Hasan and his wife around for dinner this evening and wondered if you'd like to bring Matt along as well."

"What's the catch?" Amber asked.

"What do you mean? Why should there be a catch?"

"I just wonder why you're inviting Hasan to dinner. He's creepy, borderline illiterate and really doesn't seem the type for dinner parties."

"Don't be so harsh," said Pearl. "Hamza thinks it would be good for him to socialise a little. And for his wife Fidan as well."

"I'm surprised a man like that could persuade any woman to marry him."

"This is Turkey," Pearl said with a sigh.

Her words and the sorrowful delivery note that came with them intrigued Matt. But it was not this that sparked a sense of excitement and a spontaneous, "Sounds great. I'd love to come."

Their conversation reminded him of the last time he had seen Hasan, speaking briefly to the stranger with the red worry beads. It seemed the perfect opportunity for getting to know who that stranger was.

# CHAPTER 15

Pearl and Hamza lived high up the slopes overlooking Karakent. The road there wound its way around confusing twists and turns that would have been impossible for Matt to navigate if Amber had not been in the car to direct him. Many of the streets were little more than dirt tracks, and none were named. In contrast, all the villas and apartment blocks were identifiable by names alone. They had no numbers.

It was already dark by the time they drew up outside a dull greyish-white and slightly run-down little villa. It looked to be desperately needing a lick of paint. Stepping out of the car, Matt caught an unmistakable scent on the night air that he could not place. The villa was one of the highest plots up the slope above the town, and even at night – with the moon close to full – the view over the bay was spectacular. The lights of the town far below danced around the marina. The small island beyond the mouth of the bay, silhouetted against the sheen of the moon-kissed sea, had the look of a huge grey mouse about to pounce. And between them, at the centre point of the bay, shone a solitary light that outshone the faint sparkles of the surrounding water. It was the light from Ben's boat. Matt could not imagine what his old friend was plotting in his cabin at that moment.

"Beautiful, isn't it?" said Amber, getting out on the other side.

"It looks so at peace in the moonlight," Matt said, but he knew only too well that, whatever it was which lay at the heart of the view over the bay, it was certainly not at peace.

"I meant the jasmine," Amber said. "I saw you sniffing the air when you got out of the car."

Matt only grunted in response. His mind was still on thoughts of Ben plotting in his cabin.

A sudden breeze briefly brushed away the scent of jasmine and caused Amber to shiver slightly. She pulled her cardigan tighter around her waist, folding her arms over it to keep the garment in place.

"The wind can get chilly at night when it sweeps down from the mountains," she said.

A dark cloud blotted out the moonlight as she spoke these words and, as if in response, a light went on above them that cancelled out the darkness. It came with a deep, gravelly voice.

"Hey, come on up."

Hamza was standing on the terrace above where Matt had parked the car. He leaned forward and rested his hands on the stone balustrade. Pearl appeared from behind Hamza and spread her right arm around his shoulders. Her hair glistened like copper in the terrace lights.

"You're here at last," she said. "Come on up."

Amber guided Matt around the corner to a set of steps that led up to the terrace of her sister's villa. They were greeted at the top of the steps by Hamza, as Pearl absented herself with a hasty wave of both hands.

"Be with you soon. The köfte need a little attention first," she said, and vanished from view.

"Normally, we would grill out here on the terrace," Hamza said apologetically. "But the wind is getting chilly, and with the clouds gathering over the mountains, we thought it would be best to eat inside."

"Your assistant's not here yet," Matt said.

His words were intended as a question, but they came out as an observation. He was disappointed, let down in his keenness to know who the man with the worry beads might be.

"Hasan? No, he's not here yet," Hamza said.

"One thing you can rely on with Hasan," Pearl shouted from the kitchen, "is that he will always be late."

Hamza smiled back into the kitchen at his wife with a look of embarrassment, before turning back to his guests and offering them a drink. Matt took a beer and Amber a white wine.

"Angora, if you have it," she added, as he disappeared into the kitchen.

With the breeze growing ever chillier, Amber suggested to Matt that they follow Hamza inside and take their drinks into the lounge. The room struck Matt as a peculiar mix of Turkish and English culture. The loud, ornate furniture that he imagined Hamza might have picked up through his antiques business competed with quiet, unassuming watercolours and aquatint engravings on the walls. On closer inspection, he found that almost all of them depicted scenes of Brighton and surroundings. The unmistakable Royal Pavilion crying India, of which there were several, Marine Parade with horse-drawn carriages, and East Cliff with sailboats at sea, along with Lewes Castle and scenes from the South Downs.

Both Pearl and Amber clearly clung to their childhood memories, each in their own way – Amber by moving back to the place where she had grown up, despite the trauma, and Pearl by hanging pictures on the wall as souvenirs.

"Here we are," said Hamza, returning to the lounge and a tray of drinks, which he set down on the coffee table between a garish red Ottoman-style sofa and two large matching armchairs. He joined Matt with a glass of Efes beer, while the two sisters shared the same taste for white wine.

"I couldn't help noticing all your pictures of Brighton and the South Downs," Matt said, gesturing to the walls around them as

Pearl lowered herself onto the sofa beside her sister and took her glass in her hand. "What made you leave all that behind and settle here in Turkey?"

"A broken marriage and a messy divorce," came Pearl's blunt reply, her eyes fixed on the glass in a stony gaze.

Not for the first time, Matt mulled over Thomas Moore's words. If it wasn't Luc Bennett or Hauke Schmitt, then it was Susie or Pearl. They all seemed to be running from something. An awkwardness descended on the mood around the table as Matt pondered the Irishman's observation. And for the next fifteen minutes, they skirted gingerly around any topic of discussion that might prove uncomfortable territory until the aimless conversation was interrupted by the jingle of Hamza's phone. He picked it up and muttered into the phone in Turkish. Matt could see in Pearl's eyes and the wry smile on her face that she knew who he was speaking to and understood what was being said.

"What's his excuse this time?" she asked when Hamza put the phone back on the table.

"He says Fidan's not well."

"Of course he does," Pearl scoffed. "He always does. And we all know what that means."

"I don't. What does it mean?" Amber asked with a faux innocence in her voice that irritated her sister.

"No, you don't," she agreed, making no secret of her irritation. "You don't know because you've never spoken to Fidan. He keeps her out of view most of the time."

Amber looked quizzically at her sister as she took a sip of wine.

"The name Fidan means young sapling," Pearl said. "Which is a wonderful description of the way she was when I first met her. That was before she married Hasan. She was such a sweet young woman. Very modest and quite shy. But since she married, no one gets to enjoy her company any longer, because she's ashamed to show the bruises her husband inflicts on her almost daily."

"What!?"

"It's not uncommon," Pearl hissed with a venom in her words that took Matt by surprise.

"A woman dies at the hands of her husband almost every day here," she added. "There's a certain kind of man who believes it's not only his right, but actually his duty to beat his wife. Each one a young sapling beaten and deprived of love until their blossom fades and they stop growing altogether."

Hamza looked across the table at his wife in visible embarrassment. She must have seen the discomfort, for she pursued the subject no further. But Amber was less considerate of his feelings. She cast a withering look in the direction of her sister's husband.

"How can you employ a man like that in your shop?" she asked.

"I told you, it's Hamza's way of keeping him out of trouble," Pearl insisted, audibly aware of how weak her words sounded. "And trying to protect Fidan," she added.

"The way to protect her is to report him to the police," Amber said, unimpressed by her sister's defence of her husband and becoming visibly angrier with every word. "Or is there no law to protect women here?"

"Of course…" Pearl insisted, but she was cut short by a non sequitur from Matt that instantly closed down the discussion when he turned to Hamza.

"Do you know that man he was talking to yesterday after you left Yusuf's place?"

Matt's question was greeted by a dumbfounded silence from his hosts. Only Amber knew the purpose behind his question. And she glowered at him with a look of angry frustration for distracting them from a far more important issue.

"What man?" Hamza said at last, evidently glad of the reprieve.

"When you were walking up the hill from the Zeytin together, Hasan stopped and spoke with a man sitting on a wall near the mosque."

Hamza stared across the table, his eyes wide in a blank expression, and said nothing.

"He was smartly dressed in a suit and was fumbling with a set of red worry beads," Matt added.

"Smartly dressed?" Hamza said. "No. The only people Hasan knows who are smartly dressed are council officials and, of course, the police. But he would never stop to talk with them."

"The police," Matt repeated.

"But they don't dress in smart suits and play with worry beads," Pearl chipped in. "So, I'm afraid you'll have to ask Hasan who he is, because we have no idea."

Pearl glanced at Hamza, who looked back sheepishly in a way that suggested he might actually have quite a good idea who the man was.

Pearl was audibly irritated by the way Matt had deflected the conversation with this question. Despite her defence of Hamza, it was clear from the ferocity of her earlier words that Hasan's treatment of his wife was a cause célèbre for Pearl. Had she suffered similar treatment from her ex? Matt wondered.

The ire that bore down on him now from both women in the room was palpable. It left him wary of taking the discussion any further. But Amber saw his dismay. Overcoming her own frustration with his change of tack, she quickly turned the conversation a notch further. He smiled almost imperceptibly in gratitude for the way she generously surrendered her argument.

"Ben gave me Susie's diary to read this evening," she said. "In the hope I might find a clue to her death."

"You mean the Schmitt theory?" Pearl asked wearily.

"But it seems a peculiar diary in a way," Amber added, "because from what I've seen so far, it seems to be a series of complaints about her husband almost from the word go, as if there was never any romance. It reads as if it was intended as a record of his behaviour. And it reminds me of what you were saying about

Hasan and Fidan. There's no mention of being beaten or bruised, but there is a deep undercurrent of resentment.

"Of course, I only met Susie once or twice, so I can't really judge, but she always seemed a very happy, bubbly person. A really warm-hearted, generous woman. And yet it's not the way she appears here."

"Oh, she was," Pearl insisted. "And there did seem to be a lot of romance at the beginning. Too much for my liking. It didn't seem authentic on his part. But she was so flattered by all the roses and the attentions of a much younger man."

Matt noticed a sadness in her eyes as she paused for reflection and rose from her seat to fetch the dinner in from the kitchen.

"It was her vulnerability," she continued, returning from the kitchen with a tray that brimmed with the delicious aroma of spicy dishes, "and that warm-hearted spirit. That's what led to her tying the knot so soon. But the vulnerability was not immediately obvious. Only Ahmet saw that. And he was quick to exploit it. Everyone else saw only her generosity, and the whole town took to her at once. Especially Yusuf. I think he would have married her, too, given half a chance."

Over the dinner of hummus and a smoked aubergine dip, followed by deliciously spiced köfte, the discussion continued to revolve around Susie's generosity of spirit. There seemed to be a reluctance to dwell on the darker side that she had revealed in her diary.

Matt became steadily resentful that Hasan and his connection to the man with the worry beads had long been forgotten. And he imagined Amber felt the same over the way all talk of the diary was off the table as soon as her sister took over the conversation. But he was disappointed when she said, "I'm off to bed then. I need time to go through the diary before I sleep."

He had been hoping she would return to the hotel with him.

"Can you find your way back all right?" she added, turning to Matt.

He caught a slight edge of concern in her voice. But other than this, there was nothing in her manner that could allay his sense of disappointment.

"Yes sure. No problem. Downhill all the way," Matt replied in a vain attempt to appear cool. "See you tomorrow then. At Yusuf's."

# CHAPTER 16

Matt was still fretting over Hasan and his connection to the man with the worry beads when he drew up outside his hotel and stepped out of the car. He felt the first drop of rain hit him in the eye and blinked. Looking about him, up and down the street, across the road, he scrutinised every shadow. But saw no trace of the slightest rolling motion of the beads he had come to identify with the stranger. Nor any other sign.

Had the man simply taken cover from the rain? Matt wondered. Or had he gathered all the information he needed? And if he had, then for whom and for what?

Matt carried these questions with him up the stairs. When he opened the door to his room, he found it unusually cool. Too cool even for it to be caused by the evening breeze and the brewing storm. For once, the air-con was working when it was not wanted. He switched it off and threw himself onto the bed to ponder the day's events, puzzled as to what Ben might be plotting on his yacht. But he did not get far with his thoughts before the night ferried him off into sleep.

It was already light when he woke. He checked his phone beside the bed. Gone eight already. It was the best sleep he had had all week. A good sign, he told himself. He would be fit for anything the day was about to throw at him.

He had hoped the phone would have a message from Amber. But there was none. He told himself that she had probably been poring over the diary all night and also woken late. He took a shower and ventured downstairs for the spartan Turkish breakfast that his hotel had to offer.

But at least he could enjoy the copious amounts of tea provided before he stepped out into the morning. While the street was dry, the puddles in the forecourt and along the side of the road told him that the place had been beset by a deluge in the small hours. And now that the shadows of the night had receded, he could confirm that there really was no further sight of the man with the worry beads.

Has he actually given up his pursuit altogether? Matt asked himself, as he walked on down the hill into town. Or is this simply the calm before an undeclared storm?

These thoughts were brought to an abrupt halt by the disembodied growl of a familiar voice.

"From the frown on your face, it looks like the storm kept you awake all night as well."

The words came with an unmistakable musicality. Matt turned and came face to face with Luc Bennett emerging from a dilapidated old Fiat that looked barely roadworthy. His faded red baseball cap still firmly in place.

"It did us at any rate," Luc went on, as Matt gazed at him in nonplussed silence. "We thought the roof was falling in."

"Luc," Matt said when at last he found the words to speak. "What are you doing down here?"

"Just popping into the supermarket to stock up. How are things?"

"I'm off to meet an old friend," Matt replied curtly.

He was in no mood for small talk and wanted Luc to know. But Luc was no more interested in idle conversation than Matt was.

"It occurred to me when I saw you coming down the street," he said, with a piercing look in his eyes. "That flash drive. I hope you've got rid of it by now."

Matt said nothing, but he could see from the look in Luc's eyes that the Welshman knew he was still clinging on to the USB stick.

"Where did you get it?" Luc asked, pushing Matt further.

"I told you. I was given it."

"Given it?"

The last thing Matt wanted right now was any more chit-chat, but the startled expression on Luc's face compelled him to open up.

"He was a complete stranger. A guy called Rekan," he explained, and went on to describe his journey a few days back when the bus was stopped by the Jandarma.

Luc Bennett appeared to hang on every word, as if making a mental note of every detail. Matt omitted his interrogation at the gendarmerie, but what Luc heard was evidently enough to bring a look of concern to his eyes and dig deep furrows across his brow.

"Like I said Matthew," he muttered, almost with a snarl, "you need to get rid of it. Sharp." He jabbed a finger into Matt's shoulder as if to accentuate the last word.

With this ominous warning, Luc disappeared into the supermarket and left Matt to wander on into town. It was barely into mid-morning and the restaurants were not yet open, but Osman was already sitting out in front of his tavern, framed by the bougainvillea that grew around the entrance. The gentle strings of a bağlama wafted out into the street, while yellow taxis stood idly at the rank on the other side waiting for the promise of a fare. Osman looked up as Matt passed, but if there was any sense of recognition, it did not show.

While the restaurants were not yet serving food, the bars had already opened up, and Matt was surprised to see the familiar figure of Dr Schmitt sitting outside the Utopia so early in the day. But what really took him aback was to see that he was talking to Amber. He felt a twinge of disappointment, even irritation, that she had not messaged him to say she was going to be here. She spun around in her chair when Matt approached from behind.

"Amber."

He spoke her name in a detached tone. Perhaps subconsciously designed to mask his sense of let-down and appear cool. She responded with an apologetic yet strangely nervous thrill in her voice.

"Hello Matt. I hope you managed to sleep through the storm. I couldn't."

He said nothing, but took a chair beside her. The black cahier notebook lay on the table in front of her. And he could see that she was burning to say more.

"At least, it kept me awake enough to pick my way through Susie's diary with a fine toothcomb. And I'm pretty sure I found what we were looking for," she said. There was a note of triumph in Amber's voice as she opened the notebook and pushed it over the table to Matt.

At that moment, he felt a heavy hand on each shoulder.

"So, what's your poison, Matt?"

Matt looked up to see the unshaven, sun-wrinkled face of Tom Moore staring down at him.

"It's a bit early, but I'll take an Efes thanks."

Tom Moore ambled back to the bar with the order, and Matt turned his attention to the notebook.

"It's in the very last paragraph," Amber added, pointing at the entry in question. "And Dr Schmitt agrees. It ties in exactly with his theory."

Matt could not fail to see the look of smug satisfaction that Amber's endorsement brought to Hauke Schmitt's face. He leaned forward to read the entry in the diary:

"*A. back home last night. Attempting to salve his conscience with another local speciality wrapped up in a plastic bag. Turkish horseradish. Put my nose in the bag. Really pungent. Maybe try it in the morning.*"

"There you have it," Dr Schmitt cried triumphantly. "Just as I thought."

"What do we have?" asked Matt.

"Susie loved horseradish. And Dr Schmitt is another aficionado. Grew up on it as a child, didn't you?" Amber said, turning to Hauke Schmitt, who simply nodded and allowed her to answer for him. "And he's never heard of Turkish horseradish. But there's something called aconite, which you probably know as monkshood. Apparently, lots of it grows around the Black Sea. It has pretty blue flowers and a root that's often mistaken for horseradish…"

"Indeed, a most beguiling root of pure evil," Dr Schmitt chipped in at last. He was unable to contain his own oddly muted excitement any longer.

"When Miss Baxter showed me the entries in this diary…"

"Miss Baxter?"

Matt's interruption came with a look of bafflement.

"That's me," Amber grinned. It was a smile that lit up her face so sweetly that it finally washed away any lingering sense of disappointment in Matt's eyes.

"Yes, of course," said Dr Schmitt with an embarrassed nervousness in his voice. He was rattled by the way Matt had drawn attention to his Teutonic correctness, but swiftly regained his composure.

"And when she showed me these entries," he repeated, "I was reminded of Pliny."

"Pardon me?" Matt said.

"Pliny the Elder, the Roman philosopher. And natural historian, of course."

"Of course," Matt repeated under his breath, increasingly vexed by the smugness in the way this man expounded his knowledge of the ancient classics. Dr Schmitt ignored Matt's visible irritation.

"Have you read Pliny?"

"Not in the original."

Matt's sarcasm was lost on Hauke Schmitt. He responded in the only way he knew how: with the correctness of an overbearing professor.

"But you will no doubt be familiar with Ovid's story in Metamorphoses, where Arachne was turned into a spider with the aconite that grew from the mouth of Cerberus."

Hauke Schmitt paused briefly to enjoy the blank expression on Matt's face before continuing with the lesson.

"When Pliny wrote of Ovid's story, he described how aconite grew in abundance around Heraclea Pontica. Now, you will not be aware of this," he said in a tone that marked his words out as a blunt put-down, "but Heraclea is on the Black Sea. It is known today as Ereğli."

"And Susie mentions Ereğli in her diary," Amber chipped in, her eyes sparkling with excitement. "It's where Ahmet comes from."

She paused to let this information sink in, before Hauke Schmitt took up the baton again.

"Arrhythmia, asystole, paralysis of the heart. And no clear post-mortem signs except asphyxia," he said in a serious, doctorly tone. Then added darkly, "The perfect instrument. It was known as a woman killer in ancient times. Pliny wrote that, of all the poisons, aconite is the quickest to act; that death occurs on the same day if the genitals of a woman are touched by it."

"Oh my God! Is that how he did it?" Amber looked aghast at the doctor.

"I doubt it very much. But there is really no way of knowing."

Hauke Schmitt's words came dressed with the faint hint of a smirk that appeared to unsettle Amber. Matt felt gratified that she seemed at last to be finding the man a little creepy, as if she sensed that his mind's eye was savouring that image of Ahmet administering the drug.

"This was Susie's last entry," Amber said, plainly flustered.

"Okay, so there's no hint of what she actually did with the root that Ahmet brought back for her," Amber went on, with a disparaging glance at the German doctor. "But everyone knew how much she loved to cook with horseradish. So, we can assume he brought it back with the express intention of using it to poison her food. Why else would he sell it to her as horseradish. He knew she'd be literally dying to try it."

The German doctor leaned back in his chair with a wave of the hand, as if acceding to Amber's interpretation.

"So, after weeks or months of plying her with a honey that made her more tired and sick with every day that passed," he declared, "Ahmet Karadeniz delivered the final *coup de grâce* with aconite."

The keen edge of triumph in Hauke Schmitt's voice and the glint of self-satisfied delight in his eyes put a sour taste in Matt's mouth as he sipped on his beer. But the doctor was not finished.

"He created the impression the poor woman was suffering from a chronic illness by inducing all the signs and symptoms of mad honey disease. Symptoms that are notoriously difficult to diagnose, because each one of them can be linked to so many different pathologies. Then he delivered his final blow with a poison that leaves behind nothing more than the suspicion of a heart problem.

"Quite enough to convince the local quack," Schmitt added. "Since she was a Muslim and had to be buried quickly according to tradition, the doctor's certificate was enough to proceed before a proper obduction could be performed."

"It's horrific!" Amber's eyes were alight with rage. "It's as if they actually want to make it as easy as possible for men to get away with killing their women in this country! It's unbelievable!"

"What's unbelievable?"

All heads turned at the sound of this new voice. Momentarily silenced by the intrusion, the three of them looked up like synchronised swimmers emerging from the water to see Luc Bennett at their table. He lifted his faded baseball cap, scratched his head, and grinned. It was Amber who broke the silence.

"The way men in this country are allowed to treat their women. That's what. And literally get away with murder."

She was speaking of Susie and the entries in her diary. But Matt sensed that she was also thinking of the conversation the night before, the talk of Hasan and the abuse he inflicted on his wife, Fidan. Luc rested a hand on Amber's shoulder, as if to comfort her, and glanced down at Hauke Schmitt.

"Hello Josef. Haven't seen you in a while," he said, invoking a name from the German doctor's past that Luc Bennett plainly knew would get him rattled.

Hauke Schmitt nervously adjusted the gold-rim glasses on his nose and smiled uneasily back at Luc Bennett. He said nothing and let the name drift away on the breeze. But Luc had no wish to provoke any further. There were other things on his mind.

"Matt, could I have a word?" he said.

The cosy musicality of his voice carried an oddly conflicting air of mystery as he gestured Matt to move away from the table so they could talk in private. Just the two of them.

Amber and Dr Schmitt watched in silence, she peering with a fascinated curiosity and he with deep suspicion across his face, as Luc took Matt by the elbow and guided him to the discreet shade of a eucalyptus tree on the opposite side of the road.

"I've been thinking about what you said earlier. You said a guy called Rekan gave you the flash drive."

"How did you actually know I was here?" Matt asked, ignoring Luc's words.

"Everybody knows where everyone is in this town. The walls have eyes and ears in this place."

Luc's words brought to mind again the image of the man with the red worry beads. Matt said nothing.

"Have you checked to see if there's anything else in those files? Maybe a sheet in the PDF that you missed? Maybe he said something when he gave it to you?"

"No, I'm pretty sure there's nothing else there," Matt said, growing suspicious of Luc's interrogation. "Why do you ask?"

"Because it occurs to me that Rekan is a Kurdish name. And that makes me wonder why a Kurd would have a file on the Grey Wolves and why the Jandarma would be interested, apart from the fact that a Kurd is always a person of interest. You see, the far-right fanatics are not such a big concern for the powers that be since they've been integrated into the MHP. Even their jailed mobster friends have been given free rein since the Covid amnesty.

"So, it makes me wonder what Rekan was up to. Maybe the Grey Wolves are getting restless, and he wanted to use the information somehow. Or maybe the flash drive contains other stuff as well – on the PKK or HDP, for example."

"Why do you insist on confusing things with your damned acronyms and abbreviations?"

Luc Bennett ignored Matt's irritation.

"It's just a thought. If you still have the flash drive – and I suspect you do – then check to see if there's anything else on it. Because, whatever it's all about, if the Jandarma are interested and it involves both the far right and the Kurds, that's a really explosive mix."

Matt let the trace of a smile cross his lips, but not enough for Luc to notice.

"But best just to get rid of it," Luc insisted. "All the more so these days when the Kurds are involved. That can get you into big trouble."

Luc was attempting to couch his words of caution in as casual a manner as he could muster. But Matt sensed that the flash drive in his pocket had become an obsession for the Welshman. It was clear that Luc was deadly serious, and yet Matt had the feeling that the Welshman knew he would not be persuaded to part with it and that he was simply interested in making sure he still had the flash drive.

The warning called to mind the last words Rekan had spoken before he was taken away by the Jandarma. "Murat. Only Murat". This mnemonic phrase had lodged itself in Matt's mind. And it brought a perversely broad grin to his lips that could no longer escape Luc's attention.

"I mean it Matt."

But Rekan's three words had given him an idea. He gave Luc a slap on the shoulder.

"Thanks. Much appreciated. But I really need to get going."

"Look, before you go," the Welshman said, resting his disfigured right hand on Matt's arm to restrain him. "Let me give you my number."

He seemed oddly on edge to Matt as he dragged a phone from his trouser pocket. There was a nervous anxiety in his voice that struck Matt as out of character for the former MI6 man he had come to know.

Luc keyed in his PIN, and the two of them exchanged numbers.

"Call if you need me," Luc said, adding with an earnest emphasis in his tone, "Any time." Then he turned to leave.

"Thanks. I will."

Matt watched the Welshman make his way back up the hill, pondering Luc's odd behaviour, his nervous unease, then crossed back over the road. Amber and the German doctor were also following the progress of Luc Bennett up the hill, as if in silent speculation, when Matt rested a hand on Amber's shoulder, leaned his head down and spoke quietly into her ear.

"I'll see you for lunch with Ben around twelve. Down at Yusuf's," he said. Matt gave no further explanation, but turned and strolled off down the hill in the direction of the marina, carrying a smile on his face that had been made a little less relaxed by Luc's insistence that he call him if need be.

# CHAPTER 17

There was a reason Matt had gone into the security business: having battled his postgraduate demons of alcohol and cocaine, and won, he had become deeply cautious. So, he resisted the temptation to start up his laptop and view the file on his flash drive in public. But Luc Bennett had piqued his curiosity about Rekan and the purpose behind the USB stick. So, keen to learn more, he set off to speak with the only fount of knowledge on these matters that he knew. And he preferred to do this without involving Amber.

Strolling down the hill in the direction of the marina, he stopped every so often at the souvenir shops to join the tourists and examine the local handicrafts. Then ambled on past the shady tree outside the mosque where Hasan had stopped and spoken to the man with the worry beads. He wanted to keep a discreet eye open for any suspicious movements around him. For while the mysterious stranger was no longer to be seen, having appeared to have lost interest, Matt could not be sure that he had not been replaced by someone else. Yet there was no obvious sign of anyone following him.

The mosque shone a resplendent white through the boughs of the tree. Its minaret rose above the foliage like an admonishing finger to warn of the explosive path he was on. A path that Luc

Bennett had painted into Matt's mind as one littered with a string of roadside bombs. This was in stark contrast to the tranquil backdrop of the bay beyond the minaret: the peaceful, sparkling blue of the sea that was overlooked by the bougainvillea of the Zeytin restaurant.

Belgin was spreading out the tablecloths and decorating the tables with vases of single red roses as Matt approached. He caught the sound of what Amber described as boomer music drifting out from the kitchen. It was the softly floating melody of 'Albatross' again and perfectly suited the backdrop of the bay beyond the marina.

Matt took this as a sign that Yusuf must be somewhere in the kitchen and quickened his pace so as not to find Yusuf had disappeared by the time he reached the restaurant. But there was no need: when Belgin looked up and saw Matt hurrying down the road, she ran into the kitchen and brought her father back out with her.

"Hoşgeldin!" said Yusuf, beaming his trademark grin.

He spread his arms wide and, as Matt came up to him, clasped both hands in welcome.

"It's so nice to see you again, Matthew. Please, drink a tea with me." With a sweep of his left arm, he gestured Matt to take a seat in his restaurant.

"I know it's a bit early in the day, but I'd sooner have a beer."

"Of course."

Yusuf disappeared back into the darkness of the kitchen, while Matt took a seat at what he now considered his own table overlooking the marina. 'Albatross' had given way by now to Rod Stewart and 'Sailing'. It may be dusty old boomer music, Matt told himself, but Yusuf has an uncanny way of matching the melodies to the mood and atmosphere of the place. He stared out to sea beyond the boats in the marina, to Ben's yacht in the bay.

He was dwelling on thoughts of what his old friend might have been cooking up on his boat, when Yusuf returned with a glass of cool Efes beer and a glass of tea for himself. He placed them carefully on the table and took the seat facing Matt.

"Yusuf, I've been meaning to ask you something since we first met a few days ago. Do you know the bakery up the road called Ekmek something or other?"

"What Ekmek?"

"Near the Şimşek hotel."

Yusuf's eyes lit up in recognition.

"Of course."

"It was run by someone called Murat," Matt said.

The light in Yusuf's eyes darkened. He gave Matt a quizzical look that bordered on suspicion. But said nothing. He was waiting for more.

"He died recently," Matt added.

"In the early summer," Yusuf said at last. "You know Murat?"

"No. But I heard about his death. A heart attack, I believe. And I was wondering if you knew him."

Yusuf sipped slowly on his tea, placed the glass back in its saucer, and looked deep into Matt's eyes.

"It is not wise to ask too many questions, Matthew. Murat and my brother Mehmet arkadaş." He hesitated, searching for the right word.

"Friends," he said when at last he found it. "Mehmet and Murat good friends. My brother journalist. It is his job ask questions. But he ask too many questions. Now he is guest of government in Izmir prison."

Yusuf fell silent, pensively sipping his tea. A brief gusting breeze blew up from the marina as the sun disappeared behind a cloud. It was a reminder to Matt that traces of last night's storm still lingered. Yusuf placed the tea glass carefully back in its saucer and rose from his seat.

"Kitchen wait for me."

With these words. Yusuf disappeared back across the road carrying not only the glass and saucer in his hand, but plainly a whole history in his thoughts that preyed heavily on his soul and refused to be disclosed.

Whoever Murat was, it was clear to Matt that anyone associated with him, whether Yusuf's brother, Rekan or anyone else, ran the risk of vanishing into a high-security prison. Or worse. And it occurred to him also that perhaps, like Susie, it was not a dodgy heart that had carried Murat off.

Matt's train of thought was accompanied by a change of music. Gone the boomer hits of yesteryear, replaced now by the mournful sounds of a Turkish clarinet. Matt could not shake off the feeling that the music was Yusuf's response to the unpleasant memories his questioning had evoked. The hauntingly plangent clarinet appeared almost to reflect the change of mood as Matt looked out to sea. Out to Ben's solitary yacht, which bobbed gently in the water. The sea around the boat had become a forbidding dark blue as cloud spread ever more densely over the sun.

Lifting the glass to his mouth, Matt let the doleful music guide his thoughts while he sipped his beer and gazed at the leaden sea. He was no closer to establishing who either Rekan or Murat were and what their business with each other might have been. In the meantime, out at sea, his old friend was plotting Matt knew not what.

Ben had changed since their drinking days at college. It was not a change for the better. Matt had always admired him. Envied him his energy, his commitment and his insatiable appetite for risk. But he had acquired a streak of ruthlessness since their student days. It no doubt explained his success in the city, the gleaming white yacht in the bay, and the beautiful disposable women forever on his arm.

That Ben was alone and without any sign of a glamorous female accessory on his yacht told Matt that it was Ben's ruthless side which had brought him down to these Turkish shores, that he was forging plans which had no room for frivolous companionship. This troubled Matt.

It took a gentle hand on his shoulder to kick these thoughts into touch.

"On the beer again?"

It was Amber. There was a look of concern in her eyes.

"Don't forget you're supposed to be driving over to Ahmet's after lunch."

"No worries. It's only my second."

He sensed an implicit reprimand in Amber's words. This grated on his view of her, briefly casting her in the role of a nagging partner and threatening to undermine his growing enjoyment of her company. Then she leaned forward and gave him a peck on the cheek as if to reassure him. He smiled, trying not to let it show.

"Getting serious by the look of it."

Matt and Amber turned their heads in perfect time to locate the disembodied voice. It belonged to Ben, who had entered the restaurant behind her. He stood just inside the pergola in full waterfront gear: white Ralph Lauren polo shirt, navy blue shorts, black espadrilles and mirrored shades. His mop of dark blond hair was swept back in the classic shape of a bow wave, as if to underline his yachtsman's credentials.

The clean, sophisticated image did not fit with the murky plans that Matt knew he was hatching in his mind.

"Have you ordered yet?" Ben asked.

"Give us a chance. I've only just arrived," Amber retorted, taking the seat opposite Matt that looked out over the marina.

There was a hint of discomfort and indignation in her reply. Chastened by her words, yet frowning as if uncertain why he should be, Ben took the seat next to Matt. His cool, ill-fitting image bothered him, but he was relieved of any need to dwell on it when Yusuf emerged from the kitchen.

Crossing the narrow street, beaming his trademark smile, he threw his arms out in welcome and picked up three menus that lay on the desk outside the entrance of the restaurant. The darkness of Yusuf's mood had cleared.

For all Ben's cool exterior, he was in no mood for lunch. Matt knew he was too eaten up by thoughts of the vengeance he planned to wreak on Ahmet to admit of any other kind of appetite. And when Yusuf and Belgin brought the dishes they ordered to the table, Ben could only push his food around the plate.

Matt's words did nothing to help when he tried to bring him out of his deep contemplation.

"Amber read the whole diary last night, didn't you?" he said, with an almost pleading glance at Amber across the table. But Ben continued to push the food around, seemingly lost in his thoughts.

"She's worked out how Susie died," Matt added. "Seems it was just how Schmitt had imagined it."

Ben looked up from his plate, turned to Matt, and fixed him with a look of thunder on his face.

"Peggy," he said, making a fist with his right hand and amplifying the depth of rage in his voice: "Her name was Peggy. And I don't give a toss how. Or what that fucking German doctor thinks."

After Ben's night of brooding on his boat, it was clear to Matt that he was now firmly bent on action. Amber reached a sympathetic hand across the table and rested it on Ben's arm. Yet Ben was beyond any kind of reassurance. He had long since crossed into the high-risk zone that Matt had so often witnessed in their early years together. It worried him.

"So, what are you thinking, Ben? How is this going to work? How do I get Ahmet out to you on the boat? And what happens then?"

"What time are you seeing him?"

"Around two thirty."

"Good. Can you steer a dinghy?"

Matt nodded in reply.

"Okay. So, after lunch, I'll go and find a nice dinghy for hire and moor it next to mine down there."

Matt and Amber both peered over the wall at the end of the table and scoured the harbour for Ben's dinghy. It was moored at the far end. Amber cast an uneasy smile across the table at Matt, as if wary of the mission they were about to embark on. But he had already decided that this was something he should undertake alone.

"No way!" she protested. "I'm supposed to be your wife, remember?"

"Then allow me to be your protective husband," he insisted in return.

He was trying to make a game of it. But the frenzied look in Ben's eyes and the crazed intent in his voice had brought home to Matt the danger that was brewing on that boat of his. And he did not want Amber to have any part in it.

"No. I won't allow you to. I don't need your protection."

The fury burned in her eyes at this suggestion that she could not look after herself. She continued to stand her ground, until Ben reciprocated her own gesture of reassurance earlier and rested a hand on Amber's arm.

"Matt's right," he said. "There are some things it's probably better for you to avoid."

Amber visibly seethed, but she slowly began to relent, as Matt's disquiet over the direction events were taking was nourished further by Ben's words. They had been intended to console Amber, yet only served to fuel his own concern. But he knew there was no way around it and hoped that at least he might avert the worst of worlds.

"I'd better get going then," Matt announced with a sprightly tone, attempting to inspire confidence, once lunch was done.

"Right, I'll leave the ignition key to the dinghy with Yusuf," Ben replied.

"Can I at least walk up the hill with you as far as Pearl's office?" Amber asked with a sarcastic edge to her voice. While she was resigned to Matt's decision, she was determined to register her displeasure.

"Look, Amber," he said at last, as they approached her sister's office, following an otherwise silent climb up the hill. "You don't know what Ben is capable of. Nor Ahmet come to that. I'm genuinely worried that it's going to turn very nasty. So, I really don't want you on that boat when things kick off."

"That should be my decision, Matt. Not yours," she said, then gently squeezed his hand. "But I appreciate what you're doing."

"Hopefully it'll all be done by early evening. I'll call you as soon as I can."

With these words, he gave her a peck on the cheek and turned to go. She caught his left arm as he did so to pull him back and plant her lips on his. He reciprocated, but the jitters and apprehension that were consuming him deprived his kiss of any passion.

"I have to be going," he whispered. "I'll call you later this evening."

# CHAPTER 18

ASK. Those aggressive blood-red letters splashed across the building taunted Matt as he drew up in front of Ahmet's office and climbed out of his Citroen Elysee. He pushed the car door shut with a muted thud. His heart was racing at the prospect of the task ahead. The pounding almost audible above the stillness of the dusty street. The resident Rottweiler slumbered on the pavement.

Ahmet was alone, seated behind his desk, when Matt pushed open the door. He was wearing a black, short-sleeved shirt and white tie. Now divested of his aviator sunglasses, he was so focused on the computer screen in front of him that he failed to pay any attention when Matt entered. It was not until Matt was almost standing over the chubby figure squinting at the screen that Ahmet looked up.

"Luke!" he said, getting up from his chair to walk around the desk and extend his arms in welcome.

For a brief moment Matt was thrown. Was that a 'look' weirdly screwed up by his Turkish accent, he wondered. Then recalled that he had given an alias.

"It's so good to see you again, Luke," Ahmet said.

They shook hands. Matt smiled in response to the overeffusive welcome. He said nothing.

"But where is your lovely wife?"

"She's indisposed," Matt lied, provoking a look of bewilderment on Ahmet's face.

"In where?"

"No, not in anywhere. I mean she's not feeling well."

"I'm so sorry to hear that."

Ahmet clasped both of Matt's hands together in his own sweaty palms in a demonstrative gesture of sympathy that Matt could have done without.

"Do you want to cancel?" Ahmet said.

"No, not at all. We're both on the same page when it comes to property. I know what she likes."

"A villa overlooking the bay, you said."

"In Karakent," Matt emphasised, easing his hands from Ahmet's grip.

"Exactly. And I have three villas which you and your beautiful wife will adore."

"Great. Let's go and take a look."

Ahmet took his mirrored aviator shades from the breast pocket of his shirt and placed them carefully on the bridge of his nose. With an unctuous smile, he gestured with his right arm to guide Matt out of the office. Grabbing a white jacket from a coat stand as he went, Ahmet followed him out onto the street. The Rottweiler still slumbered by the door.

"We'll take my car," Matt added as Ahmet locked up behind them. "And you can direct me."

Motoring back along the coast road, Matt enjoyed the sea air that wafted through the open window and the sight of the gentle surf as it washed against the rocks below. All signs of the night's storm had receded and, from the cloudless sky, the sun now shone down on the sparkling water, lending a mood of peace to the drive. He began to feel more at ease.

Less than half an hour later, Ahmet was directing him along the road over the promontory towards the grand villa that he had admired from Ben's yacht.

"That's spectacular," Matt said as they approached the villa up ahead. "Is it for sale?"

"That is the most expensive villa on the bay," Ahmet replied in the sullen tone of a disappointed loser that seemed to be saying it was out of Matt's league.

"The view must be stunning. I was admiring it yesterday from my boat."

Matt surprised himself at how easily he was embracing the role assigned to him by Ben.

"You have a boat?" Ahmet asked, the excitement in his voice unmistakable.

"Out there."

Matt took his left hand off the wheel and gestured towards Ben's yacht anchored out in the bay. Even from their car up on the promontory, the blue strip along the side with its brash letters BF stood out like a marker highlighting its presence.

Ahmet's gaze followed the direction of Matt's hand. The glum tone in his voice had given way to an overly keen curiosity.

"That is your boat?"

The purring satisfaction of a real estate agent about to make a killing was a pleasing endorsement of Matt's newfound playacting skills.

"A beauty, isn't she?" he said.

"I can see why you leave it in the bay. It's so beautiful out there," Ahmet agreed, and pulled a mobile phone from the inside breast pocket of his jacket to make a call. He put the device to his ear and, raising his hand to Matt, he called out, "Stop. Stop the car."

Ahmet gabbled incomprehensibly into the phone for some minutes. Matt waited, his hands still on the wheel, wondering all the while what Ahmet was up to – until he put the phone back in his pocket and smiled across at Matt.

"Are you interested?" he asked and pointed up the road to the villa that sat on the edge of the promontory surveying the bay below.

"Is it for sale?"

"It can be arranged. If you drive me back into town, I can get the keys and we can view the property together."

Matt looked across at Ahmet. It was impossible to read any kind of meaning in his eyes, hidden as they were behind his mirrored shades. Only the sly expression on his lips suggested to Matt that something not quite legitimate was going on. Without another word, he started the engine, turned the car around, and motored back into town.

Ahmet directed him to park the car on the wasteland beside the old schoolhouse opposite Osman's restaurant.

"We meet back here in ten minutes," Ahmet said, clambering awkwardly out of the car.

He clearly had no wish for Matt's company as he hurried off to fetch the key to the villa. From the secure shade of the eucalyptus tree opposite the restaurant, where Osman sat sipping çay, Matt watched Ahmet's plump little legs take him scurrying over the road and up around the corner.

It was when he disappeared from view that Matt was struck by the flaw in Ben's thinking. At that moment, it occurred to him that there was no way he could drive down here later and pick up the key to the dinghy together with Ahmet. Not only was Matt supposed to own the yacht and would have the key himself, but Yusuf could not even hear Ahmet's name without falling into a deathly silent rage. Susie had plainly been very precious to him. The risk of conflict was too great.

These thoughts prompted Matt to leave the cover of the eucalyptus tree and make his way to Yusuf before Ahmet returned. Ten minutes, he had said, which would have been more than enough. Yet barely had Matt emerged into the sunlight than those busy little legs came into view, scurrying back around the corner. Matt cursed under his breath and returned to the car. He would have to find another way to get the key from Yusuf without alerting Ahmet to the contradiction.

The Turk appeared flustered as he clambered into the car. He gave the impression that his conversation with the keyholder had not gone well. Matt started the engine, drove out onto the road and headed back up to the promontory overlooking the bay.

"This is yours to sell, right?" Matt asked as they approached the villa.

"This is Turkey," Ahmet replied with an evasive wave of the hand. "Anything is possible."

The few houses on the road leading up to the villa were elegant but modest dwellings in traditional Turkish style with classic oriel windows. But the villa, surrounded by olive trees in resplendent isolation, was built to tell a different story. Grandiose, imposing and out of place, it would have been more at home in Malibu. It was fitting then that the front door should be made of the best red cedar wood imported from California, as Ahmet explained when Matt pulled up directly in front of the villa and climbed out of the car.

It was then he noticed for the first time a mosaic plaque above the door with elaborate lettering that read Bay View. The name put Matt in mind of Pearl and struck an uncomfortable chord. Her real estate business was called Bay View Properties. Was it maybe hers to sell? Was it Pearl that Ahmet was speaking to on the phone? This seemed unlikely: not only did she have a visceral dislike of Ahmet following the death of Susie; the person he was speaking to was Turkish. But perhaps Hamza was going behind her back, lured by the promise of a fat profit?

Matt was carrying these thoughts with him when Ahmet opened the door and invited him to step inside. Even allowing for the lack of furniture, which showed at least that the villa was not occupied and so presumably for sale by someone, if not by Ahmet, the interior proved ludicrously spacious. The whole place was infused with the smell of cedar wood. Vast floor-to-ceiling windows extended over the entire breadth of the lounge and looked out onto the sparkling water of the bay, which touched the sky above like the most optimistic Mark Rothko painting he had ever set eyes on.

"And that," said Ahmet, pointing out to the bay, "is your boat."

Against the canvas of blue, Ben's yacht gleamed a pure white that was at odds with the darkness of the plans being forged on board the boat.

Ahmet peered at Matt through his sunglasses, the expression in his eyes lost behind the mirrored lenses. Matt only saw his own reflection, but he could read the Turk's dreams from the smirk on his lips.

"Let me take you down to the next level," Ahmet said.

He led Matt to the furthest corner of the room, down a cedar wood staircase to a no less spacious area and onto a dazzling white terrace. A seductive sun trap. The freshness of the autumn breeze sweeping up from the sea was instantly quashed by the warmth of the light reflected off the travertine tiles and the expanse of water before them.

"The best infinity pool in Karakent," Ahmet gushed, the smile on his face now wider than the Strait of Istanbul in the certainty that this pool would clinch the deal.

Matt was growing tired of the man and his vain attempts to make a slick sales pitch. He cast the bait.

"How much?" he asked.

"Three million."

"Three million," Matt repeated. "Is that lira?"

Ahmet threw his hands in the air and exploded with laughter. A theatrical gesture, which he quickly softened with the slippery touch of the businessman's hand on Matt's arm.

"Please," Ahmet said, stretching the word as far as it would go in a beseeching tone. It was neither plea nor request.

"This is business, Luke." Ahmet's hand still rested on Matt's arm as he spoke. "We talk pounds."

"Three million pounds," Matt repeated. He walked back indoors to enjoy the shade and give the impression he was seriously considering the price.

"Say two million and you've got a deal."

Following Matt indoors, Ahmet threw his hands in the air again and scoffed.

"Luke, you disappoint me. You know this is not possible. Look at the quality. Look at the infinity pool. For two million the builder make a big loss and I make no commission. You know this."

"Two and a half million," Matt conceded.

"No. Is not possible," Ahmet insisted. "Luke, I know you like villa. Three million is a good price."

Matt turned and walked away, heading back to the door. But Ahmet was not about to give up. He followed Matt to the door.

"I have other villas. Cheaper villas," he said. "Let me show you."

Matt stopped, a hand on the door, and turned to face Ahmet.

"Cheap doesn't interest me," he said, now thoroughly into his role. "I want this place."

"It is still three million," the Turk insisted.

Matt sank deep into a pondering pose, almost as theatrical as Ahmet's explosive laughter, then finally gave a nod of agreement.

"I'll tell you what. Two million nine hundred and ninety-nine thousand, and I'll invite you to my yacht for dinner, where we can talk about the details and close the deal."

Ahmet gave a hesitant smile. Was that consent? Matt wondered. He could see another flaw in Ben's plan beginning to open up. But after a prolonged silence, the Turk finally eased his concern.

"That is a very good idea," he agreed at last. "But I have some other business first. We drive back into town and meet later at the marina."

"Perfect," Matt said, thinking this would give him the perfect opportunity to pick up the key to the dinghy from Yusuf.

When Matt arrived at the Zeytin restaurant, Yusuf's eyes were alight and wide with excitement. It was plain that Ben had divulged something of the plan to him. The moment he had seen Matt on his way down the street, he hurried into the kitchen, re-emerging almost instantly with the key in his hand.

Yusuf threw his arms around Matt, kissed him on each cheek and wished him good luck as he thrust the key into Matt's hand. The whole impassioned gesture gave Matt the impression he was bidding him farewell on a journey from which he may never return.

"Thank you," he said as he disentangled his hands from Yusuf's. Two simple words, but the tone spoke of his unease.

Matt glanced down the road, crossed over into the restaurant and peered over the railing to the marina. Ahmet was already at the entrance, waiting. He was not alone.

"I must be on my way," Matt said with a wave of the hand to Yusuf and set off down the road to the marina.

As he walked along the promenade approaching the entrance to the marina, he saw that Ahmet was talking to a group of three men. They stood like chess pieces waiting for the next move. The king in a smart white city suit with sleek white shoes and, either side of him, two black pawns more casually dressed in T-shirts and chinos. Already the alarm bells began to ring in Matt's head. He was reminded of the mental note that he had made. And the name that went with it. Erkan Suleyman.

When Ahmet saw Matt coming, he peeled off from this group and strolled towards him with a beaming grin.

"My dinghy's over there."

Matt pointed to the other side of the marina. Ahmet's shades shifted direction as he scoured the scene in search of the dinghy. He put Matt in mind of a squat meerkat surveying its territory.

Ahmet immediately turned, and Matt guided him back the way he had come, past the threesome at the entrance. They watched as Matt led Ahmet quickly past the small yachts and fishing boats moored at the marina. Keen to get this mission over, Matt hopped into the dinghy as soon as they reached the far end. Ahmet hesitated for a moment, as if suspicious, then jumped in behind.

Matt released the mooring line and started the engine, then steered the vessel around the lighthouse on the harbour mole and out onto the open sea. The proximity of the water beneath them put him in mind once again of his student days.

He recalled the day Ben introduced him to white-water rafting. Matt was always awestruck by the power of the water, but it was the motion in the gentler reaches of the river that he enjoyed the most. For Ben, there was nothing that could quite match rafting the most fearsome of rapids. Matt only once joined him on a trip. They had come so close to overturning and being smashed against the rocks that he almost felt his heart stop beating altogether. Fearful that the two of them would never get back alive, he vowed it would be the last time he joined Ben on his extreme weekend trips.

It was these thoughts that preyed upon him now as the water grew increasingly choppy the closer they came to Ben's yacht.

# CHAPTER 19

By the time Matt and Ahmet came alongside, the sun had already started its gentle slide down the sky towards the promontory where the villa stood. Matt was first to climb aboard the seemingly empty boat. Ahmet followed. And the moment he came on deck, the doorway to the cabin filled with a strapping, athletic figure.

Matt saw a scowl of twisted satisfaction run across Ben's face, from ear to ear, as his old friend approached them.

"Nasılsın?" he said.

"Iyiyim. Ya sen?"

Ahmet's voice quaked with hesitation and mistrust.

"Bende iyiyim teşekkür ederim," Ben replied with a superior smirk.

Matt was shocked to hear his old friend, whose grasp of foreign languages had never extended beyond the most basic grasp of school-level French, engaging in this fluent exchange of Turkish pleasantries. An exchange that Ahmet plainly found anything but pleasant as he visibly squirmed throughout the polite repartee.

The Turk turned to Matt.

"You know him?" he asked.

"Oh, Matt and I go back a long way," Ben said before Matt had a chance to speak.

Ahmet muttered awkwardly to himself, stood hovering between Matt and Ben, uncertain of his next move. Or his next words.

Ben was clearly enjoying Ahmet's discomfort. He disappeared briefly into the cabin and returned almost instantaneously clutching three glasses in his left hand and a bottle of rakı in his right. Placing them with careful deliberation on the table in the middle of the deck, he stepped back and turned to Ahmet with a sweeping gesture of his left arm.

"Won't you join us in a glass of your lion's milk?"

A cool breeze whipped up over the deck as the sun moved ever lower in the sky. It was neither the time nor the place for rakı. Ahmet shifted uneasily from one foot to the other and said nothing. It was not until Matt walked over to the table to join Ben that he was finally needled into action.

"Of course, Ben," Ahmet said, following Matt and taking a seat at the table. "So, it is you who has interest in villa."

Ben said nothing in reply, but returned to the cabin and brought out a bottle of water, three rakı holders and a bucket of ice, which he placed beside the glasses. He half-filled the glasses, dropped in two cubes of ice, topped them up with water, and handed a glass each to Matt and Ahmet.

"Frankly, I couldn't give a damn about your villa," Ben said, smiling coldly and raising his glass to Ahmet.

"Şerefe," he added, and raised his glass.

"Şerefe," Ahmet said, timidly putting his own glass to his lips.

It was a weak voice. Wavering. Uncertain. Reluctant to commit. He took a sip, put the glass down and removed his sunglasses, as if attempting to take control of the situation.

"So, how's the property business?" Ben asked, placing his glass in the rakı holder.

"The market is not good now. British people not so interested. And Turkish people won't pay the prices."

Ahmet spoke so softly that his words were barely audible.

"But if you not interested in villa," he continued, his command of English weakening under the strain, "why Luke bring me here?"

"Luke?"

Ben cast a quizzical glance at Matt, who threw an artful smile back in return.

"Matthew, Luke. What's the difference? Guess I was in biblical mode."

Ahmet looked from one to the other. Far from taking control, he showed all the signs of getting ever more drowned in confusion. He picked up his glass, put it to his lips and leaned back into his chair in a show of relaxation.

If it escaped Ahmet's attention that Ben had disappeared back into the cabin, there was no way he could miss the baseball bat Ben carried with him when he returned. The Turk visibly winced, his expression transformed at once to a look of terror. He rose to his feet and stepped back, knocking his glass and aviator shades off the table as he went. His voice quaked with panic. "What you do now, Ben? What you want from me?"

"The truth." Ben growled. "That's all I want."

He levelled the baseball bat in Ahmet's direction as he moved in on his prey.

"Truth is money, Ben. You know that," Ahmet said, desperately trying to regain some composure. "I need my share, too."

"Fuck your money." Ben gave the Turk a hefty prod in the solar plexus with the bat. "And fuck your share."

Ahmet fell flat on his back, crushing his sunglasses beneath him.

"What about my sister?" Ben grunted with another fierce prod to Ahmet's stomach as he lay on the deck. "Tell me how she really died."

"I don't know what you mean, Ben. It was heart attack. You know that."

"I have a diary that tells a different story."

Ben drove the baseball bat harder and deeper into the solar

plexus. Ahmet let out a cry of pain that could have been heard from across the bay.

"What diary?" he gasped. "I know nothing about diary."

"Of course you don't. Peggy hid it from you. Her record of the torment you heaped on her every day. The poisonous gifts."

"I know nothing," Ahmet insisted, still panting for breath.

"No? Well, let's just see if we can't help loosen your memory a little," Ben growled.

He leaned forward to grab the collar of Ahmet's jacket, dragged him back onto his feet, and shoved him into a chair next to the table. He took a glass of rakı in his hand and put it to the Turk's mouth.

"Drink this," he said. "Down in one."

Ahmet took it in his hand, drank the liquid straight down, and threw the glass overboard in a vain act of defiance.

"And this one," Ben said, reaching for a second glass from the table.

Ahmet again downed the lion's milk in one and went to throw the empty glass overboard. But the defiant gesture this time lacked the same confidence, and the glass hit the deck.

Ben reached for the third glass and this time dragged Ahmet's head back by the hair to force the drink down his gasping gullet, causing him instantly to choke and splutter on the spirit. As Ahmet's head lifted in a reflex motion, Ben brought his fist down on the Turk's choking mouth. Ahmet collapsed back in the chair.

"You fucking Turkish bastard," Ben yelled into his face, unable to contain his rage any longer. "You fed my sister poison every day until she died. Come on. Say it. You killed her! Say it! You fucking killed my sister!"

Ahmet was unable able to say a word beyond a barely intelligible "No" – mumbled through the bruised lips and the blood that filled his mouth. This and the angst seared into the lens of Ahmet's eyes, the look of a cornered fox, only spurred Ben to enact the entire repertoire of revenge that he must have been playing out in his mind ever since the death of his sister.

"Matt, pass me the bottle," Ben grunted, nodding in the direction of the rakı bottle on the table. Matt hesitated.

"Ben, this isn't the best way of going about it."

"How the fuck do you think I should go about it, then?" Ben yelled, glaring at his old friend with a wild frenzy in his eyes.

"Just do it," Ben screamed.

What both he and Ben had failed to notice amid the rage that rent the air more effectively even than the gusts of wind across the deck was the sound of the small boat that pulled up alongside.

Only Ahmet caught sight of the visitors climbing aboard behind Ben. Matt saw them in the corner of his eye as he tried to talk Ben out of drowning Ahmet in the lion's milk.

There were three of them. A tall, slim figure in a smart white city suit with sleek white shoes, followed by two figures dressed in dark chinos, T-shirts and black jackets that threatened to burst beneath their biceps and pectorals at any moment.

"I understand you're interested in buying my villa," said the man in the white suit with the red pocket square, speaking perfect English. Ben swung around as the name Erkan Suleyman flashed up in Matt's mind.

"Is this your way to negotiate down the price?" he added, gesturing towards the forlorn figure in the chair. The trace of a disfigured smile crossed Ahmet's lacerated lips.

"And who the hell invited you?" Ben yelled.

Ahmet struggled to his feet as Ben advanced – fists clenched – towards the newcomer in white.

"Visitors are not welcome. So, get the fuck off my boat. Now!"

The two men in black stiffened, moved up either side of the man in white, and each pulled a nightstick from under their jacket. The smooth-talking Erkan Suleyman stepped forward, brushed Matt to one side and jabbed Ben in the chest with his fist, causing Ben to tumble back into the seat now vacated by Ahmet.

"Ahmet," he said, "I had the impression your host was keen

for you to join him in a drink. It would be impolite not to return the gesture."

He snapped his fingers at the sidekick to his left, reached for the rakı bottle on the table and handed it to Ahmet, as the goon in black rammed his nightstick hard into Ben's ribs. Ben yelled as much in anger as in pain.

"Let him drink," the smooth-talking Turk said softly as he dragged Ben's head back by the hair to allow a grinning Ahmet the pleasure of pouring the lion's milk directly down Ben's throat.

Flanked by the newcomer's escorts with their batons, Matt could only watch as Ben spluttered and struggled to cope with the stream of rakı that Ahmet gleefully funnelled into Ben's blood stream. Ben heaved and retched uncontrollably, on the brink of vomiting, hindered only by the muzzle of the goon's nightstick that dug into his chest – until Matt could watch no longer. Lunging forward to wrest the bottle from Ahmet's grip, he was greeted by the full force of the other goon's baton deep in his solar plexus, followed by what felt like the butt of a gun to his head.

Matt collapsed on the deck in an unconscious heap. He was not witness to the further torture inflicted on his old friend. The whole pageant of the brutal assault which followed passed him by.

It was not until Matt hit the water that he splashed his way back to consciousness. He floundered and choked, trying desperately to make sense of where he was, what he was doing. He flailed around, gasping for air. In a panic that he was about to go under, he grasped for a hold on anything he could find in his crazed confusion. His right hand found Ben's dinghy. It was adrift in the water alongside him, and he pulled himself into the boat.

He had lost all sense of space and time. How long he lay there in the hull of the boat, leaving his lungs to recover and the bruising to ease, he had no idea. But it was long enough for Ben's gleaming white yacht to vanish from the narrow compass of his vision. It no longer towered over the dinghy. Where once there had been an ocean-going ship was now an empty, darkening sky.

Matt raised his bruised body to peer over the side of the dinghy and caught sight of Ben's yacht heading out to sea – towards the crop of rocky islands that lay like murine sentinels at the entrance to the bay. The confusion only deepened. What was Ben up to? Where was he going?

Matt's own small boat bobbed and drifted aimlessly on the water. The lights of Karakent had already come alive as dusk descended on the bay. The gathering breeze off the water sent a chill through his wet clothes. Sensing the need to get ashore, he clambered to the rear of the boat to start the motor.

It was only then he found that he was not alone. Ben's lifeless body lay crumpled in the stern, hindering Matt's access to the motor. The shock of this discovery cast him into an instant pit of despair. The chill deepened. It came now from within. A raw iciness. And a bitter taste of guilt that he had failed his old friend.

He eased Ben's body to one side so that he could reach the motor. And caught muffled groans from the immobile heap as he did so. Matt's heart leapt with relief. He stretched down into the shadowy hull of the boat and ran his hand over the source of the groans, the drenched T-shirt, the side of Ben's face. The wetness on his skin had the thickness of blood. Ben raised an arm in an attempt to grab Matt's wrist, but the arm fell away before it reached its target.

Relieved and troubled in equal measure, Matt managed an anxious chuckle to himself at his reckless friend's survival. He started up the motor and steered the dinghy back to shore.

# CHAPTER 20

Matt beached the dinghy at the farthest corner of the bay, well away from the marina and the inquisitive lights of Karakent. Ben was still barely conscious. To bring him ashore in his present state would not only be difficult, but also raise too many questions. So, Matt felt it wise to leave his friend in the boat to recover while he went for help. He pulled a tarpaulin over Ben and set off for the Zeytin restaurant.

Amber was waiting for him. She waved excitedly when she spotted him staggering up the hill towards her. But he could see that the excitement of her wave was tinged with concern when she emerged onto the street to greet him.

"Look at you! What on earth have you been up to?" she asked in horror as Matt drew close enough for her to see the bruised and bedraggled state that he was in. "And where's Ben?"

Matt waved an arm back in the direction of the beach. And at that moment, Yusuf appeared from the kitchen.

"Matthew. What has happened?"

"Had some bother," Matt mumbled, as Amber took him by the arm.

Solicitous as ever, Yusuf guided them both to a discreet corner of the restaurant, then rushed back into the kitchen.

"You need ilaç," he said, returning from the kitchen with a glass of rakı and setting it down in front of Matt.

"No, really," Matt said. "That's the last thing I need right now."

"Ilaç. Medicine," Yusuf insisted. "Very good."

"Really, Yusuf, a large tea would be just fine."

Yusuf grinned in his inimitable fashion and vanished back into the kitchen again.

"Ben is in a bad way," Matt said, turning back to Amber. "He's taken a nasty beating."

Yusuf returned almost at once and placed a large tulip-shaped glass of tea in front of Matt. He took a seat at the table and scooped the rejected glass of lion's milk into his hand, while Matt told them what had happened: the meeting with Ahmet; the brutal encounter with the men in black and white; and his near-drowning when he was thrown unconscious into the water.

"That was Erkan Suleyman," Yusuf said, darkly.

His words were greeted with silence. Amber looked quizzically first at Yusuf, then at Matt.

"Erkan is a bad man," Yusuf said.

"Tell me about it," Matt replied. "He might look pure and innocent in his all-white outfit, but believe me, he's vicious."

Yusuf nodded.

"He has many enemies among the women in Karakent. But many friends in politics. People say he is also a friend of our president. Maybe this is true. I don't know. But I know he has friends in the Jandarma, and it is because of people like Erkan that my brother sit now in jail."

Yusuf paused and ran both hands over his face, as if to cleanse himself. His words reminded Matt of his conversation with Luc and the mobsters now roaming free after the Covid amnesty.

"But my brother was lucky. He could be lying there." Yusuf raised an arm and gestured out to sea. "In beton."

Amber's eyes followed the trajectory of his arm, and as she gazed out over the bay an awkward silence descended on the table.

Yusuf was dwelling on his brother, while Matt was impatient to get help for his old friend lying abandoned at that moment on the beach. Amber looked back at Matt.

"So, where is Ben?" she asked. "And his boat. It's not anchored out in the bay any longer."

"Sorry. I left that bit out," Matt said. "And I can't really tell you. The last I saw of the boat; it was heading out of the bay. But Ben's in the dinghy at the far end of the beach. Badly beaten and unconscious. We need to get some help."

"There's always Dr Schmitt."

"Hauke Schmitt? Are you kidding me?"

"He's a medical doctor, Matt. What else would you suggest?"

He hesitated, but he knew she was right, and they could not leave his injured friend to languish much longer in the boat.

"Do you have his number?" he said at last.

"No. I've been told he doesn't even own a phone."

"But he lives only five minutes up there," Yusuf chipped in, pointing up the street past the mosque.

When Matt and Amber rang the doorbell of the house to which Yusuf had directed them, there was no response. Yet the lights were on, and Amber was certain she had heard movement. Matt pressed the bell again. Twice. This time, the movement inside the house edged closer to the door. They heard the loud, fumbling noise of a key negotiating the lock.

Hauke Schmitt looked bleary-eyed and mildly shocked as he stood in the doorway. It was the first time Matt had seen the doctor without his trademark Panama hat. It made him appear shorter and less imposing. His grey hair was tousled. It lent an impression of volume that belied its paucity and thinness. He had the bearing of a man who had just been woken from a deep sleep. But when Amber explained the situation, his drowsy temper immediately lifted and his eyes lit up.

Leaving them to wait on the threshold, Dr Schmitt retreated into the dingy hall and disappeared into a back room, where the sound of him rifling through cupboards could be heard. An antique mustiness wafted out onto the street, testimony to the long years of anonymity spent here by the former Stasi doctor.

When Hauke Schmitt eventually emerged from the dimness of his hideout, he was carrying a large Gladstone-style bag. For a physician who, by his own admission, had long since retired from practice, he seemed to Matt to be still pretty well-equipped.

The crunching of the pebbles as they approached the boat put Matt in mind of the worry beads that had been a trailing feature of the past few days. The stranger could be lurking anywhere at that very moment. But the darkness at the far end of the beach was well out of reach for the street lights of Karakent. It offered the perfect sanctuary from watchful eyes. The used condoms that he now saw washed up around the boat told him it was also a popular retreat for lovers in search of a secluded spot – a feature of the landscape that had escaped him when he beached the dinghy here.

There was no sign of amorous couples having tried to make their tryst in the abandoned dinghy. But perhaps the sounds emanating from the boat had simply frightened any interlopers off. For when eventually they reached the boat, Ben's beaten and lacerated body was already groaning and stirring from the comatose stage of drunkenness inflicted on him by Erkan and Ahmet.

Matt heard a sharp intake of breath from Amber and a cry of "Oh my God" when they looked into the darkness of the dinghy and saw the state of his old friend. The sight that greeted her caused her to reel back in a breathless panic. She withdrew from the dinghy, trembling and weeping in the darkness.

Neither Matt nor Hauke Schmitt had time to consider her distress. Their focus was on Ben. It was clear to them that he was barely able to stand. But between them, Matt and the German doctor succeeded in getting him out of the boat and laying him face up on the pebbles of the beach. Hauke Schmitt took a torch from his bag and examined the injuries to his face as best he could in the torchlight.

"We must get him to a more comfortable place where there is light and running water," Dr Schmitt said, sighing in exasperation when the light on his torch flickered, then dimmed and finally gave up the ghost altogether.

"I'll bring the car down to the end of the promenade," Matt said. "If we can haul Ben over to the car, then maybe we can drive him up to Pearl's."

It was too dark for Matt to see any trace of tears running down Amber's face. She quietly nodded and took out her mobile to phone her sister, while Matt turned to make his way back across the pebble beach.

His path was silhouetted by the lights of Karakent, as he headed back to the hotel to fetch the car. When he returned, there was no sign of Ben or the German doctor. Only Amber graced the promenade with her presence. She sat alone at the top of the steps that led down to the beach. She was shaking and sobbing bitterly.

"Hey, what's up?" Matt said. He set himself down beside her on the steps and put an arm around her shoulders. "Where are the others?"

Amber said nothing, simply pointed out into the darkness where the dinghy lay.

"What happened? What's going on? Did Schmitt do something to you?"

Matt had never liked the German doctor from the outset. And now, in the confusion of the night, his imagination was running wild.

"No, nothing," Amber said at last through her tears. "I'm sorry."

"What do you mean you're sorry? For what?"

"I just couldn't take it. The moment I saw Ben's body in the boat took me back twenty years."

What Matt could not have known was how that moment had immediately triggered images in her mind of a different boat altogether. The chill that blew off the sea may have been sufficient to keep stray lovers off the beach that night. But it was not enough to stop a resurgence of her darkest memories of the seafront at Brighton.

Still shaking as she sat on the steps in Matt's arms, she told him how she was instantly seized by a panic, her heart in her throat, when she saw Ben's crumpled, battered body. Faced with that image leaping at her from the shadows of the boat, Amber found herself re-enacting her night of terror in Brighton when she was only eighteen.

"Look, you'd better wait in the car while I go back for Ben," Matt said, helping her up from the steps by the arm and guiding her back to the vehicle.

He found Hauke Schmitt still sitting beside Ben. They were sheltered from the chill breeze that blew off the sea by Ben's dinghy. And the German doctor made no secret of his impatience with the waiting game that had been forced upon him.

"High time," he snapped as soon as Matt came within earshot.

Matt made no apology for the delay, but silently cursed the doctor for not looking after Amber.

Without exchanging any further words, the two of them hauled Ben across the beach to the promenade, where Amber was waiting in the front seat of the car. They bundled him into the back seat, and Hauke Schmitt climbed in beside him, clutching his doctor's bag.

It was just as Matt was climbing into the car that he caught sight of a familiar image: those red worry beads glistening in the shadows. Amber sat beside him, staring blankly ahead, still visibly shaken by the reignited memory of her teenage ordeal. Her mind was plainly too preoccupied for the worry beads to register. Matt said nothing, started the engine and motored slowly back up through the town to Amber's sister.

Pearl was alone when they arrived at the house high up over Karakent. Without a word beyond an initial cry of shock, Pearl immediately took Ben from Matt's supporting arm, steered him into the bathroom with the help of Dr Schmitt, and dismissed Matt with a wave of her free arm.

As if to distract from the horrors of the evening, Amber took Matt on a tour of the pictures that hung in the lounge. Engravings and watercolours of Brighton and the South Downs in happier times, images to lighten the mood. Yet they appeared to have the opposite effect as she went into the detail of the coastline and the streets where she had grown up and steadily descended into a darkness that unsettled Matt. He sensed that she was still reliving memories that would be better left to lie untouched.

With the gloomy mood came a sudden unexpected chill when the front door opened. Hamza stood in the doorway; his large frame bathed in the glow of the porch light.

"What's going on?" he boomed.

There was a wild agitation about Hamza that Matt had not seen in him before. He closed the door behind him, shutting out the chill wind. Yet it was not the chill that had rattled him.

"Where's Ben?" Hamza asked. Deep concern was etched into his brow.

"In the bathroom," Amber replied.

"What's he doing there? His boat is on the rocks and he's here in the bathroom?" he added in a tone of disbelief, and headed along the passage in search of Ben.

Matt and Amber heard muffled voices coming from the bathroom when he opened the door. After some minutes, Pearl emerged, followed by Hamza and Hauke Schmitt supporting the hapless figure of Ben. Together they manoeuvred him into the spare room where Amber would normally have slept.

"He must rest here," Dr Schmitt insisted, "while he sleeps off the alcohol. And we will see how he is in the morning."

"You can sleep on the couch, Amber," Pearl suggested, whereupon Hamza walked over to the sofa and began removing the cushions, as if to make a bed of it. Hauke Schmitt remained standing on the periphery. His job now done, he appeared to be more interested in viewing the pictures of Brighton on the wall.

"No, Hamza, we'll do that later," Pearl said, retrieving the cushions as she dropped onto the sofa. "I need a stiff drink first."

"What did you mean, Hamza, when you said Ben's boat is on the rocks?" Matt asked.

"What I say," he called back over his shoulder as he went to fix a drink for Pearl. "Ben has driven his boat onto rocks. At the islands off the bay."

"That wasn't Ben," Matt corrected him, drawing a quizzical look from Hamza as he set a glass of wine down on the table for Pearl. He was all ears. And his brow furrowed as Matt told him the whole sequence of events that led to him and Ben winding up barely alive in the dinghy.

"You say the man was Erkan?" Hamza said at last, then fell silent.

He said nothing more for some time as he appeared to be mulling over this information. A racking tension took hold of the atmosphere around the table while everyone waited for him to speak again. From the look on Pearl's face, Matt could see that she probably knew what dark thoughts were going through her husband's mind. She looked worried.

The tension was finally shattered when Hamza brought his fist down on the table, causing it to vibrate under the force.

"Such an idiot," he growled. "Ben should never take on Ahmet in this way. Erkan will always protect his people."

He paused again, looked sternly across the table first at Matt, then Amber, and turned to Pearl seated next to him. Resting his right hand on her arm, he turned to her and spoke now in a softer, yet troubled, tone.

"Ben can stay tonight," he said. "But tomorrow morning he must go."

"Go?" Matt protested from across the table. "He can't go anywhere in this state. And where is he supposed to go? His boat's been destroyed and everything with it. He has no documents, no passport. He has nothing."

Pearl gave her husband a look somewhere between incomprehension and concern. He tightened his grip on her arm in response.

"I'm sorry," Hamza insisted. "We can't afford to make an enemy of Erkan. And Ahmet will also not let go now. When he realises that Ben survived, Ahmet will come after him. And you and Amber also, because he knows you have Susie's diary."

"If you are worried, we can take him to my place tonight," said Hauke Schmitt from behind the sofa. "My humble abode is the last place Ahmet would look."

These words from the former Stasi doctor took Matt completely by surprise. He leapt from the sofa.

"Where on earth are you going?" cried Amber, startled by this jolting surge of activity.

Matt ignored the question. Perhaps he had not even heard it. He strode across the room, slid open the window onto the terrace, and moved furtively over to the balustrade. The cool breeze that swept over the patio subsided briefly and let the fleeting scent of jasmine onto the air. It reminded him of the night before, when he had arrived here for the first time with Amber. A night of quiet promise that came to nothing. The promise this night was of a different kind altogether.

He prowled all along the perimeter of the terrace, examining the street below. The image of the stranger with the red worry beads lurking in the shadows on the promenade had taken hold in his mind. Matt had got it into his head from the outset that he probably worked for the Jandarma and had been assigned to tail him after Rekan was taken off the bus. Yet now it seemed no less likely that Mr Worry Beads could actually be working for Ahmet or Erkan and may be skulking around the villa.

Matt crept down the steps from the terrace and into the street. Clouds of dust kicked up around him, driven by the wind that blew down from the mountain. The olive trees bristled in the chill breeze. And the day's last call to prayers rose into the night sky from the mosques in the town below. But there was no hint of movement. The street was empty. He saw no sign of the man and no motorbike or car that might have followed them. Matt's sense of caution told him this would be a good time to move.

"I think you're right, Dr Schmitt," he said, stepping back into the lounge. "I think we should go now."

The smirk on Hauke Schmitt's face suggested he was quietly pleased with the respect implicit in being referred to by his doctor title. This had not been Matt's intention, and the smugness on the doctor's lips irritated him all the more.

# CHAPTER 21

By the time they reached Hauke Schmitt's place in the backstreets of Karakent, Ben's stricken body was showing signs of autonomous life. Minimal, but enough to aid the task of steering him through the hallway of the German doctor's house. A single naked light bulb lit the corridor. And Matt was struck again by the same antique mustiness that he had noticed here earlier that evening. They manoeuvred Ben into the cramped space of a room that was about big enough to fit a camp bed between piles of books stacked against the walls, then laid him on the camp bed and left him to rest.

Dr Schmitt led Matt into a larger, fresher-smelling room. He gestured his guest to take a seat, opened a cabinet and pulled out a bottle with two glasses, which he then filled and handed one to Matt.

"A poor quality of whisky," he said in an apologetic tone. "But the real thing is far too expensive here."

"It's good enough," Matt said, taking a sip. "Cheers, Dr Schmitt. And thank you for helping out with Ben."

"Please, call me Hauke," the doctor said.

These words came with a correctness that displayed all the inbred formalities of the man's native etiquette. It was a gesture of friendliness, if not friendship, and Matt smiled in response. A reluctant smile. He still did not trust the man one inch.

"Not Josef? Josef Wasenmeister?"

Matt's provocation brought only a dismissive wave of the hand from the German doctor.

"As I have said before, Matthew, you must not believe all that Bennett tells you."

Hauke Schmitt fell silent. Matt watched him pensively, considering the whisky in his glass, and waited for the doctor to speak.

"You know," he said at last. "Hamza was right when he insisted that Ben could not stay there. But he said it for the wrong reasons. He said it out of pure self-interest."

Hauke Schmitt paused again and peered over his glass at Matt, as if estimating him in some indecipherable way. Matt wondered if he was suggesting that Hamza was in hock to Erkan. After all, he seemed to know about the disappearance of Ben's yacht long before it could have been public knowledge. Or was he simply afraid of Erkan?

"Of course, Matthew, your friend cannot stay here either," he added.

Ever since Matt's mother died around five years ago, no one else had called him Matthew. Until Yusuf. Now the German doctor. And in Schmitt's case it signalled a detached kind of familiarity that left Matt feeling uncomfortable. It was not so much the words that unsettled him, as the inscrutable smile on his face as he uttered them.

"And I say that for the right reasons," Schmitt added with slow deliberation and an imperious emphasis on the word 'right'.

Matt's dislike of the German doctor grew with every ounce of smug arrogance that seemed to flow out of the man's mouth whenever he spoke.

"Contrary to what I said earlier, this is most certainly not the last place Ahmet would look for your friend. Or you and Miss Baxter, for that matter," he added, knocking back his whisky. "But it would at least be further down his list of choices, so this gives us a little time."

Hauke Schmitt rose from his chair.

"Another one?" he asked, stretching out a hand and taking Matt's glass.

"Time for what?"

"To consider your next step."

The doctor shuffled over to the cabinet, replenished the whisky and turned back to Matt, thrusting the glass into his hand. Matt looked questioningly into Hauke Schmitt's eyes.

"My next step?"

"And Ben's."

"I rather think that's a decision for Ben," Matt said. "And he's not really in any fit state for decisions right now."

"You're right. Let us wait until the morning, when he will have slept off the alcohol and we can assess his pain and his injuries a little better."

This, at least, was something Matt could agree on with the doctor. So, keen to ensure that he was there when Ben eventually woke, he insisted on staying with his friend all night.

"I can sleep on the floor," he assured the doctor. "There's just enough space."

Although Hauke Schmitt provided him with blankets to soften the boards, the air in the room made it an uncomfortable night. The mustiness of the old books stacked all around the room clawed at his throat. Every time he dropped into a state that even remotely resembled sleep, the mustiness would drag him choking from his short-lived slumber and keep him awake. Questioning. Speculating about the motives behind the German doctor's hospitality. About the role of the stranger with the worry beads. And about the flash drive that still nestled in the ticket pocket of his jeans. But above all, about the mortal threat now posed by Ahmet and his overlord, Erkan. And every train of thought was underscored by the sound of Ben faintly breathing.

It was impossible for Matt to tell what time it was when eventually he fell into a deep sleep. Or how long he had slept when he was roused at the first hint of dawn that edged its way through the shutters on the only window in the room. The very faintest of light it was, and this alone would not have been enough to stir him. Without the murmured sounds that came from the camp bed, he might not have been roused before noon.

"Where the hell am I?" Ben groaned in the gloom of Hauke Schmitt's makeshift library.

Before Matt was conscious enough to realise what was going on, Ben was already angling to navigate a way out of the canvas cocoon of his camp bed. And came rolling down onto Matt with a thud, taking the wind out of both men and drawing a cry of 'oof' from Matt and a howl of pain from Ben.

"Take it easy Ben," Matt said. "Let's get you back on the bed and I'll get some coffee."

Taking him under the arm, he eased Ben back onto the camp bed, then navigated his way through the gloom to find the kitchen. A dim light from the far end of the corridor struggled to make its presence known, but it was just bright enough to tell Matt that the German doctor had beaten him to it. He was pouring himself a cup of tea.

"How's the patient?" he asked when he looked up to see Matt appear in the kitchen doorway.

"He's awake. I promised to take him some coffee."

"I'm afraid I can only offer tea," Schmitt replied. "I don't drink coffee."

"That sounds very English," Matt remarked, moving closer into the kitchen.

"Oh, it's nothing refined like Darjeeling. Or even breakfast tea. In fact, it's very Turkish. Here, take it. It will do him good," Schmitt said and handed Matt the cup that he had just poured for himself.

Neither the lack of coffee nor the variety of tea was of any interest to Ben when Matt presented him with the cup.

"What am I doing here, Matt? And where the hell are we?" he wanted to know.

Matt's telling of the previous day's events was met with unexpected silence from Ben. But for all the unspoken anguish, Matt saw that he was seething beneath the surface. A simmering fury that swelled into a gaping hole of despair when he was told that his yacht had been scuppered on the rocks out at sea.

"You're supposed to be in security, Matt. This is what you're in business to deal with."

Ben recoiled in agony when he tried to sit up. He clutched his head in his hands, whining like a dog. The pain from the day before was not about to let go of him just yet. And news of the scuppered boat only rubbed further salt into his wounds.

Matt lost his friend's already frayed attention the moment he tried explaining that he was just a pen pusher in his security business and did little more than recruit enforcers for his clients. But Ben's head was clearly stuck too fast in the grip of his pain for such nuance, and he ignored Matt's words.

Raising himself again from the canvas bed, he swung his legs out over the side when Hauke Schmitt walked in. He cast the prying gaze of the physician over the slumped figure on the bed.

"So how is the patient this morning?" he said. "Sitting up already, I see."

With the caution of a wounded beast, Ben lifted his head and peered up at Dr Schmitt through the matted hair that hung over his eyes. He said nothing. Standing over him, the doctor glanced at Matt and adjusted his gold-rim glasses.

"If Ben feels fit enough to move," he said, "then you and he must leave as soon as possible. Ahmet knows you have the incriminating diary and will come after you with Erkan's handymen as soon as he knows you are alive and still here."

"He doesn't have the diary," Matt corrected him. "Amber has it."

"Does he know this? I think not," said Hauke Schmitt. "But no matter. I have a contact in Konya. A local woman just a day's drive from here. She will look after you while you get new documents for Ben."

"A woman," Matt said.

He knew the power of patriarchy in this country, and those two words were simply an expression of surprise that a local woman would agree to look after them. Hauke Schmitt appeared to take it differently and gave Matt a disparaging look.

"Leila will take good care of you," he said sternly. "And she speaks excellent English."

Matt wondered what connection this woman had to Schmitt. Was it a contact from his days with the Stasi? There was no time to dwell on the details. He had to call Amber and let her know what was going on. Ahmet may not be aware that she had Susie's diary. But it was more than likely that her sister did, and if Pearl knew, then her husband would as well. And Matt felt he could no longer put his trust in Hamza.

Amber was slow to pick up. She was not one for early starts and, as he spoke, Matt could picture her pulling herself up in bed and rearranging the disarray of her hair that had become entangled by the night. Her words had the garbled sound of a voice not yet primed for speech. But as soon as he explained their plans, the voice came alive. And carried more than a hint of alarm.

She told Matt that the Jandarma had called just after he left with Dr Schmitt and Ben the night before. They were looking for Ben, wanted to question him about his boat. And said they would return the next morning.

Matt recalled the words Yusuf had used to describe Erkan's curriculum vitae: the mobster's links not only to politicians but also to the Jandarma. And he had also seen confirmation of this himself when he caught sight of Erkan at the gendarmerie. Matt needed no powers of persuasion to impress upon Amber the need for her next move.

While her sister and Hamza still slept, she dressed, threw some clothes into her rucksack and wrote a short note explaining that she would be away for a few days and not to worry.

Under the early dawn sky, the chill breeze of the night had

eased. But as he climbed into his car, Matt could not fail to see the clouds that loomed over the mountains. He prayed that the heavens would not make the road to Konya too treacherous.

Within minutes of calling Amber, he was drawing up alongside her in his white Citroen Elysee and opening the door of the front passenger seat. She got in and pulled the door gently to as Matt took her rucksack and placed it on the back seat next to Ben, who was slumped behind the driver's seat.

"Morning Ben," she whispered, glancing back as she fastened her seat belt. "Are you feeling better this morning?"

Ben grunted in reply.

They motored on up the hill, past the village of Palamut and the turn-off to the Bennetts' place. A solitary tractor was heading out of the village towards the junction as they passed. Matt accelerated up the mountainside on a narrow winding road, which was in a state of some disrepair, into what was uncharted territory for all three of them.

"Are you sure this is the road to Konya?" Amber asked.

"Schmitt insists it's the quickest and safest way to go. The coast road is too slow. And when we get to the open plain, the roads are apparently so empty it will be easier to keep an eye on anyone who might be following us."

It was not only the man with the red worry beads that Matt had in mind. That stranger had since been joined by half a dozen others who had good reason to put a tail on them.

# CHAPTER 22

Matt and Amber were to meet Leila in a tea garden in the centre of Konya, not far from the shrine of Rumi. Ben would wait in the car. The swollen, bloodied appearance of his face was not the kind of image that would sit well anywhere near the resting place of the Sufi mystic.

The tea garden lay in a wooded, terraced park slightly elevated above the street traffic. It was a strangely quiet, almost rustic setting in the centre of the bustling city. The sounds of urban life were submerged beneath the chimes of water that sprang from fountains built into the terraces of the park. Each table had the air of an outdoor séparée shielded by neat boxwood hedges. Although trimmed to no more than shoulder height, Matt felt the boxwood lent a much-needed sense of peace and privacy as they sat down at the first free table they could find.

It was late afternoon when they arrived, and the park was well-frequented. But Amber's strawberry-blonde hair ensured that the two of them easily stood out from the locals, so that their contact would have no difficulty in finding them. And indeed, before they had even had a chance to order tea, they caught the sound of a voice speaking English.

"You must be Dr Schmitt's friends," the woman said with the trace of an American accent as she approached their table.

"I'm Leila."

The woman called to a waiter and took a seat at the table alongside Amber. At first glance, she did not seem the kind of person Matt had been expecting to meet. An elegant, sixty-something woman with dark, neatly coiffured hair that did not show a hint of the grey that might be expected in a woman of her age. Brown Modigliani eyes framed by a pair of designer spectacles, yet conveying an impression of someone more interested in academic pursuit than in design. And her softly spoken voice: it carried an accent that suggested she had learned her fluent English on a campus somewhere on the east side of America.

"I was told there would be three of you," Leila said.

"Ben's waiting in the car," Matt explained. "He's still feeling quite bad."

Leila nodded in a way that suggested she knew full well what had brought them to Konya. And the words that followed told him that Hauke Schmitt had already described their predicament in detail.

"There is a place east of here where you will be safe," she said. "As it's about an hour or more by car, and you've already had a long journey, I suggest we drive there tomorrow morning. You can sleep on the floor at my place tonight."

Leila rested a hand on Amber's arm with a reassuring smile.

"Don't worry, the floor is for men only. I have a spare bed for you."

After the tension of the last twenty-four hours, Leila instantly put Matt at his ease with a laid-back, carefree manner that surprised him. He had not met many Turkish women, but those he had, such as Hasan's wife Fidan, were excruciatingly shy, if not downright timid. In contrast, Leila was lively and talkative. She gave the impression that she knew a thing or two about the world. It was an image that she underlined with her East Coast American accent, her flowing hair and a cool, metropolitan sense of dress.

It became quickly clear during their conversation that Leila was anxious to move on. She urged them to drink up their tea, before guiding them out of the tea garden and back down to the fumes of the traffic.

"Where's your car?" Leila asked, carefully surveying every vehicle parked along the side of the road.

"Around the corner," Matt said. "In a side street."

"Perfect. You can leave it there. We'll pick up your friend in the taxi and head back to my place."

Before she had even finished her sentence, a car appeared from nowhere and pulled up alongside them.

"Get in," Leila said, and muttered in Turkish to the driver as she climbed into the front seat, then raised her voice to the passengers in the back once her two charges were in place behind her: "Matt, you tell us when we get to that side street."

After picking up Ben, they travelled for a good twenty minutes in the taxi to Leila's place. This lay on the outskirts of Konya in one of the more upscale quarters of town. The apartment itself was in keeping with both the district and her sense of style.

"From what Dr Schmitt told me on the phone," she said as she closed the door of her apartment behind them, "it's quite possible your pursuers will have attached a tracker to your car. So, it's best we just leave it where it is."

Her words instantly put Matt in mind of the evening before, when they had hauled Ben across the beach from the boat. And of the man with the red worry beads he had spotted as they were easing Ben into the car. That now familiar stranger had plainly been watching the entire episode. And would have had ample opportunity to put a tracking device in place.

"Don't worry, you're safe here," Leila reassured him when she saw the concern in Matt's eyes. "For the time being, at least."

Picking up a pack of cigarettes from the kitchen table, she took one out, tossed the open pack back onto the table, and lit up. With the cigarette dangling from the corner of her mouth, she set down four glasses, then opened the fridge, reached out a bottle of white wine and offered her guests a glass each.

"It may be frowned upon here in what is probably the country's most religious city," she said, before adding with an irreverent smile, "but I like to think Konya's cherished mystic Rumi would have approved."

At that moment, as if in answer, the day's last call to prayer rose into the night sky around her apartment.

"You see what I mean?" she said and stood up to close the window on the sound.

"Şerefe," she added, returning to the table and raising her glass.

Matt found it hard to envisage this woman as an associate of the dour Hauke Schmitt. Easy-going, light-hearted and chatty, she was the diametric opposite of the German doctor. Yet she hinted at the common ground between them when she launched into a potted tour of her history.

Leila was not Turkish, she explained. She was Kurdish. Her parents had been university teachers. But their anti-government views compelled them to leave the country, as life became increasingly difficult for them to the point where they could no longer find any university that would offer them a teaching post. So, they emigrated first to West Germany and then to America, taking Leila with them. After high school, Leila returned to Turkey to study science at the University of Diyarbakir, but switched to agriculture when the new faculty opened.

This snippet of her life story put Matt in mind of Schmitt's nemesis, agronomist Luc Bennett. He smiled to himself at the thought that maybe she actually had more in common with the Welshman than with her German associate. Yet this seemed unlikely in view of the anti-government views she spoke of, which suggested that she might at least have flirted with the country's communists and would have been an ideal recruit for East Germany's Stasi.

With Luc Bennett's tales still in his mind, Matt shot a piercing stare across the kitchen table in the direction of Leila.

"Has Dr Schmitt ever talked to you about his time in Zimbabwe?" he asked.

For once, the talkative Leila fell silent. She stubbed out her cigarette, emptied her glass and poured the remains of the wine bottle into it.

"There's another bottle in the fridge," she said, and glanced at Amber, inviting her to open it. Then gazed into her glass again.

"You're referring to the Harare report," she said at last.

Matt simply nodded. By now, the faint sound of the call to prayer outside had died away completely. Only the rippling sound of liquid filled the stillness that was restored to the room as Amber topped up the glasses.

"I heard about it from other sources," she added evasively once the glasses were full. "But he never spoke of his time there to me. Or of the report."

She paused. And her lips quivered faintly as if rehearsing her next words.

"I recall him talking about Africa only once," she added. "And the only reason I remember it so well is because it was so peculiar. Not connected to anything else. It just came right out of the blue and had nothing to do with Zimbabwe."

Leila paused again and looked across the table at Matt. She had his attention.

"He was talking about tropical forests in the Congo and a parasitic fungus found there which feeds off ants. *Cordyceps*, he called it."

"He would," Matt said.

"Pardon me?"

"I was just thinking," he explained. "Only a man like Dr Schmitt would know the Latin name of every fungus in the world."

"He's a very precise man," Leila replied. "I value that."

Leila had clearly caught the disparaging tone in Matt's words and wanted him to know it had not gone unnoticed.

"Of course he told me the full scientific name," she added,

"but I can't remember it now. It was what he said next that stayed with me. The hypha of the fungus, he said, penetrates the body of the ant and migrates to the brain, where it manipulates the creature and controls every aspect of its behaviour.

"Just like our leaders. Just like our media, he said. They control the way we think and the way we act. Until we are little more than zombies."

Leila paused for reflection. Or was it for effect? Matt wondered.

"That was the moment when it dawned on me that Dr Schmitt was not the trusting follower of his Soviet masters that we all thought he was. Maybe he was thinking of the Harare report when he said all that, I don't know."

Matt was not convinced. It seemed to him more likely that this was just another subterfuge on the part of Leila or Hauke Schmitt. Or both. Either way, the truth about the German doctor held little interest for him. But Leila made it plain she was not ready to let the subject lie. As if intent to burnish her old friend's credentials for Matt's benefit and dispel any doubts he may have, she hammered the message home.

"In fact, he feels such loathing that he could only be described as a Russophobe today," she said pointedly. "It's gotten really bad in the last few years with so many Russians buying up real estate along the coast. And he worries all the time they'll start moving into Karakent as well. It would be the ultimate nightmare for him."

If the aim of her words was to get Matt on side, they fell way short of their target. He was barely listening. With all the talk of the German doctor's Soviet masters, it was a different question altogether that was burning a hole in his curiosity – and in the ticket pocket of his jeans.

"Did you and he talk about the attempt on Pope John Paul's life back in the day?" he asked, changing tack as he recalled his conversation with Luc Bennett.

Leila's composure slipped for a moment. She eyed Matt across the table with suspicion, while Amber and Ben looked on in baffled silence. But Amber instantly twigged when he added, "I mean, it was suggested at the time that the Grey Wolves were involved, so that must have been big news in Turkey."

"You seem very familiar with our country's politics," Leila said. The inflection in her voice told Matt his words had done nothing to allay her suspicions.

"I wouldn't say that. But I do know a little about the Grey Wolves. And as you're a friend of Dr Schmitt's – and Kurdish too," Matt added, momentarily throwing all caution to the wind, "I'm wondering if you might know what *this* is all about."

Matt produced the flash drive from his jeans and placed it on the table.

"A young Kurdish man gave it to me for safekeeping."

Leila stared at the USB stick and said nothing. A silence descended on the room like a dense immovable cloud. Matt instantly began to question this reckless move. But it was too late. It could not be rolled back.

Leila, curious yet visibly wary, rose from her chair and disappeared down the corridor of her apartment. She returned a few moments later, with a laptop under her arm, placed it on the kitchen table and started up the device. Taking the flash drive in her fingers, she looked at Matt.

"What's on here?" she said.

"I was hoping you could tell me that. As long as it's not corrupted. It got a little wet recently," Matt said. "The password, by the way is, 0791rebmevon51."

She slipped the flash drive into the USB port on her laptop, entered the password, and opened the file. Her eyes lingered on the screen, as if hesitating, then she peered across the table at Matt with a quizzical expression in her eyes.

"Vacation snaps?"

"Scroll down to the zip file," Matt said with a hint of relief in his voice to see that the flash drive was still intact. "You'll find a bunch of files at the bottom. A PDF file, two video clips and some audio files."

He was struck by the mild excitement in Leila's eyes when she opened the PDF. She looked up at Matt.

"Am I right in thinking it's something to do with the Grey Wolves?" he asked.

"Whatever it is," she said, "it must have been put together by someone with great hacking skills. But it's not only the far right here."

She chuckled quietly to herself.

"I see other familiar names. Members of the AK party, the MHP, the Turkish mafia. And businessmen – especially in real estate and construction. That figures," she mused, as she continued scrolling through the file.

"My word, they're all here! Along with their links, their addresses, and most important of all, their bank accounts. Their money. Transactions, So-called donations. Who paid what to which party member.

"Oh," Leila hesitated. She stopped scrolling and sat riveted to the screen, as if staring into an abyss.

"What's up?" Matt said.

The troubled silence that followed was palpable. Matt could see that Leila was caught in some undefined net of disquiet.

"Are you all right?" asked Amber.

"Doctor Schmitt tells me Matt and Ben provoked the anger of a man called Erkan Suleyman," Leila said at last, her voice solemn and subdued.

"When Hauke retired to Karakent, he set up a private practice there, mainly for the tourists. He was looking for an assistant, and I suggested that my cousin's daughter might be interested as she had just qualified and was keen to get some experience. Tragically, she crossed paths with Suleyman soon after she arrived, and she's been a broken woman ever since."

"What happened?" Amber said, squeezing her words into the brief pause that Leila left for reflection.

Leila looked up from the screen, the expression in her eyes

visibly hardened. "Let's just say he doesn't take kindly to rejection," she said in her solemn tone, plainly loath to spell out the story in all its detail.

"That's what he's like. He destroys anyone who frustrates his ambition. A man who in no way lives up to the name Suleyman, man of peace. There are many other scarred women who can testify to that. The ones who are still alive, that is."

Matt could not help but notice how Amber visibly shook as she listened to the Kurdish woman's story. Imagining that she was mentally reliving her own ordeal all those years ago, he rested a comforting hand on her arm. It came as a shock when she looked up at Matt with an unfathomably cold expression in her eyes to find that his gesture brought her no comfort at all. On the contrary, he saw that her thoughts had embarked on a painful journey with an uncertain destination.

"He's close to some of our political leaders as well," Leila added darkly. "And he's here in this PDF. This file could damage the careers of many people. Maybe even bring down the government."

"And the other files?" Matt prompted her, wanting to distract Amber from the story of her cousin's daughter.

Leila opened one of the audio files, leaving her guests in suspense as she listened intently to two male voices in conversation.

"Oh my word," she said, as the audio played. "They're talking billions here. I wouldn't swear to it, but I reckon one of the voices belongs to the minister of the environment."

Leila opened the first video file. It showed a meeting of half a dozen men and had barely started when Amber pointed at the screen.

"Wow! I'm sure I know that man."

"Really?" Leila was startled by Amber's words.

"Well, I'm not that sure, but he looks a lot like someone I often saw with my ex," Amber said. "He was in the timber trade."

"That makes sense. Their illegal logging is exactly what the discussion on the audio file is all about. Lining the pockets of the politicians and generals by selling off all the timber felled in the deforestation of Kurdistan."

"Logging?" Matt said with a questioning look. "In Turkey?"

"Oh, it's nothing like Brazil," Leila said with resignation in her voice. "Logging in the Kurdish region is a political military exercise designed solely to defeat the resistance and oppress the people."

Leila opened the other video file.

"Oh my goodness. You see that man there?" Leila added, pointing at a portly, fortyish figure at the head of a long table. "He's the president's son-in-law, and flanked by the man in the audio file and the boss of one of the country's biggest building corporations. And those brown envelopes on the table tell you all you need to know about what's going on here."

Leila closed the file, removed the flash drive from the laptop, and fixed Matt with an earnest stare.

"If you're caught with this, you'll be in big trouble," she said. "But leave it with me and I can make sure it gets into the right hands."

Matt smiled.

"I was told the right hands belonged to a man called Murat. And he's dead," he said, retrieving the flash drive and tucking it back in the ticket pocket of his jeans. "Now, if you ask me, we're probably in big enough trouble already. And from what you say, I reckon this could be our get-out-of-jail card if we play it right."

"You should not take this lightly, Matthew," Leila warned. "You have no idea what you're up against."

Matt shrugged, picked up his glass and drank the last of the wine. Ben was already half asleep and slumped over his own glass.

"She's right, Matt," Amber chipped in. "But maybe we should turn in for the night and talk about it in the light of day. But I think Ben could do with your spare bed, Leila," she added. "He's still in need of some mending. And I'm happy to sleep on the sofa."

"Leaving the floor to me," Matt observed.

"Exactly," Amber said with a chuckle.

"If you're happy with that, I'll get you a blanket for the sofa," Leila said, and disappeared to fetch blankets from behind a door in the corridor and set up the sleeping arrangements.

"I hope you sleep comfortably on the sofa," she said, and retired quietly to her own room after wishing them goodnight.

Ben crawled straight into bed in the spare room without muttering a word, while Matt graciously offered Amber priority use of the bathroom. As soon as she had finished there and snuggled under the blanket on the sofa, fully clothed, she clutched her smartphone in both hands and sent a WhatsApp message to let her sister know they had arrived safely.

As she pressed Send, Matt reappeared from the bathroom and arranged his blankets on the floor of the lounge before switching off the light. In the faint glow of the streetlamp from outside, Amber watched him remove his T-shirt and his jeans and sling them over the back of an armchair.

"What are you doing?" she said from under her blanket, with amusement in her voice.

"I can't sleep with all those clothes on," he muttered in a morose, barely audible tone, and crawled under his blanket on the floor.

"Whatever turns you on," she whispered with a provocative chuckle.

"It doesn't." He was in no mood for humour. "And with all the talk of tracker devices and the sight of Mr Worry Beads lurking in the shadows when we dragged Ben off the beach last night, it's doubtful I'll get any sleep anyway."

As if to underline the prospect of the thought-racked night that lay ahead, he tossed out an idea from the obscurity of his blanket, which bore no relation to anything that had happened that day.

"But tell me," he said. "What's the name of your bookshop?"

Amber was taken aback by the non sequitur and said nothing for a while, pondering its significance.

"It's not very original," she replied at last. "I call it Bookworm. Why do you ask?"

"No reason. Just thinking of Ben's boat. Almost drowning. And how I should take a trip down to Brighton one day and enjoy the sea air on a pleasanter shore than this one here. If we ever get out of this nightmare."

A part of Amber was unsettled by these words. Yet a greater part of her sensed a sweet tingle of anticipation. Perhaps it was this that unnerved her. As she dwelt on these thoughts, she became aware of a peculiar sound. A sound of sawing logs. It was coming from the blanket on the floor. She glanced down at the bundle in the darkness and saw it gently heaving.

She smiled to herself. Her gaze wandered around the unfamiliar flat, exploring the shadows as she mulled over the past twenty-four hours. What was she doing here? Amber asked herself. Stuck with a guy who was getting himself deeper and deeper into trouble. Were they really safe lodged in Konya with Leila?

Her eyes fell on the part of the room that caught the most light from the street: the back of the chair, where Matt's clothes were draped. Once focused on his jeans, her eyes would not shift from that spot. And left her unable to sleep. Her mind dwelt endlessly on the talk between Leila and Matt. Revolved perpetually around the significance of the flash drive. The danger it posed. And Matt's blasé dismissal of any risk. It seemed to her so out of character from what little she knew of him. But it gave her an idea.

Creeping out from under her blanket, Amber tiptoed over to the chair, teased the flash drive out of the pocket of his jeans, and tucked it safely into her capris. The rigid casing pressed into her flesh as she slid back under her blanket and settled down on the sofa. Knowing that the device was now safe and secure in her own possession, she finally fell into a deep sleep.

# CHAPTER 23

The talk of tracker devices gave Matt no peace the next morning as they drove through the centre of Konya in a beaten-up old Renault that gave the impression it could fall apart at any moment.

"I keep promising myself to trade it in for a new model," Leila said, raising her voice to compete with the noise of the engine. "But I'm just so attached to this old clunker."

Matt was irritated by her casual talk of the clapped-out car she was driving while there was a possibility that Suleyman and his thugs might have found his rental car and be lurking on the streets of the city at that moment. A city that was already bustling with life – tradesmen in their pickups, boys on scooters darting back and forth in an endless cacophony of beeping horns on their early-morning errands. Matt kept a close eye on each and every one as they passed, glancing through the back window every so often in case they were being followed.

"You really don't need to worry, Matthew," Leila called out from the driver's seat with reassuring laughter in her voice, when she caught sight of Matt's nervous behaviour in the mirror. "Even if they had a tracker on your car, there is no way they can find you now."

She switched the radio to a music station that instantly filled the car with the rhythmic beat of Turkish pop music. Leila chuckled.

"Tarkan," Leila said with a mischievous chuckle in her voice. "I love it. He's a German Turk. I like to tease Hauke with this music whenever I see him. He can be so stuffy."

"How often do you see Dr Schmitt?" Amber asked, raising her voice in an effort to make herself heard above the music. But even from the vantage point of the front passenger seat, her efforts were to no avail.

Leila was now visibly lost in the music, which moved seamlessly from the urban pop of Tarkan to languorous Anatolian folk music. It was as if the radio was eerily synchronised with their journey as the car took them ever deeper into the hinterland beneath a dull grey sky that was matched almost like a mirror image by the monotonous landscape around them.

Leila's mood, too, visibly changed as their journey progressed. She seemed to be adrift in dark thoughts until she could not take the mournful music any longer and switched off the radio altogether. They travelled on in silence for some time. Spots of rain began to fill the windscreen, and she put the wipers on. No one ventured to interrupt her thoughts. Only the rhythm of the wipers moving back and forth interrupted the silence.

"This is the Konya Plain," she said at last. There was a weariness to her voice. "It will mean nothing to you, of course, unless you've read a book called *In the Land of Blood and Tears*."

She looked in the rear-view mirror, then across to the passenger seat at Amber, and was met with blank expressions.

"Everyone talks about the genocide of Armenians," Leila said. "I'm sure you've heard about that."

"Which Turkey denies," Amber said with a nod of the head.

"They can deny it all they like," Leila insisted. "But there were witnesses. And the same witnesses saw the genocidal treatment of the Kurds at the same time, when whole groups and families were herded across the Konya Plain in the middle of winter. It gets very cold here at that time of year. And when the deported families reached a village here one evening, they were forced to spend the night in the rain and snow. The next morning, mass graves were dug for all the Kurds who had frozen to death."

The rain had already stopped. Leila switched off the wipers, and silence descended on the car again.

"I don't know exactly where it happened. No memorial to those crimes has been erected here, of course. But every time I drive this way I can't help thinking of those poor people."

It was soon after this sombre history lesson from Leila that she swung left off the main highway and onto an unmetalled road that was little more than a track. There were no signposts to indicate where they were heading. Matt had the impression it had been laid there for farmers. He checked behind again as they rattled their way over the rough track. There was not a vehicle to be seen anywhere on the landscape that stretched away on all sides of them.

After ten minutes or so, the farm track petered out into a barely marked trail that only looked fit for an off-roader. But Leila's ancient Renault clattered on ever deeper across country for a good twenty minutes or more, testing its suspension to the extreme.

"This is karst country," Leila said when at last she brought the car to a standstill at a ridge overlooking a vast crater in the ground. "I think you call it a sinkhole in English. There are many of them in this region. And over the years people often built cave dwellings into the side. This is a really old one."

"Like in Cappadocia," Amber said.

"Exactly. Which is also not very far away," Leila said, turning to Amber as she climbed out of the car, slipped a bag over her shoulder and added, "We must walk from here."

A chill October wind whipped up over the ridge as she led Amber down a narrow path into the sinkhole. Matt followed behind with Ben. He could well imagine what it must be like here in the dead of winter – how the Kurdish deportees must have suffered all those years ago when they were dragged across the plain and dumped in the snow with no shelter.

The path down the side of the sinkhole was precarious, and Ben depended on Matt's support to negotiate it safely. His gait was at least close to normal now. But he still signalled an audible discomfort and weakness in his left leg that made it prone to give way unannounced and threatened to send him over the side without a helping hand from Matt.

Matt felt a drop of rain and glanced up at the darkening clouds that loomed over the rim of the ancient sinkhole. They were already around fifty metres below the ridge and followed Leila for a good ten minutes longer before they came upon a row of bushes lining the path. Opposite the bushes stood an inconspicuous wooden door in the rocky limestone wall of the crater. With the rain coming on stronger, both Amber and Ben let out a sigh of relief when Leila pulled a key from her shoulder bag and opened the door.

Matt hung back as the other three disappeared through the doorway. He eyed the path they had just walked and scoured the ridgeline of the sinkhole. Seeing no sign of movement anywhere, he followed the others inside and closed the door behind him.

He found himself in a large chamber. The cold austerity of the place was accentuated by the light from an oil lamp that Leila had just lit. It was still struggling to produce a flame of any note. A single light bulb hung from the stone ceiling, suspended by an ancient-looking cable.

"We used to have an old generator here," Leila said when she saw Matt's eyes following the line of the cable with a quizzical expression. "But it packed up some years ago, and we've had no electricity here since."

"There are also plenty of candles over there," she added, pointing to a large box under a wooden frame.

This was matched by three other wooden structures along the wall on the left and the wall facing the door. They clearly served as basic, makeshift beds. No sprung mattresses. Only slats of wood to lie on. And on each of these beds a rolled-up sleeping bag.

The centrepiece of the room was a rough-hewn wooden table where the oil lamp stood. It was piled with tins of food, beneath which were a dozen or so large bottles of water. On the other side of this table, against the wall on the right, stood a cooker and alongside this a large blue gas cylinder almost as tall as the cooker itself. It was the only element of colour in an otherwise dour place of sanctuary.

"So, here we are," Leila said, as Ben took a seat at the table, and Amber sat down opposite him with a deep sigh of relief.

"Did you carry all that stuff down here yourself?" Matt asked, his eyes still fixed on the large gas cylinder.

"You will see that I only put two sleeping bags in here," Leila said, ignoring Matt's question, then turned to Amber: "This is not a place for you. I think it best if you come back with me and stay in the apartment while we sort this out."

"Ben, would you stand up for a moment?" Leila said.

Ben's eyes were a picture of confusion as he rested an arm on the table and rose shakily to his feet. Reaching into the pocket of her jacket, Leila took out her cell phone, walked over to Ben, and snapped a picture.

"Not the best," she said, examining the shot, "But we can get it touched up. Now what I need from you is your personal details. Then we can get a convincing new passport for you in a couple of days."

"Damn it. I don't need a fucking passport!"

Ben slumped back into the chair. They were the first words he had uttered, aside from incomprehensible grunts, since they had met Leila the day before. She was taken aback by his anger.

"I just need to get fit, damn it! Ahmet has to be sorted once and for all."

"Leila's right," Matt said. "You could land yourself in trouble if you don't have a passport."

He was thinking of his bus ride from Istanbul.

"And the best way to get fit," Leila added, "is to stay here, out of sight, for a few days. By which time we will have your passport anyway."

For all Ben's impatience, he had no choice. He sank back in silence, waiting for Amber and Leila to take their leave.

"I'll be back in two or three days," Leila added as she opened the door. The bushes outside bristled in a gust of wind that sent a chill into the room.

"Are your phones sufficiently charged?"

"Not a problem," Matt said. "I doubt we'll be using our phones down here anyway."

"Well, just to be sure," she said, pulling a device from her bag and handing it to Matt, "take this power bank. I'll give you a call before I come over. I assume you have Matthew's number, Amber?"

Amber nodded, and Leila pulled the door to as they slipped back out into the damp October morning. An uncomfortable silence filled the rock-hewn shelter the moment they left.

The tension that embedded itself in the quietness was palpable. Matt sensed the anger and impatience that was eating up his old friend. He rummaged through the tins and jars on the table, hoping to find something he could offer Ben that might ease the tension.

The smell of the oil lamp right next to him on the table clawed at his throat, which only added to his unease. The flame was burning wildly and churning soot into the air. Matt adjusted the wick, then continued his search of the countless tins and jars, until his eureka moment. With a show of mock elation, he lifted one of the jars above his head in triumph to present his trophy.

"Nescafe! I'll put the kettle on."

"Don't do that on my account. I'll have some of this," Ben muttered. He kicked one of the water bottles under the table with his right foot, rose from his chair, and went to lie down on the makeshift bed closest to the door.

Ben winced as he lowered his body onto the bed. The pain from his beating had a way to go before he could relax. But the impatience that showed in the growl he let out told Matt he would have his hands full keeping his old friend on a tight leash. Fortunately, there was nowhere he could go anyway for now. Sequestered in this remote sinkhole, he and Matt would have to sit it out until Leila returned.

Yet Ben's frustrated fury would not be stilled for a moment. The rage bled from his eyes with the caustic power of his longing for vengeance. It ran deep, like a menacing flow of magma on the brink of eruption. Matt knew it might explode any moment.

He poured a glass of water from one of the large bottles and handed it to his old friend. He attempted a look of sympathy, but it was heavily coloured with exasperation and resentment.

"Look Ben, when you asked me to locate a man called Ahmet in Turkey, I was happy to go along with it because I owed you. I dread to think what would've become of me if you hadn't given me the help you did when I most needed it."

"Well, you wouldn't be cooped up here in this cavern, that's for sure." Ben gave a wry smile. "Look, if you're trying to say you want out, Matt, that's fine. It's up to you. I understand."

"I'm not saying that. I just wish you'd warned me what kind of a guy Ahmet is. I didn't know we'd be going up against the Turkish mafia."

"You know, the first time I met Ahmet was the day he married my sister," Ben said, adopting a more pensive tone. "And I got a hint of what a nasty small-time bully he would turn out to be even then."

He paused, and Matt sensed a mass of thoughts flashing through Ben's mind.

"Peggy's wedding day of all days." Ben paused again. "It was a strange affair. I'd never been to a wedding like it. I watched the happy couple take to the floor, and I have to say she did seem so incredibly happy as they danced together."

Matt saw the trace of a tear in Ben's eyes as he spoke.

"Then the other guests joined them and danced for ten minutes or so before all the women peeled off and left the men to dance alone together. It was totally bizarre, but then it got weirder still when this young guy walked up to my table and pulled me onto the dance floor. Can you imagine?"

Matt said nothing. He was curious to know where this story was going.

"Do you know a guy called Hasan?" Ben asked. "And his wife Fidan?"

Matt recalled Hamza's sidekick. The memory brought images of the man with the worry beads rushing back.

"Well, he was there. On the dance floor. With Pearl's husband, Hamza. They were dancing together to this upbeat Turkish music. Looking very cool. The beat getting faster and faster. They were totally wrapped up in the moment, when Fidan walks up to Hasan. They exchanged a few words and then, out of nowhere, he lashed out. Slapped her so hard in the face she almost went down.

"It was horrific. Looking back on it, I was ashamed and embarrassed that I did nothing, said nothing. But I was a stranger and a guest, and nobody else batted an eyelid. I turned to Ahmet hoping he could fill me in. And you know what? He was smiling that greasy smirk of his. Smiling with approval. I couldn't believe it.

"And you know what he said? 'She should know by now that you don't just walk up to Hasan and disturb his concentration like that. Especially if you're his wife.' That's what he said. And the look on Peggy's face when he said it will stay with me forever."

Ben's rant flattened out into an uneasy lull, where no words could usefully fill the vacuum. The anger in his expression said everything that needed to be said. And the two of them sat sipping on their drinks in silence until Matt found the words to bring his old friend back from the bitter ferment raging inside him.

"Okay, he's a nasty, small-time bully. But we've seen the kind of friends he has. So, we need to be cautious, because there's no way I want out. I'm with you all the way, Ben. Now that Amber's been dragged into it, too, I feel a responsibility for her as well.

"And let's face it, with the retired intelligence communities of East Germany and Turkey – or whoever Leila works or worked for – all busting a gut to help us, it would seem a tad ungrateful if I walked away now."

"So, who is this Leila woman anyway?" Ben said. "Are you sure we can trust her? I mean, this guardian angel who appears from nowhere, a complete stranger. Why should she even get involved?"

Matt fell silent. He had no answer. He could not deny that she was an unknown quantity foisted on them by the German doctor. He recalled the long conversation he had had with the Welshman about Hauke Schmitt, a man he had said was not all he might appear to be. A man who once called himself Josef Wasenmeister. So, where did that leave Leila? Was she also not what she appeared to be?

These thoughts reminded Matt that Luc Bennett had given him his number, and he pulled his phone from the pocket of his jeans.

"Who are you calling?" Ben asked.

Matt said nothing in reply as he waited for Luc to pick up.

"Hello Matt," came the melodious tone of the Welshman's voice. "To what do I owe the pleasure?"

The familiarity of the voice gave him a curious sense of comfort in their chilly hideaway. He caught the sound of barking in the background, which told him that Luc must be at home with Betty in their dog sanctuary. It seemed such a long time ago that he was sitting up there sharing a beer with the Welshman amid the olive trees.

"Hi Luc. I've been mulling over that conversation we had about Hauke Schmitt."

"Okay," Luc Bennett said, drawing out the second syllable in a way that spelled a searching curiosity.

"Did you ever come across a Kurdish friend of his called Leila?" Matt asked.

"Look, can you hold the line a second, Matt?" Luc said, and vanished into the background.

He left only the sounds of indefinable activity behind, but the noises gave Matt the impression he was withdrawing to his office, perhaps wanting to avoid interruption from Betty. It was a good two or three minutes before Matt caught the sound of someone picking up the phone again.

"Hello. Are you there, Luc?" Matt said when no words came from the other end of the line.

"I'm getting a peculiar echo, Matt. Where are you calling from?"

"Well, did you?" Matt repeated, ignoring Luc's question. "Come across a woman called Leila?"

"Kurdish, you say? No, can't say I have. But I'll tell you what, Schmitt and Kurds sounds like an unhealthy mix to me. So, what's this all about, Matt? Don't tell me you're getting mixed up with the PKK now as well."

"No, no, it's all good. Just wanted to know if you knew her that's all."

"No, afraid I can't help you there, Matt." Luc left an unmistakable pause that gave Matt the feeling he wanted to say more.

"And the rest of you?" Luc said at last.

"The rest of me?" Matt repeated.

"Well, the lovely Amber of course."

"We're all good," Matt said.

"Well, you just take care."

The edge of genuine concern in Luc's voice did not escape Matt. Nor the hint of a gnawing suspicion. It left Matt feeling puzzled by the Welshman's manner.

"So, who's Luc?" Ben asked when Matt eventually put down his phone.

"You haven't met him?" Matt asked. "His wife runs a dog sanctuary up in the hills outside Karakent."

"And where does he come in? Why should he know this Leila woman?"

"Maybe he doesn't. But he knows Schmitt from way back, and she knows Schmitt from way back, so I just thought Luc might know her too."

Matt explained to Ben what Luc Bennett had told him about the history of Hauke Schmitt in Africa, painting in as much detail as he could recall.

"Well, well. If she mixes with people like that," Ben said, "I'd say we're right to be suspicious. But what the hell, let's see where the journey takes us."

"If you recall," Matt said. "Leila insisted that Schmitt gave up allegiance to his masters in East Berlin long before the wall came down. He'd seen the light. And you can't deny that he was the one who treated your bruises and got us out of Karakent."

"But it's not just him, is it?" Ben said, turning to Matt with the disquiet now etched in his eyes. "What about the Bennett guy? What's an MI6 man even doing here?"

"Ex-MI6," Matt corrected him, wondering why his friend might be so troubled by the involvement of someone from intelligence.

Ben paused, sank into quiet reflection for a moment. There was a look of concern on his face. Then he turned to Matt.

"Can I borrow your phone?"

"Why?" Matt asked, passing his mobile to Ben.

Ben eased himself to his feet, keyed in a number, and hobbled over to the door with the device pressed to his ear. Faltering as he opened the door, he shuffled out into the fresh air.

"Tony?" he said, "Is it done?"

What followed was a prolonged silence, sporadically punctuated by a series of grunts, sprinkled in turn with emphatic and ever louder protestations of "oh no!" He engaged in this one-sided conversation for a good five or ten minutes until Mat finally heard Ben explode.

"No, Tony!" he yelled. "Just do it. Just close the fucking deal."

"What was that all about?" Matt asked when Ben returned and handed him back his phone.

The anger was still written on Ben's face. He ignored the question, sank into a pool of reflection and said nothing more, leaving Matt only to speculate.

Matt knew it was pointless to gate-crash his thoughts. He left him to brood and let the rage in his eyes slowly fade. A good few minutes passed until Ben peered out from his gloom. As if refreshed by this brief time-out, he gave what seemed to Matt like a phony smile of amusement.

"So, you have feelings for Amber?"

"Don't change the subject, Ben. What was that phone call about?"

"I thought you were supposed to be married," Ben said with a smile, ignoring the question.

At least Ben's burning rage appeared to have tempered, which came as some relief to Matt. But whether due to Ahmet or to the phone call, there was still a tender edge of fury there. It fluttered, faintly but perpetually, in the way leaves bristle on the trees in the build-up to a storm. This worried Matt.

# CHAPTER 24

The journey back to Konya in the beaten-up Renault was almost devoid of any conversation between Amber and Leila. They had each been dragged into something that was not of their making, yet both acted as if driven by a sense of duty to handle it. Arriving back soon after midday, Leila dropped Amber off at the apartment.

"Make yourself at home," she said, handing over the keys as Amber climbed out of the car.

"I'll be back at three," Leila added, then turned the car and drove back the way they had come.

The apartment in daylight made a different impression on Amber. She had not had much of a chance to get a picture of the place before. Now in the noontime light, it appeared more spacious than she remembered it. The pictures on the wall reminded her of Pearl's lounge furnished with scenes of Brighton, except that these were mostly old photographs of unfamiliar scenes, aside from one that seemed oddly out of place: the Statue of Liberty in New York. Was it intended as a souvenir of Leila's younger years in America?

What fascinated her in particular, was Leila's bookshelf. For Amber, the books people read hold a clue to their inner selves. So, she would always make a beeline for the bookshelves in a person's home. And here in Leila's apartment she had time to leaf through every book on every shelf. It was not a large collection, but it revealed her to be a well-read woman. And yet, after hearing Leila's story, Amber had fully expected to find works on Kurdish history or maybe her specialist subject of agriculture. There was just one, *In the Land of Blood and Tears*, which she had mentioned the day before, as they journeyed over the Konya Plain.

There were no Turkish books. Everything on the shelf was mostly English or German. The only German name she recognised was an author Amber had read herself: Hermann Hesse. The English ranged from Jane Austen through Upton Sinclair and William Faulkner, all the way to John le Carré. Of which there was a great deal. And then there was a solitary French title, *Pâques à New York* by an author Amber had never heard of called Blaise Cendrars.

With Amber's limited knowledge of her host, this collection of books and the absence of any literature she might have expected to find here painted an intriguing picture of Leila. One that featured her as a cosmopolitan polyglot but, at the same time, airbrushed out a particular side of the woman, concealing the deeply held feelings that Amber knew she had about her country, about her roots and probably about herself as well. The bookshelf, in other words, told Amber little about Leila, except that she was a very private person.

But it was not only privacy that was important to her. So too, it seemed, was punctuality. At exactly three o'clock, there came a knock on the door. Amber peered through the spyhole. It was Leila.

"So, now we have to wait," she said as she hung up her coat in the hallway of the apartment.

"For what?"

"A passport for Ben. They said it might take a few days."

"Who are 'they'?"

Leila gave a cagey smile, but offered no words in reply except a questioning, "Coffee?" as she made for the kitchen, calling back over her shoulder as she went, "But I don't do Turkish coffee in case you're wondering."

"You don't seem to do much Turkish anything," Amber said, wandering over to the bookshelf and running her fingers over the books. "I notice you don't even have any Turkish literature here."

"My little gesture of protest, I guess," Leila said, then went quiet and concentrated on the coffee, until the kettle sang.

"It's always been difficult for Kurdish people," she added, pouring the boiled water into the mugs. "But it seems so much worse now with the government always trying to deny the Kurds a voice. Almost denying our existence.

"They've depopulated and destroyed thousands of communities. And now they're even deforesting whole areas and selling off Kurdish timber. Before long, the region will be a wretched wasteland."

Leila paused and reflected for a moment.

"You know, there's an old proverb that says 'when the ox comes to the palace, he does not become a king; the palace becomes a barn'. And you can go to prison for saying it. That's Turkey today."

She paused. The look of sadness and resignation in her eyes was not lost on Amber.

"After Cizre and then the jailing of our HDP leader, I'd had enough. I'm too old now for demonstrations and protest marches, which are getting more violent by the day. So, I simply threw out all the Turkish books I had instead.

"And anyway," she added, "I prefer English literature."

There was a casual lack of conviction in Leila's voice as she set the mugs of coffee down on the table in the lounge.

"And German," Amber noted.

"I went to school in Germany. That was my first introduction to literature."

"Was that when you were introduced to Steppenwolf?"

The smile that now lit up Leila's face was of a different kind this time. Not cagey as before. This was a private expression that carried a hint of affection in her eyes.

"Have you read it?" she asked, taking the book off the shelf.

"It's the only one of your German books I have read. In translation, of course."

"It was a gift," Leila said, her smile now warmer still as she placed the book on the table alongside the coffee. "From Hauke Schmitt."

Amber said nothing. She picked up her mug of coffee and left Leila to meander through unspoken memories, seated on the sofa opposite, coffee mug cupped in her hands. Her manner gave the impression of a very close relationship with the German doctor. Amber was reminded of his pompous exchanges with Matt and found the thought of intimate relations between Leila and Dr Schmitt quite implausible. But the way she sat smiling so fondly at her memories suggested that the thought was not as farfetched as Amber imagined.

"I first met him in Urfa," Leila said at last. There was a quiet chuckle in her voice. "It must have been sometime in the mid-eighties. He was touring the archaeological sites in the country and seemed quite sad and lonely. He told me he had no family, no home, and a job he hated.

"I laughed. Said he made himself sound like Harry Haller in Steppenwolf. It was years since I'd read it, but the way he presented himself reminded me so much of that character. You know what Hauke's like. He's very correct and quite stiff. So you can imagine that he was deadly serious and didn't take at all kindly to the comparison. So, it was not the most auspicious of starts to a friendship. But we stayed in touch. And then one day, a year or so later, after I had moved to Ankara, he turned up out of the blue with a copy of Steppenwolf in his hand and said I was quite right, that he was just like Harry Haller, so he had bought a copy for me. And signed it *Hauke Haller*."

She picked up the book, opened it at the first page and stretched her arm across the coffee table. Amber took the book in her hands to examine it with the care of a museum curator holding a precious manuscript.

"That's so romantic," Amber said, passing the book back to Leila. "I never would have imagined such a gesture from him. But I'm surprised you say he hated his job. He seems a very caring kind of doctor."

Leila placed the book down on the table with an uneasy expression in her eyes.

"When I first met him, he was at a stage in his life when he was questioning a lot of things. I think he felt that he was not putting his skills as a doctor to their best use. He even began to explore things like Sufi mysticism. Not that he is at all religious. And nor am I. But he discovered a beauty in Sufism that we both find very appealing. He often visits me still mainly to lose himself in Sufi music and meditation.

"There's a performance of dervish music in town tomorrow if you're interested," she added.

"You mean whirling dervishes and that sort of thing?" Amber said in a tone of almost child-like excitement.

"And that sort of thing," Leila repeated with a nod and a look of amusement on her lips.

"It will be a good way to spend our time together while we wait for your friend's passport," she added. "But in the meanwhile, what about dinner this evening? Have you ever tried an Urfa kebab? It's a speciality of mine."

"Oh, I love it."

Amber's eyes lit up. She was thinking back to the rooftop dinner she had enjoyed with Matt. That was just a few long days ago. She could not have imagined then how complicated life was about to get. And the light in her eyes dimmed again, as she wondered how Matt and Ben must be feeling at that moment in their stone-cold hideaway.

Leila rested a comforting hand on her arm. It was as if she knew what was going through Amber's mind.

"Then I'll get the food ready," she said, getting up from her chair and donning an apron. "I don't know about you, but I'm starving. So, let's have an early dinner."

While Leila was preparing the meal, Amber drifted into the lounge. She pulled a slim volume from the bookshelf that she had escaped her attention earlier. It was the title that struck her: *Flowers for Hitler*. A collection of poems by Leonard Cohen that she had never heard of before. She only knew his songs.

"That goes back to my high school days in New York," Leila said, glancing over from the kitchen as Amber sat down on the sofa and opened the book. "To my days of rebellion, when I revelled in the dark and provocative."

"You surprise me."

"Oh, I dropped all that melancholic self-absorption after returning to Turkey. I discovered a sense of optimism here at university and was swept up by all the activism for the Kurdish cause. But it didn't last. My parents got wind of it and urged me not to get involved, otherwise I'd land in jail. They were right, of course, so after graduating I found another way. I kept quiet about the Kurdish issue and supported the cause passively from the government department I joined after my studies."

"How did that work?"

Leila glanced nervously across from the chopping board where she was dicing onions with a fearsome-looking knife. And said nothing.

"Do you always use such terrifying implements to dice your vegetables?" Amber asked.

She was keen to tack away from Leila's backstory, not least for fear of the damage that knife might inflict in her seemingly nervous distraction.

"This is nothing compared to its much fiercer cousin," Leila said, nodding towards the wall behind where Amber was seated.

Amber turned to see, displayed on the wall, a magnificent curved dagger that she had not noticed before.

"A traditional Kurdish jambiya," Leila said, as she continued dicing the onions. "I'm told it belonged to my great-great-grandfather."

At last, a small trace of Leila's roots, thought Amber, feeling oddly comforted by this find. Placing the book of Leonard Cohen poems back on the table, she looked across at Leila, who was now fully engrossed in her creation for dinner. She seemed a box of contradictions to Amber.

"You said you met Dr Schmitt when he was touring the ancient sites of Turkey," Amber said. She was curious to know more about these contradictions and ventured down a different avenue in the hope that Leila would open up.

"Well, let's say I was assigned to show him around."

"Assigned? That sounds intriguing. Who assigned you?"

Leila put down the fearsome kitchen knife, took a deep breath and removed her apron.

"Do you remember last night I mentioned the time Hauke talked about the parasite which feeds off ants and manipulates them to control their behaviour?" she said, lowering herself into the seat opposite Amber on the other side of the coffee table.

"How he compared them to our leaders. How they control the way we think?" she added and took the Leonard Cohen book in her hands, leafing through the pages.

Amber nodded.

"He was part of a small East German team that had been advising our department for some years."

She paused, as if uncertain whether to continue. But Amber was gripped. She so wished Matt were there to learn about her German doctor friend.

"He never told me what his team did or why he was actually there," she said. "But as time went on, he began making offhand remarks about his colleagues. It was clear that he was becoming more and more resentful. And even questioning why he was here."

"What sort of remarks?" Amber asked.

Leila fell into a studied silence. She began to flick back and forth through the pages of the book, visibly ill at ease.

"I need to get on with the kebab," she said, put down the

book, returned to the kitchen and slipped her apron back on.

No further words were exchanged on the subject of Hauke Schmitt. When the Urfa kebab was ready, they sat over dinner together and steered clear of anything that might prove awkward. Amber spoke of her life in Brighton, omitting the painful part that initially drove her away from the city, while Leila talked in no less sanitised terms of life in Turkey. And once dinner was over, they moved into the lounge to spend the rest of that evening drinking wine and sharing their views on favourite literary works.

Amber remained intrigued. She was keen to know more about the relationship with Hauke Schmitt. But she had to accept that, for the time being, they would not be going any further than an anodyne discussion on nothing in particular.

# CHAPTER 25

It was not lost on Matt that Ben had seemed on edge ever since he had learned of Luc Bennett and Hauke Schmitt's background in intelligence. And he could not help thinking it was this as much as the pain from his injuries that accounted for Ben's mood. He wondered if it had anything to do with his phone call to the mysterious Tony.

The morning wind could be heard gusting around the sinkhole outside as Matt rustled up the meagre breakfast of fried eggs, beans and fried bread from the supplies left behind for them. He put his own plate on the table and handed the other to Ben, who was now sitting up on the side of his bed. The wind whistled under the poorly fitting door. It was a day to stay inside.

Ben could only finish the egg on his plate. He let the rest lie untouched.

"I need some fresh air," he said, laying the plate down behind him and pushing his beleaguered frame up from the makeshift bed. He moved haltingly towards the door, unlocked it and stepped out into the cool morning air.

"For God's sake Ben, come back in," Matt shouted. "We need to keep our heads down till they get back."

Sporadic gusts of wind jolted the door into a swaying motion

228

on its shaky hinges. And stifled Matt's words. Ben was unmoved, defiantly taking in the cool air, arms outstretched to the sky as if in worship.

Matt darted out through the doorway, grabbed his old friend's right arm to drag him back into their hideout. He slammed the door shut behind them and guided Ben back to his breakfast on the table. The weight of Matt's hand on his shoulder brought a scowl to his face as he sat down.

"You were already out there too long yesterday on the phone. We need to stay out of sight till they get back."

"It's a desert out there, for fuck's sake. There's no one there to see us."

"You don't know that."

"So how long do we have to stay?"

"For God's sake, just stop moaning," Matt said. He was close to losing patience with his old friend. "We're stuck here for now, so let's just keep our heads down."

"That's just it, Matt," Ben cried, and smashed a fist on the table. "We're stuck here for fuck knows how long. Just waiting. But I don't have that luxury. I need to get back to Ahmet before Ahmet gets back to me."

"And how do you plan on doing that? You're in no fit state to go anywhere. Your best chance of getting back to Ahmet is to sit back and wait."

"You don't get it," Ben growled.

"No, I don't," Matt said, eyeing his old friend with a long, questioning stare. "I'm not even sure it's all about Peggy any longer."

"Oh it is. It's one hundred percent about Peggy."

"Then why do you act like a bull in a china shop, damn it? Why does it feel more like a hundred and ten percent? What's the other ten percent about?"

Ben was cowed into silence, like a wounded animal cornered by its own folly. He rested his head in his hands and said nothing more. Frustrated by Ben's refusal to speak, Matt rummaged through his own mind, recalling the events of the past two days since his friend's arrival – until he came to the ill-fated scene on his yacht.

"Ahmet made a strange comment on the boat," he said at last. "Truth is money and he wants his share. What was that all about?"

Ben's head sank deeper into his hands at these words. Matt was not hopeful of a response as he waited for Ben to stir. It was a long wait, punctuated by the repetitive whining of the wind outside. It rattled the latch on the door, incessantly. Clattering and shaking as if someone was trying to get in. And it rattled at Matt's patience, until he could wait no longer.

"For God's sake, Ben. You dragged me into this mess. The least you can do is be up front about what's going on."

"Okay," Ben said at last, raising his head from his hands with a pained expression in his eyes. "Yes, it's about money too. But that was all for Peggy as well."

"How do you mean?" Matt said. He was unable to conceal a hint of suspicion in his voice, as he began to question Ben's true motives for the first time.

"It was obvious soon after the funeral that he had a hand in her death," Ben said. "The way he immediately secured all her property and assets for himself. So, without letting on, I offered him an investment opportunity with no intention of paying out. It's my way of getting back at least some of the money for her daughter Kyra."

"So, it's not the diary they're interested in," Matt said. "It's the money."

"I've no doubt Ahmet wants to get his hands on the diary," Ben assured him. "The problem is that Erkan Suleyman got wind of things. And he invested a hell of a lot more than Ahmet, so he wants his money back too. It was no great surprise…"

His words were abruptly suffocated by the wind that blew right into their cavern when the door crashed in. It came with the kind of ferocity that went with the name Erkan Suleyman. He did not show in person. But his goons were there in the doorway. Two of them. All in black, silhouetted against the light outside. These were not the same gorillas that Erkan had brought with him onto Ben's yacht. They were bigger still. And masked. But they carried the same swagger. The same menace. Wielding baseball bats.

"Who the fuck are *you*?" Ben cried, instantly restored to his angry self as he leapt to his feet taking his chair in his hands and brandishing it at the intruders.

Matt picked up the oil lamp from the table, threw it at the two men and took his own chair in his hands. It was a pointless gesture. The baseball bats shattered both their chairs to splinters, compelling Ben and Matt to retreat. But the two goons simply advanced either side of the table, smashing everything in their path as they went, until their prey were forced back deeper into the cavern.

Ben stumbled when his legs reached the makeshift bed against the wall. Rolling to the side, he yelled, "Get the bed Matt!"

Matt knew at once what he meant. They grabbed the bed at each end and charged forward with it, like the raised blade of a snow plough, as the two gorillas bore down on them. But the wooden frame was no match for their assailants. It simply splintered into pieces the instant it made contact with the baseball bats.

The men were supremely skilled in their art. Ben was instantly thrown to the floor, hooded and cuffed with cable ties, before Matt, at the other end of the splintered bed, had any chance to respond. He was pinned against the wall by the barrel of a baseball bat across his throat. Barely able to breathe, he brought a knee up into the groin of his attacker. To no effect. The bat across his throat restricted him, and the target of his knee was out of reach.

Like Ben, he was pushed to the floor, hooded and cuffed with cable ties that cut into his wrists. Not a word was spoken. Denied any sight of what happened next, he was only aware of being dragged out into the cool morning air, taken to what felt like a van at the top of the sinkhole and forced into the back.

# CHAPTER 26

Leila was not one for early starts, so breakfast the next morning was not finished until well after ten. She was clearing the dishes from the table, when she heard the ping of a WhatsApp message from her phone. She dashed back into her bedroom.

"Good heavens! That was quick," Leila said, returning to the kitchen with the phone in her hand. "Ben's passport will be ready later today. They'll deliver it this evening."

"But it's not genuine, is it?" Amber said.

"It will do the trick for now. So, once we've cleaned up here, let's get going. We'll have plenty of time to visit the Mevlana mausoleum, where Rumi is buried. It's quite beautiful. Then we can have a light lunch before the whirling dervishes start their performance."

Amber was not disappointed they drove past the tea garden where they had first met Leila and into the centre of town, where the majestic building came into view. Alongside the mosque stood a tower with a conical dome that was adorned top-to-bottom with turquoise green tiles, broken only by a thin line of blue tiles inscribed with Arabic writing around the base of the cone. Even under the grey morning sky the tower glistened sublimely. Amber could well imagine how supremely beautiful it must be in the bright sunshine.

They entered through the gardens behind the mausoleum. The peace and tranquillity Amber found there was evidently enjoyed to the full by the locals. In the centrepiece of this garden, a young couple was posing for photographs. He in a smart dark suit and tie, she in full white matrimonial splendour. Leila stopped and contemplated the scene in silence for a minute or two.

"Have you ever been married, Amber?" she asked.

"No."

Amber gave Leila a quizzical sideways glance. She had the impression that the question concealed a private sense of loss or regret and wondered whether this might have involved Hauke Schmitt. But, perhaps wishing to put it to the back of her mind, Leila gave her no time to dwell on the thought. She took Amber's arm to guide her through the garden and into the mausoleum.

Leila spent a good hour or more explaining the history of the place to Amber. Showed her the shrine of Rumi himself with a reverence that surprised her and examined in great detail the inscriptions and ancient scriptures on display, which included some of the oldest existing copies of the Koran, she said.

"But I have to confess that I can't decipher most of the texts displayed here, as my knowledge of the Arabic script is very limited. It's quite frustrating," she added.

For all Leila's insistence that she was not religious, Amber had the impression that she had a keen and passionate interest in the history of Islam at least, if not in the religion itself.

But, as with all things theological, the entire visit went over Amber's head. She even found the atmosphere in the museum slightly oppressive. It was in such contrast to the freshness and tranquillity outside. So she felt a sense of relief when eventually they emerged from the building and returned to the gardens.

The wedding couple had long since moved on from their photo shoot, and the gardens were now empty. Amber suggested they sit for a moment and relax as the sun began to show signs of breaking through the cloud. They remained seated there to enjoy the warming air as the sun spread over the whole area around the mausoleum. Leila sat in quiet contemplation, leaving Amber to wonder what was going through her mind. Whether she was going over the talk of Hauke Schmitt the previous evening. Or was she deep in mystic meditation inspired by their location?

"It's beautiful in the sun, isn't it?" Amber said, jogging Leila from her thoughts.

Leila looked up, confused and startled by the sudden interruption.

"The mosque," Amber said, pointing at the turquoise green dome, which gleamed now in all its glory.

"It is. I never cease to admire its beauty."

Leila paused, as if still gathering her thoughts, before adding, "And with the sun now breaking through, it occurs to me that there is a perfect restaurant not far from here where we can enjoy our lunch outside in the garden."

The setting proved to be perfect. But what startled Amber as they approached the restaurant were the three letters above the door. AŞK. In bold red letters. She was instantly put in mind of Ahmet. Although the S carried a cedilla, unlike Ahmet's business, those three letters briefly threw her into a panic. She could not escape a sense of trepidation as they entered the restaurant.

They lingered over lunch for a good two hours or more, before Leila took Amber on a short tour of the city to while away the time before the concert performance began. But the image of those three letters remained ingrained in Amber's mind all the while, and a sense of nervousness clung to her as they wandered around Konya. Past street vendors selling their sesame rings, and pigeons that pecked furiously at the ground where any stray sesame seeds might fall. Past a little Catholic church that looked oddly out of place in this most Islamic of cities in Anatolia. And through the many streets of the bazaar.

When eventually they arrived at the concert hall, they had only five minutes to spare before the start of the performance.

Despite the emptiness of the arena, the musicians gathered on a rostrum to Amber's right, suggested that something was about to happen. Apart from she and Leila, there was a small group of people seated on the tribune opposite the rostrum, and a few isolated figures spread out around the arena. This was the extent of the audience, which made for an eery sense of bareness when the dervishes drifted into the arena.

Dressed in black cloaks and tall felt hats, they entered in single file with the languid motion of a dark, slow-moving river and lined up opposite the orchestra. The first of them took up position apart from the others. He was distinguished from the other dervishes only by his hat. Amber assumed this singled him out as the leader of the group.

"That's the sheikh," Leila whispered, as the gentle haunting sound of a Turkish reed flute weaved a way into the silence of the arena. This single flute was soon joined by the bewitching intonations of a voice, plaintive and mysterious, before the other instruments in the orchestra added their own melodic rhythms.

Amber looked on spellbound, watching the dervishes in tall hats remove their black cloaks, file past the sheikh, each bowing as they passed, and then begin slowly to rotate. Folding their arms over their shoulders as they went, they then gradually opened out each arm like a flower opening up in spring. With both arms now raised and head cocked to the right, they whirled in silent meditation as the mysterious plaintive music continued to play.

"Do you see the way they're holding their arms?" Leila said. "They always hold their right palm upward towards heaven and the left palm down towards the earth."

Amber was captivated. The dervishes maintained their mesmerising circular motion, like human gyroscopes, for what seemed like forever. When she turned to Leila, she found her companion, too, was in almost as deep a trance as the dervishes below. Eyes closed. A look of serenity on her face. Amber pictured Leila and Hauke Schmitt immersed together in this beguiling display of devotion and meditation. It was a slightly comical image. Yet deeply moving at the same time. She could not imagine what Matt might think of this unknown side to the East German doctor.

The performance in the arena lasted a good hour, possibly much longer. The flute, the hypnotic voice and the percussive rhythm of the Turkish drums wove a tangled pattern of emotions in Amber that merged into a euphoria she had never known before. Her sense of time had been completely lost in the music and the endless whirling motion of the Sufi mystics.

It was the extreme depth of this rapture which magnified the moment of shock that hit her when she spied a familiar figure. A sight that had become a leitmotif since meeting up with Matt. The fidgeting motion of the man's fingers on a set of red worry beads.

He sat on the far side of the arena. But it was unmistakably the same man who had been following Matt every step of the way. Leila was still immersed in the performance, but Amber's sharp intake of breath and involuntary flinch instantly dragged her from her trance. Her eyes sprung open, and she turned to her companion.

"What's wrong?"

"We need to go," Amber said, and grabbed Leila's arm.

Leila's expression was a mixture of concern and confusion.

"I'll explain outside," Amber replied, tugging now at Leila's arm as she rose from her seat.

Leila followed her out into the early evening air. The freshness of the atmosphere outside helped Amber to catch her breath. But her sense of panic remained.

"Let's walk," Amber said, and set off at pace, dragging Leila with her by the arm.

"Can you tell me what's going on?" Leila said in bemusement.

"I saw a familiar face in the hall," Amber said.

Leila's eyes were infected at once with the same disquiet that had caused Amber's heart to race.

"A familiar face? Here in Konya?"

"On the opposite side of the hall."

Amber told the story of the man with the red worry beads. Of how the stranger had been following Matt everywhere he went since he first arrived in Turkey.

"And you have no idea who he is?"

"Matt initially thought he might be working for the Jandarma. But I think he's come around to the idea that he's probably one of Erkan's men."

"Quite possibly both," Leila said in an ominous tone. "Do you think he saw you?"

"Why else would he have been there?" Amber said, glancing around to see if they were being followed. She could see no sign of him.

They drove back to the apartment in silence, each contemplating the implications of the sighting. Leila parked the car a few blocks from her apartment and kept a constant eye on the street behind as they walked the rest of the way. But Amber was conscious of the stranger's flair for hiding in the shadows. She felt her heart pounding with every step they took.

Once in the apartment, Leila went straight to the window in the lounge, which looked onto the street. She peered through the net curtains, up and down the road.

"It's all clear," she said, and went to the kitchen, where she took a bottle of white wine from the fridge and poured a glass for each of them. Amber was not so certain and, as they sat in the lounge together sipping on the wine, she fell into a troubled silence that hung tenaciously over the mood. They spent the rest of the evening saying little more on the topic.

Leila took her glass back into the kitchen with her and rustled up a meal of köfte with onions, peppers and bulgur, along with a side of Turkish salad. This usually included too much parsley for Amber's taste, but Leila had thankfully given it a twist of her own and left out the parsley altogether.

"I think red would go better with köfte," she said, finally breaking the uneasy silence, and opened another bottle of wine before they sat down to eat.

During and after dinner, they talked about their shared tastes for literature and music. But neither of them touched on the subject that was clearly at the back of both their minds: the man with the red worry beads. Not until the night was almost over.

It was just before dawn. Amber had endured restless hours going over and over the image of the familiar stranger playing with his beads while the dervishes rotated in their trance. The constant fidgeting motion. It played in her mind like an animated GIF on an endless loop. Over and over it ran, as she weighed the implications of his presence in Konya.

She had sent a WhatsApp message to Matt in the middle of the night, but there was no sign of him having read it.

Unable to remain in bed with her thoughts any longer, Amber took her phone and wandered into the kitchen to make a cup of coffee. The languid light of dawn stretched its fingers like grey vipers slithering slowly over the rooftops. A sky still poisoned by the picture in her mind of that stranger. And the threat he posed.

"Good morning, Amber. Can I help?"

Amber span around.

"I was just looking for the coffee."

"By the look of you, your night was even worse than mine," Leila said.

Amber let out a nervous laugh.

"I was a bit restless," she said, as Leila reached the coffee jar down from the cupboard and put the water on to boil.

"Just couldn't get the man with the worry beads out of my head," she added. "It occurred to me that if he was watching when we bundled Ben into the car, he would have followed us to Dr Schmitt's place. And if he knows he's a friend of yours, they will come looking for us here after finding the car in Konya."

Leila put a comforting arm around Amber's shoulder.

"You really don't need to worry. You're quite safe here," Leila said.

But the expression Amber saw on her lips flickered nervously as Leila turned to pour the coffee. It was a troubled expression. A look that gave Amber every reason to feel worried.

"I suggest you phone your friends and let them know the situation," Leila added, "And you can tell them that Ben's passport will be here this evening."

"I sent Matt a WhatsApp in the night, but he still hasn't read it," Amber said. "But you're right, I'll give him a call."

"Matt," she said, breathless with anticipation when she heard his voice, then realised it was his voicemail recording.

She tried again. This time, the phone was dead. There was no response at all.

"We need to get out there now," Leila snapped. The sudden urgency in her words startled Amber.

Leila strode over to the window that looked onto the street. She scrutinised every corner of the neighbourhood below between the net curtains, then turned and reached for her keys on the coffee table.

"Forget the coffee. We should go now," she said.

The jitters in her voice were not lost on Amber.

# CHAPTER 27

It was a different sky that morning when they drove out of the city. The wind that had blown across the plain two days earlier had now died away. It left dense-white cotton wool clouds to hover in the blue, while sunlight shone on the yellow-brown fields which stretched away into the distance either side of the road. There was a sense of warmth in the air again.

It might have given Amber cause for optimism, had it not been for the mood coming from the driver's seat. Leila simply kept both hands on the wheel all the while, tapping it now and then with her fingers. She said nothing. Amber became ever more fearful of interrupting her concentration, and left her to drive.

Not until the car came to a stop at the ridge overlooking the sinkhole did Leila utter a sound. Clambering from the car, she let out a mumbled string of words. They were not intended for Amber, spoken as they were in Turkish, or more likely Kurdish. She could not be sure, and simply followed on behind, as Leila led her down the narrow path to Ben and Matt's hideaway.

The contrast with the last time they had been here forty-eight hours ago could not have been starker. The chill wind and rain had passed, their place taken now by warm sunshine on their backs. The dust that had been held in place two days earlier by the rain kicked up now behind Leila as she walked. The scene was imbued with a freshness that belied the sense of apprehension Amber felt as they made their way deeper into the sinkhole.

All at once, a curious hooting sound filled the air. Amber almost missed her step and stumbled. Out of the blue, a group of magnificently crested birds rose from scrubland in the crater. They carried their exotic whooping call with them as they flapped around, then descended again and disappeared behind the bushes. Leila stopped, turned and smiled.

"Hoopoes," she said. "Hauke tells me that in Germany, they were once seen as evil birds. But we're in Sufi country now, and for Sufi mystics, the hoopoe is a leader on the path to enlightenment. So that must be a good sign."

Amber had the impression she was trying to lighten the mood. If so, she failed miserably. Amber's sense of apprehension only deepened further, and she was cut to the quick as soon as they came within sight of the cavern. Leila stopped in her tracks.

The door hung from its frame. Suspended like a sheet of iron on a single thread, it looked about to come off its hinges altogether.

"Matt!" Amber cried out. "Ben!"

Not a sound came back in reply. Leila edged up to the doorway, peered cautiously around the corner, and saw at once that the room was abandoned. Empty cans and broken glass littered the floor. One of the makeshift beds had been shattered and lay now in a heap of splintered planks. A smell of propane gas lingered in the air.

"What on earth happened here?"

The distress in Amber's voice was palpable. But Leila remained cool.

"Very few people know about this hideaway. And that's rather concerning."

Leila spoke these words with a calmness that seemed oddly detached, almost disinterested. And yet, it was something much deeper than concern that Amber saw in Leila's eyes. They flickered with fear.

"One thing's for sure," she added, inspecting the damage around her as she wandered the room. "Your man with the worry beads is smarter than we thought."

Leila checked the cooker, kicked the broken glass to one side as she went and picked up the bottles that were still intact.

Amber remained in the doorway, moving from one foot to the other, her hands tightly clasped in nervous distress. Behind her, she caught the desultory sounds of the hoopoe, taunting her, as if signalling a dark message. This was no path of enlightenment they were on.

Against the background noise of the birds, Amber's agitation invaded every tiny cranny in every word she uttered, making each one seem to splinter and crackle when she spoke.

"What do you think they've done with Matt?" she quaked. "And Ben? Where do you think they are?"

"There was obviously a struggle," Leila said, continuing her audit of the damage. "At least they're not here on the floor in pools of blood. So, I guess they've been taken."

She bent down to lift up a large rod from amidst the broken glass. Amber saw at once that it was a baseball bat. Leila weighed the bat in both hands, examining the inscription and the symbols on the barrel.

"And there's no trace of blood here either," Leila said. "But how come they left this behind?"

She tapped the barrel in the palm of her left hand, her eyes fixed on the inscription.

"Makes me think it might be intended as their calling card."

She raised her eyes from the weapon and looked Amber in the eye with a sudden urgency in her expression.

"You know, we should get back to town right away. There are people I need to speak with."

The hoopoes were gone as they traipsed back up the side of the sinkhole. And as if to underline their absence, grey clouds began to gather over the ridge.

The two women hardly spoke on the drive back to town, each too absorbed in their own unease and speculation. Amber suspected that Leila's fears went far beyond the whereabouts of Matt and Ben. She wondered whether it might involve Hauke Schmitt in some way, but she kept her thoughts to herself.

By the time they arrived back in Konya, it was already approaching noon, and the cloud cover was complete. The sun had vanished for the day. Leila drew up outside her apartment block to let Amber out.

"I might be some time," she said, "so be patient. And please stay in the apartment. Don't go anywhere. And don't open the door to anyone."

Amber hesitated.

"If it's all right with you, Leila, I'd sooner come along for the ride."

Leila looked across the car with an expression in her eyes that Amber was unable to fathom. She appeared to be searching for the right words, as if considering the consequences of Amber joining her. Or perhaps silently pleading for her to stay.

"You know, Leila. I've spent much of my life either looking over my shoulder or being asked to wait for others to decide what's best for me. And in the few days I've been here, I find myself subjected to both."

Amber punctuated this last word with a click, as she quietly pulled the car door to.

"So, I'd really prefer to come with you."

With a deep sigh, Leila relented, put the old Renault into gear and drove back the way they had come before turning off into a warren of streets where Amber had never been before. She had the impression Leila was taking a deliberately circuitous route around the centre of the city. They drove a good half an hour before she eventually pulled up and parked the car in a quiet side street that ran into what looked to Amber like a busy traffic hub.

"But you really must stay in the car," Leila insisted when she switched off the engine. "There is no way you can get in without a badge."

There was a snappy nervousness about the way she spoke that aroused Amber's suspicions.

"I might be some time," Leila added, as she opened the glove compartment, grabbed a lanyard with what looked like an ID, and stepped out of the car.

Amber watched her stroll down the street and turn right into the square ahead. She waited until Leila was at the end of the street before getting out of the car herself and hurriedly following after her. She arrived at the corner just in time to see Leila disappear into a building fifty metres along the square.

It was an inconspicuous building, a modern concrete structure, but not so modern that it couldn't do with a lick of paint. Its original yellow had become dull and faded over the years. When Amber reached the steps leading up to the glass doors of the entrance, they gave no clue as to what lay inside. There were no names, nor even a number on the wall.

She approached the entrance in the expectation that the doors would open automatically. They remained firmly closed. It was only then she saw the access control system to the right. This was what Leila meant when she said there was no way in without a badge. But why had she been so furtive, Amber wondered. Surely she could have managed to get them both in on her ID.

She was left with no choice but to wait, until she caught the first drops of rain on her face. She then turned and hurried back to take shelter in Leila's beaten-up old Renault. Amber reached the car just in time to avoid the deluge and pulled the door behind her as the rain began to bucket down, quickly turning the street into a torrent.

She checked her phone. It was a futile gesture. Amber knew there was no chance that Matt would have left a message. But maybe her sister. Maybe Pearl had heard from him or Ben. But there was nothing. No missed call. No message.

She hardly knew Ben, and had only known Matt a few days longer. But still, she felt that a gaping hole had already opened up in her life since their disappearance. The sudden loss of Matt's company in particular upset her in a way she had not expected. And it was only now he was missing that she realised what his absence meant.

Her mind became entangled in speculation and the wildest visions of where Matt and Ben might be at that moment. Plumbing the darkest depths of her imagination, these visions led her inescapably to the fear that she may never see either of them again, when her thoughts were interrupted by a knock on the car window. And the car door opened. It was Leila, looking drenched.

"Well, that's Ben's new passport sorted," she said, breathlessly sweeping her fingers through her wet hair. "All we have to do now is find him, and hope he's fit to make use of it."

Amber did not appreciate Leila's idea of black humour. But her use of the word "we" told her at least that Leila had no intention of leaving her in the lurch. So, she ignored the flippancy, as Leila started the engine and drove them back to her apartment.

"We must head down to the coast," Leila said, closing the door of the apartment behind them. "In all likelihood, your friends have been taken back to Erkan Suleyman."

"Suleyman?"

Leila paused for a moment. Amber had the impression she was gathering her thoughts, as if unsure where to go next. Then with slow deliberation, as though laying out her cards in a game of patience, she said, "When Hauke called me and explained your situation, he spoke of a man called Ahmet and an incriminating diary."

"I have it with me," Amber said, almost in a whisper, with an excited nod of the head.

She opened the blue shoulder bag she carried with her and pulled out the black notebook that Ben had entrusted to her.

"It belonged to a friend of my sister called Susie," she said. "Susie was Ben's sister and Ahmet's wife."

"You speak in the past."

"Susie died."

She sensed herself well up as she placed the notebook on the kitchen table. Then, as Leila took it in her hands, Amber corrected herself.

"She was killed. By Ahmet."

Leila flashed a look of concern across the table, then slowly opened the notebook with what looked to Amber like a wary curiosity in her eyes.

"It's all in there," she said. "How he neglected her, persuaded her to make a will, and slowly poisoned her."

While Leila leafed through the pages of Susie's diary, Amber explained the whole story. From the exotic honey that Ahmet had plied his wife with to the mad honey disease that Hauke Schmitt had described. And the final lethal dose of monkshood that left Susie dead and Ahmet the proud owner of her properties.

Leila was so absorbed by the entries in the diary that Amber was not sure she was listening until she interrupted the telling of the story with, "Kurtboğan we call it, monkshood," then continued leafing through the notebook. She did not once look up.

As the dark clouds outside caused the light to dim, Leila switched on the kitchen light. A good hour passed while she pored over every entry, running her fingers back and forth over the script as she went.

With uncanny timing, her deep absorption in Susie's diary was eventually broken by the shrill ringtone on her phone at the very moment she reached the final entry. When she answered the call, speaking German, Amber assumed it must be the doctor on the other end. She was right.

"That was Hauke," Leila said, putting the phone down on the kitchen table. "There are rumours that Ben and Matt are back in Karakent. Or somewhere nearby."

"What do you mean rumours?"

Leila seemed on edge.

"He said he'd been talking to a man called Hamza…"

"Hamza? Where does he come into it?"

"I don't know," Leila said, but Amber detected a fluster in her voice that made her suspicious.

"Look, we'll drive down there tomorrow and…"

"Tomorrow? We need to go now," Amber insisted. "Why wait until tomorrow?"

Leila rose from the table and put an arm around Amber's shoulder.

"Look outside, Amber," she said. "It's dark already; the roads are treacherous, and neither my old Renault nor my old self is fit for a night drive through the mountains. We will set off early in the morning. Meanwhile, Hauke will keep his ear to the ground and try to establish exactly where Ben and Matt are."

# CHAPTER 28

Amber sucked in the cool, fresh air with relish when they stepped out of the apartment early the next morning. Leila looked around the street cautiously as they made their way to her car. The distant barking of a dog was the only sign of life to intrude upon the street, along with the raw sound of a two-stroke motorbike a block or two away. Approaching the car, Amber was startled to see Leila go down on her knees and scrutinise every cranny in the chassis of the vehicle before unlocking it.

"Just checking," she said. "I doubt they'll be interested in us now they have your friends. But better safe than sorry."

Even after Leila had assured her there were no tracker devices of any kind, these words gave Amber no sense of security as they climbed into the car. She recalled Hauke Schmitt intimating that, when Ahmet finds neither Matt nor Ben have Susie's diary, he and his henchmen would come after her as well. And it did not escape her attention that Leila kept looking nervously in the rear-view mirror as they drove out of the city. It was plain that she felt no more secure than Amber.

They had been on the road for a good two hours, heading out of Konya province towards the mountainous region north of Antalya, when the road took a sharp bend to the right. Steering the car around the corner, Leila turned sharply off onto a dirt track.

The abruptness of the move took Amber by surprise. Her sense of insecurity came racing back.

"What's going on? Where are we going?" she cried.

Leila said nothing, but simply smiled as she continued up the dirt track. It led to a small house overlooking the road. When they reached this building at the end of the track, she stopped the car, climbed out and looked down at the road, which lay a good fifty metres below them.

"Why are we stopping?" Amber asked in a tone fraught with impatience and anxiety.

In her agitation, she failed at first to notice the plump, head-scarfed woman in floral pantaloons who emerged from the house as soon as the car pulled up. The woman greeted Leila with open arms, and they chatted for a minute or two, while Amber stared down on the road below and mulled the purpose of their stopping here.

When she finally turned to join Leila, the woman in the headscarf smiled, muttered a coy 'Welcome' in English, and vanished back into the house.

"We need a bite to eat before we continue," Leila said, guiding Amber onto a terrace which overlooked the road. "Have you tried gözleme?"

Amber shook her head with a look of disbelief in her eyes.

"How can you even think of food?" she said. "We need to get back to Karakent."

"Take it easy, we have to eat," Leila said, then launched into a quick-fire stream of words that sat oddly with her insistence they just sit back and relax.

"And she makes the most delicious pancakes in the whole of Konya province. Okay, they're not really pancakes, they're actually flatbreads. Stuffed with spinach, cheese and herbs. Heavenly. Out of this world. You must try them."

Amber caught the nervous tension in her speech, a sense that the talk of food was merely a distraction to mask some undefined disquiet.

"And the beauty of this place is that we can keep an eye on the road as well," Leila added.

It was only when she said this that it struck Amber how Leila had been surreptitiously watching the road over her shoulder all the time she was speaking. She did not remotely relax until the pancakes arrived.

They were delivered to the table by a girl of around twelve or thirteen who Amber assumed to be the head-scarfed woman's daughter. Leila took one of the pancakes in her hand, rolled it up like a wrap, and took a bite.

"Mmm, delicious," she said, as Amber rolled up her own pancake in imitation of Leila.

"I've been thinking of that memory stick Matt showed me," she added, before taking another bite of her wrap.

Amber looked up from her pancake. She cast a questioning glance at Leila.

"It's such a shame," Leila said. "We could have put it to good use. Now that Matt's been taken…"

"No reason why we couldn't," Amber interrupted with a spark of excitement in her voice at the thought that Leila might have a plan.

"What do you mean?"

Amber put down the pancake, reached for her bag, and dipped a hand deep into a side pocket in the bag. With a look of triumph, she placed the flash drive on the table.

"That's a relief," Leila said. "Do you mind if I look after it?"

She reached over and took the flash drive in her hands before Amber had barely registered what was happening.

"Hey, hang on! No, I mean yes, I do mind. Matt doesn't even know I've got it. If he knew I'd let anyone else have it, he'd be furious."

"I think Matt will have other things on his mind at the moment."

"But I still want it back," Amber insisted, snatching the device from Leila's hand and zipping it firmly up in the side pocket of her bag again.

Leila stared hard into her eyes with a look that Amber was unable to read.

"You should trust me, Amber," she said, as she rose from the table, turned and walked over to the modest house-cum-tavern.

"Where are you going?" Amber called out.

Adrift in the middle of Anatolia with only Leila and her car to rely on, Amber knew she had little choice but to agree; she had to trust her. But the anxiety in her voice betrayed the weakness of any trust she might have.

"I need a toilet before we continue," Leila said, and disappeared through the door of the house. "You should take this opportunity as well. We still have a long drive ahead."

Again, Amber had to agree, and followed her into the house.

By the time she re-emerged from the washroom, Leila had already settled the bill and was sitting at the table. A mountain chill had begun to creep over the terrace in the short time they were there. And as there was no reason to hang around any longer, they got back in the car and resumed the journey.

When eventually Leila's old Renault rounded the last bend of the last mountain and began the descent, they were greeted by an azure seascape that sparkled for them in the afternoon sun as if in welcome.

For Amber, it was a moment of release, almost a sense of homecoming. The freshness of the shimmering water beneath the clear blue sky put her in mind of the coastal views around Brighton, of standing on Beachy Head drinking in the breeze. She wound down the window to breathe the sea air.

After the dark menace that had hovered over Konya for most of the time she was there, the clarity of the air and the sparkling water filled her with a feeling of liberation. But this was not allowed to linger for long. As they motored through the last town on the coast before Karakent, she was taunted by the sight of a familiar office block.

"That's Ahmet's place," Amber said. Her voice quaked with an agitation that bordered on alarm.

Leila slowed down as they passed this last building on the road out of town, three blood-red letters splashed across the front. ASK. For Amber it was a painful reminder of the reason why she was back in Karakent so much sooner than expected. For Leila, it was a place to be scrutinised, and Amber wondered what was going through her mind as they drove slowly past.

"Looks empty," Leila said, and pulled up by the roadside.

Amber watched as Leila got out and walked around to the pavement on her side of the car. In the corner of her eye, she glimpsed the Rottweiler asleep, still tied up outside the office.

"It may seem empty," Amber called through the car window. "But Ahmet's dog is there. And I can see his wife at the desk, too."

"His wife?" Leila gave Amber a look of surprise.

"Didn't I tell you he married again – a young girl – soon after Susie's death?"

"No, you didn't. Do you know her?"

"I met her a few days ago."

"So she'd recognise you," Leila murmured, almost swallowing her words, as she remained lost in her scrutiny of the dog, the building, and Yamur sitting at the desk.

Amber watched as Leila strolled casually up to Ahmet's office. When she crossed the road and stepped onto the pavement, the Rottweiler promptly raised its head and fixed its eyes on the approaching stranger. Only when she stopped at the window and made a show of examining the properties on offer did the dog lose interest and return to its daytime slumber.

After some minutes, Leila turned, smiled to herself, and strolled slowly back to the car. Amber had the impression she was gathering her thoughts with a particular purpose in mind.

"Come on. We must get going," she said, getting back behind

the wheel. And drove on in pensive silence until they were on the outskirts of Karakent.

"Hauke sent me a message to say he will be in the Zeytin restaurant at five for an early dinner. Do you know it?"

Amber nodded. But said nothing. She was still pondering what was going through Leila's mind.

"I've not been here in such a long time," Leila added. "I can't keep up with all the restaurant names."

"No problem. It's down near the marina."

Leila drove her Renault into the central car park overlooking the bay and navigated it into one of only two spaces left. She switched off the engine, took the key from the ignition, and sat in quiet hesitation before turning to Amber.

"The thing about places like this," she said, "is that it's almost impossible to go unnoticed. Someone is going to see you."

"I'm just a tourist, Leila. Few people know me here. And Ahmet has only met me once very briefly."

"You're an attractive young woman, Amber. For a Turkish man, there's no such thing as an encounter too brief to remember."

"Okay, we'll take the back exit over there," Amber said, pointing to the far corner of the car park as she clambered out of the car. "That way we can avoid the main streets."

She led Leila to a small metal gate in the wall of the car park, rusted by the sea air and years of neglect. It gave the appearance of being rarely used, an impression that was enhanced by the lack of any clear path through the grassy wasteland on the other side. The path led down to a steep flight of steps, which brought them into a maze of back streets so narrow they could only possibly admit sunlight for a few minutes of the day. Without the sun to warm them, the gentle breeze that drifted through the lanes carried a disconcerting chill.

The alleyways eventually led them alongside the mosque and out onto the street above the Zeytin, where a familiar melody wafted up the road to greet them: 'Albatross'.

"That old boomer music," Amber muttered to herself, thinking of Matt as she whispered the words.

"Pardon me?"

"Oh nothing. Just talking to myself."

Amber looked down the street to where the music was coming from. That head of white hair was unmistakable. Yusuf was outside his restaurant in animated conversation with an elderly couple. All beaming grin and welcoming arms outstretched in a way that only Yusuf could affect. But his charisma was not enough to entice the elderly couple into his restaurant. They moved on with a wave of the hand, and he watched them stroll on down the hill, arm in arm, to the marina.

"Yusuf!" Leila cried out as she and Amber approached. "You have a new restaurant."

Yusuf span around to greet them.

"Leila! Welcome. You make me so happy," he beamed. "And Amber, also. You know each other."

He emphasised the word 'know' in a way that made a statement of what Amber assumed to be a question.

"Yes," she said, and gave no further explanation.

He wrapped both arms around Leila in a warm embrace, mumbling to her in their local language. And, as if designed to accompany this moment, the background music changed to the gentle rhythms of a Turkish melody.

"The contract on my old restaurant finish," Yusuf explained with a sigh, returning to English when the welcome ritual for Leila was complete. "So I open here with new name."

"A good move," Leila said with a sweeping gesture of her right arm, "You have such a beautiful view over the marina here."

Yusuf gave a humble smile and nodded in agreement.

"How is Belgin?" she asked.

"Belgin is good. Very good. She is in the kitchen."

"I'm glad to hear it," Leila said, and looked about her.

"I see Hauke's already here," she added, when she spotted the

German doctor in his Panama hat seated in the far corner of the restaurant.

He was sipping on a glass of tea, almost obscured from view by the blaze of colour from the pink bougainvillea that trailed up around the pergola. It was the movement of his newspaper flickering in the sunset that had caught her attention.

Amber followed Leila onto the restaurant patio. She was intrigued by the excitement in the Kurdish woman's voice the moment she set eyes on Hauke Schmitt.

"Leila!"

The broad smile on his face was not something Amber imagined she would ever see in this dour and permanently serious doctor. But her sense of surprise was in for a further shock. Putting down his newspaper, he instantly rose from his chair, took Leila in his arms, and gave her a peck on both cheeks. It was a scene that reaffirmed Amber's earlier speculation on the possible intimacy between them.

"Miss Baxter," he said, and gave Amber his hand once he had released Leila from his arms. "Leila has told me all about the events in Konya."

At that moment, Yusuf emerged from behind them and placed two glasses of tea on the table, along with three menus for lunch. He then pulled out the chairs for Amber and Leila. Amber slung her bag over the seat opposite Dr Schmitt and sat down, but Leila refused the gesture.

"You say Belgin is in the kitchen?"

Yusuf nodded; they exchanged some muttered words that Amber was unable to understand, and Leila then disappeared into the kitchen with her own bag slung over her shoulder.

Against the background of gentle music that wafted from a concealed speaker, Amber watched Hauke Schmitt shifting uncomfortably in his seat as they waited for Leila to return. The speaker was suspended from the pergola behind the lush leaves and blossom of the bougainvillea. And the drifting melody that rippled out beneath the foliage sang of the breeze and breaking waves. It put Amber in mind once again of Ben and his yacht.

The German doctor gave the impression he was aware of being watched, until his discomfort eventually prompted him to fold his newspaper, push it to one side and peer over his gold-rim glasses at Amber.

"I have made some discreet enquiries," he said. "It would appear that Ahmet Karadeniz received some guests yesterday evening. Including two Englishmen."

"Matt and Ben?"

"It is likely. But no names were mentioned."

"When you say he received them, you mean at his real estate office?"

Amber's eyes were seized by desperate panic, a look that Leila picked up from afar the instant she re-emerged from the darkness of the kitchen.

"What's happened?" she asked, hanging her bag over the back of her seat.

As the bag swung into place, Amber saw a sliver of light gleaming from inside. Looking closer, she saw what looked like the blade of Leila's fearsome kitchen knife. But why would she bring a kitchen knife with her? Amber wondered.

"I was telling Miss Baxter that Karadeniz received some guests yesterday," Hauke Schmitt said. "Probably her friends."

"At his office," Amber added, putting her thoughts around the knife to one side. There was desperation in her voice. "So, we just drove right past them!"

"That is not what I meant to say, Miss Baxter," he corrected her. "The information I have is that they were taken to Erkan Suleyman. Exactly where I don't know."

Leila rested a hand of comfort on Amber's arm. But Dr Schmitt's last words did nothing to calm her fears.

"But now we know they're here, surely the police can help?" Amber insisted.

"As I've already explained," Leila said, "the most you're likely to get from the police is a parking fine. And the Jandarma here are in the pocket of Erkan Suleyman. So, contacting them is only going to land you in trouble."

The steely earnestness in her voice was new to Amber. It showed within the space of a few minutes a completely different side to Leila. This easy-going Kurdish companion had become a different person in the presence of Hauke Schmitt. It gave Amber no comfort. Only a deep sense of anguish.

"So, what do we do? Am I supposed to just sit here, enjoy the view over lunch and a cool glass of wine?"

Hauke Schmitt lowered his gold-rim glasses and peered over them at Amber. She was close to tears. But he offered no words of encouragement. Simply fidgeted with the newspaper at his side, then picked up the menu and studied it in embarrassed silence. Amber felt driven to despair by the hush that descended on her table. Like a solitary outsider mocked by the chatter and the clatter of cutlery on the tables all around.

"Look," she persisted. "All he wants is Susie's diary. Which I have. So, why don't we just hand it over?"

"Then everyone will be happy," she added when her words met with further silence.

"Ben won't," Leila said. "He wants justice for his sister. And will die in his vain attempt to get it. Like he almost did last time. Almost taking Matt with him.

"And that's the problem," she added. "From what I hear, Ben is like a bull in a china shop."

"His friend Matthew is not much better," Dr Schmitt chipped in.

Amber was visibly wounded by this remark. Leila cast a disapproving look at Hauke Schmitt, unaware of the mutual antipathy between the two men. The doctor raised his hands in an unspoken show of apology.

"Aside from the diary, though," Leila said, "Erkan Suleyman will be after something else. From what Matt told me about how he came into possession of that flash drive and was then questioned by the Jandarma, I'm pretty sure Erkan knows Matt has some compromising stuff on him. So, it's not only about the diary.

"But Hauke's not entirely wrong," Leila added, turning to Amber. "In Turkey, where social media channels like YouTube and Instagram – or even Wikipedia – are constantly monitored by the government, there are subtler ways of approaching a problem like this. So, I think we can find a way to get a kind of justice for Ben's sister."

"What do you mean?"

"I'm thinking of that memory stick."

There was a fire in Leila's eyes as she spoke. It drew a look of intense curiosity from Hauke Schmitt. Amber could not miss the way his ears pricked up. He shot an inquisitive glance at Leila, but she said nothing more. And when he switched his glance to Amber, she offered only a blank expression.

A pregnant pause descended on the table as each one waited for the other to speak. It was eventually the German doctor, unable to contain his frustration any longer, who broke the silence.

"Well, shall we order then?" he said.

He cast a questioning look across the table at Amber as if to ask whether she was ready. She stared back at him aghast, then at Leila, in speechless disbelief. When at last she found her voice, the words came out in a pitch of such frenzy they gave the impression of being strung together in a single outstretched balloon of a word.

"Matt and Ben are in terrible danger just down the road how can you even think of food?"

"All to his time, Miss Baxter," Hauke Schmitt said in a mangled kind of English that gave Amber the sense he was more flustered beneath that cool exterior than he cared to admit.

"We need nourishment if we are to plan our next move with proper care," Leila said.

Amber felt this was an effort to save her doctor friend's

embarrassment more than it was to explain the need for lunch. Yet she saw no point in resisting. So, when Yusuf came to take their orders, she reluctantly went with the flow and opted for a quick light lunch.

"Lahmacun for me – with some of your spicy Turkish rocket leaves," she said, and fondly assumed that Leila and Hauke Schmitt would not linger too long over their own chosen dishes.

How wrong she was. Her hopes were immediately dashed when they both ordered a feast of hummus, aubergine dip and other mezes, along with a stuffed aubergine main and a Turkish salad. As soon as Yusuf had taken their orders, they chatted to each other in a mixture of German and Turkish. Now and then, Hauke Schmitt would glance over at Amber as they talked – and smile. An enigmatic smile that seemed to be born more of scepticism than amusement.

What are they saying? Amber wondered. Why the need to shut me out with words I can't possibly comprehend? Why the secrecy? What are they hiding?

Amber gazed out over the marina to the sea beyond, and to the islands offshore where Ben's yacht had been scuppered. There was no evidence of it there any longer. And the absence of the boat only served to heighten her irritation, acutely aware as she was that Ben and Matt were in mortal danger at that very moment, while her companions gossiped over lunch.

She sat for a good five minutes in this isolation, pensive and pondering the reasons for her exclusion, until Yusuf brought the mezes in a display that filled almost the whole table. From the look on their faces, Amber could see it had the mouths of both Leila and Hauke Schmitt watering.

The German doctor turned to Amber and spoke in English. The need for secrecy had now plainly passed.

"Do you have any idea of the chequered history this vegetable has had?" he said, as he dipped his bread in the smoked aubergine and held it up for inspection.

"Would you like to try some?" he asked, holding the dipped

bread temptingly before Amber with a curious smile on his lips and a slightly disturbing look in his eyes.

She declined with a shake of the head. And her refusal was greeted with an expression of disbelief on Hauke Schmitt's face.

"If you're worried about those tales that Avicenna thought the aubergine to be poisonous," he declared in his pompous manner, "there is really no cause for concern."

He paused as he popped the bread with the dip into his mouth and let a look of pure pleasure spread from ear to ear.

"In fact, it was Renaissance man who called it 'mala insana' – the 'mad apple'," he added. "Nothing to do with the Persians at all."

After his earlier stories about mad honey disease and the woman killer in Ancient Rome, it seemed to Amber that he was uncomfortably familiar with poisonous foods. His digression into ancient botany served only to add a thick layer of disquiet to her irritation, which was heightened all the more when Dr Schmitt's main course appeared.

"İmam Bayıldı," he proclaimed, both hands outstretched as if in welcome to the dish that Yusuf laid before him.

"In case you're wondering, Miss Baxter," he said, leaning towards Amber with an inscrutable expression behind his gold-rim glasses, "that means 'the priest fainted'. It is widely assumed this is because the imam found it so delicious. But I have a different theory, which has more to do with Renaissance man."

Amber had the impression he was deliberately trying to unsettle her for some reason. And to add to her frustration, Yusuf brought more food to the table just as she imagined that Leila and the German doctor had had their fill.

"Sütlaç!" Leila cried with delight. "Yusuf, you're a gem."

"On the house," Yusuf said with his trademark smile. "I know how much you like it."

"Rice pudding," Leila said, turning to Amber. "Would you like to try some?"

Amber shook her head as much in irritation as in refusal.

"This is no ordinary rice pudding, Miss Baxter," said the German doctor in a tone that sounded to her like a put-down.

"They make it with mastic," he added, now back in his teacherly mode. "A resin from Pistacia lentiscus. Second only to the resin from the turpentine tree, according to Pliny. But on that I have to disagree with the great man. Mastic is the finest."

This was the pretentious kind of talk that so infuriated Matt. And only maddened Amber all the more, especially when Leila seemed so stubbornly oblivious of her frustration.

"Just like old times, isn't it?" Leila said, exchanging flirty looks with Hauke Schmitt.

"When we've finished here," Leila said, "I suggest we meet up at the timeless Utopia bar. If only to complete the nostalgia."

"Meet up?" Amber said, raising her voice. "What do you mean? I thought we were supposed to be figuring out what to do about Matt and Ben."

"Be patient, Amber. There's something I must do first," Leila said, as she rose from the table and made to leave.

As Leila spoke these words, the music was drowned out by the sound of the call to prayer from the mosque up the road. It instantly blasted the alien music from the airwaves. Yet came with a splurge of acoustic feedback to reveal the lie that this was not a live call to prayer, but a duff recording.

The comical effect was not lost on Hauke Schmitt and Leila. They both chuckled over their shared appreciation of the mishap.

But for Amber, the comedy of the moment carried an air of foreboding. Like the creepy menace of a clown lurking in the background.

# CHAPTER 29

Hauke Schmitt shifted awkwardly in his chair when Yusuf brought coffee to the table. And said nothing. He did not even acknowledge the restaurateur, but simply stared at the coffee. This was not like the correct German doctor that Amber had come to know. She had the impression he was discomfited, irritated perhaps by Leila's departure on some undisclosed mission before the coffee arrived.

"Have you seen my sister since we left? Or her husband Hamza?" she asked, when eventually she felt compelled to break the silence.

She waited for what seemed like forever to get a response, her fingers playing with the glass of water that stood beside the coffee cup.

"No, why do you ask?" he said at last.

The question came with a curious sideways glance that gave Amber the feeling he knew something. And was intent on hiding it.

"I was just wondering," she said, her fingers still toying with the rim of the glass. "I haven't heard from her since we left. And it's just not like her."

"There is sure to be a simple explanation," he said, slipping into his mouth a small cube of the Turkish delight that came with the coffee.

"Your sister was here this morning," Yusuf said.

"This morning?" Amber looked up, startled by Yusuf's voice. She had no idea he was still standing by their table, listening in on the conversation.

"She told me that she has meeting with Russian man this afternoon."

"Russian?" Hauke Schmitt said.

His face blanched a peculiar kind of white, enhancing the hint of horror and foreboding that Amber detected in his voice. She was reminded of the conversation in Konya: a Russophobe was how Leila described the German doctor.

"New customer," Yusuf explained. "He looks for land to build hotel."

"Russians building here in Karakent? Are you serious?"

Yusuf turned to Amber, dismay and incomprehension written across his face. He was visibly shocked by the horror in Dr Schmitt's voice.

"Russians bring only gloom. Gloom and misery," Hauke Schmitt hissed with an angry defiance that Amber would never have expected to hear from the scrupulous German doctor.

"And death," he said, riveting her attention with the unexpected fury of his words. There was a hint of saliva in the corners of his mouth as he murmured to himself in his native German: "*Der Tod ist ein Meister aus Russland.*"

Removing his gold-rim glasses, he fixed Amber with a look that sent a shiver down her spine. She shuddered, and the touch of the glass in her fingers turned cold as ice. She gripped the rim to take a sip of water. But her nerves conspired against her. As she picked up the glass, her hand caught the handle of the cup beside it and sent the coffee shooting across the table. The dark brown liquid spread like a river in flood, flowing rapidly in the direction of Hauke Schmitt and dripping into the crotch of his linen trousers.

"Oh my God, I'm so sorry!" Amber cried.

The German doctor sat in shock, staring down at the instant stain in the linen, but said nothing. However, the exasperation and anger in his eyes was not lost on Amber. She reached into her handbag for some tissues. Without a word, he took a handful, mopped the stain as best he could and wiped the drips from the edge of the table, before throwing the tissues into the dark brown lake to soak up what remained of the coffee.

It was when Amber went to put the unused tissues back into her bag that she saw the yawning gap, the inside pocket that was unzipped. It gaped wide open like a mouth lost for words. She plunged a hand into the pocket, feeling around for anything she could find. She found nothing. The flash drive was gone.

"Leila!" she cried.

Hauke Schmitt shot a look of dazed surprise at Amber as he continued struggling to find a comfortable position in his damp trousers.

But she had no time for his discomfort now. She was retracing the events of the day in her mind. Leila must have taken the flash drive during the toilet break at the pancake house, she told herself. Only now did she realise the significance of Leila's smile outside Ahmet's office, and the words she muttered when she saw Yamur at her desk: "So she would recognise you."

Amber slung the handbag over her shoulder and leapt up from her chair.

"I'm sorry, Dr Schmitt. I must go," she said, and left a visibly bemused Hauke Schmitt still struggling with the damp patch in his crotch.

Turning to give him an apologetic wave as she left the restaurant, she saw the doctor's mouth hanging slightly open in his bewilderment. Much as she wanted to explain, she had no time. She had to catch up with Leila, and hastened up the hill, past the mosque, to the taxi rank across the road from Osman's restaurant.

She was a good ten minutes behind Leila and pressed the driver to get her there as quickly as possible. A broad grin crossed his face in response. He was clearly more than happy to oblige. They careered around the twists and turns along the coast at such speed that Amber began to fear they might run off the road into the sea. So, although the gleam of those familiar blood-red letters ASK in the dark seemed especially sinister that evening, she felt a sense of relief when eventually they came into view.

But what shocked her when the taxi rolled up in front of the building and she climbed out of the car was not that Leila was already there, it was that Yusuf's daughter, Belgin, was with her. The two of them were taunting the Rottweiler under the yellow light of the street lamp outside Ahmet's office.

So focused were they on provoking the dog that Leila failed to see Amber getting out of the taxi. She was not aware of her presence until Amber strode up to them and grabbed the stick they were using to rile the creature from Leila's hands. The chained beast snarled and snapped at his tormentors.

"Amber!" Leila cried in shock when she turned to see who it was that had commandeered her stick. And with her cry came a fierce growl from the dog.

"What the hell are you doing, Leila?" Amber yelled.

But her shrieking voice was drowned out by the beast as it rattled off a full-throated volley of ferocious barking at all three of them. Straining to fight off its tormentors, the animal tugged so fiercely at the chain that Amber feared it would soon come off the wall. The flaking plaster around the wall anchor showed hints of movement as the dog tugged ever harder on its fetters.

Like artillery fire, the barks and howls of the Rottweiler echoed around the quiet town. And brought Ahmet's wife, Yamur, out onto the street. Amber saw the woman instantly, first panic, then anger in her eyes, as she ran over to them screaming.

She yelled a stream of what Amber assumed to be abuse at the three of them, as she tried pushing them away. Belgin lost her balance in the face of Yamur's onslaught and fell to the ground, whereupon Ahmet's wife turned her fury on Amber. She pushed and shoved and screamed in Amber's face. As Amber drew back from the assault, she caught a brief glimpse of Leila creeping off the battlefield and sneaking into the office from which Yamur had just emerged.

With one girl down, another AWOL and the Rottweiler's owner in support, the ferocity of the dog's bark slowly softened into an ugly snarl. But Ahmet's wife would not let up. She continued to shout incessantly in Amber's face – so close she could feel the spray of spittle in her eyes – until Amber attempted to step out of Yamur's range. But the woman was unrelenting. She grabbed at her hair as Amber tried to move away. And it was at this moment that a new light pierced through the fury in Yamur's eyes. It was the light of recognition.

Ahmet's wife let go and stepped back, as if confused, unsure what she should do next. Hesitating for a second, she took her mobile phone from the pocket of her jacket, held it to her ear and began babbling an incomprehensible stream of words into the device. By now, Belgin had picked herself up again and made herself scarce.

Convinced that Yamur was speaking to Ahmet, telling him that Matt's 'wife' was here tormenting their dog, Amber snatched the phone out of her hands. Yamur shrieked with rage at this invasion and lunged forward in a bid to grab it back. It was a forlorn effort. Amber stepped nimbly out of her way, causing her to stumble.

As Yamur struggled to keep her balance, Amber caught sight of Leila reappearing from the office. Glancing across at the unfolding conflict with a look of satisfaction on her face, she headed back to her old Renault. It was parked on the other side of the road, and Amber could see now that Belgin was sitting in the passenger seat. With Yamur still visibly dazed by the confrontation and the Rottweiler left to growl from the sidelines, Amber turned tail and followed Leila to the car.

"Get in," said Leila, holding the door open as she chuckled to herself. Belgin joined in the laughter.

As soon as Amber had slipped into the back seat, Leila started the engine and drove off to leave the dwindling figure of Yamur in her rear-view mirror, gesticulating from the pavement under the yellow light of the street lamp.

"What are you playing at, Leila?"

"What do you mean?" the Kurdish woman said, looking in the mirror at Amber while Belgin still chuckled to herself in the front.

"You took Matt's memory stick."

"Relax."

Leila smiled into the mirror and stretched her right arm back as best she could towards Amber, holding the flash drive between her fingers.

"But I would destroy it now if I were you," she added, when Amber took the device in her hand. "It's served its purpose."

There was a smug self-assurance about Leila's manner that irritated Amber.

"Shall I destroy this as well?"

"What's that?" Leila asked, glancing down at the palm of Amber's hand reaching forward.

"That crazy woman's phone," Amber said.

A broad grin spread the breadth of Leila's face. It filled the entire rear-view mirror.

"Ahmet's wife?" Leila said. "That's perfect. You're getting the hang of this game."

Whatever she meant by this remark, Amber found it slightly patronising – all the more so when she added, "If you let Belgin have it, she'll put it to good use."

Feeling resentful of the way Leila had taken to shutting her out, Amber hesitated for a moment.

"It'll provide the perfect finishing touch," Leila said when she saw the hesitation on Amber's face in the mirror, then exchanged a few words with Belgin.

Yusuf's daughter nodded, turned and stretched an arm back between the front seats. Amber stared down into the waiting hand and sighed, before finally dropping the phone into the palm of Belgin's hand.

It was a bright moon that reflected off the sea as they motored back along the coast to Karakent in silence. Amber wanted so desperately to see in this a good omen.

# CHAPTER 30

Matt had lost all sense of time when eventually the door opened. The sound of footsteps, leather soles on a wooden floor, echoed in the emptiness of the room as they entered. Even before the hoods were lifted from their heads, Matt had a good idea where they were. It was the sweet woody fragrance in the air, the smell of cedar wood, that gave the game away. They were somewhere in the Malibu-style villa that he had been shown around by Ahmet Karadeniz.

The room itself was unfamiliar. The lack of furnishing revealed nothing more about the four walls he and Ben were held in than a statement that they were not there for relaxation. Only the air-con on the wall behind them gave any clue that it was originally built for comfort. And the unease that came with this message was underlined by the mirrored aviator sunglasses staring down at Matt and Ben, each shackled to a chair.

"Welcome!"

There was a reptilian quality in the grin on Ahmet's lips as he spoke, extending his arms in a false kind of welcome that invested the word with an undercurrent of evil.

"So, Ben," he continued, pulling up the only other chair in the room and settling into it opposite his two captives. "The last time we saw each other, I recall that you spoke of my wife's old diary. Now, I have no knowledge of this, but if she kept a diary, as you say, then I want to see it."

Ben yanked at his shackles in reply. He was in no mood for conversation. Ahmet pulled a pack of Marlboro from the pocket of his tight-fitting jacket, placed one pensively between those lizard-like lips, and let a silent tension build in the room as he puffed on his cigarette. He was over halfway to the stub before he spoke again.

"Well, I'm sure you will agree that all the property of my first wife – and that includes her diary – must now fall to me," he said. The words were met only with a snarl from Ben.

"This is written in the will we signed before she died," Ahmet added.

His hands and feet firmly shackled, Ben could only sit and suffer the rage boiling inside him. The veins on his forehead bulged in a bitter ferment of anger that would not be quenched until Ahmet was destroyed. But he was powerless to do anything about it.

"You won't get away with this, Karadeniz," Ben growled in desperation.

Ahmet smiled.

"I think you'll find I will," he said. "And if you let me have that diary, you and your friend here will also get away unharmed."

Matt glanced at his old friend with a nervous look in his eyes. It was a look which could tip into fear at any moment. He knew this, and he could see in Ben's expression that his old friend knew it too. But Ben was in no mood to throw in the towel. He fixed Ahmet with a stare of pure contempt.

"It's up to you, of course," Ahmet said.

He rose from his chair and ambled towards the door with the rolling gait of the little fat man that he had become since he married Ben's sister. With his hand on the door, he paused for a moment, then turned and added with a sneer on his lips, "I will leave you for a moment so that you can discuss it between you. If you are still undecided when I return, my assistants will be happy to help you reach a decision. I think you will agree they can be very persuasive."

Ahmet closed the door behind him. Ben let out a sneering cackle when he heard the sound of a key turning in the lock.

"Why lock us in, Ahmet?" he yelled. "Where the fuck do you think we're going, chained up like this?

"So, how do you reckon you're going to get us out of this one?" he grunted, turning to Matt on his right, and tugged on his shackles.

"By letting him have what he wants maybe?"

The bitter irony in Matt's words went right over Ben's head.

"After we've come this far?" He raised his voice in disbelief. "You've got to be joking. We don't even have the diary to give him, anyway."

"But we know who does. And she's seen what these people are capable of; she knows what'll happen if he doesn't get what he wants."

"And Peggy? What about my sister? What fucking satisfaction does she get if we give up the only evidence we have against him?"

"That's just illogical bullshit, Ben. And you know it. You weren't too bothered about evidence before, when you just wanted to kill the bastard. Face it, the only satisfaction you're talking about here is yours, not your sister's. And if we don't let him have the diary, we're totally screwed anyway and gonna wind up seriously dead."

"Oh, fuck your logic," Ben snarled.

Only the sound of the chains against the metal chair legs was left to echo from the walls as he yanked at his shackles in frustration.

Sitting side by side, shackled in their cell, the two of them went quiet. Matt could not escape the sound of his friend's rapid breathing. And the twitching of the legs in the corner of his eye.

For Matt, there was no question. Why get themselves killed over a diary? Could Amber even use it to bring down Ahmet if they were dead? There was no logical reason for holding on to it. But he knew that Ben was on a different track altogether. He was driven by the obsession of revenge. And was ready to tough it out.

It was a good hour before they heard the clatter of a key in the lock. Ahmet ambled back into the room, leaving the door open behind him, and positioned himself threateningly in front of Matt and Ben. Yet, with stubby hands on hips and little fat legs splayed in a wannabe power pose, it was a posture that Matt found more comical than menacing.

He looked up into the mirrored shades and pre-empted any threats from Ahmet with a brazen fabrication.

"Look, we don't even have the bloody diary. It was handed over to the Jandarma," he said, and paused to let the message sink in, before adding: "After a copy was sent to the British police."

For a brief moment, Matt saw a quiver of uncertainty on his captor's lips. Ahmet said nothing as that tremor of concern settled down and slowly spread into a broad reptilian grin of amusement.

"Ha, that is a lie. It is not possible," he snapped.

The jingle of a phone peppered Ahmet's words as he spoke. He took the phone from his pocket, eyed the number, then turned and left the room. Matt caught the sound of his voice on the other side of the door. And while the conversation was way beyond the grasp of both Matt and Ben, it became clear who he was speaking to when they heard him repeatedly call the name Yamur, Yamur.

There was an agitation in his tone that was unmistakable in the brief conversation, which was followed by a long silence. Just as Matt was expecting the Turk to reappear at any moment, Ahmet's voice made itself heard again. It was more tempered in this second call, and Matt had the feeling he was talking to someone else altogether. The call lasted less than a minute. When it finished, Ahmet almost instantly reappeared in the doorway.

"So, Ben, where were we?" he said, with a smirk on his lips. "Oh yes, my wife's diary."

Whenever anyone spoke of Ben's sister as Ahmet's wife, Ben visibly seethed. And when the Turk spoke those words, Matt sensed his old friend quaking with such rage that he seemed on the point of boiling over altogether. Clearly so blinded by his anger, he appeared not to see the new arrivals. Matt recognised the two men at once. Suleyman's lackeys. They followed Ahmet into the room, quietly closing the door behind them, as he walked up to Matt and Ben to pose again with his fat legs splayed before them in his comical demonstration of power.

Matt's heartbeat quickened to a rate he'd not known since the day he went white-water rafting with Ben and almost died. It was not Ahmet's power pose that had his pulse racing, but the new arrivals behind him that did it for Matt. And the crushing blow of the baseball bat that finally did it for Ben.

Constrained by his shackles and unable even to double up with pain, he could only scream. Matt winced at the sound.

Ahmet smirked as another blow went for Ben's left shin. The chair leg took most of the force, but together with the savage pain already punishing Ben's gut, it was enough to turn Ahmet's smirk to a chuckle.

"Fuck!" Matt cried in horror. "Stop this fucking crap! You'll get nothing out of Ben. He'd sooner die for the memory of his sister than help you out."

Ahmet peered down through his aviator shades at Matt and let a broad smile spread across his plump face. The expression in his eyes was lost through the mirrored sunglasses, but Matt sensed that their tormentor had detected weakness in his words. Ahmet dipped his head to the side, as if giving his goons the nod. And in the same instant, a crushing blow to the solar plexus brought a shriek of pain from Matt.

Through the moaning, spluttering noises that poured from Matt's mouth, Ahmet appeared to catch another sound altogether, interrupting his pleasure at the torment heaped upon his guests. He raised his hand, cocked his head to listen out, and his gorillas froze like statues.

Ahmet turned, stepped back towards the door, eased it open just enough to peer through the crack, and left the room. His sidekicks remained stock still and continued to hover threateningly over their captives. Yet there was something about the menace and Ahmet's hurried exit that gave Matt the feeling none of these three were at ease in their role. He wondered if the interruption was down to an unwanted intruder. Perhaps a passing gendarme. Or maybe Erkan Suleyman himself.

Nursing their pain for what seemed like forever, Matt and Ben could only sit and wait, shackled in their chairs, until Ahmet returned to enjoy his sport. When at last he hurried back into the room on his chubby little legs, he headed straight for Matt, taking a baseball bat of his own into his hands as he came.

Closing the door firmly behind him, Ahmet swung the bat around in his right hand as he strode up to Matt, still slumped in pain from the blow to his solar plexus.

"So, where were we?" Ahmet said, shoving the barrel of the bat beneath Matt's chin and using it to lift his head. He leaned forward to enjoy the tortured expression in Matt's eyes.

"Of course, my wife's diary," he said. "But to hell with that. We both know you have some information that is much more interesting."

Matt understood at once what Ahmet meant. He had no time even to consider how the Turk might have got wind of the flash drive in the ticket pocket of his jeans, as the crushing impact demolished any room for speculation. He felt the pain even before the baseball bat ploughed its way down into his groin.

"And you're going to tell me where it is," Ahmet growled.

# CHAPTER 31

As soon as the car pulled up in the centre of town, Belgin clambered out and disappeared into the night, without a word. Leila and Amber strolled on down to the Utopia to meet Hauke Schmitt. From a distance, the place appeared empty. Only the vague figure of Thomas Moore was to be seen busying himself in the gloom of the bar. They failed to see the German doctor, still in his Panama hat and concealed by the shadows of the terrace, until he held up an arm and waved.

Impeccably polite as ever, he stood up to greet Leila and Amber, pulling out a chair for each of them. After leaving him drenched in coffee, Amber was surprised and embarrassed by the generosity of his welcome.

"A very good evening to you ladies," came the voice of Thomas Moore. "What will it be?"

"White wine for me please," said Amber.

"And for me," Leila said.

As he returned to the bar with their orders, Amber was struck by how unusually quiet it was that evening. None of Tom Moore's customary music from the seventies blasting out from the bar. The mood of the place was infused instead with the sounds of a clarinet weaving a gypsy-like melody through the clear evening air. But not from the bar. The music floated weightlessly down the street from Osman's restaurant. It reminded her all too painfully of the brief moments she had spent with Matt in the short time she had been here. And of the perilous situation he must now find himself in. She fell silent with these thoughts while they waited for their order and Hauke Schmitt savoured his çay.

Amber felt the beginnings of a breeze waft up from the sea and pulled her cardigan around her shoulders. Awakened by the sudden chill and the quiet when the sound of the clarinet died away on the breeze, she grew impatient to break the silence – to say anything that would put those thoughts to the back of her mind.

"Leila, didn't you say that you and Dr Schmitt once worked together?"

"Mm, yes," Leila said with a sceptical nod of the head and cast a sideways glance at Hauke Schmitt.

"But you never actually said what you did."

Amber was in no mood for small talk, but she was ready to seize on any opportunity for distraction from the plight of Matt and Ben. And she was genuinely intrigued by the shared history of Leila and Dr Schmitt. But he looked discomfited by her question. Holding onto the brim of his Panama hat as the breeze morphed into a stiff gust, he threw a suspicious glance in her direction.

At that moment, Tom Moore appeared, placed the glasses of wine on the table with a discreet but cheery "Enjoy" and returned to the bar.

"I worked in a government department for agriculture," Leila said at last, evading a direct answer to Amber's question.

As she spoke, the bright moon vanished behind a dark cloud that had swept in over the sea unnoticed. Amber shivered, slipped her arms into the sleeves of her cardigan and folded them across her chest. The cold glance she caught from Hauke Schmitt on the other side of the table told her it was pointless to pursue her prying interest any further. The curiosity was anyway too shallow to compete with her deep concern over the whereabouts of Matt and Ben.

But it was not the retreat from her line of questioning that cancelled out the expression in the doctor's eyes. It was the slap on his shoulder, causing him to leap abruptly to his feet.

"Um Gottes Willen!" he screamed, and sent his chair crashing to the floor behind him.

Startled by the sudden shriek from this otherwise softly spoken German, Amber looked up to find the unexpected sight of Luc Bennett at the table. He was standing just to the side of a hapless Hauke Schmitt, whose arms were extended in dismay, and eyes fixed on his linen suit. It was not the same suit that she had spilled her coffee on; he had plainly changed while they were at Ahmet's place.

"I'm so sorry Josef!" said the Welshman.

The amusement in his eyes betrayed the insincerity, but it was lost on Hauke Schmitt. Luc offered him a tissue to wipe the tea off his suit.

"That is not helping," the German doctor grumbled. "This is tea. Black tea. I will have to get the whole suit cleaned."

"I really am sorry," Luc repeated.

Hauke Schmitt said nothing more. He quietly picked up his chair and threw the tissue into the ashtray in a cantankerous gesture that told Luc his apology had been noted, but not accepted.

"Hello Amber," Luc said, pulling up a chair. "Have you heard from Matt?"

There was an air of awkwardness about his manner that mystified Amber. She said nothing, simply glanced across the table at Hauke Schmitt, who was still consumed by irritation. Luc had got the German doctor's hackles up.

"What do you want, Bennett?" he snapped.

It was Luc's response that caused Amber's ears to prick up.

"I had a strange call from Matt a couple of days ago," he said.

"What?" Amber flashed an expression of shock across the table. "He called you?"

"He seemed a bit peculiar." Luc nodded. "But then the signal was weak and I couldn't hear him too well."

"Why? What did he say?"

Amber was baffled. A couple of days ago was when they had left Matt and Ben in the bowels of the sinkhole on the Konya Plain. Was it the phone call that gave away their location? She wondered.

"Why did he call you?"

"He wanted to know if I knew someone called Leila," Luc said at last, and peered at Hauke Schmitt as he spoke, waiting for a reaction.

Amber caught a glimmer of movement in the eyes behind those gold-rim glasses, saw the hint of a smile on the German doctor's lips and a look of amusement in Leila's eyes. But neither of them said a word. And the smile on Hauke Schmitt's face slowly morphed into something more sinister. To Amber, it had the look of a sneering scowl as he braced himself to respond.

"Leila," he said at last, "allow me to introduce you to Mr Bennett."

"Oh," Leila said with a look of surprise on her face, and gave him her hand. "So, you're Luc Bennett. Hauke has told me all about you."

"I bet he has," Luc said, reciprocating with a handshake and an irony in his voice to match her tone of surprise. "And all very flattering, I'm sure."

The cheerful expression on Leila's lips faded into a look of self-conscious discomfort. But any embarrassment was saved by the frustration of Amber, who glared first at Hauke Schmitt, then at Leila, when Tom Moore appeared at the table to take Luc's order.

"I'm sorry," she cried, "but when are we going to stop sitting around here drinking and actually do something?"

"What is it Amber? What's going on?"

The soft musicality of Luc Bennett's words initially conveyed a sense of concern for Amber. Yet it conflicted with the prying tone of his next question. For her, it was almost as if he had a pretty good idea what was going on and was simply looking for confirmation. He made such a show of astonishment that she felt sure he was feigning ignorance as to what was happening. This only added fuel to her impatience.

Leila rested a hand on Amber's right arm. "You don't need to worry, Amber. It's all settled."

"What do you mean settled?" Amber said.

"Yes, Leila," Luc chipped in. "What *do* you mean?"

Amber glanced at the Welshman to see his face turn a curious pale at Leila's words. His feigned confusion now looked disconcertingly genuine. She wondered what was going through his mind when Luc turned to the German doctor.

"Do you know what they're talking about, Josef?"

Hauke Schmitt nodded gently with a look of smug satisfaction on his face. It was as if he was relishing the moment when he finally got one over on his old Cold War nemesis.

"As I think you also know, Bennett."

Luc Bennett raised both hands with a shrug of the shoulders in a gesture of innocence. The distrust and contempt in Hauke Schmitt's eyes were not lost on Amber.

"You may not know the precise details, and I confess that neither do I," he said, before adding cryptically, "but I know you understand the motion of the wheels. It is only the journey's end that remains unclear. No doubt Leila can enlighten us."

He turned to Leila. She simply smiled.

# CHAPTER 32

Holding the barrel of the baseball bat in both hands, Ahmet thrust it hard against Matt's throat. The agony in his groin still dug deep into the gut. From under the smothering screen of pain, Matt caught a fleeting glimpse of Ahmet's lips in motion. But the only words he heard spitting from his mouth were "… Rekan", over and over, as he felt the hyoid bone press hard against the base of his tongue. It was only when Ahmet realised Matt was unable to speak that he released the pressure. Matt spluttered and choked for air. And in the corner of his eye saw the baseball bat come crashing down. He rocked his chair to the side in a vain attempt to avoid the worst of the blow, but still felt a searing pain when the bat hit his shoulder.

He caught the sound of Suleyman's pigs snorting with relish when they heard what they doubtless thought was the cracking of a bone. It was the metal frame of Matt's chair as it hit the floor. Fired up by the action, they hoisted the chair back up to let Ahmet take another swing, this time at Matt's arm.

But the way Ahmet slid a hand into his pocket instead, smiling down at him with a look of pure evil on his face, Matt saw at once that he had something else in mind. And when that hand re-emerged from the Turk's pocket, he knew exactly what it was. He froze. Even the pain from the beating he had taken was benumbed, as Ahmet flicked open the plastic bag he was holding.

"Are you a diver?" he said.

Despite the numbness of his mind, Matt was acutely aware of the baffled expression on his face as he looked into Ahmet's ugly scowl. His heart raced nineteen to the dozen. But he said nothing.

"Do you dive?" Ahmet repeated.

Still no response came from Matt.

"I have heard that some divers can hold their breath for five or ten minutes," Ahmet said, opening out the mouth of the plastic bag as he walked slowly around Matt's chair.

"But people with no experience of water can quickly…"

Ahmet's last words were lost on Matt as the bag was pulled tight over his head and twisted around his neck, blocking out the slightest trace of any air.

Unable to move and seized by panic, he struggled to catch what breath he could, and fell deeper into his pit of terror as the bag tightened its grip on his face. Every ounce of air had been shut down. He was swallowing plastic. Images of his near-drowning when he was thrown from Ben's yacht flashed through his mind, his lungs felt fit to burst. His head, hot with sweat, began reeling – until he lost all sensation and everything went black.

It was the sensation of cool air that brought Matt back after Ahmet whipped off the bag. He spluttered with relief, felt his lungs fill with oxygen, then the pressure of a heavy hand that clasped his head and forced it back. Ahmet stood beside him, holding the plastic bag in his hand.

"You have a memory stick," he growled. "From a man called Rekan. Kurdish."

Matt was still in recovery mode, yet still alert enough to wonder how Ahmet could possibly know this.

"So where is it?" Ahmet insisted when his words brought only a defiant silence from Matt.

Ahmet flicked the plastic bag in Matt's face. The meaning was clear. But it provoked only truculence from his captive.

"That's not gonna get you what you want," Matt said. "You kill me and you don't get to know where it is."

Ahmet glanced at Ben, still slumped in the chair beside Matt.

"I have other options," he said with a vicious smirk on his lips.

"You really don't," Matt assured him. "Ben has no idea where it is."

Ahmet hesitated only briefly before the smirk turned to a look of intense irritation. Swiftly pulling the bag back over Matt's head, he held it tight around the neck. Matt was forced to swallow plastic again in a desperate terror as he gasped and struggled to get air.

Amid the bedlam of terror in his mind, he almost missed the thunderclap that had the door rattling. The almighty crash that followed instantly loosened Ahmet's grip. Matt felt the air rush in as Ahmet let go of the plastic bag and wheeled around to tear open the door. Whatever he expected to find on the other side, it was certainly not the dark squad that had smashed their way through the front door. A good dozen of them, armed to the teeth, in black helmets and full body armour. Crunching over splinters of wood and broken glass, they yelled and screamed, their weapons directly aimed at Ahmet. In his semi-conscious haze, Matt saw them through a gap in the doorway as they shoved Ahmet against the wall, slapped him in handcuffs, and dragged him out of the building.

The invasion was so sudden, so quick and so loud that Matt was left in a state of blurred bemusement. All he could hear was shouting and the commotion that comes with collective streams of activity and movement. It was not until the outer room had been completely trashed that three of these invaders finally ventured into their cell, battering the door off its hinges with a terrifying barrage of screams. Weapons raised – Armalites as far as Matt could judge – and trained on Ahmet's henchmen. The two thugs instantly dropped the baseball bats, and the invading trio shoved the two men against the wall then swiftly cuffed them too.

Looking woefully weak and inadequate without their bats, Ahmet's gorillas were dragged out of the room. Matt and Ben remained shocked, bewildered, and still shackled to their chairs. But the relief Matt felt once their tormentors had been swallowed up in the commotion outside was eclipsed by the intense pain that still stabbed and gnawed away deep inside. The inner calm and stillness that came with the knowledge that their torment was over seemed oddly to accentuate the pain all the more.

The confusion and agony were only fractionally quelled when another black-clad figure appeared in the doorway. He was unarmed, but followed by two more members of the cast, weapons raised, as he entered the room. Standing over the two captives chained to their chairs, he barked out a stream of sounds that said nothing to Matt and Ben. Then switched to English.

"Who are you?" he snapped. "What you do in Turkey?"

"Matt Quillan," came the barely audible reply. "This is Ben Braithwaite."

Impatiently tapping a gloved hand against his right thigh, he waited for more. Matt had nothing more to give. Neither of them had the energy for words. Their interrogator signalled his armed sidekicks to remove the shackles. Within seconds, a pair of heavy-duty wire cutters were delivered to the room. As soon as they had done their job, his two sidekicks finally lifted Matt and Ben out of their chairs and led them out of the building.

"Mr Quillan."

The voice was familiar. The genial smile that came with it even more so. They belonged to the suspicious three-star gendarme who had given Matt the third-degree soon after his arrival in Karakent. He wore the standard gendarme uniform with a beret, not the helmet and combat gear of his black-clad colleagues.

"Is this your friend who look for villa and a little romance?" he asked, nodding in the direction of Ben, who looked more beaten than a flogged horse.

"And who drive his boat too close to rocks maybe?" he added.

Matt simply nodded. He had no energy for explanations.

The gendarme turned, spoke a few words to a member of the armed squad, then turned back to Matt and Ben.

"You come to station," he said, and took Matt by the arm. Matt winced with pain. The gendarme released his grip and guided him to a van standing by the roadside. The vehicle put Matt in mind of his bus ride from Istanbul on his first day in Turkey. He was suddenly seized with panic by this memory and felt the ticket pocket of his jeans. It was gone. He searched every pocket of his jeans. Nothing. The flash drive was gone.

"Have you lost something?" said the gendarme.

"What? No. No, it's all good," Matt muttered, and flinched as he was helped into the van. Ben followed with the support of another gendarme.

The station was the same building where Matt had been questioned shortly after he arrived in Karakent. Set in the same incongruous garden of oleander bushes, it held the same feel of menace now as he and Ben were escorted up the same path and taken to the same interrogation room: barely furnished with only three wooden chairs; a desk that had seen better days; and the solitary barred window. Only the praying mantis was missing.

The two gendarmes who escorted Matt and Ben into the room pulled up a chair for each of them, sat them down and stood behind their chairs. They waited in silence, until Ben could not take the tension any longer.

"What the fuck are we doing here?" he mumbled.

It was the first sound he had uttered since his howls of pain from the baseball bats. Before Matt could reply, the door opened and the three-star gendarme swept in. He threw a file onto the desk, sat down and glared at the two bruised figures opposite. Matt repeated Ben's question.

"Why are we even here? We need treatment, for God's sake."

The gendarme ignored the question, continued glaring at them, then slowly opened the file in front of him. He picked up what looked to them like a passport, flicked through it, examining every page, then looked at Ben.

"Benjamin Oscar Braithwaite," he said with slow deliberation.

"This is you," he added, waving the passport back and forth.

"Where the hell did you get that?"

Ben was shocked. Both he and Matt assumed it had sunk with the boat. The gendarme only smiled.

"How you know Ahmet Karadeniz?" he asked.

"He was my fucking brother-in-law."

"Brother?"

Bewilderment was written all over the gendarme's face.

"In law," Ben repeated, shouting now with growing frustration. "He married my sister. Then he fucking killed her!"

Until now, the gendarme had remained calm and composed, but Ben's last words brought a look of shock to his face.

"Killed her?" he repeated, eyebrows raised.

"People here knew his sister as Susie," Matt chipped in.

A spark of recognition flashed in the gendarme's eyes.

"Susie," he repeated slowly, then "Karadeniz", as if fitting the pieces of a puzzle together.

"Yes, I remember," he said, and looked Ben straight in the eye. "Your sister?"

Matt and Ben looked on as the gendarme continued fiddling with Ben's passport and visibly digesting this information. Matt had reckoned on some sort of a bounce, a sign of excitement, the kind of commitment and energy you might expect from a police officer at the mention of murder. Yet all they got was the quiet contemplation of a man who looked suddenly out of his depth.

He stopped playing with the passport, shoved it across the desk to Ben, and turned to Matt.

"Are you still at the Kelebek?" he asked.

Matt nodded.

"I suggest you take your friend and get a room for him there. My men will drive you," he added, and rose from the desk.

"And Ahmet?" Ben said. "What about Ahmet?"

Turning to Ben as he opened the door to leave, he looked at Matt, then back at Ben with a long, hard glare.

"Please stay in town for now. We need to speak with you again," he said in an ominous tone. "About the boat."

The three-star gendarme made no further mention of Ahmet and left the room.

# CHAPTER 33

When Matt and Ben finally dragged themselves into the Kelebek, the chorus of cicadas around the hotel was in full swing. The desk was occupied by the same young woman who had checked Matt in when he first arrived. She greeted him with the same bright smile he had seen that day. But tinged now with concern as they approached the desk.

"Merhaba. Welcome," she said and then, as they came closer, "Are you okay?"

The last time she had seen Matt, he was a person of interest to the Jandarma. Now he walks in with a sidekick, both of them looking as if they have suffered a nasty accident. Her smile evaporated.

"It's okay," Matt said. "We just need a shower and a brush-up. Do you have a room for my friend here?"

She looked at Ben and hesitated. Matt had the impression she still had the Jandarma in the back of her mind. But she relented.

"Passport?" she said at last, yet the concern in her eyes showed no sign of easing.

Ben pushed his rediscovered passport across the desk. She photocopied it, handed it back to him, and reached down a key from the cabinet behind her.

"Room number 12. Next to Mr Quillan's room," she said, placing the key on the desk, before adding, "I hope we don't see the Jandarma back here again."

"Don't bank on it," Matt said as Ben picked up the key.

He and Ben agreed that a few hours of healing was called for and took to their beds for the rest of the afternoon. Matt fell to sleep instantly. It was the ringtone on his mobile that woke him when the light was already starting to fade. He checked the display. Unknown number.

"Hi, is Ben there by any chance?" came an unfamiliar voice.

"Who wants to know?"

"Sorry. I'm Tony. A colleague of Ben's. His phone's been dead these last few days, and this is the last number he called me from."

"He's not here, I'm afraid," Matt said, instantly stung with suspicion as he recalled Ben's secretive phone call in their hideout on the Konya Plain.

"Well, could you give him a message when you see him? Could you tell him it's all good and the deal's done?"

Matt agreed, put down the phone and stripped off for a shower. Once he was cleaned up and dressed, he went to check on Ben. His old friend had evidently taken longer to recover and get himself into shape. When he opened the door with his towel still around him, the bruises on his arms and chest glared at Matt like tattoos gone badly wrong. Against the pristine white of his towel, they gave the appearance of a misconceived fashion statement.

"So," Ben said as he stepped into his underpants. "What the hell was that all about, Matt?"

"What was what all about?"

"That rapid fucking reaction squad. Or whatever it was."

"I've no idea. But I didn't get the impression they were looking for us. They seemed pretty surprised to find us there."

"So, you reckon it was Ahmet they wanted?"

"No idea, Ben," Matt insisted. "But after accusing him of killing your sister, you can be sure they'll investigate now he's been arrested."

"Come on Matt," Ben scoffed. "Let's face it, killing women is no big deal in this country."

There was a fierce rage in the way he zipped up his jeans and drew his belt aggressively tight around his waist. Matt disregarded his friend's rising temper.

"Tony called," he said matter-of-factly.

Ben fastened his belt and glanced up: his eyebrows raised.

"Tony?"

"Said to tell you it was all good and the deal was done."

Ben's anger ebbed away into a look of relief at these words.

"At least that's a bit of good news at last," he said.

"So, what's this Tony got to do with it?" Matt said.

"What do you mean?"

"I mean this whole business with Erkan Suleyman and Ahmet."

A look of bewilderment spread across Ben's face.

"Why should my work colleague have anything to do with them, Matt? I do have another life you know."

"You surprise me," Matt said.

It was not intended to sound mean and sarcastic, but he could see that was how his friend took it. But he ignored the hurt on Ben's face. There were more pressing matters on his mind. He took his phone out from the back pocket of his jeans.

"Sorry, Ben. I need to call Amber. She'll be wondering where the hell we are."

"We don't even know for sure he's been arrested." Ben scowled as he pulled on a black T-shirt that perfectly matched the bruises on his arms. "And if he has, that guy Erkan's probably secured his release already, they're all so fucking corrupt here. But he'll pay. Whatever it takes, that bastard will fucking pay."

The two of them were now on diverging tracks, each paying little attention to the other as they parted ways. Ben still driven by his sole ambition to see Ahmet destroyed, and Matt intent on tracking back to a quieter life.

"Amber!" Matt said into the phone in a voice that spoke of

both relief and surprise. "Where are you?"

"Matt! Oh my God. Thank goodness. We've been so worried about you."

The softness of her voice, even in that moment of excitement, was like a balm for his bruises.

"But more to the point," she added. "Where are you?"

The surprise when Matt learned that Amber was also back in Karakent hit him like a bolt of lightning.

"Okay, see you soon," he said, put the phone back in his pocket and turned to Ben.

"Amazing. She's back here already. With Leila and Hauke Schmitt at her sister's office."

Ben continued to stew in his frustration and anger. He showed no sign of acknowledging Matt's news.

"You feeling fit?" Matt said, opening the door onto the corridor.

Ben said nothing. But, with a grudging reluctance in his walk, he followed Matt along the corridor and out of the hotel. The street was already in darkness. The last time Matt walked onto this street, a sense of suspicion and apprehension had hung in the air. A feeling spawned by the presence of the stranger with the worry beads lurking in the shadows.

For the first time since his arrival in Karakent, Matt caught a freshness in the air, a huge sense of release, enlivened all the more by the sweet smell of jasmine that he had never noticed around the hotel before.

While it was end of season for Karakent, the place was alive with the hum of tourist shops when they reached the centre. Bay View Properties was no exception. The lights were ablaze and the office full of chatter. Pearl was busy with prospective buyers and too occupied to notice Matt and Ben when they walked through the door. But Amber had been looking out for them ever since the call. The moment she caught sight of them, she leapt to her feet, ran over, and embraced Matt with a warm hug. He winced.

"Oh God, I'm so sorry." Amber drew back in horror at the bruises on them both. "They really put you through it, didn't they?"

"It could have been worse," Matt said.

It was Amber's expression of horror that attracted the attention of Hauke Schmitt and Leila. They broke off their conversation. A big smile spread across Leila's face. She instantly got to her feet.

"I'm so glad to see you're both safe," she said.

With a hesitation that Matt took to be reluctance, the German doctor also rose slowly from his seat to join the welcome party. The expression from behind the gold-rim glasses remained as inscrutable as the pages of a notebook dredged up from the depths of Lake Van. Matt almost had the impression that Dr Schmitt was disappointed to see him back.

"So, are you going to tell us all what happened?" Pearl chimed in. She had already lost her prospective buyers, who had beaten a quiet retreat amid the general clamour of the reunion.

"I was never going to make a killing with them anyway," Pearl shrugged, when Amber apologised for chasing customers away with all the noise. "They were just into property porn."

"You know," said Matt with a glance in Ben's direction. "The first thing we need is a nice, cool beer. So, Utopia or Zeytin?"

"Utopia sounds the perfect place after what you've been through," Amber said.

Only Hauke Schmitt held back, insisting that he needed an early night. It took Leila's power over him to persuade the German doctor to tag along. Pearl suggested they go on while she locked up for the night and assured them she would join them later.

As this motley group approached the Utopia, an old blues number from the sixties or seventies blasted out into the night air. Matt took it to be Tom Moore's evening choice. It seemed about the right era for him. But it jarred. As all the tables at the bar were empty, he imagined that it also grated with everyone else in town. But for Ben, it was a shot in the arm.

"Peggy loved this kind of music," he said once they had sat down and ordered their drinks. "She often wrote to me of this place that played such great music. She just loved the soulful kind of stuff."

"Whoever 'she' is, you could be talking about Susie," Tom Moore said as he placed the drinks on the table.

"He *is* talking about Susie," Matt said brusquely, recalling now the warm impression she had made on him when they met all those years back at Ben's business jamboree.

"Oh, I'm sorry. I didn't mean to butt in like that," Tom replied, highlighting the lilt in his voice as if to lend the apology a hand by charming Matt with his Irish accent.

He failed. Matt ignored him while Ben scowled.

"Well, she had great taste, that woman," Tom muttered, wandering back to the bar when it dawned on him at last that his presence was not welcome.

This interruption had cast a cloud of embarrassed silence over the table. It did not disperse until the arrival of Pearl some fifteen minutes later.

Matt took this moment as his cue. He was conscious of how Amber in particular was keen to learn how they came to vanish after she and Leila had left them in the safe refuge of a sinkhole that Leila insisted few people even knew about.

"Except for Erkan Suleyman, it seems," Matt said, with a glance across the table at Leila. She smiled awkwardly.

He explained how the door to their cave dwelling came crashing in when Erkan's goons kicked it down around midnight.

"That must have been Mr Worry Beads' doing," said Amber. "We saw him in Konya after we left you there."

"He may well have followed you to Konya," Hauke Schmitt chipped in. "But he was not the one who tracked you down to the doline."

"The what?" said Matt.

"He means the sinkhole," Leila whispered, her shoulder bag still resting on her lap. Matt caught a glint of metal peeking out from the bag as a tense silence descended on the table and all eyes rested on the doctor.

He fiddled with his teaspoon and said nothing more. Matt had the impression Schmitt was toying with them, basking in knowledge to which others were not privy, in the same way he enjoyed flaunting his knowledge of ancient classics.

"Hauke?" Leila said at last.

The German doctor gave her a sideways glance, as she lifted the shoulder bag, slung it over the back of her chair and with it the glint from her knife, which vanished into its dark interior.

Schmitt turned his gaze first to Matt, then to Ben, peering over his gold-rim glasses. He was visibly mulling over what he was about to say, perhaps even whether he would say anything at all. When the words eventually came, he delivered them with slow deliberation.

"If you want to know who tracked you down, I suggest you ask your friend Luc Bennett," he said.

"Luc?" Amber chipped in with a look of shock in her eyes. It was the expression of someone mentally flicking through the pages of the day's events.

"He did seem very odd when he was here last night," she added. "The look on his face when Leila said it was all settled. He went so pale."

"He might well have done," said Hauke Schmitt. "When he told you Matthew had called him, he forgot to mention that he still has friends in the business. Even here. Once an MI6 man, always an MI6 man. It was that phone call that gave you away."

"Come on," Matt objected, then recalled the array of electronics at Luc Bennett's house and his strange behaviour when they last met. "But that's absurd. Why would he even want to do that?"

"He may not want to," Hauke Schmitt conceded. "But it's well-known that Erkan Suleyman blames him for the death of his precious dog. And he will always demand compensation for the wrongs that are done to him."

"What? Deliver us to Erkan over a dog?"

Matt winced as he shifted in his seat, visibly struggling with the memory of the beating they had both taken.

"Well, at least they got you out of there safely in the end," Leila said.

"And saved Ahmet from facing justice," Ben scoffed, still seething with anger.

"Oh, don't worry, Ben," Leila assured him. "He will go down for a very long time."

"But he won't die, will he?" Ben shot back, raising his voice a few notches. "He won't die for killing my sister."

Leila recoiled in her chair from his fury, knocking her bag off the back of her seat. The dull thud when it hit the ground and the glint of metal spilled out into the light again, was not lost on Matt. He put an arm around Ben's shoulder, partly to restrain him, partly to calm him down.

"You have Matt to thank that Ahmet was even apprehended," Leila added, as if to bolster the force of Matt's gesture. "Without his memory stick, you and he would not be sitting here now."

Matt threw a questioning look at Leila. Then at Amber, who looked sheepishly into her glass.

"There was such explosive stuff on that flash drive," Leila said. "But as I said before, we couldn't just go to the police with it. Erkan's control over everyone in this town meant the information would simply disappear, especially when they found Erkan's own involvement. So, I asked Yusuf's daughter to help us. Belgin's very tech savvy and posted the video clips and all of the audio recordings on social media for the whole country to find. Then I snuck into Ahmet's office and copied the files onto his computer.

"We didn't have much time. I thought all was lost when I had to enter a password. But Ahmet's not the brightest, and I got lucky when the password hint came up. Kurtboğan. I tried aconite. No luck. Then monkshood, and I was in."

"The bastard!" Ben growled in the background.

"And the phone you grabbed from Ahmet's wife," Leila added, smiling across the table at Amber, "was the cherry on the cake. When we got back, Belgin used his wife's phone to warn the Jandarma about the social media post and tell them where they could find the files. The rest is history."

"So, Ahmet goes to jail for treason," Hauke Schmitt chipped in. "And they will be certain to put Suleyman back inside as well."

"Don't be too sure of that," said Leila. "His name only appears once or twice in a pretty innocuous piece of information. It's more likely he'll worm his way out."

"To hell with Suleyman," Ben yelled. His voice rocked the air, almost smothering Howlin' Wolf's plaintive 'Born under a Bad Sign' that blasted out from the bar. He scowled at Leila across the table.

"Are you saying all that action man stuff with the riot squad was down to you?"

She looked sheepishly at Ben, whose face appeared a livid blue beneath the street lights. He was incandescent with rage.

"And Ahmet dies in prison for treason. If we're lucky. So, fucking what?"

Ben brought his fist crashing down on the table with a seismic force that set the drinks shaking. Leila's glass toppled over, but she saw it coming and escaped the stream of wine that flowed over the table.

"He needs to go down for killing Peggy, not for some trumped-up fucking lie. I should have finished him off when I had the chance."

"Killing is never a satisfactory path to vengeance," said Leila.

Ben scoffed at Leila's composure. But Matt sensed she was speaking from personal experience. And the suspicion was not allayed when she added, "Believe me, Ben. However justified it might seem at the time, it will weigh on you for the rest of your life."

The table around them had fallen quiet, leaving only the last words of Howlin' Wolf to hang in the air – Born under a Bad Sign,

Born under a Bad Sign – until the song slowly faded away, and nothing could be heard but the bristling of the eucalyptus trees across the road.

From behind the bar, Tom Moore stared with the look of a nightjar watching out from its nest for predators. Perhaps he was too focused on the quiet around the table, for he showed no sign of noticing the familiar figure that wandered out of the darkness further down the hill. No one else around the table saw him either until the figure approached the group and rested his hand on Pearl's shoulder. It was Hamza.

"Have you heard the news?" he said. There was an oddly muted gruffness to his voice.

"What news?" Pearl asked.

"Fidan."

"What about Fidan?"

"She was found dead outside their apartment today."

"Dead?" Pearl repeated, only half in disbelief. "That's dreadful. How? What happened?"

"Hasan said she fell down the steps. He called the ambulance, but she was already dead by the time it got there."

Hamza paused. The quiet around the table grew deeper and darker, stretching into the night, until he spoke again.

"Hasan is heartbroken," Hamza added. "He was wailing like…"

"Like Ahmet the day after Susie died?" Pearl said, eyebrows raised as if to mark out the irony in her voice.

It was clear that Hamza knew exactly what she meant. He said nothing in reply. The rest of the table was too much in shock to speak. All except Amber.

"Did you say Fidan?" Amber cried. "Oh my God!"

Matt saw the anguished expression on Amber's face morph slowly into a trance-like daze. She began to mutter quietly to herself in what seemed like a ritualistic mantra. No one else around the table appeared to notice, but Matt sensed she was reliving her own past traumas, perhaps counting her blessings that she had survived, until the incantation gradually took on the shape of words.

"Another sapling beaten and deprived of love," she whispered, echoing the words her sister had used to describe the young woman compelled to become steadily invisible to the world around her.

"Little by little they take away that beauty: little by little the sapling withers," Hauke Schmitt mumbled in reply, peering over his gold-rim spectacles at Amber.

"Really Hauke, this is not the time or place for Sufi mysticism."

It gave Matt a curious pleasure to see the German doctor put in his place at last. He smiled quietly to himself at Leila's rebuke.

"So now what?" Ben said, still fuming. "They call in some quack doctor who pronounces accidental death or whatever, and the man is free to crush another sapling. Just like Ahmet crushed my sister.

"Is it so different back home?" Amber said. Her tortured tone brought a quizzical glance from her sister.

Her words cast an awkward silence over the table. Hamza pulled up a chair next to Pearl and took her hands in his as he sat down beside her. At that moment, a flower seller appeared at the table, carrying a metal can full of roses. Pearl flashed a look of scorn at the blood-red flowers, perhaps recalling her early encounters with Ahmet. Amber waved him away in irritation. Matt saw that she was still struggling with the turmoil brought on by rekindled memories.

Further up the street, a huge white bus expelled a whoosh of air as it pulled up outside Osman's restaurant and opened its doors onto the street. A solitary passenger emerged from the bus, turned and walked up the hill into the darkness. The scene put Matt in mind of his first day here and his ride down from Istanbul. He imagined Rekan now languishing in jail somewhere – unaware of just how useful his flash drive had proved.

Matt's rambling thoughts blinded him to the other figure swaggering down the street past Osman's place. But he had not escaped Ben's attention.

"So, you were right about Suleyman," Ben said, glancing at Leila as he nodded in the direction of the familiar figure all in white coming their way.

"How long before we see Ahmet strolling after him?" he growled.

Matt looked up, then glanced at Amber. She had plainly spotted the man as well and appeared to be sinking back into a state of detachment. Alone with her thoughts. Her eyes fixed on the white suit, white tie and the handkerchief bleeding from his breast pocket. Walking free and heading in their direction. His face a picture of pure evil in the street lights above. They appeared to be deliberately lit to accentuate the menace of his grin.

To Matt, it was as if she knew that grin. That face. The outline of his white suit etched against the evening darkness. The purest white. Like all those years ago in Brighton.

The man in white was not alone. Talking with him as they strolled together was a portly stranger. He was a lot shorter than Erkan Suleyman, but gesticulated with an air of authority that spoke of power and influence.

"Antonov," Pearl said when suddenly she caught sight of the two men coming down the street. "That's Yuri Antonov. He was in my office earlier today."

"The Russian," said Hauke Schmitt.

Pearl shot a glance across the table at the German doctor. The alarm in Schmitt's voice roused Matt briefly from his concern for Amber. He flashed a look in the direction of Leila. Her eyes reflected the doom-laden tone of the ex-Stasi man's words. But their meaning was lost on Matt. He was more troubled by Amber's state of mind.

She seemed oblivious to everyone around her, as her gaze remained fixed on Suleyman, the white suit and the handkerchief bleeding from his breast pocket. She was plainly too immersed in her thoughts to hear Ben's words.

"The bastard. If he hadn't interfered in the first place, I'd have finished Ahmet off on the boat."

Swaggering down the road in the company of the gesticulating Russian on his left, the man in white drew ever closer.

"As I said before," Leila chipped in, "violence is really not the most satisfactory way to exact revenge."

Matt had the impression she was speaking from experience, but it was Amber that still troubled him.

"Believe me, Ben," Leila repeated. "Killing him would have been a most pyrrhic revenge."

"What? Killing who?" Amber called out, as if from a disturbing dream.

Matt flashed a look of bemusement at Amber, but Leila ignored the interruption.

"Don't forget, Ben, Ahmet knows you know. And he will be seething with the injustice of getting life for something that had nothing to do with him. That's the sweetest kind of revenge you could ever have."

"And if Ahmet soon walks free like him," Ben bellowed, nodding in the direction of Suleyman as he brought his fist down on the table. "How sweet will that revenge be when he kills his new wife or some other poor bastard?"

The clamour from the table distracted Suleyman's Russian companion. He glanced up from their conversation, peered suspiciously at Ben, and offered Pearl a brief smile of acknowledgement as they passed. Matt was struck by the way Hauke Schmitt grimaced at this gesture and Leila smiled reassuringly at the German doctor, as if she understood his discomfort.

But the Russian was not alone in his distraction. The shock in Suleyman's eyes told Matt the Turk had only now become aware of Ben's presence. He stopped, turned to glare at Ben, and let a grin of pure evil spread across his face as he strode over to the table.

"Good evening, Ben," he said with a smirk. "Enjoy it while you can because it's not finished yet."

Ben moved to get up from his chair. Matt placed a restraining arm on his, and the smirk on the face of the figure in white grew wider still. In the corner of his eye, Matt caught the movement of Amber's arm as she slipped her hand inside the bag that was slung over the back of Leila's chair. She rose from her seat and slowly drifted around the table.

"It is now," she muttered, as she plunged the blade into the gut of the man all in white, punctuated only by the red handkerchief bleeding from his breast pocket.

Suleyman looked down at the knife, clasped his stomach – the smirk now frozen in shock – and slumped to the ground. Amber quietly gazed at the thick stream of blood that flowed from the wound. Watched with a satisfied smile as it trickled out over the white jacket and into the dusty road where he lay. It sparkled in the light from the street lamp above.

"Oh no!" Matt cried and sent his chair crashing to the ground as he leapt to his feet. "We need to get you out of here right now."

He bent down, calmly removed the knife, and wiped it clean with the red pocket square from the man's jacket. Without another word, he then took Amber in his arms and steered her away from the scene.

The Russian looked on from afar in baffled silence.

"Amber!" Pearl cried. But her sister had already vanished into the shadows with Matt.

Like the Russian, the rest of the table watched the spectacle in static silence, muted by the shock. Only Leila smiled quietly to herself, as Tom Moore's music moved into the twenty-first century, and the sound from the Utopia bar serenaded the scene with the mournful tone of 'Where the Wild Roses Grow'.